Book 1

The Marital Scandal

JONITA MULLINS

ISBN-13: 978-1718994713

ISBN-10: 1718994710

First Printing May 2018

Published by Candleshine Publishing
Muskogee, OK

Cover photo by Richard Atkinson
www.photographsbydixie.com

Printed in the U.S.A.

List of Characters

The Couples
Cornelia Tuttle
Her parents Jonathan and Julia Tuttle
Edmund Webber
His brother and sister-in-law Walter and Bettie Webber

Harriet Gold Boudinot
Her parents Benjamin and Eleanor Gold
Elias (Buck Watie) Boudinot
His mother Susanna Watie and his brother Stand Watie

Sarah Northrup Ridge
John Ridge
His father Major Ridge

The Missionaries
Samuel and Ann Worcester (Brainerd Mission, Tennessee)
Cyrus and Electra Kingsbury (Mayhew Mission, Mississippi)
Cephas and Abigail Washburn, Jacob Hitchcock, James Orr, Cynthia Thrall (Dwight Mission, Arkansas Territory)
Hannah Sanders, Delight Sergeant, Ermina Nash (New Echota Mission, Georgia)

The Tennesseans
Oliver Ackley
His family Dolly Ackley, Daphne and Jason Edwards
Sam and Eliza Allen Houston

The Cherokees
In Georgia
Chief Pathkiller and Peggy
Chief Charles Hicks
James Starr, Lem Starr, John Ross

In Arkansas

Chief John Jolly
His children Price and Colista Jolly
Rabbit Ballard
His daughter Lucinda Ballard
Chief Blackcoat, Sequoyah, Spring Frog, Old Blair, Patsy Blair, John Flowers, John Rogers, Tsiana Rogers Gentry, Thomas Chisholm, Jesse Chisholm

The Creeks

Jane McIntosh Hawkins
Her family Chilly McIntosh, Roley and Muskogee McIntosh
Hawk Childers, John Davis, Benjamin Perryman

Others

Mr. and Mrs. Carroll, the Tuttle servants
Mrs. Huddleston, Corrie's employer
Colonel Matthew Arbuckle, Lieutenant James Dawson, Fort Gibson officers
McKee Folsom, Josiah Doak, Choctaw delegates
Ophelia Buchanan, Oliver's aunt
Jessie Russell, the Buchanans' housekeeper
Colonel David Brearley, Creek agent
Persis Lovely, widowed farmer

The Marital Scandal

CHAPTER ONE

Cornwall, Connecticut
June, 1825

Angry voices rose and fell as Cornwall's citizens surged toward the street corner near the Congregational Church. The crowd of angry men seemed to be waiting for something.

Cornelia Tuttle and her best friend Harriet Gold waited too. The two young women stood at the window of Cornelia's darkened upstairs bedroom. Through the waning daylight they watched the crowd gathering in the town square.

Soon a figure emerged out of the shadows and Harriet gasped. Her brother Stephen hurried to join the mob. He was carrying two hay-stuffed figures of a bride and groom. The bride represented Harriet and the groom her fiancé Elias.

The last rays of sunlight threw the scene into relief. Deep shadows contrasted starkly with a golden glow reflected in the windows of the brick buildings that lined the square. The mob now rushed along the cobblestone street like an angry beast seeking its prey. They were headed across town toward the home of Harriet's parents.

Harriet stood quietly but tears streamed down her face. The two friends watched from the shadows of the unlit room as the angry, shouting mob hurried past the Tuttle house. Whipped into a frenzy by the scurrilous editorial in this morning's newspaper, Cornwall's rabble had spent the afternoon gathering on the square to loudly denounce the impending marriage of one of their citizens to an Indian.

Concerned with the anger building among their neighbors, Harriet's parents had secreted her away to Pastor Tuttle's home. Cornelia and Harriet had been friends since childhood. The Tuttle family was more than willing to provide refuge for the frightened young woman.

What normally would have been a quiet summer evening in the small New England town had become dark and ugly. The dying embers of daylight made the shadowy figures look larger than life. It must have seemed as if they were to Harriet. To watch her own brother carry an effigy of herself and her fiancé while the mob shouted words of hatred must have been devastating. Cornelia could only imagine her pain.

"I told myself I wouldn't cry if he did it," Harriet said in a choked whisper. "But honestly I thought it was just a threat to badger me into relenting. I never thought Stephen would actually join that mob."

Cornelia pulled the nineteen-year-old woman into her arms and Harriet fully gave in to the tears. Gradually the sound of the angry voices died away and a silence that seemed even more ominous remained.

Harriet pulled back from her friend's embrace. "I'm glad Elias was not here to witness this," she said as she wiped the tears from her cheeks. "He was so pleased to come to the Mission School. So grateful for the opportunity. He would be hurt by this ugliness."

"I hate that you have to bear the brunt of it alone," Cornelia said as she pulled her friend to sit beside her on the little green brocade settee in the corner.

"I'm not alone, Corrie," Harriet said. "I've had you right beside me since we first laid eyes on those Cherokee boys. Remember, at the Fall Social?"

Corrie smiled, glad to see that Harriet was no longer focused on the rabble outside. "How could I forget? It was life changing. At least we thought it was at the time."

The two women were quiet for a long moment each remembering the event from four years ago. They had been fifteen-year-old freshman at the Cornwall Female Academy and thrilled to be invited to the annual Fall Social. It included the Westminster Male College and the Foreign Mission School, a school for indigenous young men from around the world.

They both felt quite grown up as they rode in the Tuttle carriage to the meeting hall on the Westminster campus. Corrie tugged at her lace gloves and tried to calm the butterflies in her stomach. She and Harriet sat across from her parents, Jonathan and Julia Tuttle, who would serve as chaperones at the dance.

Mrs. Tuttle smiled at the two girls who could barely suppress their excitement. The Fall Social was a rite of passage for Cornwall's young people and many a marital match had begun at the event.

"I hope you girls will be friendly toward the students at the Mission School," Julia reminded them. "I don't want them to feel ostracized or shut out of the activities. Some folks in town were not happy to have those young men come here."

"Like that awful Mr. Bunce?" Corrie asked.

She saw two different reactions on her parents' faces. Her father tried to hide a smile while her mother frowned.

"Don't say 'awful,' dear. It's slang, a low class sort of word."

"Probably something Bunce would say," Jonathan added, almost under his breath. At this her mother did smile. Isaiah Bunce was the publisher of the local newspaper and had strongly opposed the opening of the Mission School by the United Foreign Mission Society. Since Rev. Tuttle was on the board of the school, he too had been criticized by the editor. Mr. Bunce was no favorite in the Tuttle household.

"Should we ask those boys to dance?" Harriet looked to Mrs. Tuttle for guidance.

"No, dear, the young men are to do the asking. But you can certainly engage them in conversation. Make them feel welcome."

"What do we talk about?" Corrie asked. In her mind, she often imagined these boys from distant lands dressed in their

native costume, speaking languages unknown to her. It was all very exciting, but a little daunting as well.

"Ask them about their home or their family," her mother advised. "When you are far away from home, you like talking about such things, I think."

"Will they be able to speak English?"

"Yes," Rev. Tuttle spoke then. "It was a requisite for attending the school. They must have a rudimentary knowledge of the language the classes will be conducted in. Most of them received their primary education at English-speaking schools."

They arrived at the grand meeting hall and Mr. Carroll, their driver, pulled into the line of carriages letting out the guests for the dance. Rev. Tuttle helped the ladies step down and then held open the door for them to enter the candlelit hall.

The girls grasped hands for a moment as they stepped into the glittering room. Mirrors placed strategically along the walls made the candles seem to double in number. Students from the three schools mingled around the room while a chamber orchestra tuned up at one end of the long hall.

"Have a good time, girls," Julia said before taking her husband's arm. They strolled toward the refreshment table to join a group of board and faculty members.

Corrie looked around the room, suddenly feeling shy. "Do you see anyone we know?"

Harriet nodded toward one end of the room near the orchestra's platform. "There's Sarah," she said, already pulling Corrie toward their friend who was a sophomore at the ladies' school. "She's with her Cherokee beau."

"He's not her beau, really, is he?" Corrie couldn't keep the sound of shock out of her voice.

"He sits with her family at church, doesn't he?"

"Yes, but I didn't know they were courting."

"Surely they are if they sit together every Sunday." Harriet didn't seem to find the idea shocking at all. "I think his name is John."

They reached the young couple where they stood talking with two other young men who also appeared to be Indian. All the men were dressed in dark suits looking as refined as any of the boys from Westminster. Corrie felt just a twinge of disappointment that these young men didn't look as darkly exotic and uncivilized as editor Bunce accused them of being.

"Hello, Sarah," Harriet greeted the tall blonde girl who wore a soft peach-colored dress that complimented her fair complexion.

Sarah Northrup greeted the two girls and then introduced the man who apparently was her date for the evening. "This is John Ridge. He's from Georgia and is a junior at the mission school."

John made a slight bow as they all exchanged the proper pleasantries. Then he clapped a hand on the shoulder of the young man next to him. "This is my cousin, Elias Boudinot."

Corrie felt her eyebrows fly upward before she could stop them. Elias Boudinot was the name of a very influential Congressman from New Jersey. Her surprise at hearing the man's name must have been obvious to the young Cherokee, for he offered an explanation.

"My birth name was Galagina *Watie. . ."*

"Which means Young Stag in our language," John interrupted. "But we called him Buck at our primary school in Georgia."

"It is our tradition to adopt an adult name," his cousin went on. "So I chose the name of my patron. You must have known him."

"Yes, Representative Boudinot was a guest in our home a few years ago," Corrie said, "when he came to observe the school and offer his support. Besides an endowment, he planned to give a scholarship to an incoming freshman every four years."

"Yes," the younger Boudinot said. "I received that scholarship. Before I came to Cornwall, I paid a call at Mr. Boudinot's home to thank him. He was so welcoming and encouraging I decided to take his name to show my respect."

"I still have to remind myself to call him Elias rather than Buck," John added.

"What an interesting tradition," Harriet remarked.

Corrie felt her eyes drawn to the third young man standing in their group. He looked younger than the other two and was probably a freshman like she and Harriet. He was tall but solidly built and wore his dark hair to his shoulders. He had yet to say anything.

Elias followed her gaze and offered the introduction. "This is Edmund Webber from Arkansas Territory. His brother Walter is married to my sister Bettie so we are kin of kin I guess you could say."

"My pleasure, ladies," Edmund bowed. Of the three young men, Webber seemed the least sure of his English. His words had a different rhythm to them revealing that English was not his first language.

"Arkansas Territory," Corrie repeated. "You are certainly a long way from home." All she knew of Arkansas was that it lay beyond the Mississippi River.

"It does seem very far away," Edmund agreed. He tugged uncomfortably at his high white collar.

"Oh, the music has started," Sarah said, throwing a not very subtle hint toward John that she wanted to be asked to dance. He obliged her by offering his arm and they moved onto the dance floor.

Elias turned to Harriet. "Your manner of dance is very different from ours," he said, "but I am learning the steps. Would you care to join me?"

"I'd love to," Harriet smiled. The two of them walked together to join the line of dancers.

Corrie and Edmund were left standing in awkward silence.

"I am sorry, but I do not know the dance steps," Edmund said at last. "Please do not let me stop you from joining your friends."

"Well the dance is for couples," Corrie said, feeling her face grow warm. "But I'm not very good at the dance steps

either. Why don't you tell me about your home and family. You have a brother?"

"Yes, my brother Walter is married to Elias's sister. Walter is paying my way to school."

"You have English names," Corrie noted.

"Our mother is Cherokee so we are Cherokee," Edmund explained. "But our father is Scottish so we have both English and Cherokee names. It is not so unusual in our culture to have more than one name."

"Like Elias," Corrie added. She cast an eye toward the dance floor to see that Harriet and her dance partner seemed to be enjoying themselves.

"Yes, we choose an adult name from something important in our lives. Perhaps I shall change my name to 'He Met a Pretty Girl.'" There was teasing in his voice, but also admiration in his eyes.

Corrie blushed at the charming compliment. For the rest of her life she would never forget that moment.

"They're probably at Papa's house by now," Harriet's voice pulled Corrie from her reverie back into the present.

"I'm sure editor Bunce must be pleased," Corrie grimaced.

"No doubt he is," Harriet agreed.

Mr. Bunce was, in fact, quite pleased that his editorial had created the mob protesting the impending marriage of that Cherokee to Benjamin Gold's youngest daughter.

The balding man stood at a window of his apartment above the newspaper office where he had watched the chanting crowd hurry by. There was satisfaction in seeing how powerful the pen could be.

It was true that there were few of the good Christian folks of Cornwall among the mob. Most of these rabble-rousers had joined in only after Oliver Ackley had visited the taverns and pressed a few coins into palms. Some of the Westminster lads had joined in purely for a lark, though they seemed to harbor resentment toward the Indian boys at the mission school.

"This should put a stop to the wedding," Ackley observed as he stood next to Bunce downing his second snifter of brandy. "Even the girl's own brother is against it."

"Perhaps," Bunce said without conviction. "But don't count on it. Mr. Gold and Pastor Tuttle have made their positions quite clear on the subject. I can't believe the New Haven paper actually printed their letters. I certainly refused to do so."

"It doesn't matter what they wrote," Ackley said as he helped himself to more brandy. "The tide of public opinion is turning against the school. It will be closed soon, mark my words. I've written to Lyman Beecher. He's their most influential board member. I suggested to him that these Southern Indians would start bringing their slaves to school with them. He's a flaming abolitionist and he won't stand for that."

"I doubt that any of them own slaves," Bunce mused. "They're poor, uncivilized Indians."

"Don't think it," the other man countered. "Some are quite wealthy. That John Ridge has slaves, I'm sure. Their labor built his plantation home in Georgia where he took his Cornwall bride last year. What was her name? Sarah something."

"Northrup," Bunce supplied. "I thought surely the scandal surrounding her marriage would end the school."

"It might have if Gold and Tuttle hadn't stood firm. Now Gold is paying for his tolerance. His own daughter is shaming the family. Engaged to Elias Boudinot," Ackley practically spat the man's name. "Trying to make himself respectable by taking on such a respected name."

"You certainly hate the Indians," Bunce observed as he turned away from the window. The crowd was long gone now and the street lay quiet and empty.

"You'd hate them too if they had killed your brother."

The newspaper editor studied the young man from Tennessee who had taken a seat near the cold fireplace and now stared moodily into his glass. Bunce poured himself some of the dark liquor and sipped it slowly.

Oliver Ackley had showed up at the newspaper office shortly after the mission school opened. He had convinced Bunce to use his paper to stir up opposition to educating young indigenous men. Ackley hated Indians as much as Beecher hated slavery. And it all went back to Horseshoe Bend.

"Your brother was killed by the Red Sticks," Bunce said referring to the Creeks who had gone to war against American expansion into Alabama. He knew some of Ackley's story. The Battle of Horseshoe Bend in 1814 had made a name for Andrew Jackson. He ran for President on his reputation as an Indian fighter.

"General Jackson ordered a charge against their breastworks across the peninsula on the Tallapoosa River," Ackley said. "My brother was shot as he topped the barricade; might have been mutilated if Ensign Houston hadn't dragged his body away. Houston took an arrow himself."

"Yes, I remember. Congressman Houston was at Horseshoe Bend, wasn't he? And didn't the Cherokees fight alongside the Tennessee militia?"

"Yes," Ackley downed the last dregs from his glass and set it on the table by the chair he occupied. "Sam Houston probably only joined the fight because the Cherokees were in it. He thinks of himself as being Cherokee." Ackley's tone was snide.

"And some Creeks fought against the Red Sticks as well, didn't they?"

"You know a great deal about it for a Yank," Ackley's dark green eyes narrowed.

"I'm a newspaper man," Bunce explained as he took the seat on the other side of the hearth. "I cover the news."

"You also create the news," the younger man said with approval. "You created a mob today. It should put a stop to this marriage and put an end to that school."

Bunce shook his head but said nothing for a moment. "It won't be that simple," he offered at last. "The trustees have met and expressed their disapproval of the Gold girl's engagement. But they didn't shut down the school. From what

I understand Pastor Tuttle convinced them to keep it going at least for another year."

"Tuttle would have a different view if it was his daughter betrothed to an Indian."

Bunce grunted, "Perhaps he would."

At his home next to the Congregational Church, Jonathan Tuttle still stood at his parlor window even though the mob had passed from view. Across the room his wife sat at her spinning wheel, her hands guiding the wool thread being pulled from the carded fleece in her lap. The gentle sound of the treadle and the steady tick of the mantle clock were all that could be heard now that the angry voices had died away.

"Thank God it's not our Corrie facing such ugliness," the minister said as he finally turned from the window.

"It very well might be," Julia warned. "She's still corresponding with Edmund Webber. He may have returned to Arkansas Territory, but I think there is an attachment there."

"Has she told you that?"

"Not in so many words. But Corrie always gets the mail on her walk home from Mrs. Huddleston's house. I see the pleasure on her face when there is a letter from him. It's been that way since they graduated last year."

Tuttle paced across the wool rug his creative wife had made for their home many years ago. The strain of the scandal surrounding the Gold-Boudinot engagement was showing with new lines on his face and more gray around his temples.

"Corrie would tell us if he had proposed marriage, wouldn't she?" he asked.

"I'm not sure she would," Julia said with a frown. "Not after what has happened to Harriet. When the Golds refused to give her permission to marry, that poor girl made herself sick with heartache. If Benjamin and Eleanor hadn't relented and agreed that she could marry Elias I think she might have died."

"Well, she made a remarkable recovery once their permission was granted." Jonathan didn't keep the ironic tone out of his voice.

"I don't think she was feinting illness, dear," Julia chided. "When Corrie and I visited her all last autumn I could tell she was genuinely sick. She simply had no will to get better."

"Not until she got her way," her husband added.

"The heart wants what the heart wants," Julia shrugged. "I'm afraid Corrie's heart may be in Arkansas. And if it is, I for one will not stand in the way of her happiness. I will not teach her to practice tolerance and acceptance and then hypocritically refuse to offer it myself."

The pastor's wife was a strong-willed woman and Jonathan had learned not to challenge her sense of fairness or determination to do what she believed was right.

"Nor will I, my dear," he concurred. "But even you must agree that tolerance can only go so far. I daresay you wouldn't want our daughter to marry any of those men who just passed our house this evening."

"No, of course not," Julia conceded. "There are reasonable limits to acceptance. But we have had Edmund in our home. He has sat at our dinner table with other students from the mission school. We know him to be a fine, decent young man."

"Certainly he is," the pastor said as he finally took a seat having walked off some of his agitation. "Yet I cannot help but hope that distance will cool any passions that might exist between Cornelia and Edmund. No father wants to see his daughter subjected to the kind of hate that we have witnessed tonight."

"I don't want that either," Julia sighed. "I hope Corrie was able to keep Harriet from seeing it."

Upstairs Corrie crossed her room and opened a bureau drawer to take out one of her lace-trimmed handkerchiefs. She handed it to her friend who took it gratefully and mopped her face of the still-flowing tears.

"I'm sorry I can't seem to stop crying," Harriet sniffled.

"You need to try, Harriet," Corrie said. "You'll make yourself sick again."

"No, I won't," Harriet smiled wanly. "I promise I'll be alright. Especially with Elias coming for a visit next week. He has graduated from Andover and he's coming here before going home to Georgia."

After completing his studies at the Foreign Mission School, Boudinot had enrolled at the Andover Theological Seminary in Massachusetts. He planned to become a minister.

"You've warned him about what's going on here, haven't you?" Corrie asked. "He knows to be discreet?"

"Yes, he knows. It's the same thing that happened when Sarah and John were married. We both anticipated that this might happen. Elias even offered to end the engagement to spare me, but I wouldn't have it."

"No, I suppose not." It was Corrie's turn to give a faint smile as she sank down onto the settee beside Harriet. Her friend's determination to marry the man she loved had taken her nearly to death's door. She admired such a commitment but feared she could not be so brave.

"I wonder if Elias and I could meet here instead of at Papa's house," Harriet asked. "That way Stephen won't know about it and cause some scene."

"I'm sure that will be fine. I'll ask mother in the morning."

"Oh, Corrie, you have been such a dear friend to me through all my trials," Harriet reached for her friend and pulled her into an embrace. "Thank you. I'm so glad there is someone for you as well. And I pray you and Edmund don't have to face what Sarah and I have. Surely the people of Cornwall can't be scandalized a third time."

Corrie returned the embrace but when the two young women parted, she could not quite look Harriet in the eye.

"Edmund and I have no understanding," she said glancing at the dainty writing desk next to the settee.

"But Edmund cares for you deeply, I'm sure," Harriet countered. "I have no doubt that a marriage proposal will be forthcoming. You'll see."

"I don't know . . ." Corrie let her voice trail off.

"Well, I do," Harriet said firmly. But soon her shoulders drooped. "This day has simply drained me, Corrie. I know it's not late, but I think I'll retire for the night. Do you mind?"

"Not at all. You need your rest."

The women rose and Corrie stood between her friend and the desk. Then she walked with her to the bedroom door. The two bade each other good night and Harriet stepped across the hall to a guest bedroom.

Corrie sighed and walked slowly to the little desk. She stood behind the chair and looked down at the envelope that rested on her ink blotter. It was addressed to her in Edmund's florid penmanship. She ran her fingers across the looping letters of her name. Then she quickly tucked it under the blotter, not able to look at it any longer.

Edmund had asked her if she might visit him in Arkansas Territory. He had described the beautiful mountains near his home and wondered if she might like living in such as setting. It seemed as if a proposal might follow depending on how she answered him.

But Corrie did not have Harriet's courage or determination. She didn't know if she wanted to continue her correspondence with the charming Cherokee man living on his brother's plantation in Arkansas. How could she contemplate marriage when it might mean facing hateful opposition from her own neighbors?

So many emotions swirled inside her. She crossed the room to once again look out her window. The last rays of sun gave the world a golden glow. But as she watched, the sun slipped behind the hill beyond where the Foreign Mission School stood. Quickly her world was plunged into darkness as her own tears coursed down her cheeks.

CHAPTER TWO

Illinois Bayou, Arkansas Territory
June, 1825

Edmund Webber tallied the trade in a ledger at his brother's store on the Illinois Bayou. A Cherokee couple who lived on a nearby farm had brought in a few rabbit and possum pelts as well as two dozen eggs to trade for a bolt of calico fabric, two plugs of tobacco and a large brimmed felt hat.

He tried to politely converse with the couple about the upcoming dance scheduled for the Green Corn Moon. But his mind was distracted. He had heard the steam whistle of the big paddle wheeler called the *Neosho* and knew the boat would be tying up at the Dardanelle dock. It would carry a packet of mail for sure. He had been waiting for weeks for a letter from Connecticut.

When Rattling Gourd and his wife finally left the store, Edmund hurried around the counter and reached for a sign hand-lettered in both English and Cherokee that would tell patrons the store was closed. He set the sign in the window, closed the door but didn't bother to lock it, and walked as quickly as his long legs would carry him toward the river and the waiting steamboat.

Edmund had made it his task to collect the mail packet that arrived each week with the *Neosho*'s regular run upriver to Fort Smith. He would take the few pieces of mail to Dwight Mission which operated the only thing close to a post office in the area.

Mail was still something of a novelty for the Cherokee settlements that occupied the north bank of the Arkansas River between Dardanelle and Fort Smith. But the Cherokees now had a written language thanks to a gifted silversmith named Sequoyah. As more Cherokees learned Sequoyah's syllabary, more correspondence passed between Arkansas and the Cherokee back east.

Edmund was a little winded by the time he reached the wooden dock. He was not the only person who had come to meet the steamboat. Absalom Simms who operated a store at the bluff above the river was collecting a shipment of supplies for his post. Thomas Chisholm who made his living in the fur trade had a large pack of bison hides to be shipped to New Orleans.

Edmund slowed his pace after stepping onto the wharf then stopped to wait among a group of men who appeared to have come to the river simply to observe the activity that always surrounded the arrival of a steamboat.

"*Osiyo*," he greeted the men in Cherokee. They all spoke or nodded a return greeting. Edmund knew most of them, for the Cherokee settlement at the Illinois Bayou was not a large one with only about a dozen families. Most of them traded with the few stores near the river between Dwight Mission and Dardanelle.

Soon a steward from the *Neosho* stepped onto the wharf carrying the familiar canvas mail bag. He glanced around for Edmund and when he located him he tossed the packet to him. It was then that the young Cherokee noticed that Jacob Hitchcock from the mission was also among the onlookers at the dock.

Hitchcock was superintendent of Dwight Mission which was located a few miles above the Arkansas River on the west bank of the Illinois Bayou. He had apparently brought outgoing mail which he handed to the boat's steward.

Edmund edged his way through the onlookers to reach Hitchcock.

"I did not know you would be here today, Mr. Hitchcock," he said.

"I normally don't come down unless I'm expecting supplies or have mail that needs to go out," the older man replied. "Today I had mail."

Edmund nodded. "I will hand this pack off to you then. But you would not mind if I check for mail for the Webbers."

"No, certainly not," Hitchcock said. He took the small canvas bag Edmund held out, untied the string that bound it and reached in to pull out a handful of letters and three copies of the *Arkansas Gazette* newspaper. He handed the letters to Edmund while he checked the recipients of the newspaper.

"I don't know why I always check?" he chuckled. "The mission, Chief Jolly and your brother have the only subscriptions to the *Gazette*." Not many of their neighbors could read the English newspaper.

Edmund smiled, but was distracted. He had looked through the stack of letters twice. There was a letter for his sister-in-law from her mother in Georgia and an envelope for him from Boudinot's Andover address. But that was all for the Webber family.

He hadn't realized he had heaved a disappointed sigh but Hitchcock noticed it. "Not what you were hoping for?" he asked with a quirk of his eyebrow.

Young Webber did not want the missionary to know that he was pining for a letter from a certain pretty girl. It was not that Hitchcock was nosy and he certainly was no talebearer. He had always shown an interest in Edmund and was only expressing friendly concern. But the Cherokee was not willing to share this particular disappointment.

"I guess we always want more mail than we receive," he said with a forced laugh.

"Now that's the truth," Jacob agreed as Edmund handed back the letters. The man quickly glanced through them. "Only two for folks at the mission," he observed. "There will be disappointment at Dwight as well."

Then he handed one copy of the *Gazette* to Edmund, tucked all the rest of the mail back into the pack and tied it once again. He tucked it with another package under his arm.

"Will you stop by the store?" Edmund asked.

"No, I need to get back," Hitchcock said as he joined Edmund in weaving through the boat watchers to find his horse tied to a low branch of an oak tree on the river bank.

"There's quinine in this pack," he explained. "I need to get it to Dr. Weeks. The fever's starting again now that it's turned so hot."

He mounted the horse and turned its head toward the mission. "I'll see you for Sabbath services," he said to Edmund.

"Bettie and I will be there," Edmund returned. His sister-in-law usually attended the Sunday morning service at Dwight where Edmund served as the interpreter for Rev. Washburn, the director of the mission. His brother, on the other hand, wanted nothing to do with church.

"Take care then." Hitchcock tugged at his hat brim and then nudged his horse into a trot.

The Cherokee man watched for a few moments as Mr. Hitchcock rode along the river path. According to a recent issue of the *Gazette*, funding had been approved for a real road to be constructed between Little Rock and Fort Smith and then on to Fort Gibson located further upriver.

A surveying crew from Fort Smith had been working on setting the road's alignment, a fact that angered some of Webber's neighbors. Surveys were bad work as far as many Cherokees were concerned. They always brought more people wanting more land and pushing the Cherokees further west.

Edmund walked briskly back to the Webber trading post. When he arrived at the store he found Old Blair dozing in a cane-bottom chair on the covered porch.

"You need something?" Edmund asked of the elderly Cherokee.

"Just shade," he grunted around the long stem of his pipe. "Too hot."

"Yes, it is," Edmund agreed. His mind had been so much on other things he had not noticed until now that the afternoon had grown quite warm. He was glad to step into the dim interior of the store where it was cooler.

Bettie was inside visiting with Patsy Blair the old man's daughter-in-law. Their conversation ceased when he entered as if they had been caught gossiping. He wondered if they were talking about him.

Edmund knew that some of his neighbors eyed him suspiciously. He was the first among them to get a secondary education. He could not only speak English but could read and write it as well. That alone made him "different." He felt sometimes as if he must be very careful about what he said and did.

He walked to a desk at the back of the store to be out of earshot of the women so they could continue their conversation. After a fire had burned his brother's trading post last year, Walter had rebuilt it and made it much larger. But it was still stuffed to the rafters with any trade item the locals might have need of. Webber was a canny businessman like their Scottish father.

At the moment, his brother was away and Edmund and Bettie watched the store for him. With Chief John Jolly, Walter had traveled to Fort Gibson for a treaty signing. The Osages, who had a long-running feud with the Cherokees, had finally been induced by the government to move out of an area known as Lovely's Purchase. The western Cherokees used this area as a hunting outlet to the prairie where game was still abundant. It was Chief Jolly's hope that when the Osages moved this land would be permanently ceded to the Cherokees.

Edmund sat at his desk, glumly staring at the *Arkansas Gazette* but not really seeing it. The newspaper had printed the entire inaugural address given by President John Quincy Adams this past March. It took a long time for news to reach them out on the frontier.

The young man heard Bettie bid Mrs. Blair goodbye and walk with her to the door. Then his sister-in-law made her way to where he sat.

"Letters?" she asked, but quickly spied the two envelopes Edmund had tossed on the desk. She picked them up and smiled broadly to see the one from her mother, Susanna Watie. She handed the other back to Edmund.

Glancing around the many shelves she finally spotted what she was looking for. She unsheathed a hunting knife and with it carefully pulled the sealing wax away from the envelope. She did not want to tear it. Paper was scarce and even an envelope could be reused in some way. She returned the knife to its holder.

"Careful, Bettie," Edmund teased. "Walter will say that knife is used now and he'll be forced to discount it."

She laughed for they both knew that her husband would not take a penny off the price of an item in his store.

"So do not tell him," she countered.

Carefully she pulled out the sheets of thin paper in the envelope. Her mother had covered both sides of each in the Cherokee script that the eastern and western factions of their nation had quickly learned.

There was silence for a while as Bettie read her letter. Edmund used the time to unsheathe his knife and also carefully pry off the bright red wax Elias had used to seal his envelope. He pulled out a single sheet of paper written in English but with an occasional word added in Cherokee.

"Not good," Bettie shook her head. Edmund set down his letter and turned his attention to her. "Mother is sad," she added.

"Why?"

"Buck," she said, nodding toward the letter her brother had written to Edmund.

"Don't you mean Elias?" Edmund continued to tease.

"Yes, Elias," the woman responded. "He is still Buck to me. And he still plans to marry that Cornwall girl. Even though there are plenty of bad feelings against it."

Edmund cast his eyes downward lest Bettie see his own feelings about marrying a Cornwall girl. Suddenly his desire to tease was gone.

"I thought you said he should be able to marry whomever he wants."

"He should," Bettie nodded. "But Mother says his children will not be Cherokee. So he must marry a second wife – a Cherokee – to have children who are Cherokee. But he says no he will not. Christians do not marry two wives at the same time. Is this true?"

"Yes," Edmund said.

Bettie had attended Sabbath service with him since he had returned from school. But she was still new to the faith.

"So Buck's children will not be Cherokee. This is so much sad."

Lineage was passed through the mother in Cherokee culture. So even though his father was Scottish, Edmund was still thoroughly Cherokee because his mother was Cherokee. This would not be the case for Elias or for John Ridge. Marrying a Cornwall girl had deeper ramifications than just bad feelings or even someone's moral objections.

Edmund felt this conflict like a twisting knife in the pit of his stomach. It was one of the reasons that he had not found the courage to speak of marriage to Cornelia Tuttle. When he had carefully broached the subject with his brother, Walter had expressed outrage that Edmund would even consider such a possibility.

Since his graduation from the mission school, Edmund and Elias had corresponded over the long distance. Elias had shared his own soul-searching in deciding to marry Harriet Gold. He had ultimately decided to follow his heart and marry the woman he loved even though there were many objections to such a match.

Elias and his cousin John Ridge had made the decision to marry women who could not give them Cherokee children, but Edmund was hesitant. John and Elias were willing to assimilate into American culture. During their debates at school, they had always maintained that doing so would protect their nation from being overrun and their land from being stolen. They were adamant that the Cherokees and other tribes not give up any more land.

But Edmund agreed with his brother on this. It was better to move west and retain their traditions, language and sovereignty than to try to prove that they were no different from their Georgia neighbors. Look at the anger their choice had brought to Elias and his cousin.

So Edmund was still hesitating, knowing that to marry Cornelia would not only anger the people of Cornwall but his neighbors and his own brother as well. Sometimes he regretted that he had ever gone back east for his schooling. If he had not, he would by now be settled with a Cherokee wife and Cherokee children. Instead he ran to the dock each Wednesday hoping for a letter, waiting for an answer to a question he didn't have the courage to ask.

In his last letter to Cornelia he had vaguely wondered if she might like to live on the frontier some day. He could not bring himself to ask if she could live among the Cherokees where she and her children would be regarded as foreigners. Could she live with him as his wife? He felt as if he were being torn in two.

Though his eyes were downcast, Edmund could feel Bettie watching him closely. He knew she suspected that he had a Cornwall girl of his own that he cared about. She had seen the letters that Cornelia had written over the past year. She likely had noticed that those letters had stopped even though Edmund still hurried to the dock each Wednesday.

"You trust God, don't you?" his sister-in-law asked quietly.

He looked up to see compassion in her eyes.

"Yes, I try."

"Then give him time to work this out," she advised. "Mother says there is trouble in Cornwall. Give things time to get quiet again. Then you will hear from your Cornelia."

"Thank you, Bettie," Edmund said, trying to take hope from her words. "I will try to remember that."

Their conversation ended then for the snap of the front screened door told them someone had entered the trading post. Soon Bettie's young sons, Walter, Jr. and Charles, came rushing through the crowded store to find her. Trailing behind them was Jennie, the Negro house slave whose job it was to look after the boys.

Immediately Edmund felt uncomfortable for an entirely different reason. Having received four years of schooling among staunch New England abolitionists, he had come to question the morality of owning slaves.

It was a long tradition among his people and the slaves were, as a general rule, treated humanely. His brother owned several slaves. Though Edmund had resolved to never own slaves himself, he nevertheless benefited from their labor on his brother's plantation. He knew how Cornelia felt about this. Discussing it once while he visited her parents' home had brought them to their only exchange of angry words. This was another reason he hesitated to marry the pretty Cornwall girl.

CHAPTER THREE

Cornwall
June, 1825

Cornelia raised her parasol to protect against the warm afternoon sunshine as she stepped out of the Huddleston house on Jewell Street. She was employed as a governess to the six Huddleston children ranging in age from five to sixteen.

Because Corrie lived only a few blocks away, Mrs. Huddleston did not require her to live in. So now that she had fed the younger four children their supper and helped the oldest two daughters dress for the evening meal with their parents she was free to walk home for the day.

She was anticipating a quiet supper free from the clamor of rambunctious children and the drama of chanting mobs. The turmoil of the last few weeks, since Harriet's engagement had been announced, had left Corrie feeling drained.

She almost walked past the post office without stopping in as she usually did. She knew she owed Edmund a letter and she felt terribly guilty that she had not written to him while trying to help Harriet navigate the storm of scandal. Corrie didn't want to tell him about how ugly things had become here and didn't want to answer his questions about her visiting Arkansas.

She didn't want to respond because she did not want to hurt him. Yet she knew her silence might hurt him as well. Instead of happily anticipating another letter from him, she felt a guilty dread. One part of her wanted a letter; the other part feared receiving one.

So Corrie quickened her pace as she approached the post office. But before she could clear the door, a man stepped out and nearly collided with her.

"Oh," Corrie gasped and quickly pulled her parasol out of the way. She had nearly poked the man in the eye with it. "I'm sorry."

"My fault," the tall young man said. "It is I who should apologize. I wasn't watching where I was going. Are you alright, Miss?"

Corrie looked up into his dark green eyes. "Yes, I'm fine."

He didn't move so Corrie was forced to stand still as well. He seemed to be studying her and it made her self-conscious.

"Well," he finally said, while tugging at his hat brim, "have a good day." Then he started across the street toward the newspaper office.

Without thinking, Corrie turned to go into the post office. She hesitated before entering to look back at the stranger she had just encountered. He was looking back at her as well. Blushing, she hurried inside.

"Well, good day to you, Miss Tuttle," the gray-haired postmaster greeted her. Mr. Scott knew everyone in town and usually knew their business as well, just from the mail. Corrie suspected that he held letters up to the light to try to read their contents.

"Good day, Mr. Scott," Corrie said as she wrestled her parasol closed and then approached the counter where the paunchy man stood in his shirtsleeves and a dark vest.

"Only a few letters for you today, Miss," the man said as he turned to pluck those letters from a slot marked "Tuttle."

"One's all the way from Georgia," he told her. His curiosity was written on his face. "From the girl who married that rich Cherokee."

"I see," Corrie said while holding out her hand to receive the letters.

"Nothing from Arkansas Territory though," Scott went on.

Corrie squelched her irritation at the busybody. "Well, the mail can be slow from the frontier," she said forcing a calm smile to her face. She pretended to be indifferent to the lack of mail from Arkansas.

"Ayuh, I suppose," the postmaster conceded, "though it's getting better now that there are regular steamboats running out that way."

"Yes," Corrie politely agreed, still holding out her hand for the Tuttle mail.

Mr. Scott handed it to her somewhat reluctantly. Many of his patrons would read their mail right there in the post office and share tidbits of information with him. But Corrie had no intention of doing so.

"Thank you, Mr. Scott," she said, as she turned to go. "Have a good evening."

"Same to you, Miss." Mr. Scott watched her step out the door with clear disappointment on his face. They didn't get too many letters from Georgia around here.

Across the street, Oliver Ackley also watched Corrie as she emerged from the post office.

"Who's that girl?" he asked Mr. Bunce.

The editor looked up from his desk and squinted into the afternoon sunshine. "That's Pastor Tuttle's daughter," he said then returned to his writing.

"Attractive young woman," Ackley observed.

Bunce looked up again but this time he studied Ackley. "You can meet her by attending church this Sunday. She'll be there no doubt."

Ackley pulled a face at the mention of church then turned away from the window. "Afraid I won't be here this Sunday," he said. "I leave tomorrow to return to Tennessee. General Jackson has asked those of us who worked on his last campaign to meet at the Hermitage. He's already strategizing for a second campaign."

"For President, you mean?"

"Certainly, what else?"

"I thought perhaps another military campaign against the Creeks or the Seminoles," Bunce shrugged. "I assume that's the kind of campaign you'd like to join."

"Hardly," Ackley said with a bitter tone. "I wouldn't follow Jackson into battle. But I want him in the executive office. I share his goal of removing the Indians from the states."

"President Adams may achieve that himself."

Ackley shook his head. "He's too influenced by New England do-gooders who want to educate the Indian."

The young man paced as he often did when he was agitated over Indian affairs. "Once they are educated it will be twice as difficult to persuade them to move. That's why it's imperative that we get Jackson into office."

"That shouldn't be too difficult," Bunce leaned back in his chair. "He won the popular vote last year. If Henry Clay hadn't persuaded the House to break the Electoral College tie in Adams' favor, Jackson would now be president. But he'll still have to overcome his marital problems."

Ackley waved a hand as if the vicious gossip about the Jacksons was of no consequence. But Bunce knew otherwise. Adams' supporters had made it an issue in the last election. They would certainly try it again if Adams ran for a second term. The fact that Mrs. Jackson had not been legally divorced when Andrew Jackson married her had filled the newspapers with lurid accusations.

Bunce hadn't been above covering the salacious news in his own paper. He might oppose having a mission school in his town, but he still favored a New Englander for President. He had not been upset to see Jackson lose the House vote. But he wouldn't tell Ackley that.

"So you leave tomorrow?"

"I'll take the first stage out," Ackley confirmed. "Keep me abreast of conditions here. I hope to hear from you soon that the Golds have put a stop to this marriage. We cannot allow these Indians to marry their way into acceptability and influence. They'll use it to keep from moving west."

Bunce said nothing for a moment, shaking his head silently at the single-minded, vengeful focus of this Tennessean.

"I should send correspondence to the Hermitage?"

"No, I'll only be there a day or so. You can reach me at my father's farm near Lynchburg – Grove Hill."

Bunce had done his research on Ackley's family and knew that his father's "farm" was actually a 300-acre plantation lying west of Chattanooga very near the lands of the Cherokees. Oliver Ackley might couch his hatred of Indians in his desire for some sort of justice for his dead brother, but Bunce knew an equal motivation was the desire for more land. The Ackley plantation could not grow as long as the Indians remained on the land around it.

Ackley would likely be quite satisfied in knowing that the Savannah newspaper Bunce had received today carried the news that the Creeks had just been induced to sign a treaty giving up their lands in Georgia in exchange for land west of the Mississippi. But the editor wasn't inclined to share this news.

Bunce watched the young man through narrowed eyes. Ackley thought he was using the editor and his newspaper to further his cause. But Bunce would not be pushed any farther than his own scruples allowed. And he would not be sorry to see Ackley leave Cornwall.

"So I will bid you farewell then," he said, rising from his desk to offer a hand to the younger man.

"Oh, yes, of course," Ackley said, taking the offered hand. "Well, I'll be off then to my room at the inn."

"Good evening," Bunce dismissed the man, even holding open the door for him to leave. He stood and watched as Oliver strode away from the church square in the opposite direction of Miss Tuttle making her way home. He saw Ackley turn to look at the young woman once. But she was unaware of it and seemed to be absorbed in reading a letter.

Corrie was scanning the three pages from Sarah Ridge quickly as she walked past the church toward the rectory sitting beside it. She could tell that even after a year of married life in Georgia Sarah was still a bit homesick for Cornwall.

The letter was filled with the day-to-day activities at Running Waters, the Ridge plantation, but she also wrote that the sultry summer days made her long for the cooling breezes of New England. Corrie finished the letter and then hurried up the steps to the house. She entered the kitchen to find her mother and their housekeeper, Mrs. Carroll, finishing supper preparations.

Julia looked up from the pan of potatoes she was emptying into a serving bowl. Through the steam she saw the letter in her daughter's hand and she smiled.

"A letter from Edmund?" she asked.

Corrie kept her voice casual. "No, it's from Sarah Ridge," she said as she laid it and the other mail on the dining table. Then she hung her parasol on a stand by the door and added her bonnet with it.

"How many for supper?" she asked as she opened the cupboard to take out the dinner plates.

"It's just us three tonight," Julia answered, keeping her own voice light. She knew something was wrong between Corrie and Edmund, but she wouldn't pry. It had been too long since a letter had come from Arkansas.

Corrie completed the three place settings and then took a pitcher to get water from the big barrel that sat in the mud room off the kitchen. They did not have a well or cistern at the rectory so Charlie the water hauler delivered a big barrel of spring water every other day except Sunday. From the pitcher, she filled three water goblets and helped her mother set the serving dishes on the table.

Mrs. Carroll, at Julia's insistence, always dished up a plate for herself and her husband to eat together in their rooms above the stable. Mr. Carroll kept the Tuttles' grounds and livestock and acted as gardener, driver and general handyman for the rectory and the church next door.

After the housekeeper had said good night and departed out the back door, Julia called to her husband who sat in his study off the front parlor.

"Jonathan, supper is served."

The minister emerged shortly, rubbing his eyes, then stretching his arms above his head. He had sat all afternoon immersed in a book of sermons.

"Smells delicious," he complimented his wife as the three of them took their seats. After saying grace, they passed the serving dishes and began the meal. Rev. Tuttle glanced through the mail, but he did not open any of it. Reading at the dinner table would be the height of rudeness.

"So you've heard from Sarah Ridge," he observed. "How are she and John doing?"

"Well, enough, I guess," Corrie said as she buttered a bit of the yeasty rolls Mrs. Carroll had baked. "They have finally finished their house and it sounds lovely from her description. Two stories with a verandah and Belgian lace curtains at every window. John didn't spare any expense."

"Nothing like the mud and stick lodge Mr. Bunce said she'd be forced to live in, eh?" her father observed wryly.

Julia smiled at the comment but pressed Corrie on her answer. "Why do you say she is 'well enough'?"

"She sounds lonely," Corrie explained. "John was hired as the official translator for the Cherokee government. So he's quite busy and away much of the time. He and his father went to Washington last year right after the election. And before that he was in Alabama for a time, helping the Creeks with translation as well."

"He speaks Creek also?" Julia sounded surprised.

"He's a master linguist," Tuttle interjected. "He's proficient in Greek and Latin as well. Graduated top of his class. Headmaster Daggett says John is one of the most brilliant students he's ever educated."

"Sarah says she's learning Cherokee so she can help John with translation," Corrie added.

"Sarah is quite as bright as John," Julia observed. "If she were a man she could have pursued any profession she wanted."

"Instead she will do what many women do," Jonathan said.

"And what is that, dear?" Julia asked with a quirk of an eyebrow. She looked prepared to defend those of her fair gender.

"She will make her husband look good," Jonathan smiled while sharing a conspiratorial wink with his wife.

Corrie was aware of the look that passed between her parents though she kept her eyes on her plate. She knew that her father often used the ideas and writings of her mother in his Sunday sermons.

She waited a moment before announcing, "Sarah asked me to come for a visit."

"To Georgia?" her mother sounded surprised. "Were you thinking of going?"

"No," Corrie said slowly. "It's much too far. I'd have to be gone for weeks and I couldn't leave Mrs. Huddleston without help for that long. But it was nice to be asked."

"Well, I wouldn't want you traveling that far by yourself," Julia mused. "But I don't want you to feel trapped here at home. Perhaps you can go next year after Harriet has settled in Georgia as well. It would be nice to visit both of them. You should never be afraid to travel." She paused and then added, "Should that be something you ever wish to do."

Corrie knew that her mother was thinking about her traveling to Arkansas, not Georgia. But she let the subtle hint hang in the air without responding to it. The table was quiet for a time and Corrie realized it would be up to her to move the conversation along.

"Don't forget, Mother, that Elias and Harriet will be here tomorrow. He's coming in on the morning stage."

"I haven't forgotten," her mother assured her as she passed more bread to Jonathan. "Were you able to get some time off so you can visit with them?"

"Yes, Mrs. Huddleston said I could leave a little early in the afternoon. So I'll have about an hour with them before Elias has to leave."

"It's a shame he couldn't spend the night," Tuttle stated. "We would have gladly let him stay here. I would love to hear about his final year in theology school."

"Harriet says he wants to get home before the Green Corn ceremony. It's an important event, I guess, for the Cherokees."

"Well, I can't wait to see Elias," Julia said as the three of them finished their meal. The pastor took his mail to the study to be perused while the women cleared the table.

Corrie was quiet as she helped her mother wash and dry the dishes. She knew Harriet was probably beside herself in anticipation of seeing her beloved. But Corrie had no such hope. She wasn't going to Arkansas and Edmund seemed lost to her forever.

Early the next morning before daylight Elias sat at breakfast at the hostelry in Hartford. Across the table from him was a friend and fellow graduate from Andover named Samuel Worcester, a tall man with curling dark hair.

Worcester had joined Elias on the stage for the three-day journey from Boston to Hartford. The newly ordained minister had received an appointment from the American Board of Missions to serve at Brainerd Mission among the Cherokees near Chattanooga. He would wait in Hartford while Elias took a side trip to Cornwall.

From Hartford the two men would continue on to the Cherokee lands. Worcester planned to spend the summer getting set up at the mission before bringing his bride Ann to the site following their wedding in August.

Elias absently stirred his cooling coffee while he flipped open his pocket watch to check the time. The stage was late and he was impatient.

"That's the fourth time you've checked your watch in the last five minutes," Worcester grinned.

Elias looked up at his friend. "It is late," he defended himself. "I do not want Harriet to worry. I fear her health is still precarious."

Worcester sobered in sympathy with his friend. He knew Miss Gold had been quite ill last year and Elias blamed himself for the distressed situation she had faced after he had proposed to her. Samuel and Ann had prayed with Elias for her improved health on many occasions, often joined by their study group at Andover.

"I thought Miss Gold had fully recovered," Samuel said. "And the stage isn't late; it's not even seven o'clock yet."

"She says she is fine now," Elias confirmed, but worry lines creased his forehead. "But I will not be convinced until I can visit with her. She was so sick at Christmas that her parents would not even let me see her."

The young Cherokee checked his watch again then stuffed it back into his vest pocket. The two men were quiet as the hostel owner cleared away their breakfast plates after pouring them both more coffee.

"Am I doing the right thing, Worcester?" Elias asked. "Harriet writes that people in Cornwall are angry about our engagement. But she refused my offer to call it off. She is quite determined."

"Be glad she is, my friend," Worcester advised. "She will be a stalwart companion in the midst of life's trials."

"But do I have the right to ask that of her? Her family is furious and mine is less than thrilled. If we begin our marriage in such a trial does that bode well for our life together? I will be taking her away from everything she knows."

"Do you love her?"

"With all my heart," Elias answered with conviction.

"Well, she obviously loves you," Worcester smiled. "And you prayed about this for over a year. Trust the Lord. Everything will work out."

"I hope you are right," Elias said somberly. But his face brightened when through the window he saw the stage with its six big draft horses pull out of the nearby livery.

The two men stood and Worcester walked with Elias to the stable. They shook hands before Elias climbed the two steps into the leather-bound interior of the coach.

"God speed," Worcester said, as the driver closed the door and checked the latch. Then the stout man climbed into the high driver's seat and released the brake.

The two friends nodded to one another then Worcester moved back as the fresh, rested horses stepped lively to begin the drive to Cornwall. He watched the coach until it turned out of sight, then went back inside the hostelry for another cup of coffee. He would write a letter to Ann, his own stalwart companion.

In Cornwall that afternoon, Corrie glanced at the clock on the mantle in the Huddleston nursery. She patiently wiped the youngest child's face. Their afternoon tea with biscuits and jam was finished and she would be free to leave in another few minutes.

All day she had imagined Harriet's happy reunion with her handsome fiancé and Corrie was anxious to be home so she could visit with Elias as well. During her school years, the Tuttles had welcomed all the boys from the mission school to their home. Corrie had met Osages from Missouri, two Choctaw brothers – Israel and McKee Folsom – from Mississippi and a few lads all the way from the Sandwich Islands which they called Hawai'i.

But the three Cherokee students were most often at the Tuttle home along with Harriet and Sarah. They had all become good friends with good memories of their school days. Before John and Sarah had become engaged, the people of Cornwall had been far more accepting of the indigenous students.

Corrie was tying her bonnet strings as the clock struck four. With a wave to her small charges, she slipped downstairs and out the door. Today she would bypass the post office and be home within just a few minutes.

She stepped into the kitchen to find Mrs. Carroll testing the oven's temperature by holding her hand inside it. With a nod, she then slid in a roasting pan containing a cut up chicken. Checking the clock for the time, she then moved to the counter to begin dicing the turnips, carrots and onion that she would add to the chicken later.

Corrie greeted the woman while she hung her parasol and bonnet. Glancing through the dining room into the front parlor, she could see Harriet and Elias sitting side by side on the brocade sofa her mother always offered to guests. Across the room, Julia and Jonathan sat in two matching wing chairs. Corrie hoped her parents had given the two young people some privacy while Elias had been here.

She checked her hair in the little mirror above the umbrella tree and then made her way to the parlor.

"Oh, here she is," Julia said with a smile at her daughter.

Elias and Jonathan stood as Corrie entered the room. She went to Harriet and gave her friend a hug then shook hands with Elias. As the men were seated again, she moved the little footstool by her mother's chair and sat it next to the sofa by Harriet then was seated as well.

"It's so good to see you, Elias," she said. "I hope you had a good journey here."

"It was tolerable," he said, smiling at his fiancée. "But the horses could not move fast enough for me."

Corrie noted that their fingers were intertwined on the sofa though they maintained a respectable distance between them. She captured a sigh before it could escape. It reminded her of how Edmund had held her hand in church the last Sunday before graduation. How wonderful it had felt. No wonder Harriet wore such a contented look on her face.

"Elias has been telling us about his traveling companion, Samuel Worcester," her father said. "They'll be continuing south together from Hartford. Rev. Worcester has been appointed to Brainerd Mission in Tennessee."

"That's the mission cousin Cyrus started isn't it?" Corrie turned to her parents. "Before he went to Mississippi?"

"Yes, that's it," her father said. "It sounds like Rev. Worcester will be a good addition to Brainerd."

"As soon as he learned he was assigned to Brainerd, he asked me to help him learn Cherokee. He's almost as proficient at the written form as I am," Elias laughed. "He wants to immediately start translating hymns and scriptures into our language and have them printed. His father is a printer so I think Worcester has ink in his blood."

"Will printing be possible in Cherokee?" Jonathan asked.

"Not without special type being made."

"It doesn't use the English alphabet?"

"It uses English, Cyrillic, and a few symbols that the inventor simply made up. It took me a while to learn it, though Edmund tells me that children at the mission school learn it quite quickly. I have been corresponding in Cherokee with Edmund, Corrie. He knows it better than I do since he lives near Sequoyah, the man who created it."

"Sequoyah must be quite a scholar," Julia noted.

"You would be surprised," Elias countered. "He has no formal education at all. He does not read or write English; I am not sure that he even speaks it."

"That is amazing," Jonathan said. "And he is a neighbor to Edmund?"

"Yes, they both live on Illinois Bayou near Dwight Mission. Isn't that right, Corrie?"

"Yes," Corrie said simply. She did not want to talk about Edmund.

"What do you hear from him these days?" Harriet asked.

Corrie refrained from rolling her eyes in annoyance. She could tell that her mother was watching her closely. "He's very busy, I think," was all she would say.

"Yes, that is what I hear too," Elias added. "His brother is away so Edmund and my sister must see to running the business."

"What is your brother-in-law's business," Julia asked politely.

"Primarily the fur trade, I believe," Elias said after a moment's hesitation. "Walter also has a general merchandise store on the bayou and that seems to be doing well. And he grows a few crops."

Corrie knew what Elias wasn't saying. Those crops were grown by slaves. She hoped that Edmund had nothing to do with that part of his brother's business.

"Edmund is primarily employed by Dwight Mission as an interpreter," Elias added as if reading her thoughts. "I believe he finds that work very satisfying."

"From their annual reports to the Board, I gather that Dwight is growing," Rev. Tuttle added. "It's seems to be the most successful of any in the Neosho District. The Osage missions aren't faring as well."

"The Osages are not yet agriculturists," Elias offered, "as the Cherokees are. My sister tells me there is bad blood between the western Cherokees and the Osages. And unfortunately Walter has been in the middle of the conflict. I am praying the missionaries will be able to bring reconciliation."

At this time Mrs. Carroll stepped into the parlor to announce that supper was ready to be served. Corrie and Julia stood quickly to help the housekeeper set the table. The others followed more slowly to the dining room. Elias and Harriet were still holding hands until he pulled out her chair for her.

After saying grace, the talk turned to wedding plans for the young couple. They had chosen a date in March when roads would be passable for travel. They planned a quiet, private ceremony at Harriet's home. Then they would leave for Georgia to the home Elias would spend the next few months building.

"My brother Stand will help me cut the timber for the house this summer," he explained. "We'll take it to the Vann's sawmill at Spring Place, then raft it downstream to the Watie land."

"Will you start a church there?" Rev. Tuttle asked.

"Not at this time," Elias answered. "I have been offered a job as a teacher at the Oothcaloga Mission near New Echota."

"Oh, you'll be teaching," Julia smiled. This was an occupation she highly approved of. She had taught school for a time before her marriage.

"Yes," Elias said. "I will begin after the corn harvest."

As the meal drew to an end, Corrie noticed that Harriet had grown quiet. Elias would have to leave soon to catch the last stage to Hartford tonight. It must be very hard for her to have only a few hours with her fiancé.

When the dessert was finished, Julia spoke to her husband. "Dear, help me clear away these dishes."

"Me?"

"Yes," she gave him a certain look. "Corrie will help too."

Leaving the young couple alone to say their goodbye, the three Tuttles picked up the serving dishes and exited to the kitchen.

When they were alone, Elias reached for Harriet's hand and raised it to his lips.

"I hate saying goodbye," he sighed.

"Oh, so do I," Harriet agreed. "I wish you weren't going to be so far away."

"I considered getting a teaching position somewhere in Connecticut for the fall term. But I want to have our home built before you move down. I need to be in Georgia."

"I know," Harriet said. "Don't worry over it. I'll stay busy with wedding plans and getting packed."

"I hope to be able to come for a visit when school breaks in November for the fall hunt," Elias told her.

"I will look forward to that. And in the meantime we can write to each other just as we did while you were at Andover."

Rev. Tuttle walked into the room then. "I'm sorry, Elias, but the stage will be pulling out soon. I'll walk you to the station if you would like."

The two young people understood what wasn't being spoken. It would not be wise for Harriet to accompany Elias across town to the coach station where townspeople would be sure to see them. Their goodbye had been said here and that would be all they would have until he could visit again in the fall.

Elias helped Harriet to stand and they all walked to the front door of the rectory. He retrieved his hat then took Harriet's hand for a last lingering moment before stepping outside into the late afternoon sunshine. The three women watched as the pastor and the young Cherokee passed down the walkway to the street and then turned toward the town square.

Corrie slipped her arm around Harriet's. She had expected her friend to cry, but there were no tears in her eyes. She simply looked resigned and very determined.

"Would you like me to walk with you home?"

"That would be wonderful, Corrie," Harriet agreed. "I don't want to walk alone."

CHAPTER FOUR

Hartford, Connecticut
June, 1825

Elias reached Hartford late that evening but found that his friend was waiting in the hotel dining room for him, sipping buttermilk and reading a book. The two agreed to meet for breakfast early the next morning to catch the stage for New Haven.

From this seaport town they boarded a small merchant ship that hugged the eastern seaboard southward on its way to Savannah. The two young seminary graduates spent the warm days on deck, discussing conditions among the southern Indians and each one's plans for work at their respective Cherokee missions.

"How long since you've been home, Elias?" Worcester asked one day as they passed the Carolina outer bank islands. "I know you didn't go home at Christmas break."

"I paid a visit last summer when you were home in Vermont," the young Cherokee responded as he stretched out his long legs in the sunshine. "I chanced to be there when my sister Bettie was visiting as well."

"Where does she live?"

"Arkansas Territory now. Her husband and his family were among around a thousand Cherokees who moved west seven years ago. Her brother-in-law was a fellow student at the Cornwall school. Edmund received his primary education at Spring Place in Georgia just as I did. We've corresponded since he returned to Arkansas after graduation."

"He didn't want to pursue a university education?"

"There is little use for university degrees on the frontier. Edmund clerks for his brother and acts as interpreter at Dwight Mission. And he gets to do plenty of hunting and fishing. He describes the mountains where he lives as being as beautiful as the Blue Ridge. I almost envy him."

Elias smiled for a moment but then the smile faded. "But even on the frontier, the Cherokees are being pressured to move further west."

Worcester shook his head. "Why can't the states respect Indian sovereignty? You have treaty rights! I'm telling you, Elias, the Cherokees need to challenge the states in court."

Elias now smiled at his friend's fervor. "We could not win in a state court."

"Then take it to the Supreme Court."

The Cherokee clamped his hand on Worcester's shoulder. "Perhaps we will have to someday," he said. "Will you stand with us, if we do?"

"Without a doubt," Worcester confirmed. "You know I will."

They arrived in Savannah a day later to find the city sweltering in the summer heat. Here Worcester purchased a wagon and two thick-chested roan horses using funds gifted him by his future father-in-law. The men loaded their trunks in the wagon bed and set out north on the road to Marietta.

On the second day of their journey they saw a survey crew working off the side of the road. Elias frowned at the sight.

"You don't look happy," Worcester noted.

"This is Creek land," Elias explained. "They would have no use for surveyors. Like the Cherokees, they hold their land in common and only mark boundaries with stones at the corners. I do not think this is a good thing."

"I read in the Hartford paper that the Creeks had signed a treaty exchanging their lands in Georgia for land out west."

"I know from John Ridge that this treaty was not agreed to by the majority of Creeks. He helped them draft a letter of protest to be sent to the President. The protest leader, named Yahola, believes men were bribed to sign it."

"So it isn't a legitimate treaty, but the folks in Georgia are already seizing Creek land and having it surveyed."

"It appears so."

The men continued their journey in thoughtful silence for a long while. When they arrived at the ferry landing on the Ocmulgee River, they noted a knot of men dressed in traditional Creek attire who seemed to be in a serious discussion. All along the dusty road, at crossroad trading posts and town council grounds they saw other gatherings of Creek citizens. Clearly there was an unsettled atmosphere in the Creek lands.

In the early evening they arrived at a tavern located at the Indian Springs ferry on Big Sandy Creek.

"I have stayed here before," Elias told his friend as they pulled into the yard of the tavern which served meals and offered rooms to overnight guests. "The McIntosh family owns it. They are Creek."

"Sounds Scottish," Worcester observed with a grin. "Like me."

"Yes, there is much intermarriage with Scottish traders among the Creeks." Elias also grinned. "As with us Cherokees. They are the 'Blue-Eyed Clan.'"

Both men were laughing at the joke as they stiffly climbed down from the wagon seat, secured the horses and stepped inside the public house. A few other guests sat in plain wooden chairs at square tables. The place was clean but unadorned, catering to the traveler just passing through.

A young Creek man set down a coffee pot and crossed the plank floor to greet them. He was dressed in a white trade shirt that had been adorned with bright ribbons and wore a woven belt over the long shirt and dark trousers. Beaded moccasins and a shell and stone necklace completed his colorful attire.

Elias spoke to him in *Muskoke* and the man directed them to a table. "I will bring you stew and cornbread with coffee soon."

"Do you have any spring water? We'd like something cold."

"Yes. I will bring it."

The friends were seated and removed their hats, pushing back sweat-soaked hair. The interior of the unlit room was only slightly cooler than the June sunshine.

"I didn't know you spoke Creek, Elias."

"I know a little *Muskoke*, but I am not fluent in it as John is. The Cherokees and Creeks have been neighbors for long years. Our words have crept into each other's language. When we are not fighting each other, we trade and intermarry some." His tone held some irony. "The first wife of William McIntosh was Cherokee, I think. His next two wives were Creek."

Worcester quirked an eyebrow. "Was he married to three women at once or one at a time?"

"There may have been some overlap," Elias smiled. "Does that shock your Christian sensibilities?"

"No," Worcester shook his head. "Well, perhaps a little. I know I have some adjustments to make."

"It is less common than it used to be. It is actually the white traders who often have an American wife and an Indian wife."

"That would be scandalous in New England," Worcester observed.

"There is much that is scandalous in New England." Elias could not keep a little bitterness out of his voice.

Worcester grimaced. "Sorry to have brought that up."

Elias shook his head, but said nothing. He looked around the room where another young man was serving the few guests present. "I usually see McIntosh here when I visit. Or his son Chilly. I wonder where they are."

Soon their server brought out bowls of thick, steaming soup and cold slabs of cornbread, along with crystal-clear spring water. He introduced himself as Hawk Childers and told them to let him know if they needed anything else. Then he returned to pouring coffee around the room.

He was dressed in American clothes, not Creek clothes, so they did not recognize him. Now he must hide."

Elias leaned back in his chair, dismay on his face from the tragic story. "I am sorry that such division among your people would end this way. I do not believe John would have intended such a consequence."

Their host nodded. "I will be going west as soon as possible. I did not sign the treaty, but I am known to work for McIntosh. I do not want trouble here. The Okfuskees come nearly every day still searching for Chilly."

At that moment a young woman stepped into the dining room from the back. She wore a traditional calico dress, but had a black shawl tied across her shoulders. She nodded to Childers then left.

"Mrs. Hawkins has your room ready whenever you wish to sleep," the young Creek told his guests. "But it will be hot now. You are welcome to sit here or on the porch until it is cooler. We have peach cobbler if you like."

"Thank you, Childers," Elias said. "We are sorry for the trouble you are experiencing. And, yes, we will take some cobbler out on the porch."

Boudinot and Worcester sat on the porch until the sun had set and the locusts had begun a racket in the trees along the creek. They spoke in quiet tones about the state of Creek affairs, noting how much they paralleled those of the Cherokees. Pressure to move west was mounting more each day. No one knew how long the Indians could resist it.

The two started out early the next morning, waiting their turn to pull onto the ferry and cross the creek. Once across, Worcester urged the horses up the ramp cut in the bank. When they topped the bank the horses immediately shied and balked when two Creek warriors stepped into the road.

"Whoa," the minister called as he gripped the reins to keep control of the startled animals.

The man who had waylaid them also grabbed the bridle of one of the horses to try to calm it. He carried a musket pointed downward and wore streaks of paint across his face.

"They are from Okfuskee Town," Elias breathed quietly to his friend.

The man looked Elias over carefully and then stepped away from the horses. "You are not *Muskoke*," he said.

"I am Cherokee," Elias responded. "My friend is American."

The man nodded. "Please excuse us. We did not mean to trouble you. We are seeking a fugitive."

Though the man's voice held a conciliatory tone, his eyes held suspicion. His companion circled to the back of the wagon, lifting the canvas that covered their trunks and boxes of supplies. Satisfied that no one was hiding underneath the heavy cloth, he nodded to the other man.

"Please excuse us," he said again as he moved off the road. "May your journey be safe."

Nodding, Worcester flicked the reins and started the horses moving on the dirt road. They encountered no more difficulties before reaching Marietta. They arrived at New Echota three days later weary from the journey and eager to rest at the Watie farm.

Elias was driving as they pulled up to the frame two-story house where his parents lived. He set the wagon brake quickly and jumped down then hurried into the house. Samuel climbed down more slowly and followed him, but he paused at the open front door.

"*Etsi*," Elias called to his mother as he walked through the house to the kitchen out back. "Where is everyone?"

An older woman with jet black hair looked out from the kitchen door. She quickly grabbed a towel to dry her hands and came to meet her son.

"Buck!" she said with clear excitement as she pulled him into an embrace. "When did you get home?"

"We just arrived. Are you here alone?"

"Everyone is at the council grounds for Green Corn. I am just finishing my grape dumplings to take down there. You come too. Everyone will be so happy to see you."

"I have my friend Samuel with me," Elias said as the two stepped back into the kitchen. "I wrote you about him."

"Where is he? Did you leave him standing outside?"

Elias looked embarrassed. "Yes, I guess I did."

"Well, he can come too. Take this pan for me. We will walk to the grounds. Stickball will be starting soon. You know they will want you to play."

Elias obediently used a towel to lift the large enamel pot from the fireplace. His mother's dumplings still bubbled hot inside. He breathed in the fragrance of his childhood. His mother made the best grape dumplings of anyone among their Cherokee neighbors.

Susanna Watie grabbed her fringed dance shawl as they walked through the house to find Samuel still at the front door. Elias made the introductions and then the three of them followed a well-worn path to the New Echota council grounds where most everyone in the area had gathered for the Green Corn Festival. This annual gathering was a time of feasting, games, dances and storytelling.

The smell of the roasting ears of corn and the smoke from several fires filled the air. Elias set his mother's pot on a table where she directed him. Quickly he was surrounded by friends and neighbors to welcome him home.

Mrs. Watie took Samuel around to introduce him to some of the men who stood at the fires watching with anticipation as the women roasted the fresh ears of corn just gathered from the common fields.

It did not take long for Elias to be pulled into the stick ball game underway in a clearing near the council lodge. Samuel and Susanna joined a group who sat on the ground to watch the rough and tumble game that reminded him of lacrosse.

Samuel winced as Elias was knocked flat in the midst of the wild game that seemed to have few rules. After about twenty minutes, the players called for a break and they took turns getting a drink of water with a gourd dipper hanging from a large barrel placed at the edge of the field.

Elias joined his mother and friend, pulling on his shirt which he had discarded for the game. He flopped down beside Worcester, still breathing hard.

"I have grown soft at school," he said ruefully. He gingerly felt of his ribs.

"You're going to be sore in the morning," Worcester noted.

"No doubt."

"I will rub you with liniment," his mother offered.

"*Wado, Etsi.*"

The players were returning to the field to resume the game. A young man passed them on his way, a stick in his hands.

"You coming, old man?" he asked Elias with a smirk.

"I do not wish to die on a ball field," Elias shook his head. "You will have to represent the Watie family today, brother."

The other Watie son trotted to the field and play was quickly resumed. Elias and Samuel watched the game with interest while Mrs. Watie visited with nearby friends.

"Your brother is good at this game," Worcester noted.

"His name translates into English something like 'he takes a firm stand.' So we just call him Stand." There was evident pride in Elias' voice. "When he sets his feet to toss the ball, no one can move him. It is like running into a rock. He is just as firm in his mind – stubborn," here he lowered his voice to a whisper, "like our mother."

"I heard that," the woman chuckled.

"You know it is true, *Etsi*. I mean no disrespect."

Samuel joined in the laughter, enjoying the obvious friendship the mother and son shared. They continued to chat together until a caller announced that the food was ready. Then there was silence for awhile as everyone enjoyed the freshly roasted corn and other traditional dishes passed among them.

As the sun slipped below the horizon, the drum was set and the songs and dancing began. Elias declined to dance, preferring to sit with his friend and explain the meaning of the various dances. Fireflies danced too in the surrounding woods, like sparks rising up from the fires. Soon a full moon could be seen peeking through the trees casting a warm light over the celebration.

"Green Corn Moon," Elias said quietly, pointing toward the glowing orb. "You can fall in love under a moon like that." Then as if embarrassed by the remark he added, "Cherokees everywhere are feasting tonight."

"It's a good tradition," Worcester said.

"Yes," Elias smiled.

The moon was rising over the celebration in Arkansas Territory, throwing a shimmer over the waters of the bayou. The dancing was about to end and some of the women were packing what little remained of the feast. Edmund declined Bettie's offer of more cobbler but rose to help her set pans and dishes in her wagon.

He threw his ball stick into the wagon as Price Jolly, another player, walked by.

"Good game, Webber," his friend said. "You gave us the winning score."

"Yes," Edmund nodded. "You played well too."

Then he climbed into the wagon to join Walt, Charles and Jennie. Bettie went in search of her husband and Etta the other house slave.

While they waited, Edmund watched some of the young women helping mothers and grandmothers pack family wagons for the journey home. Moodily he supposed he should stop looking for a letter from Connecticut and simply seek permission to court one of these nice Cherokee girls.

Edmund's thoughts were interrupted by a groan from his nephew. Walt wrapped his arm around his stomach. "I do not feel so good," he said.

"You ate too much corn," Jennie scolded.

"I know," the boy readily agreed. "But it was so good."

Edmund smiled at the youth. He could remember stuffing himself during the Green Corn feast when he was a boy.

"Better hope you do not feel this way in the morning," he warned. "Your mother will take you to see Dr. Weeks at the mission. He will make you take castor oil."

Walt made a face. "I will feel better tomorrow," he promised.

His parents arrived at the wagon to hear his comment. Bettie checked his forehead for fever, but finding none she patted his aching stomach. "You must say a prayer tonight that you are better in the morning."

The boy's father made a disparaging noise as he climbed into the wagon. He waited for Bettie to climb up beside him and for Etta to join Jennie and the boys.

"He will be fine," Webber grunted as he started the horses forward. "If not we will get him some of the black drink from Spring Frog. That will make him right."

Walt groaned again and made a face. The threat of the powerful laxative would motivate him to feel better even more than castor oil. Edmund sent up a prayer of his own that Walt truly would be recovered by daybreak.

As they drove the trail that paralleled the bayou the moon seemed to follow them. It grew brighter as the last vestiges of sunlight disappeared and the song of the tree frogs thrummed in the still night air.

"Sure is pretty," Jennie commented.

Edmund nodded but said nothing. The moon spoke to him a memory that made his heart ache.

CHAPTER FIVE

Cornwall
July, 1825

Corrie and Harriet sat on the back porch of the rectory where a bit of a breeze made it cooler than the house. The two friends had spent all evening poring over the sketch book from Miss Fernell's dress shop while sipping cider and enjoying molasses cookies.

Harriet had narrowed her wedding dress choice down to two styles sketched in great detail in the dressmaker's book. But she struggled to make a final decision.

"I wish I could have both," she sighed as she flipped through the book one more time. "But I don't dare ask Papa for more than one dress. I am fortunate that he's even willing to pay for one."

"Most young women get at least two dresses," Corrie countered. "One for the wedding and a traveling suit for the wedding trip."

"I know," Harriet agreed. "But I'm not going to press for more. The whole family is at odds with one another over my marriage. I don't want to add another potential conflict about the expense. I'll just choose a dress that will serve both needs."

"Well, I'd go with the one with the narrower skirt then," Corrie advised. "It will be far less cumbersome for traveling."

Harriet studied the sketch of the narrow skirt topped with a form-fitting waist length jacket. It was attractive and would certainly serve her well as a Sunday dress after she moved to Georgia. With a last goodbye to the flowing gown she also wanted, she said, "It's settled then. The narrow skirt it is. Now all I have to do is decide on the fabric."

Corrie nearly rolled her eyes. She hoped she was not this indecisive when it came time for her to choose a wedding gown. If she ever had such an opportunity. It was looking unlikely right now.

They spent the next half hour holding up the various fabric swatches that Miss Fernell's clerk had also delivered to Harriet. The bride-to-be finally settled on a nubby silk the color of the molasses cookies they had consumed. It suited the color of her warm brown hair and eyes.

That decided the young women settled back into the deep, woven-cane chairs in the shade of the porch. The waxing moon hung like a disc in the sky, scudded occasionally with clouds.

Suddenly Harriet giggled as if a memory had tickled her mind.

"Remember when we snuck out of the house to watch the lunar eclipse?"

Corrie covered her mouth to suppress her own laughter. Her mother might still be working in the kitchen and she didn't want her to hear this part of their conversation.

"I still can't believe we didn't get caught," she said in a whisper. "It's a good thing your parents' bedroom is on the other side of the house from yours. They would have heard those boys for sure and we would have been locked in our rooms for a month."

"It would have been worth it," Harriet smiled. "And we didn't do anything wrong . . . not really. We wanted to see if Elias was right. He calculated the exact time for the eclipse just from the information in his science textbook."

"I have to admit I was skeptical," Corrie confessed. "And sneaking out with boys! That would have given the good people of Cornwall something to talk about."

"John, Elias and Edmund were perfect gentlemen."

"You and I know that, but we would have had a hard time convincing anyone else that we simply climbed the hill and watched an eclipse occur . . . at midnight on a school night."

"It was so romantic though, wasn't it? Elias wanted me to be with him when he was proven right. No one in his class believed him. And he knew we would need to be chaperoned so he asked you and Sarah and Edmund and John to come too."

"It was exciting," Corrie admitted. "I certainly never would have witnessed an eclipse if we hadn't sneaked out. But we can never tell anyone about it."

"Oh, I plan to tell our children, "Harriet nodded with determination. "And you can tell yours and Edmund's children."

Corrie sighed. She had tried to let her silence inform Harriet that she and Edmund had ended their relationship. But her friend was determined to believe that all three couples watching the moon that night would end up married.

"There isn't going to be a wedding for me and Edmund, Harriet," Corrie said at last. "I haven't received a letter from him for well over a month and I haven't written to him either. I don't plan to."

"Oh, Corrie, did you have a spat?"

"No. It just wasn't meant to be for us. Arkansas is very far away and I don't know that we could make it work. We are simply too different."

"No more so than Elias and I or John and Sarah."

"No, Edmund isn't like John and Elias. He is far more traditional in his thinking, in his ways. And look at the troubles you and Sarah have had. I don't have your courage, Harriet. I don't want people to hate me and call me ugly names. I just can't do it."

Harriet looked at her friend in sympathy. She knew Corrie wasn't adding that what she did reflected on her father, the town's pastor. He could find himself in trouble with his congregation if Corrie joined Sarah and Harriet and married an Indian.

"I'm sorry, Corrie," she said. "I think you and Edmund were meant to be together. But I understand your fears. I've had to wrestle with them myself and it wasn't easy. Forgive me for being so wrapped up in myself that I wasn't aware of your struggle."

"It's nothing compared to yours. Let's just forget about it, please."

"I won't say anything more," Harriet promised. "But that doesn't mean I can't pray. It may seem hopeless for you and Edmund now, but who knows what the future may hold."

Summer passed quickly with the work of preparing for weddings and new homes. In early August, Samuel Worcester paid a quick visit to Elias down at New Echota to admire the half-completed frame house he was building for Harriet.

"Do you think she will like it?" Elias asked as they walked through the rooms smelling of sawdust and fresh cut lumber.

"Having never met your young lady, I couldn't say," Worcester answered truthfully. "But it is a fine house and she no doubt will make it a beautiful home."

"And you are settled now at Brainerd?"

"Yes, with the help of the staff already there. I've been working with David Brown on writing a simple spelling book in Cherokee. I'm going to check on ordering type for Cherokee while I'm in Boston."

"You will travel to New England soon?" Elias asked as the two men exited the frame house and walked back to the Watie farm where Susanna had promised Worcester dinner.

"I'll board a steamboat at Ross's Landing day after tomorrow. I should be in New England in a month. And I must confess I am getting anxious to get home and see Ann."

"The separation can be hard," Elias smiled. "I will be thinking of you on your wedding day with good wishes for you and Ann."

"Thank you, my friend."

After the meal, Worcester set out to return to Chattanooga. He was already packed for his journey to New England and was anxious to be on his way.

Worcester arrived early at the waterfront on the day he was to leave for Boston. The dock at Ross's Landing was not yet busy and the steamboat *Tennessee* would not leave for an hour. After stowing his travel valise in his cabin, he made his way to a little tavern overlooking the waterfront to order coffee and read until it was time to board for the river journey.

Sitting at the next table was a well-dressed young gentleman looking over a sheaf of papers offered to him by an older man who wore the uniform of a government clerk. Samuel couldn't help but overhear their conversation, for the dining room was quiet at such an early hour.

"You can see that Governor Troup has laid out his position quite firmly," the clerk stated. "It is imperative that Secretary Barbour receive this correspondence before he meets with the Creek delegation."

"Yes, of course," the gentleman with dark green eyes said somewhat impatiently. "I understand. That is why General Jackson asked me to personally deliver this to the Secretary of War rather than trusting the mail. I'll arrive in Washington City well before the Creeks do. I know for a fact that they're still in their council meeting at Wetumpka."

The clerk seemed nervous. "Barbour should not know of your connection to the general, Mr. Ackley. The two men don't share the same views regarding the Indians and their removal."

"I'll be discreet," Ackley assured him. "This whole affair would have already been settled if Chilly McIntosh had not been allowed to escape and run to Washington seeking protection. Now President Adams wants a whole new treaty drawn up."

"He may find it difficult," the clerk worried. "The Creeks in Alabama do not look favorably on a treaty of any kind."

"The Alabama Creeks are less educated than those in Georgia. They will be easy to manipulate," Ackley predicted.

"Don't count on it," the clerk warned. "They've hired a couple of Cherokee lawyers to act as their 'secretaries.' The Indian Commissioners will not find it so easy to deceive them into signing a treaty that gives away their land in Georgia. Expect several months of wrangling before this deal is done."

Ackley frowned at this information. "Who are the Cherokees they've hired?"

"John Ridge and David Vann," the clerk supplied. "Both are sons of wealthy men and have been educated in New England. They are dangerous because they know the law."

"I've heard of Ridge. He married a girl from Cornwall."

"From what I have heard he is quite vocal against ceding Indian lands. He will no doubt advise the Creeks against doing so."

Ackley tucked the sheaf of papers into a case beside his chair. "Then we'll have to find a way to silence Ridge," he said with an edge to his voice.

Samuel watched as the two men stood and Ackley dropped money for his tab on the table. Then they exited the dining room and walked toward the *Tennessee*. It seemed he would be traveling with the man called Mr. Ackley.

The minister rose more slowly, paid for his coffee, then also strolled to the boat where a buzz of activity told him that boarding would begin soon. He wore a pensive look on his face.

When he had been interviewed by the mission board for the position at Brainerd Mission he had been full of enthusiastic plans for work among the Cherokees. He assured the board of his belief that education and the gospel message would help secure peace for the people he had already come to view as his friends.

Ann had tried to temper his excitement with a more down-to-earth understanding of the pressures the Cherokees faced. In a month he would be back with his new bride and together they would share these challenges alongside their Cherokee friends.

Samuel and Ann Worcester arrived back at Brainerd Mission as several neighbors were leaving for New Echota. The Cherokee annual council meeting was being held at the Cherokee capital in Georgia.

Chief Pathkiller presided over the week-long meeting of Cherokee leaders. Debate on the issues was spirited but respectful and attended by both men and women. John and Elias had been asked to act as clerks at the council and were kept busy taking notes during the many speeches.

After the last day of the council John and Sarah walked with Elias to his home where they had stayed during the week of meetings. It was too far for them to travel back and forth from Running Waters so they had accepted Elias' invitation to stay at his newly completed home.

Elias carried a satchel full of papers covered with his cramped writing. The three friends would spend the evening transcribing the men's notes into both Cherokee and English while their memories of the proceedings were still fresh. His bedraggled quill pen was tucked into the strings tying the satchel closed and a leather bag holding a bottle of ink and a blotting rag daggled from his ink-stained fingers.

"I hope you did a better job than me at taking down your father's speech, John," Elias said as they approached his home. "I was so wrapped up in listening to his argument that I found myself forgetting to take notes."

"I think I have it," John said. "But if I missed anything, Sarah will remember." He smiled at the pretty blonde at his side who was dressed in a fashionable navy walking outfit.

"I was listening very closely to the debate," Sarah confirmed. Since she was the unnamed topic of discussion, Sarah had following it closely. Living for over a year among the Cherokees had given her a good grasp of the language.

John's father, Major Ridge, had introduced a proposal that children born to Cherokee fathers be afforded recognition as Cherokee citizens just as children born to Cherokee mothers. The major wanted his grandchildren to be Cherokee. Chief Pathkiller had been skeptical at first and several of the more traditional members of the council spoke against it, but in the end the resolution was adopted. Ridge had pointed out that such children would have Cherokee grandmothers and that convinced the majority. Elias was elated not only for himself and Harriet but also for his friends.

They stepped inside the house and all set their hats on a little table by the door. Elias had sparsely furnished his home, knowing Harriet would enjoy choosing the décor herself. Sarah had chided him for having no curtains on the windows but he had simply shrugged. Few of the isolated farm homes in the area had such niceties.

"I'll let Harriet choose," was all Elias had to say.

The men spread their notes across the dining table while Sarah heated the soup Susanna Watie had left in the kitchen for them. Then while they ate they arranged the notes and discussed the day's events.

"I will write to Edmund soon to tell him about this new law," Elias said after they had finished their meal. He was already copying his notes onto a fresh sheet of paper. "Perhaps he can convince his brother or Chief Jolly to enact something similar for the Cherokees in Arkansas. Or if not, Edmund could move back to Georgia and he and Corrie could marry and live here. I know Harriet would be thrilled to have her best friend close by."

John shook his head. Sarah saw the stubborn set to his jaw and took that moment to walk to the kitchen for more coffee.

"They all should move back," he said forcefully. "Does it not bother you to refer to someone as chief other than Pathkiller? The Cherokees should not be two nations. It weakens our position here. I don't know how many times I have had this thrown in my face by Georgia officials. Cherokees should never have agreed to move west."

Elias looked surprised at his cousin's vehemence. "John, we have family who moved west. They wanted to be free from the harassment we must deal with every day back here."

"We must face it as a united people," John said as Sarah poured more coffee into his cup. "And you and I both know that the harassment didn't end for those who moved to Arkansas . . . or even to Texas. We experienced it in Connecticut. We cannot change our skin and for some people that will always make us different and despised."

Elias saw the pained look that crossed Sarah's face before she went back to the kitchen. His cousin felt things passionately and knew he could express himself honestly in the Boudinot home. But he didn't seem to realize that his words could hurt his Connecticut wife.

"You make Sarah sad," Elias said quietly.

John looked surprised, then he glanced toward the kitchen. "I forget sometimes that she isn't Cherokee," he admitted. "I will apologize to her."

Elias looked out the window at the setting sun. "It is getting late and you need to get an early start tomorrow," he said. "Perhaps we should retire for the evening."

"You are sure it is no inconvenience to see Sarah home in the morning? I really need to reach Spring Place by noon. David will be waiting for me to begin our journey to Washington City."

"My mother and I are happy to escort her home. She will give me decorating instructions the whole way I am sure."

The men smiled at each other and then rose from the table. "You will join the Creeks in Washington?" Elias asked.

"Yes, Yahola and Menawa want us to translate for them. They don't trust the Indian Commissioner and frankly neither do I."

"Do you think the Creeks will stand firm against the Indian Springs Treaty?"

"I believe that is their intent," John said as he rolled his shoulders to ease the tension that had built up while sitting hunched over his notes most of the day. "But I know what the politicians in Georgia and Washington want. They want every acre of Indian land they can get. I hope I can help them avoid any more loss of Creek land."

"I hated to hear about what happened to McIntosh," Elias said quietly as the two of them carried their coffee cups to the kitchen. "The death penalty was harsh don't you think?"

"McIntosh knew the consequences," John replied. "He made his choice."

"And now your father is pushing for the same policy for Cherokees. Is this wise, John?"

"We must take a stand," John said stubbornly. "And live with the consequences."

"Or die?" Elias dropped his voice to a whisper so Sarah wouldn't hear.

"No one needs to die," John responded, in an equally quiet voice. "If we just stand together." Then he smiled as he handed Sarah his dishes. "I want my Cherokee children to grow up here on Cherokee land."

"Oh, you do?" Sarah asked, returning his smile. "Then we'll just have to see to that."

Elias slipped out of the kitchen, leaving the couple alone. He walked upstairs to his bedroom and paused to look out the window toward the trees by the river. He heard the hoot of an owl and it gave him a shiver. Though he didn't believe in the superstition that the presence of an owl portended death, he could not shake a sense of dread.

At Chief John Jolly's house overlooking Spadra Creek, Edmund joined a group of other Cherokee men saddling their horses for a ride to Fort Smith. He looked across the back of his horse as he tightened its cinch, noting that his brother Walter and good friend Spring Frog were already mounted and ready to start the two-day ride.

The two men were engaged in conversation in Cherokee. Though Walter understood English fairly well he refused to speak it. Spring Frog spoke it only a little and Chief Jolly was somewhat proficient in the language. But only Edmund could read English. So he had been asked to join the Cherokee delegation attending a boundary discussion at the fort.

The Arkansas Territorial government wanted a better definition of the area that had been promised to the Choctaws in Mississippi in a treaty signed at Doak's Stand back in 1820. The offer had been confirmed with another treaty early this year.

Arkansas politicians did not like the fact that sections of their territory were being offered to the southeastern tribes without their knowledge or consent. With each new treaty, the western boundary of Arkansas was shifted eastward. Edmund thought it ironic that the Arkansas leaders were indignant at this "great land grab." They failed to see that this was exactly what the Indians faced.

To calm flaring tempers, the commander of Fort Smith and Fort Gibson had invited all concerned parties to a meeting to discuss the boundary established by the Choctaw treaties. Colonel Matthew Arbuckle was the government authority for Indian relations in this part of the country. His assignment of keeping peace on the frontier seemed to involve endless meetings with angry men.

When Jolly exited his front door to mount his waiting horse, Edmund used the reins and a fistful of his horse's mane to climb onto his own horse. With a click of his tongue he started the sturdy paint and directed it to fall in line on the trail behind his brother.

The ride was pleasant in the cool morning air with the hardwood trees in the mountains putting on their autumn colors. More than once they startled a covey of quails into flight and Edmund wished he was on a hunting foray instead of traveling to a treaty meeting.

They followed the northwesterly course of the Arkansas River and camped for the night by a small tributary called Mulberry River. Edmund and Spring Frog walked the bank of the river looking for any ripe mulberries on the trees that lined the narrow stream. Most of the trees had been picked over by birds, but they found enough of the ripe, black berries to fill the small grapevine basket Bettie had packed bread in. The men enjoyed the fruit with their jerky and cornbread that evening.

They arrived at Fort Smith the following afternoon. Jolly led his delegation to the headquarters building. A corporal at the front desk greeted them and took their names. He informed them that Colonel Arbuckle was expected to arrive shortly and the meeting would begin in about an hour. They were welcome to set up their camp on the parade grounds. Then he called for a private to show them around.

As they walked across the garrison, Edmund thought he heard someone call his name. He paused to look around, wondering who might know him here.

"Edmund Webber, is that you?" a voice called again. He turned to find a classmate from the Mission School walking toward him, hand extended.

Edmund offered his own hand and the two men exchanged a handshake.

"McKee," Edmund greeted the man who had been a year ahead of him at school. He could not recall his last name but remembered that he was Choctaw.

"Folsom," McKee supplied.

"Sorry. It's been awhile."

"Yes, it has," the Choctaw fell into step with Edmund and they continued toward the parade ground. "What brings you to Fort Smith?"

"I'm with the Cherokee delegation," Edmund explained, waving a hand toward the others of his group. "We were invited by Colonel Arbuckle."

"For the boundary talks?"

"Yes. I think there may be some Cherokees still living in Miller County. They'll be expected to move now that this area is being given to Choctaws. Are you an official delegate?"

"Yes, I'll be interpreting. Just as you will, I suppose."

"Chief Jolly speaks English, but he wanted me to help with reading any documents that might be drawn up."

"The same for me. My brother and father speak the language as does Josiah Doak, our other delegate. But I have the most schooling so I am to review the documents."

By this time they had reached the area where tents had been supplied by the Seventh Infantry for their Indian guests. Edmund and McKee introduced the other members of their respective delegations. After the Cherokees had stowed their packs in the tents, they all made their way back toward headquarters.

All interested parties gathered in a large meeting space on the second floor of the log building. Besides the Choctaw and Cherokee delegations, there were Arkansas Territory officials and three men from Shawneetown representing residents of the territorial county that spanned the area between the Arkansas River and the Red River. Edmund could not miss the looks of animosity being directed toward him and the other Indian delegates by the Miller County men.

Shortly Colonel Matthew Arbuckle stepped into the room, followed by two lieutenants. One immediately sat at a small desk at the front of the room, took out writing supplies and prepared to keep notes for the meeting. The commander made his way around the room, introducing himself to those individuals new to him.

A balding man with a beaky nose, Arbuckle was only of average height, but he had an imposing presence. He was clearly in charge of the meeting and even the politicians from Little Rock were deferential toward him.

After making introductions, Arbuckle invited everyone to take a seat. A large table that ran down the length of the room had wooden chairs around it. There were not enough chairs at the table for everyone so Edmund and McKee took seats in chairs along the outer wall.

The colonel began with a welcome speech from President Adams and Secretary of War James Barbour. He stated plainly that the cession of most of Miller County to the Choctaws was not up for debate. The Senate had ratified the treaty that had been completed earlier in the year.

"Our effort today is to ensure that the boundary lines for the Choctaw land is clearly defined and understood by everyone involved. Anyone who wishes to speak to this issue may do so now."

Edmund settled back into his seat. He knew that an invitation to speak to the Indians meant each one of them would speak. Oratory was an important skill and speeches could wax long as an entire history of a matter would be told. They would likely be here for hours.

McKee saw Edmund's gesture and smiled. "The Americans think we Indians are taciturn," he said softly. "Most have never heard us give a speech."

Edmund chuckled quietly. "I wish I had a cup of that coffee." He nodded toward an urn sitting on a table along the opposite wall. He had caught its aroma when they entered the room.

McKee nodded and also settled back for an afternoon of speechmaking.

It seemed that few of the men in the room were happy with the fact that Miller County was soon to be occupied by the Choctaws who were to be removed from Mississippi. Especially angry were the men from the county seat of Shawneetown. Several dozen families were farming or running fur traps in the region. They would be required to move within a year's time.

"We're getting up a petition," one of the men stated. "We're gonna let President Adams know exactly what we think about being driven off our land. It ain't right!"

"Then you know exactly how we Indians feel," Josiah Doak interjected. Though he was actually English, he had married a Choctaw woman and had long traded among her people. He had already moved west and had established a new trading post near Fort Towson down by the Red River.

His statement brought a rush of angry words from several of the delegates forcing Arbuckle to rap on the table to restore order.

"Gentlemen, I think we need to take a short break." Then he turned to his subordinate. "Summers order a pot of fresh coffee brought in."

The lieutenant nodded and stepped out of the room. Soon two privates arrived carrying another urn and a tray of thick white china cups. Setting them on the side table, they retrieved the first urn and then slipped out of the room.

Edmund and McKee joined the other men in gathering around the coffee table. After they had poured themselves a cup they retreated to a corner for quiet conversation.

"What have you done since graduation?" Edmund asked.

"I am clerking in my father's trading post," McKee replied. "Got married two years ago and we just had a son earlier this year."

"Congratulations," Edmund said, hiding a twinge of envy.

"*Yakoke*," nodded McKee. "Thank you. And what about you? Did you marry the pastor's daughter as everyone expected?"

Edmund stared into the black depths of his coffee cup. "No," he said. "It was not going to work for us. It seems not strange for an Indian woman to marry a white man. But no one wants an Indian man to marry a white woman."

"I thought John Ridge had married Mr. Northrup's daughter."

"Yes," Edmund confirmed. "But John wants the Cherokees to embrace white culture. He believes it will enable us to keep our land back east. But I don't believe it will. I don't want to have to stop being Cherokee to have my rights respected."

McKee nodded. "I know. Sometimes I feel as if I am straddling two worlds and I shall be split in two for it."

Edmund sighed, knowing that feeling well. He had experienced it all the years he had attended school. He had chosen an education and Christianity. He was grateful to have received both. But at times it made him feel at odds with himself and most certainly with his brother. He had tried to come back to Arkansas and return to living as a Cherokee. But he could not make his heart come back from Cornwall.

McKee must have sensed Edmund's change in mood for he excused himself to get more coffee. By this time Arbuckle was calling for the meeting to resume. He unrolled a large map prepared by the army engineer and spread it out on the table.

"Here, gentlemen, are the boundaries of the new Choctaw nation. It begins 100 paces east of Fort Smith, then runs directly south to the Red River . . ."

Edmund barely heard the rest of the discussion. He stared out the window toward the west and could see the "Belle Point," the jut of land between the Arkansas and Poteau Rivers. Beyond the rivers rose layers of blue mountains to the south. It made him homesick for Georgia. It made him wish he could roll back time and simply be a Cherokee again.

CHAPTER SIX

Ross's Landing, Tennessee
February 1826

Some months later at the Chattanooga waterfront, Elias sat in his small wagon waiting for the steamboat *Tennessee* to dock. He turned up the collar of his coat against a cold wind that made the water of the Tennessee River choppy. He was waiting for his cousin John to disembark from the boat, returning home after his lengthy stay in Washington City.

Elias had come the day before expecting the *Tennessee t*o arrive in the afternoon. But the boat had been delayed by a storm so he spent the night at Brainerd Mission, visiting with Samuel and Ann. They were full of enthusiastic plans for printing their Cherokee spelling book and anxiously awaiting the newly cast type to arrive from Boston. Samuel had convinced the American Board of Missions to pay for the type and for a printing press. Both would arrive later this year.

Now Elias sat in the morning cold, wishing he had a covered carriage instead of this open farm wagon. To pass the time, he reached into his pocket and pulled out a letter from Harriet. He had read it immediately when he picked up the mail at New Echota. But he would enjoy reading it again several more times before he would leave for Cornwall in a month.

He smiled at Harriet's hurried penmanship, her excitement over wedding plans spilling onto the pages. She was marking off the days until they would be married, she confided, keeping a secret calendar where no prying eyes would see it.

She told him her wedding gown was completed and she was thrilled with how beautiful it was. She shared a few menu items she planned for the wedding supper after the ceremony at her parents' home. The Golds' cook and Mrs. Carroll, the Tuttles' housekeeper, would work together to prepare the meal. The guest list would be small – only her parents, one of her sisters, the Tuttles and the Northrups, Sarah's parents, would attend.

The rest of her family was still against the union and her brother Stephen was watching the stage station and threatening to waylay Elias when he arrived. For that reason, she advised, it might be best if Elias came another way or wore some sort of disguise.

The teacher frowned at this portion of the letter. He worried about what grief Harriet was being given by her family and others in the community. He was angry that he could not shelter her from the scorn he knew she faced and prayed again for the time to pass quickly until he could marry her and take her away from the wagging tongues of Cornwall.

"You look the way I feel," a voice interrupted his thoughts.

Elias looked up from the letter to find John standing at the wagon wheel.

"John," he exclaimed while quickly returning the letter to his pocket. "I did not see you leave the boat."

"You were somewhere else," John replied as he stowed his bags in the wagon bed then mounted the wheel to take a seat beside Elias.

"A letter of ill tidings?" he asked.

"No," Elias said. "Well, only somewhat. Harriet warns me that I will not be welcomed with open arms by the people of Cornwall next month."

"No surprise there," John said as Elias took up the reins and released the brake of the wagon.

"Do you need to get something to eat before we leave Chattanooga?"

"No, just get me home," his cousin stated as he clawed at the silk cravat that held his high white collar around his neck. His actions revealed agitation or anger. He wrestled with his tie, nearly growling as he tore it off and stuffed it into his pocket.

"What did that tie do to you?" Elias asked, amused but also concerned.

"I'm tired of trying to pretend I'm not an Indian," John stated flatly. "It has not served me well."

"What happened in Washington?"

"The Creeks signed away nearly every acre of their land in Georgia!"

"What?" Elias asked in disbelief. "I thought they were determined to undo the Indian Springs Treaty. Why did they change their minds?"

"I do not know," John shook his head, his frustration visible. "We arrived in Washington City in agreement that they would disavow what McIntosh had signed. But the negotiations had scarcely begun when their demeanor toward me changed. I suspect the Indian Commissioner told some lie about me to undermine my influence. Whatever he said worked. Yahola was still willing to listen to my advice, but Menawa was not. He barely tolerated my presence as did Secretary Barbour."

"So the Creeks were persuaded to sell their Georgia lands." It was more a statement than a question. Elias could understand why John was so angry.

"The argument Barbour made was that Georgia officials would do everything in their power to suspend the sovereignty of the Lower Creeks. It would be better for them to either move to Alabama and join the Upper Creeks or move west. The government will pay the expenses of moving and rebuilding for anyone who chooses to go west. Someone from the McIntosh group will be sent out there to select a location for them in the land the Osages are to vacate."

Elias shook his head. It was like the chess game he had seen played by some of the fellows at the mission school. And the Indians were the pawns.

For the first time since his sister had moved to Arkansas, Elias wondered if the Webbers had made the better choice. No matter how conciliatory the Creeks and Cherokees tried to be, the government always seemed to want more.

"More?" Corrie asked Harriet, as she held up a bow she was fashioning out of white tulle. They were creating the bows to adorn the candles holders in the Golds' front parlor. This would be the only decorations for the ceremony that was now less than a week away.

"No, this will be enough," Harriet replied as she tucked the bows into a box, careful not to crush them. She would keep them hidden in her bedroom until the morning of the wedding. The fewer people who were aware of the wedding preparations the better. The Golds had a very real fear that someone might try to stop the ceremony from taking place. Stephen Gold had hinted at it more than once.

Corrie could tell that Harriet's thoughts were not on pretty bows or white wax candles.

"Are you worried?" she asked quietly as she folded the remaining fabric.

"I'm trying not to give in to fear," Harriet sighed. "I know Stephen would never hurt me, but if he does anything to Elias . . . ." She left the sentence unfinished but her eyes flashed with anger.

"Your brother has always been more bluster than action," Corrie offered. "He wants to look tough to the other boys at Westminster."

"That's just it," Harriet said. "I think he's being taunted by those boys. He thinks he has something to prove. What if they all decided to kidnap Elias . . . or worse? I'll just die if anything happens to him because of me."

"Don't borrow trouble," Corrie advised, going to sit beside her friend on her big four-poster bed. "Elias is smart and careful. He's not going to let those boys get to him. Remember how he would sneak up on us when we were studying on the school lawn. We never saw him or heard him until he was standing right behind us. Then we'd scream like silly school girls."

Harriet giggled at the memory. "And he would always feel bad that he scared us and would apologize and leave us some little gift later."

"He left you little gifts," Corrie corrected her friend with a smile. "All I received was the apology."

Harriet tried to look contrite but did not succeed. Corrie's words had helped to allay her fears and now she looked happy again. She crossed the room and sat on the small chintz-covered stool beside her bureau to check her hair in a hand mirror.

"I know Elias will use caution when he arrives. He didn't even tell me exactly which day he planned to reach Cornwall, only that he would be here well before the time of the wedding."

"So there you see," Corrie encouraged. "He'll slip into town and no one will be the wiser."

"Isn't it terrible that he must be so secretive?" Harriet sighed. "But I know there is talk in town. Miss Fernell let it slip to Mrs. Graham that she had finished my wedding gown. Now everyone in Mother's Ladies' Aide Society has been asking her about it. They are none too happy that Mother hasn't convinced me to end my engagement."

Corrie was quiet for a moment. Even her own employer had mentioned the impending wedding and made it clear she didn't approve of Harriet's plan to marry an Indian. Mrs. Huddleston also made it clear that she didn't like the fact that Corrie was Harriet's good friend and was standing by her in this decision. Corrie had been extra careful the last few weeks to say or do nothing that would stir up the woman's hard feelings.

"Well, the secretiveness will all be over soon," Corrie said at last. "And you'll be Mrs. Elias Boudinot of New Echota, Georgia."

Harriet turned to face her dear friend. "Thank you, Corrie," the young woman said with a slight catch in her voice. "I don't know what I would have done all this time without your constant encouragement."

Corrie waved away the sentiment to keep from crying herself. "Just think, Harriet. Only four more days until Tuesday. Then all this hardship will be forgotten."

Elias tossed aside the newspaper he had been trying to read in his room at a small hostelry in Danbury. He chafed with impatience on this Sabbath morning. He was within 30 miles of Harriet but could not travel on this day of rest. And no reputable businesses were open on Sunday so he was forced to wait here at the lodging house with nothing to do.

He tried to pray and had read from the Scriptures when he awoke at dawn, but now the rest of the day stretched before him. He pulled out his pocket watch to check the hour again. It wasn't even time yet for the noon meal which he knew would be a cold spread of meats and cheese with bread and cider in the dining room.

He walked to the tiny window that needed a good cleaning and looked across the street to a hat factory. Its windows were dark and the door padlocked. The street was empty except for a few folks who were likely walking to church. Elias had considered attending service at one of several churches in town, but had thought better of it. He couldn't be certain that someone from Cornwall might be in town and might recognize him from his days at school.

In his mind he ran through his plan for tomorrow. He had rented a small wagon and horse for the drive to Cornwall. He had packed some old clothes to wear including a wide-brimmed hat and neckerchief. He wished the roads were dusty for that would give him an excuse to pull the scarf over his mouth to hide more of his face. But the roads were still a bit muddy from snow melt. His worn, high boots would likely be splattered with mud by the time he reached his destination.

He had written to a friend named Isaiah Hicks who was a senior at the Mission School. Isaiah would allow Elias to spend Monday night in his dorm room and then would join the groom at the Golds' home and serve as his witness for the wedding.

This thought made Elias turn from the window and cross to the bed where his leather valise sat. Once more he reached to the bottom of the bag to assure himself that the small box holding Harriet's ring was still there. He smiled ruefully at his action. The box was exactly where it had been the last time he checked. He could imagine Sam Worcester laughing at his nervous gesture.

He set the valise on the floor and flopped onto the bed with its creaky springs. He took up the newspaper again determined to read every single item in it to pass the time and hopefully hurry it along.

The next morning, he rose before light after a restless night in the drafty room. He donned his "freighter" clothes and heavy boots, slapped the hat on his head and tried to walk quietly down the stairs so as not to awaken other guests.

In the dining room on the main floor, he greeted the innkeeper. She held up a hand to indicate he should wait and then hurried into the kitchen. Shortly she returned with a small, lumpy cotton sack. He had asked Mrs. Campbell to pack a breakfast for him so he could leave at daybreak.

"I 'ave a few biscuits for ye with some slices of ham and cheese," the woman explained rather breathlessly. "There's an apple as well and a slice of me gingerbread." She handed the sack to him and he took it gratefully. She also held out a tightly closed sorghum tin and when Elias grasped it he could feel its warmth and knew it held hot coffee.

"Thank you, ma'am," he said. "I will return the tin on my way back through."

"Oh, no need," Mrs. Campbell said. "I 'ave dozens of 'em. Yous can keep it."

"Thank you."

"Yous have a safe trip now . . . where'er you're goin'." Curiosity was written on her face. The innkeeper probably knew every regular freighter who came through this area, but Elias was new to her and she likely had noticed his Georgia drawl and his Indian features. It was obvious that she wanted to ask about his business in Connecticut, but good manners kept her from doing so.

"You are kind, ma'am," was all Elias would say. Normally he wouldn't have minded taking a moment to chat with the woman, but today he was anxious to be on the road. And though news of his presence in Danbury couldn't reach Cornwall before he did, he still felt it would be best to say nothing of his destination or his reason for being here.

With his hands full now, he could only nod his goodbye, catching himself before he said something in Cherokee. He was scolding himself for the mental lapse as he walked to the nearby livery where his horse and wagon waited.

A stable boy walked the horse out of its stall and helped Elias hitch it to the wagon. The livery owner ambled over so Elias could settle up.

The teacher pointed to an old barrel with a missing stave that sat by the stable doors. "Would you sell me that old barrel?" he asked.

"It won't hold anything," the liveryman replied. "It's worthless. You can have it and take it off my hands."

"Thanks," Elias picked up the barrel and set it near his valise in the wagon bed. Then he covered it with the canvas tarp that came with the wagon. He ignored the curious looks of the man and his hired helper. He placed the sack and tin that Mrs. Campbell had given him under the wagon seat, then pulled himself up onto the bench.

"Good day to you," he said with a pull of his hat brim. Then he took the reins and started the horse up the road that would take him through Washington, Connecticut and then on to Cornwall. He would keep an eye out for other "freight" along the way to fill the wagon bed and make his disguise believable.

Elias ate his breakfast while keeping a steady pace and reached Washington by mid morning. It was too early for dinner, but the horse needed a rest so he stopped for coffee at a tavern by the road and asked for bread and cheese to eat later.

So far the young Cherokee had encountered no difficulties but as he continued toward Cornwall he grew more wary. He had been gone from the town for two years and didn't know if he would be easily recognized, but he would take no chances as Harriet had advised.

He entered the small village and directed the horse toward the one livery in town. This was also the stagecoach way station so he decided to drive by slowly rather than stopping right away. He approached the large barn and saw nothing amiss at first but just as he was about to stop he caught a glimpse of a figure standing near a shed where the liveryman stored bags of oats.

Elias glanced at the sun. It was close to the time when the stage from Hartford usually arrived. It appeared to him that the man by the shed wasn't waiting to catch the stage. He was waiting to catch someone on the stage. Elias kept driving, while tugging his hat a little lower.

As he passed the other side of the stable, he caught sight of another man wearing a sweater in the crimson color of Westminster Academy. He couldn't be sure, but he thought it was Harriet's younger brother.

He ducked his chin into his neckerchief, hoping it would hide most of his face. Elias kept the horse at a steady pace so as not to call attention to himself. He continued on toward the town square, passing the post office. His eyes scanned the doorways and alleyways but saw no one watching him there. He continued past the church then turned the horse into the driveway of the rectory next door.

Catching sight of Mr. Carroll, Elias stopped the wagon and hopped stiffly down from the bench. He walked to the back of the house where the older man was working to loosen the soil of the large garden he planted each year.

"Mr. Carroll," Elias said quietly as he approached the caretaker.

Looking up from his work, Carroll squinted to study the young man approaching him. "Is that you, Mr. Boudinot?"

"Yes, sir. I have just arrived in town."

Mr. Carroll looked Elias over from up to down. "You aren't your usually dapper self today, I see," he observed.

"No, sir. I thought to wear something more suitable for travel and for not drawing attention to my arrival."

"Ayuh," the man nodded, "I understand."

"Is Pastor Tuttle home?"

"No, he's gone to visit a sick parishioner," Carroll replied, while leaning on his rake. "Mrs. Pastor and my wife have taken food over to the Golds' home for your wedding feast tomorrow. And Miss Cornelia is at work right now."

Elias nodded and looked thoughtfully at the house. "Would it trouble you if I left my horse and wagon here? Perhaps in your barn? The horse is tired and I don't want to overwork it."

"No trouble at all. I'll see to it if you want to go calling on your young lady."

"First I would like to change clothes. I have a friend at the mission school who will let me stay with him. I will go there first."

The Cherokee paused and glanced toward the street. "Have you seen Harriet's brother around here?"

"He's been by once this morning. I suspect he's up to no good."

"So do I and so does Harriet. I need to get to the school without him seeing me."

"Take the alley over to Jewell Street and then circle around along the brook," Carroll suggested. "There's plenty of tree cover there."

"Yes, I remember that," Elias nodded. "Thank you."

He walked over to the wagon and lifted his valise out of the bed. Then he sat on the back stoop and pulled off his boots. Reaching into his bag he pulled out a pair of deerskin moccasins and slipped them on. The soft but sturdy material would be quieter and would enable him to run should it become necessary.

He set his boots on the porch, wondering ruefully how many other grooms had to go to such lengths to marry. It reminded him of all the tales of star-crossed lovers that were a staple among the folks who lived in the mountains of Georgia and Tennessee. Like the play by Shakespeare he had studied in his literature class, these stories never had a happy ending.

He shook off the dark thought and sent up a prayer instead. Then he took off his hat and coat to rid himself of any unnecessary weight. He did not feel fear; he was simply determined to avoid violence if possible. If that meant running, then that was what he would do.

He didn't want to get into a fight with Stephen Gold or any of his young friends. He was probably in better physical condition than those schoolboys after having spent months felling logs and building his house. But he had nothing to prove and didn't want to stir up any more anger among the townspeople. He would use his hunting and running skills to slip around town to the school on the hill. Hopefully no one in town would even be aware of his presence.

"Please tell the Tuttles I am here," Elias asked of the caretaker.

"Ayuh," Mr. Carroll nodded. "Godspeed to you, young man."

The caretaker watched as Elias tossed his valise over the back fence into the alley. Then he backed up a few steps to get a running start and in a single movement vaulted over the brick wall.

Mr. Carroll watched in amused admiration. "Try to catch that, young punks," he chuckled as he went to move the wagon into the barn.

To get to Jewell Street Elias would have to go back to the town square. He kept to the alley behind the church and stealthily moved from building to building to the other end of the block where the post office stood. He would have to cross the street here so he paused to study the situation.

People came and went along the sidewalks that lined the square, conducting business at the meat market, the dressmaker's shop and the apothecary's. No one seemed to be looking his way, so he gripped his valise more firmly and sprinted silently across the cobblestone street to the alley on the other side.

He made it to the shadows behind the butcher's shop and was about to resume his steady walk to the next street when he heard a voice call. "Hey, it's Boudinot!"

Without even looking to see who had spotted him, Elias began to run. He was used to running. He had learned the art of pacing oneself for the hunt or for battle. He knew how to move through the woods silently and almost effortlessly. He had one more block to reach Jewell Street then after passing a few houses he would cross an open field to reach the woods that lined the brook.

He could hear footsteps pounding after him and he smiled. The heavy shoes his adversaries wore would slow them down and wear them out. He settled into his stride and reached Jewell Street within seconds. He raced past the Huddleston home and glimpsed Corrie sitting on the front porch while her young charges played on the lawn. He raised a hand to her, but did not slow his pace. He saw her rise from her chair, shock on her face.

He wished her could tell her not to worry. He could already tell that the boys chasing him were losing ground. Elias was actually enjoying himself. But he feared Corrie would see Harriet before he did and he knew this episode would frighten her.

The Cherokee sprinted past the remaining homes and darted across the field toward the tree line. His eyes searched the stretch of woods along the small brook. Quickly he spotted what he was looking for. A large maple tree, likely more than a century old, stood to his right toward the school road and its bridge over the brook.

He reached the trees just as Stephen and his cohorts were at the edge of the field. In the dim light of the timber, he slipped behind the maple, set down his bag and flattened his back against the bark. He could feel his heart pounding from the run and he forced himself to take deep, but quiet breaths.

He waited as the boys crossed the field, their feet pounding the grass and their labored breathing sounding loud in the still air. All the woodland creatures had gone silent at the approach of this crashing, bellowing beast. Elias reached to the small of his back where he had tucked a knife sheathed in a leather pouch. He did not intend to use it but he felt reassured that it was there.

The boys slowed their pace as they entered the timber and jogged past Elias without seeing him. They were intent on crossing the brook and splashed noisily through the water.

Elias shook his head at their actions. If this had been a real battle situation, they would be in serious trouble. He almost felt sorry for them.

Taking up his valise again he walked along the bank of the little stream, keeping his feet quiet. He reached the bridge and vaulted over its rock wall, crossed the steam, and then began a slow lope toward the school.

To his right he could see Stephen and his four friends. They were attempting to cross Farmer Boulware's newly plowed and very muddy field. Elias knew from his school days that the farmer always liked to get his fields plowed early and allow the last snow to melt and soften the earth before he sowed his seed.

He knew exactly when his adversaries saw him. They plowed to a stop and then made a pivot toward him. But those heavy shoes were now wet and caked with mud and must have felt like lead.

Elias slowed to a walk as he approached the brick dormitory. School was out for the day and a number of students lounged on the wide stone steps of their quarters. They had watched Elias as he ran and were aware of the Westminster boys as well.

The Cherokee teacher scanned their faces hoping to recognize students who would have been freshmen when he was a senior. One stood as he approached and came down the steps.

"Is that you, Boudinot?" he asked.

"Hello, Isaiah. Yes it is."

"Did you run all the way from Georgia?' the boy asked with a smile.

"Just from Jewell Street." Elias offered his hand and Isaiah shook it.

"I see you outran your welcoming committee."

"It would seem so. But they will still wish to express their displeasure at my presence."

"Then we will give them our own welcome," Isaiah said with a nod to the other fellows. He took the elbow of his friend and led Elias up the stairs and through the double doors of the dorm. The other students closed rank behind them, filling the steps with a gauntlet of crossed arms and solemn faces.

Stephen stopped on the sidewalk some distance from the mission students. He bent and grabbed his knees in exhaustion. "This isn't over, Boudinot," he growled with ragged breath.

Elias didn't even look back.

The groom shared the story of his run over supper that evening at the Tuttles. He downplayed the ease with which he had bested the Westminster lads, but Corrie couldn't help but grin at the image his tale conjured up.

Harriet sat next to her fiancé, a look of dismay on her face. "I'm so sorry, Elias," she said.

He shrugged and gave her hand a squeeze. "No harm was done," he assured her. "I needed a good run after sitting on that hard wagon bench for five hours."

"But it isn't right for you to be treated in such a way." Harriet looked ready to cry. She turned to her parents who sat opposite her at the dinner table. "Papa, you simply must make sure Stephen doesn't do something at my wedding tomorrow."

"Don't worry," Benjamin Gold said. "I will personally visit the school tomorrow and I will insist that the headmaster keep Stephen in class all day. He will be confined to his dormitory as punishment for missing school today."

Julia Tuttle spoke then. "Might I suggest that we move the ceremony up tomorrow? Instead of having it at two o'clock we could have it at eleven. Most of the food for the meal has been prepared already. We'll simply serve it at noon instead of for supper."

"Are you sure that's no trouble?" Eleanor Gold asked.

"None at all. We had planned to spend the whole day with you tomorrow. This way Harriet and Elias can begin their journey earlier and be gone before Stephen is out of class."

"I think that would be best," Benjamin confirmed and Pastor Tuttle nodded his agreement.

"Can Corrie spend the night so she can help me get ready in the morning?" Harriet asked.

"Of course," Julia agreed.

"I have the whole day off from Mrs. Huddleston's," Corrie confirmed. She did not share that her employer had not been happy to allow her the time off. Corrie knew she was skating on thin ice as far as the woman was concerned and hoped that once tomorrow was past she could breathe a little easier.

After supper, Jonathan and Benjamin walked with Elias back to the mission school, keenly aware of the hard looks they were receiving from those townsfolk they passed on the street. Jonathan promised to return in the morning to walk with Elias and Isaiah to the wedding.

Mr. Carroll accompanied Eleanor Gold along with Harriet and Cornelia to the Gold's home on the south side of town. Julia walked up the street to the Northrups' home to tell them of the change of plans.

Mrs. Gold went to bed immediately after her arrival home, complaining of a headache. But the two young women stayed up several more hours. They were both too excited and a little fearful about tomorrow.

"Please pray, Corrie," Harriet begged when at last they blew out the lantern lights. "Pray that nothing bad happens tomorrow." The bride twisted the end of her loose braid in a nervous gesture.

"You're not having second thoughts now are you?" Corrie asked as they settled under the patchwork quilt on Harriet's bed.

"Not about the wedding. Not about Elias," Harriet whispered. "But sometimes I feel guilty about causing so much trouble for him. He's such a good person, Corrie. He shouldn't be treated this way – especially not by my own family."

"Family care the most – whether for good or for bad. They are the most concerned about what happens with us. I think Stephen will look back someday and very much regret his behavior. Especially after you are happily settled in Georgia."

"I hope you're right."

"Are you nervous about moving so far away?"

"No." Harriet shook her head though it was too dark for Corrie to see her. "It will be better for us to be away from the scandal and the anger. But I will miss Papa and Mother . . . and you, of course. Promise you'll come for a visit sometime."

"I'll try," was all Corrie would say. She knew she would have to wait several months before she dared asked Mrs. Huddleston for time off again. Even then she doubted that her employer would be willing for her to be gone for over two months. It was quite unlikely that she could ever travel anywhere as long as she worked for one of Cornwall's only wealthy families.

She said nothing of this to Harriet because she did not want to give her friend something else to be concerned about. Besides, who could say what the future would hold.

Corrie wanted very much to be happy for her friend, but this wedding reminded her that she had no prospects for a wedding of her own. She blinked hard to keep stupid tears from forming and hoped Harriet did not hear her tiny sniffle.

She lay quiet and still for a long while, praying about tomorrow; praying for Harriet and Elias . . . and for Edmund.

The morning broke with birdsongs in the still-bare trees outside Harriet's window. Corrie came awake to find her friend standing at the window with the curtain pulled back slightly.

"It's foggy this morning," Harriet said when she realized Corrie was awake. "But I think the sun will burn it off. Then it should be a glorious day."

Corrie could tell that Harriet had found peace sometime in the night. Perhaps she had prayed for long hours as well.

They both pulled on workday dresses and made their way downstairs for breakfast. Then there was a whirlwind of activity to give the front parlor and dining room a thorough polishing before decorating with the candles and tulle bows. Julia and Mrs. Carroll arrived to help with last minutes details on the food then returned home to get dressed for the wedding.

It was nearing eleven o'clock as Corrie helped Harriet tuck a length of pale pink ribbon into the mahogany curls she had arranged at the crown of her head. Mrs. Gold had just gone downstairs after helping her daughter into her wedding gown.

While Corrie worked, Harriet fiddled with the little nosegay she would carry. They had kept the pansies and violets in their pots until the last minute to ensure they wouldn't wilt.

"Check again, will you, Corrie," Harriet requested.

Corrie went to the upstairs landing one more time to see if Elias had arrived. She had lost count of how many times she had stood at the top of the stairs listening to the voices below. This time she recognized those of Elias and her father.

"They're here," she said as she hurried back to Harriet's room.

Harriet gave a little squeal of nervous excitement and grasped her friend's hand for a moment. "Is is finally going to happen?"

"Yes," Corrie smiled. "Your wait is finally over."

Harriet drew a deep breath to steady her nerves. Shortly they heard footsteps on the stairs and then Harriet's father tapped lightly on her bedroom door. He stepped inside at Harriet's call.

"Everything is ready downstairs," Benjamin said. "Are you ready, my dear?"

"Yes, Papa."

Corrie took this as her cue to leave father and daughter alone for a few moments. "I'll be at the foot of the stairs waiting for you."

Harriet nodded and Corrie stepped out of the room.

Mr. Gold offered Harriet his arm and she slipped her hand through it. But before they too left her bedroom, the father paused for a moment.

"You look lovely, my dear."

"Thank you, Papa."

"Forgive me, daughter," he said, hesitation in his voice. "But I feel I must ask one last time – are you sure this is what you want to do?"

Harriet looked up at her father and smiled. "Yes, Papa, I am quite sure. I love Elias and I know he loves me. I didn't make this decision lightly. I know all the attitudes and arguments against our union. I know people have condemned us in the name of God. But I know that those people are wrong."

"What gives you such courage, Harriet?"

"I prayed very much about this decision, Papa. I searched the scriptures for the answer. And I found it."

"Where?"

"Do you remember when Miriam and Aaron criticized Moses for marrying an Ethiopian woman?"

"Yes, I suppose." The furrows in the man's brow said he was struggling to remember the particular incident Harriet referred to. It was rarely spoken of in the pulpits of New England.

"That told me how God felt about my marriage to Elias. There are many things that the Bible condemns and calls an abomination. But marrying someone whose skin is a different color than your own is not one of them. God sided with Moses in that instance and Miriam was struck with leprosy."

"Ah, yes," Benjamin nodded. "That is true."

"I know Elias and I will face criticism and probably many other challenges. But we will face them together and I believe that we have God's blessing."

Benjamin's eyes seemed bright with tears as he bent down and kissed his daughter on her forehead. "And you have your mother's and mine as well," he whispered. "Shall we go down?"

Harriet nodded with a tremulous smile. She seemed unable to speak at that moment, sharing her father's emotion.

The two of them came slowly down the stairs and paused to give Corrie time to walk into the parlor and then stand by her father near the fireplace. Corrie smiled at Elias who looked elegant standing across from her in his black suit and white shirt and cravat.

Then everyone turned to watch his bride enter the room and make her way to him. The two only had eyes for each other from that moment until Rev. Tuttle closed the brief ceremony with a heartfelt prayer and pronounced them husband and wife.

The few guests joined Harriet's parents in surrounding the couple and offering congratulations. Corrie stood back and watched them, feeling a swirl of her own emotions – both happiness and sadness. Her best friend would leave with her husband today for her new home in Georgia and Corrie could not know when or if she would ever see her again. The twenty-year-old felt adrift and even frightened as her own future held only uncertainty.

Harriet's joy made her seem to glow and Elias kept his hand at her waist as if he did not want her to ever leave his side. Corrie shook off her dark thoughts and went to the kitchen to help her mother and the housekeepers set out the meal that had been kept warm on the stove.

Over the lovely dinner the conversation centered round the young couple's plans for their new life in Georgia.

"Will you continue to teach, Elias?" Julia Tuttle asked.

"For at least another year," he responded. "The school is growing and the National Council has even agreed to help with the mission's expenses in educating our youth. I expect we will hire more teachers next semester."

Here he gave his friend Isaiah a nod as if he were trying to encourage the young man to be one of those new teachers.

"I hope the mission will move into New Echota," Elias continued. "Then I hope to persuade Sam and Ann Worcester to transfer there from Brainerd Mission. It would be good to have his printing press located in our capital."

As everyone enjoyed a piece of wedding cake with coffee after the meal, Mr. Carroll slipped out to harness the Golds' big gray horse to their stylish black carriage with bright yellow wheels. The hostler, with the help of Isaiah, had already carried out the young couple's luggage and stowed it in the boot of the carriage.

Mr. Carroll came inside and joined the men who had retired to the parlor while the women cleaned up the dining room and kitchen. Mr. Carroll caught Pastor Tuttle's eye and the minister stood and walked to the door.

"I just saw a couple of ruffians watching the house from across the street," Carroll said quietly. "Then they headed up the street toward the stage stop."

Jonathan nodded, then returned to his seat and explained the situation to the other men. "Under the circumstances, I don't think Elias and Harriet should try to leave from the Cornwall stage. There may be trouble waiting there."

"We could drive down to Washington," Elias suggested. Benjamin nodded his agreement. "I'll travel with you, just as an extra precaution," he offered.

"Why don't you take my larger rig?" Jonathan said. "I'll drive yours, Benjamin, over to the livery and distract anyone waiting there."

"I don't want you to be at risk," Elias said. "Are you sure you want to do that?"

"I don't believe anyone will try to harm me. It will just be a ruse to give you a little more time to get out beyond the town limits before anyone realizes you've left."

With this plan agreed upon, Mr. Carroll and Isaiah went out again and shifted the luggage to Pastor Tuttle's two-seater carriage making sure that no one was watching them. Inside, Harriet's mother insisted that she would travel to Washington also. Corrie volunteered to ride with her father to the stage stop.

They all gathered at the doorway and Pastor Tuttle led a prayer for everyone's safety. Then Corrie gave Harriet a long, tearful hug. "Write me as soon as you're settled," she reminded her friend.

"I will. I'm going to miss you, Corrie. You've been such a dear friend."

All Corrie could do was nod. She didn't trust her voice at the moment. They all donned their coats and walked to the waiting carriages. Corrie's father helped her up onto the red leather seat of the surrey then stepped up into it from the other side. He started the gray on a slow pace toward the livery.

The Golds took the front seat of the pastor's enclosed carriage while Elias and Harriet settled into the shadows of the back seat. Then Benjamin snapped the reins and the two roan matching horses began the drive south. Mr. Carroll followed in the wagon Elias had rented for his journey to Cornwall. The hostler would take it to Danbury and then return by stage.

As she rode with her father, Corrie resisted the desire to look back for a last glimpse of her best friend. She kept her head down, hoping her bonnet would shadow her face in the bright afternoon sunshine. In such a small town as Cornwall, everyone would recognize the Golds' rig. It would be best if she and her father weren't identified, at least not until they reached the big barn where the stage would soon arrive.

They reached the livery without incident and Jonathan pulled the carriage alongside the building. He set the brake and they sat quietly to appear as if they were waiting for the stagecoach. Suddenly rough hands grabbed Corrie's arm and jerked her out of the carriage. She gave a little scream in shock at being manhandled in such a way. On the opposite side, her father was also being hauled out by two men.

"Let me go," Corrie demanded, when she found her voice.

"What is the meaning of this?" her father said with equal vehemence.

The taller of the men who had taken hold of Jonathan stepped back in surprise. "Pastor Tuttle!" he exclaimed. Then he looked at the carriage and checked to see if anyone else was in it.

"So you think to fool us, eh?" the other man said. "Where are they?"

"I can only speak for myself and my daughter," the pastor said. "We are here being treated poorly by you. Have you nothing better to do than accost a minister?"

"We didn't know, Pastor," the tall man said. "Sorry." He backed away from the carriage and gave a nod to the other fellows. They release Jonathan and Corrie and then all three hurried up the street back toward the Golds' home.

"Are you alright, Cornelia?" her father asked as he stroked the gray which had grown skittish in the altercation.

"Yes, Father. Are you?"

"I'm none the worse for it," the minister said. He came around to help Corrie back into the surrey. "Let's hope we gave the others time enough to avoid those miscreants."

Corrie and her father traveled back to the Gold house, picked up Julia and Mrs. Carroll and returned home to wait for the Golds to get back from Washington. They all were quiet as the afternoon hours passed, each sending thoughts and prayers for the young couple with the courage to follow their own hearts and defy an angry town.

CHAPTER SEVEN

Cornwall
March, 1826

The next morning, Corrie walked quickly from the rectory to the Huddleston home. She was grateful that Benjamin and Eleanor had arrived in the late evening to let them know they had reached Washington without incident. Elias and Harriet had been settled at a little roadside inn where the great general himself was reputed to have slept. They would catch the stage this morning for Pittsburgh, then board a steamer bound for Chattanooga.

While she was relieved that her friend was safely on her way to her new home, Corrie felt uneasy as she walked to work. Was it her imagination or were folks in town giving her odd looks and angry stares as she passed the post office?

So they are married now, she thought as she kept her steady pace toward the Huddlestons'. *The self-righteous citizens of Cornwall need to move on to some other scandal to whisper about behind their hands.*

Despite her defiant thoughts, the governess gave a sigh of relief as she turned onto Jewell Street. She hurried into a side door of the federal style home with its two-story white columns. She was climbing the staircase to go to the children's classroom, already pulling at the ribbon ties of her bonnet, when she heard her employer's call.

Mrs. Huddleston stood in the doorway of a small parlor she used as her office for managing the household.

"Miss Tuttle would you join me for a moment, please." The woman's tone was polite, but as Corrie turned to come back down the stairs she read trouble on the woman's face.

"Yes, ma'am?" the young woman said when she reached the bottom stair. Her heart hammered in her chest.

Mrs. Huddleston, impeccably dressed as always, took a seat near the white marble fireplace of the room where a low fire crackled. With a wave of her hand, she indicated that Cornelia should also take a seat. Corrie sat on the edge of a dainty Louis XIV chair, crossed her ankles demurely and clasped her hands tightly in her lap to still their trembling.

"There is talk in town, Miss Tuttle," the older woman began. "My husband brought it home from the law office yesterday afternoon."

"Yes, ma'am. I am aware. But . . ."

"It reflects poorly on your father and on you," Mrs. Huddleston interrupted, "therefore as your employer it reflects poorly upon me."

"I'm sorry, ma'am. It was not my intention . . ."

"I cannot have my, or more importantly my husband's, reputation tainted with gossip."

"Certainly not, ma'am." Corrie gave up trying to explain. She simply steeled herself for the reprimand that she knew was coming.

"I think some distance might be advisable."

"Distance?"

"As you are aware, I had planned for Susan and Lydia to take a tour of the continent this summer. We have arranged for them to be introduced at court."

"Yes, I know Susan and Lydia are very much looking forward to it."

"I have decided that all of the family will visit Europe with them. I've grown concerned about entrusting them solely to their aunt, my sister."

"I see." In fact, Corrie didn't really understand what Mrs. Huddleston was saying. Was she to travel to Europe with them to give them all some distance from Cornwall?

Mrs. Huddleston went on but she would not look the governess in the eye. "Therefore, your services will no longer be required beginning a month from today."

Corrie felt stunned. "You are dismissing me?" she said, breathlessly. She could not, in fact, seem to draw a breath at all. She had expected a "disappointed in you" lecture from the woman, but never an outright dismissal.

"I'm sorry, Miss Tuttle," her employer said. "Your work has always been exemplary, but I feel this is for the best."

Mrs. Huddleston stood then, indicating the matter was closed. Corrie stood too and felt dizzy for a moment. What was she going to do?

"The children will be waiting for you, Miss Tuttle," their mother said. "You were planning a walk to the park today, weren't you?"

"Yes, ma'am," Corrie said in a daze. "I'll go upstairs now if there is nothing more."

"No, that is all."

Corrie left the room feeling dazed. She slowly climbed the back stairway, her mind racing as she reviewed the conversation that had just taken place. If only Mrs. Huddleston had let her explain.

But then, what could she say? She had stood with Harriet at her wedding to a Cherokee. She and her father had engaged in a ruse to protect the young couple. All of that was true and apparently meant that the newlyweds were not the only ones with a price to pay for defying convention and marrying against the wishes of nearly everyone who knew of it. This marital scandal had now cost Corrie her livelihood.

Edmund stood on the porch of the Webber trading post, enjoying a light spring breeze that scattered the petals of the flowering plum trees growing along the bayou. He was about to walk the three miles to Dwight Mission for a meeting with the new president of the mission board. But he was waiting for a letter.

Bettie had made him promise not to leave until she could write a letter to her new sister-in-law. He would take it to the post office at Dwight since he no longer rushed to meet the steamboat at the river landing. To pass the time, he squatted to a hunter's crouch on the edge of the porch and let his eyes scan the landscape before him.

A beaten path ran in front of the log store roughly following the wanderings of the Illinois Bayou. It trailed into the tree line now taking on the bright spring green of new leaves. To the north lay the home of the silversmith Sequoyah.

To the south and west the Webber plantation spread out over the rich river bottom land where cotton, corn and tobacco grew in abundance. The common fields lay in the center of the Cherokee settlement where the women planted food crops – corn, beans, gourds like squash and pumpkins, and sunflowers.

Edmund loved this time of year when it seemed as if nature were reawakening. Life was stirring and he felt the stirring inside him like a restlessness he couldn't quell. Slowly the smile left his face and he sighed.

Inside the store he could hear his brother Walter talking with a customer. He couldn't catch everything that was being said but Edmund gathered that Walter was complaining to Old Blair about the slowness with which the Osages were moving from Lovely's Purchase. Their former government agent, William Lovely, had arranged a deal to transfer that section of Arkansas Territory from Osage to Cherokee control. Walter was hoping to build a second trading post in this area.

Edmund might not agree with his brother on many things – his disdain for Christianity, his hatred of the Osages, his practice of slavery among them. But he had to acknowledge that his brother was a smart businessman.

While his mind wandered over this Edmund saw a young Negro boy running up the trail from the south. He carried a white envelope in his hand and as he approached the store, his bare feet made a splat, splat on the damp ground. He was dressed in a too-large muslin shirt and his pants were wearing through at the knees.

"Hey, Harry," Edmund greeted the boy when he reached the porch.

"*Siyo*," Harry returned. He thrust out the envelope. "Miz Webber send this. She say sorry to take so long and make you wait."

"That's fine, Harry." Edmund took the envelope in one hand while reaching into his pocket with the other one. He fished out a penny and gave it to the boy.

Harry's eyes lit up with pleasure. He took the coin and held it up to admire it in the sunlight. "*Wado*," he said. "Can I buy some candy with it?"

"Is that what you want to do with it?"

Harry nodded emphatically.

"Go ahead then," Edmund nodded toward the door. In a flash Harry was inside with the screen door slapping shut behind him.

Edmund could hear the haggling going on between the young lad and Walter. His brother always haggled. But Harry soon emerged from the store with a small brown paper bag clutched in his hand and a bulge of something sweet in one cheek.

"What did you get?"

"Molasses drops." Harry held up the sack as if to show Edmund what a good bargain he had struck in the store.

"Share them with your brothers and sisters."

"I will." Harry ignored the stairs to the porch and jumped off it then hit the trail on a run and soon was out of sight.

Edmund watched him go, wishing the boy had chosen to save the penny rather than spend it on candy. But he supposed that would have been his own choice at that age.

The Cherokee man always paid his brother's slaves for any work they did for him. Walter and most of their Cherokee neighbors had no problem with their slaves earning their own money. It afforded some of them the opportunity to buy their freedom.

The Cherokees' approach to slavery differed from others in the south. Cherokee-held slaves built their own homes, raised their own livestock and gardens, even hunted with their own firearms.

Edmund knew slavery had been practiced by every culture on every continent in every century, but the Christian teaching he had received challenged acceptance of this institution. He wished he could convince his brother to free his slaves but Walter ridiculed the idea as being disrespectful of their ancient way of life.

The younger brother shook off the thought and glanced down at Bettie's letter. She had addressed it to Harriet Boudinot, New Echota, C.N. He knew the initials stood for Cherokee Nation but doubted most mail handlers would know. He pulled out a pencil from another pocket and added "Georgia," to the address.

Then he stepped off the porch and began the walk to Dwight Mission. Except during bad weather, he always walked to the mission where he worked as the interpreter for the mission's director, Cephas Washburn. This meant attendance at all preaching services and at the Bible class Washburn taught each Wednesday. Edmund was paid for his service and was glad to have income independent of his brother.

Most of the classes for the young Cherokee students were conducted in English but the mission teachers were also making an effort to learn Cherokee and its written form. Rev. Washburn agreed with Elias' assessment that the Cherokees would soon be as literate a people as any other and would be in need of services such as a newspaper. Progressive Cherokees like the Ridges and Waties welcomed this development while traditionalists like Walter and their second chief Blackcoat bemoaned the change.

Edmund was of two minds on the matter. Certainly he valued his education which Walter had paid for, yet he too hated to see the Cherokees lose their traditions. Having his feet planted in two cultures made him feel unbalanced and sometimes uncertain.

Today he wore the traditional long calico shirt trimmed with multi-colored ribbons. A woven wampum belt was tied at his waist and his moccasins were beaded with a pattern he had created himself. His long straight hair swirled in the April breeze and as he walked along the tree-shaded path he shook off his uncertainties and embraced a sense of peace. He loved this season and spent his walk planning a fishing trip before the coming Sabbath.

He reached the Dwight chapel where the meeting was to be held just as Miss Thrall, the mission cook arrived there as well. With one hand, the older woman held a coffee pot with a folded towel and with the other balanced a tray of blue speckled enamel cups. Edmund hurried to hold open the door for her. She smiled her thanks as she stepped inside the large room.

"Is everyone here already?" he asked in a low voice as he followed her. He hoped he hadn't held up the meeting.

"Yes, I think so," the dark-hair woman responded. "Rev Kingsbury just arrived by steamboat from Phillips Landing."

"Kingsbury?"

"Yes, do you know him?"

"I heard his name while at school. He helped to found the United Mission Society and the school at Cornwall."

"Mrs. Washburn told me Kingsbury was joining Rev. Greene here and then they'll be touring all the western missions."

"So this is an inspection?"

"I suppose it is. I hope we pass," she said with a twinkle in her eyes. She continued across the room to place the coffee and cups on a table where three pies waited.

Rev. Washburn turned from speaking with a man Edmund didn't know and greeted the interpreter.

"Good of you to come, Webber," he said.

"I hope I am not late. I was waiting on Bettie to finish a letter so I could post it here."

"No, no," the mission director assured him. "Hitchcock just got back from the dock where he met Rev. Kingsbury." He waved a hand toward the man beside him. "Have you two met?"

"No," both said in unison. Washburn made the introductions then went on to say, "Edmund attended the mission school in Cornwall and we have put his considerable skills to work here."

"It's always good to meet a graduate of Cornwall," the minister said as he shook hands with Edmund. "But you didn't bring back a Yankee bride?"

"No," Edmund felt his face flush. "John and Elias took care of that."

"Yes, so I hear."

Edmund wasn't sure if he heard disapproval in the missionary's voice.

Washburn cleared his throat to get the attention of everyone in the room. Most of the mission's workers were present. "I think everyone is here now so let's get some refreshments and then we'll start the meeting."

Abigail Washburn joined the cook in cutting the dried apple pies and pouring coffee. "These pies look wonderful Cynthia," she complimented the woman.

"Thank you, ma'am."

Compliments from others in the room soon echoed Abigail's. The group settled on the short wooden pews while Rev. Washburn strode to the plain pulpit at the front of the room.

"We are privileged to have two distinguished guests today," he said. "Rev. Cyrus Kingsbury comes to us from Mayhew Mission in Mississippi where he has been working among the Choctaws for the past few years. Before that, as you know, he helped to establish our mission society. And Rev. David Greene joins us from Boston. He is secretary of the American Board of Commissioners for Foreign Missions. They are here to explain some of the changes we'll be seeing as to our funding and administration. So I will turn the meeting to them."

Cyrus Kingsbury bounded to the pulpit as if eager to address the group. "It is wonderful to be here with you today," he began.

Edmund thought that if he had not already known it, he could have guessed the man's occupation from his "preacher voice" – big, exuberant and smiling.

"I'm sure you've heard that there are changes coming as our two mission societies are merged and you've probably felt some concern about how matters will all shake out. Will some of the missions be closed? Will reporting requirements change? Questions such as that. David and I felt it was important that we come and address your concerns in person and help you understand the reason behind these changes."

The man drew a breath and then continued. "Let me assure you that Dwight Mission will not be closed. You are one of the most successful missions in our society and certainly the most successful in the Neosho District. In fact, we've come to discuss with you and Chief Jolly the possibility of opening a second mission in this region of Arkansas Territory."

Murmurs of excited approval rippled through the group. Edmund leaned forward and rested his arms on his knees. This was better news than he had expected and he felt a sense of relief.

"I'm going to let David talk now," Kingsbury went on, "And then we'll answer any questions you might have."

David Greene was a smaller, less florid man, dark haired and wearing spectacles. He walked quietly to the pulpit and thanked Kingsbury.

"As you may be aware," he said in a soft voice, "the United Mission Society has experienced some controversy with regard to the school in Cornwall. The result has been a serious drop in donations. For that reason both societies have voted to merge and continue operations under the American Board name. So you will now report to our Commissioners in Boston."

Edmund studied the yellow and blue beads on his moccasins. He wondered if John and Elias might have chosen differently had they known their marital scandals would have such far reaching consequences.

Rev. Greene continued, "You should not see any major changes in operations. As Kingsbury said, Dwight Mission is a shining beacon out here. We're very pleased with how well you are working with the Cherokee people and we have heard nothing but compliments from the Cherokee leaders and from the Secretary of War."

"We appreciate hearing that," Washburn spoke for all of them. Edmund nodded along with the others in the room.

"What about the other missions out here?" Jacob Hitchcock asked. "Union, Hopefield, Harmony?"

"Unfortunately the fate of those missions is less clear and we'll be discussing that with them as we travel out that way. The death of Rev. Chapman at Union and the new treaty that the Osages signed last year means changes will be coming. Union may have to move; Harmony will likely be closed."

"Will you replace it?" Dr. Weeks asked.

"Yes, we plan to set up a new mission west of the Missouri state line somewhere along the Neosho River. This is where the Osages are already settling and Chief Pawhuska has welcomed a new mission among them."

Edmund thought about Walter and his long-running feud with the Osages. Walter would be happy when they all were removed to the northern section of the Neosho. This small clear river flowed southward to join the Arkansas River where Fort Gibson sat.

"Do you have a director in mind for a new mission near us?" This question came from their farm director James Orr. He was married to Rev. Washburn's cousin Minerva who was one of the teachers.

Kingsbury turned from his seat on the front pew. "We were thinking of asking Dr. Marcus Palmer at Union if he would have an interest in it. He has been preaching at Fort Gibson and we're going to encourage him to get his ordination."

David Greene added, "I doubt that a new mission will be established quickly but we want to start laying the groundwork. We'll have to secure approval from the Adams administration as well as the Arkansas government."

"Any ideas about where it might be located?" Washburn asked.

"We were hoping you might make some recommendations."

The mission director turned to Edmund. "What do you think, Webber?"

Startled to be asked, Edmund hesitated a moment while considering the question. "There are a number of families along the Mulberry River," he finally said. "Perhaps there should be a school near them."

"Good idea," Washburn agreed. "That would be about half way between Dwight and Fort Smith," he explained to their visitors. "We can take you over if you'd like to consider a location there."

Both of the visiting ministers gave their assent and they agreed to an early start the next day. Edmund was asked to go along for this scouting expedition.

The meeting drew to a conclusion when Miss Thrall returned to announce that supper was ready to be served. Edmund joined the mission staff and their boarding students for a meal of sliced ham, potatoes and carrots from the root cellar and cornbread. Afterwards Edmund decided to walk back home rather than spend the night. He would bring his own horse for the trip to the Mulberry settlement.

Elias tried to mimic the bird songs he heard as he made the walk home from New Echota. It was the last day of school before the spring planting break. He was looking forward to a visit from the Worcesters next week and he carried three letters in his satchel for Harriet. She would be happy to receive them.

He knew his wife was homesick though she never complained. She never compared Georgia to New England and never compared the house he could afford on a teacher's salary to the one John had built for Sarah.

Harriet gladly took cooking lessons from his mother and like Sarah was working to learn Cherokee. He thought she was happy here despite missing her mother and best friend. So he was glad for her sake that these letters had arrived.

He pulled the three envelopes from the satchel as he stepped into the kitchen and held them behind his back while Harriet greeted him with a kiss. She smelled of grape dumplings and *kanuche* – a soup made with ground hickory nuts and rice. It made his mouth water.

With a dramatic flair, Elias held up the three letters.

"Are those for me?" Harriet quickly grabbed a towel to dry her hands.

"For no one else," Elias teased. "I certainly never receive such a volume of mail."

"Oh," Harriet practically squealed and snatched the letters from his hands. "I wonder who they're from." She studied the handwriting on each one. "This is from mother. And this is from Corrie. But I don't recognize this writing." She held it out to Elias.

"Looks like my sister Bettie's," he supplied.

"Oh, how nice of her to write to me."

"Yes," Elias grinned as he set his case on the table. "Bettie rarely ever writes to me. I am more likely to get a letter from Edmund."

"Do you mind if I read these before we eat?"

"No, go ahead," the teacher smiled.

They both sat at the little dining table. Harriet used a kitchen knife to pry up the sealing wax on each envelope, while Elias pulled out a copy of the Savannah newspaper. Each read in silence for a while until Harriet gave a little gasp.

"Oh, dear," she said, distress in her voice.

"What is it?"

"Corrie has lost her job," the young woman said. "Mrs. Huddleston has dismissed her."

"But why?" Elias set down his paper, sharing his wife's concern for a friend.

"She says the Huddlestons are going to take a European tour this summer and chose not to continue her employment."

"I would have thought they would want a governess along to keep their children occupied and safe."

"Perhaps Mrs. Huddleston didn't want the expense," Harriet surmised with a frown. "But Corrie has had no success in finding other work. Cornwall is such a small town and there are few families that can afford a governess. She says she may have to try in Colchester or even Fairfield."

"I am sorry to hear that," Elias sympathized. "We will have to pray for her."

"I wish we could find something for her here," Harriet said thoughtfully, looking at her husband hopefully.

"They are talking about hiring another housemother at the New Echota Mission," he said. "It's primarily a day school, but some students board there because of the distance from their homes. Student enrollment is growing. Do you think she would like that type of work?"

"She might," Harriet nodded. "It's similar to the work of a governess. May I write to her and let her know about it?"

"Yes," Elias agreed. "Given who her father is, I have no doubt the mission society would agree to hire her."

"Good." Harriet clapped her hands in pleasure. "I'll write to her after supper."

"Good," Elias smiled and folded the newspaper anticipating the evening meal. But Harriet had one more letter to read so he opened the paper again to finish the article about the upcoming Congressional race.

"Oh, dear?" Harriet said again.

"What is it now?"

"Your sister says that Edmund is unhappy. She thinks he still cares for his 'Cornwall girl.' Does he ever write anything to you about Corrie?"

"No he never mentions Corrie. I assumed their parting was a mutual decision."

"I think it was but I don't think either is truly happy with it."

"Then perhaps we should find her a job at Dwight Mission."

"I'd rather have her here in Georgia," Harriet countered. "Perhaps we could convince Edmund to return to New Echota."

Elias said nothing, but the thoughtful look on his wife's face as she cleared the table for supper told him there would by many more letters exchanged in the coming months.

CHAPTER EIGHT

Cornwall
June, 1826

Oliver Ackley entered the tavern of the inn at Cornwall. The dining room that served most of the stagecoach travelers was crowded this morning. Standing in the shadows of the stairs, the young Tennessee man let his eyes roam over the room.

He knew from Mr. Bunce's newspaper that the board of trustees for the Cornwall Mission School was in town this week for their annual meeting and to attend graduation exercises at the school. He assumed that many of the men in this room were board members but he knew few of them by sight.

Finally his eyes fell on the man he had hoped to meet. He recognized Rev. Lyman Beecher from a lithograph he'd seen in some newspaper. The pastor of the Congregational Church in nearby Litchfield was making a name for himself with his fiery sermons that were often reprinted by the press.

There was an empty seat at the table Beecher occupied so Oliver edged around the other tables to inquire if he might join the men dining with the pastor.

"Certainly," one of the men said. "Quite crowded this morning, isn't it."

"Yes," Oliver said. "Something going on in town today?"

"Graduation," another man at the table supplied.

The tavern keeper placed a plain china cup and saucer in front of Oliver. "Tea or coffee?" he asked.

"Coffee, please," the young man said and watched as his cup was filled.

"Ham steak, potatoes, brown bread," the server stated more than asked. He was too busy to run through the morning's menu. Everyone would take what he offered or wait.

"That's fine."

The man hurried off to get Oliver's order while a woman, presumably his wife, made the rounds of the crowded tables topping off cups with more coffee.

The men at Beecher's table made small talk about the warm weather and the need for rain.

"We've gone three weeks without a drop of rain in Boston," a small man with glasses stated.

"You've traveled a ways for a graduation," Oliver noted as a plate of hot food was placed in front of him. "Someone in your family finishing at Westminster?"

"We're here for the mission school graduation," Beecher explained. "Most of us," he waved his hand toward the crowded room, "are on its board."

Oliver nodded as if this was new information to him. "I've heard of that school," he said carefully. "Doesn't have a very good reputation."

The men he spoke to shared looks among themselves.

"What have you heard?" the man with glasses asked. "From your speech I gather you're not from New England."

"No," Oliver admitted. "I'm from Tennessee. I'm here on business with a couple of textile mills. But even at home we've heard of the scandals. The school and the good people of Cornwall have been poorly used by certain students."

Beecher sighed and looked around the table at his fellow board members. "I told you," he stated cryptically but offered no explanation to Oliver.

That was fine with the Tennessean. He'd planted his seed of mistrust and doubt and hoped the harvest would be the closure of the school. Graduates like Ridge and Boudinot were gaining too much influence in Georgia. He wanted no more graduations from the Foreign Mission School of Cornwall.

While he finished his meal, other diners rose and paid their tab then exited the tavern. Oliver took his time to finish a last cup of coffee then also rose to leave the establishment. He did not plan to stay in Cornwall long but would have to wait for the next stagecoach to arrive mid-morning. He'd walk to the market and purchase something for dinner to be eaten on the road.

As he approached the mercantile, he saw the young woman that he had nearly run over at the post office last year. What had Bunce called her? Pastor's daughter, but he could not recall her name. She also was walking toward the general store. Oliver slowed his pace to time his arrival after hers.

Corrie stepped into the overstuffed mercantile and was quickly greeted by one of the daughters of the store owner. Katie Banks finished wrapping a purchase in brown paper and tied it with a length of string she pulled from a spool at the counter. While she did so, Corrie browsed the aisle where bolts of fabric, ribbons and lace were displayed.

The customer turned from the counter and Corrie realized it was Jerusha Johnson, one of the teachers at the girls' school. The young woman wasn't much older than Corrie herself.

"Hello, Miss Johnson," she greeted the teacher.

"Why, Miss Tuttle, it's good to see you," Jerusha returned. Then she lowered her voice as a tall, blond stranger opened the door and stepped inside, removing his hat as he did so.

"How goes your job search?" she asked.

"Not well, I'm sorry to say," Corrie replied. "There haven't been any vacancies at the school, have there?"

"I'm afraid not."

Neither young woman could resist watching the stranger pass by them as he made his way to the back counter where barrels of apples and crackers stood.

"It seems there is nothing to be had in Cornwall," Corrie sighed. "I feel I am becoming a burden to my parents."

"I'm sure they don't think so," Jerusha commiserated. "I could inquire at some other schools. "Are you willing to travel?"

"Yes, I've always wanted to and mother has encouraged me to do so. She was more disappointed than I when the Huddlestons decided not to take me to Europe with them." Corrie smiled, hoping that would ease the teacher's concern.

"What about a mission school?" Jerusha asked. "My sister has been teaching at Union Mission in the Osage lands. She has come to love it out on the prairie."

"Well, as a matter of fact, I've been informed of an opening at a mission in Georgia. But I have hesitated to pursue it. Georgia is such a long way from home."

"Perhaps the fact that there are no openings here is a closed door from God," Jerusha said, laying a hand on Corrie's arm. "He may have a work for you in Georgia."

Corrie looked thoughtful for a moment, glancing briefly at the stranger who seemed to be taking a very long time in choosing an apple.

"You may be right, Miss. Johnson," she said. "Thank you for your words. They have been a help to me in knowing what I should do."

"I'm glad," the teacher smiled. "I wish you the best." She squeezed Corrie's arm and then said goodbye and left the store.

Corrie walked to the back counter where Katie straightened shelves while waiting for her customers to decide on purchases.

"I'd like a pound of coffee beans please, Katie," the pastor's daughter said.

"Certainly, Miss Tuttle," the girl replied. She measured out the fragrant beans on a scale hanging over the counter. "Is your mother entertaining all those preachers in town?"

"Yes, exactly," Corrie smiled. "We'll have them over for supper after their meeting at the school. In spite of it being warm, she's sure they'll all want plenty of coffee."

"Well this should take care of them," Katie said. She used a scoop to transfer the beans into a brown paper sack.

Corrie paid for her purchase then turned to leave. Unbeknownst to her, the young man, with apple in hand, was now standing behind her. She nearly plowed right into him.

"Oh, pardon me," she said startled by his closeness. She caught the scent of tobacco on the light-colored coat that hugged his broad shoulders.

"My fault, miss," the handsome stranger said. "I do apologize. I seem to make a habit it running into you."

Corrie also caught his Southern drawl. "Running into me?" she repeated quizzically.

"Yes," he explained. "Last summer . . . at the post office. I suppose you don't remember that."

"Oh, yes," Corrie said slowly, trying to recall the occasion. "I remember." She remembered that she had been worrying about a letter from Edmund.

"I failed to introduce myself which was very rude of me. My name is Oliver Ackley." He waited expectantly as if hoping to learn her name.

Corrie hesitated. It was considered quite forward for a young, unmarried woman to introduce herself to a man, but there was no one here who could make the proper introductions. "I'm Miss Tuttle," she said at last. She did not offer her hand to shake.

"Miss Tuttle," he made a slight bow. "It's a pleasure to make your acquaintance."

Katie watched the exchange with a bemused smile on her face. At that moment, Mrs. Farnsworth, the town gossip, entered the store. Corrie knew better than to be caught in conversation with a stranger. So with a nod of her head, she excused herself. "I'm afraid I must be going."

She greeted the older woman on her way out and left Oliver standing at the counter watching her once again.

Later that afternoon Corrie helped her mother put out the place settings for supper. The mission school's board members had arrived a half hour ago but had sequestered themselves in her father's study. Occasionally the women could hear raised voices but could not make out the words coming from the closed room.

"Cyrus is not happy," his wife Electra Kingsbury stated as she stood in the doorway between the parlor and the dining room. She had offered to help with supper, but Julia Tuttle wouldn't put a guest to work even though Electra was her cousin.

"You can tell, can you?" Julia asked.

"Cyrus is like a bulldog," Electra explained. "He has a big growl though he usually is harmless. But if he sets his jaw onto something he does not let go." Her eyes twinkled behind the thick spectacles she wore.

Corrie had always secretly felt sorry for her cousin for the thick glasses marred her looks. She had been given up as a spinster until she had agreed to travel to Mayhew Mission in Mississippi to help a young widowed missionary with his children.

Electra had a wicked sense of humor and a lively personality and it hadn't taken long for the missionary and his children to fall in love with her. They had been married two years now and seemed quite happy. Electra's story gave Corrie hope. Perhaps there was some lonely missionary in Georgia waiting for her.

Which reminded her that she needed to tell her parents about her decision. She still felt a few qualms about moving so far away, but she wouldn't be alone. She had friends there.

"Do you think they're going to close the school," her mother's question interrupted Corrie's thoughts.

"I don't doubt it," Electra confirmed. "That's why Cyrus is not happy. The American Board didn't start the school. They have no vested interest in it. And it won't matter how much my husband growls. Rev. Greene may seem like a meek little man, but he's just a smaller bulldog."

Corrie and her mother smiled and even Mrs. Carroll hid a grin when she stepped into the dining room in time to hear Electra's comment.

"Should I set out the food," the housekeeper asked.

Julia checked the watch she wore on a pendant. “It’s almost six o’clock. I told Jonathan I planned to serve supper promptly at six. I hope he doesn’t let the growling continue much longer.”

“I’ll go interrupt if you want me to,” Electra offered. “I’m not afraid of a bunch of bulldogs.”

“If they’re not done soon, I’ll take you up on that.” Julia agreed.

But Pastor Tuttle must have had an eye on the clock in his study for just as Electra was about to cross the parlor, the door opened and the board members filed out. Julia nodded to Corrie and Mrs. Carroll and they hurried to set out the piping hot food.

Though conversation around the crowded dining table was polite Corrie felt a certain tension in the air. She could tell that her father and Cousin Cyrus were not pleased with the decision the board had made. The mission school was to be closed.

The main course was finished and Julia and Mrs. Carroll cut slices of raisin pie garnished with sweetened cream. Their guests all paid compliments to the meal while Corrie poured coffee for them all.

“I recently received a letter from Sam Ruggles, all the way from the Sandwich Islands,” Cousin Cyrus was saying. “He tells me that the mission there is printing the grammar and dictionary that Henry Obookiah worked on while he was a student here. They believe his work will lead to a complete conversion of the Hawaiian people.”

“That is great news,” Rev. Greene said.

“Yes, great news,” Lyman Beecher concurred. “That is what the school should have been about. Not creating uproar and censure over scandalous marriages.”

Corrie saw her father’s face go red. He had conducted the wedding ceremonies for both couples and it seemed as if the outspoken minister meant censure toward the pastor. Corrie saw a flash of anger in her mother’s eyes but neither of her parents said anything.

Mr. Northrup interrupted the strained silence that had settled over the table. "There is the matter of the endowment Congressman Boudinot provided the school. Since he and his wife are now deceased we cannot ask their preference for how the money will now be used."

"I would suggest setting it aside for the new mission we are planning in the Neosho District. The Osages will be moving away from Harmony and we want a mission closer to their new villages." This came from Rev. Greene.

"That seems like a good use for the funds. I'm certain the Congressman would have been amenable to that arrangement," Cyrus agreed. The other men around the table also nodded their approval.

"We can put that to a formal vote at our meeting with the headmaster tomorrow. Then we can announce it at the graduation in the evening," Greene stated.

Having finished their meal, the board members took their leave after thanking Mrs. Tuttle for her hospitality. Cyrus and Electra remained behind. They would spend the night at the Tuttle home. Rev. Kingsbury had planned a month of preaching engagements around New England before the couple would return to Mississippi. His children were spending the month with his parents and all would enjoy a summer visit up north.

The Tuttles and Kingsburys lingered in the parlor for a while, enjoying Mrs. Carroll's cranberry spritz kept cool in the root cellar. After Cyrus and Electra retired for the night, Corrie asked her parents if she might speak with them.

"What is it, dear?" her mother asked as the all took their seats again in the parlor.

"I've made a decision about the job at New Echota," Corrie said, still feeling a bit uncertain.

"The position of housemother?" Pastor Tuttle asked.

"Yes," Corrie confirmed. "I plan to write to Harriet to let her know of my interest. If you think I should. And you could inform the mission board, Father."

Julia looked torn. "I know you've hesitated to take a job so far away," she said softly. "And to be honest, I will certainly miss you when you go. But I support your decision. You know your father and I, in our way, are very committed to the work of these Indian missions."

"Yes, I know," Corrie nodded. "I am too. I've prayed about this and I think it is what I should do."

The smile on both parents' faces made Corrie feel more certain of her decision.

"I'll tell Rev. Greene tomorrow," Jonathan stated.

"Make sure Rev. Beecher hears you," Julia said dryly. "Won't that turn his collar around?"

Jonathan tried to hide a smile, but didn't succeed. "We may have lost the school," he said, "but the board cannot turn back the tide on its revolutionary work. We have given young men from many nations the scriptural principles of freedom, equality and justice. They will return to their own people empowered with these truths and it will make a tremendous difference among them."

"And you, dear daughter, will continue that work," Julia said, reaching over to embrace Corrie. "If envy wasn't wrong, I would envy this adventure that you are about to embark upon."

"Thank you, mother." Corrie returned the embrace feeling grateful to have such understanding and supportive parents. She rose and crossed the room to give her father a hug as well.

The following morning, over breakfast, Corrie shared her plans with Cyrus and Electra.

"This is providential," Electra exclaimed. "You can travel south with us when we return to Mississippi. We were planning a visit to Brainerd Mission in Tennessee anyway. Since Cyrus started that mission he's always had a tender spot in his heart for it."

"I want to see how the Worcesters are doing," Cyrus agreed in his deep rumbling preacher voice. "I'm hearing good things about their printing efforts. Brainerd is close enough to New Echota that we can make sure you get there safely."

"Oh, that will make me feel much better about Corrie traveling so far," Julia said.

"I hope it won't be any trouble for you," Corrie added.

"Not at all," both Kingsburys said at once.

"You'll travel as our guest," Cyrus continued. "We'll be leaving Connecticut on the first of August. Will that give you enough time to be ready?"

"Oh, yes, I'll be ready," the young woman nodded emphatically. For the first time, Corrie felt excitement about the journey she would soon embark upon. What would wait for her in land of the Cherokees?

"You planning a trip?" Edmund posed the question to the Chisholm brothers who had spent the past hour in the trading post. A pile of supplies waited on the counter where he stood.

"We will travel the river," Thomas replied, with a nod of his head toward the Arkansas, "to the great mountains."

"Are you going to run trap lines?"

If the men were planning that they were missing the main supply they would need – traps.

"No," the younger brother said. "Furs are playing out. The animals have been overharvested by the Osages and Pawnees, Kickapoos. Need to let the herds recover."

Thomas leaned on the counter and lowered his voice to let Edmund know he was speaking in confidence. "We hear about gold in the mountains. We want to find out if this be true. Before the government pushes all the Indians out here. Do you hear such things too?"

Edmund nodded slowly. At school he had learned of the efforts of the Spanish and French to find gold and other precious minerals out west. He knew little had been found in the fabled mountains and so they had settled on exploiting the area of its furs. He had doubts about the rumors of gold that still passed among the mountain men who had traveled that far across the prairie.

"I know a Delaware warrior named Black Beaver," Jesse Chisholm went on when Edmund said nothing. "He has been to the western ocean. He knows. He says the Arkansas Rivers starts in the mountains where the gold is."

"So you are going to find it?" Edmund couldn't keep a bit of skepticism out of his voice.

Thomas shrugged. "It no hurt to look. Maybe so we will find it."

"You come too," Jesse said.

Edmund hesitated. While he sincerely doubted that there was gold to be found, he had always been curious about the great craggy mountains that formed the backbone of the turtle. To the Cherokees the land of the continents was like the back of a turtle sunning in the water. For a moment he was tempted to join the Chisholm brothers if just for the adventure.

"When will you leave?"

"In two sleeps," said Thomas.

Edmund felt the tug of desire. But his practical nature and Scottish frugality overruled the thought. "I can't," he explained. "My brother is in Fort Smith and he expects me to watch the store. He does not want to miss a sale," he smiled to show the brothers he held nothing against them, "especially not such a big one as this." He gestured toward their pile of goods.

"Why he go to Fort Smith? He in trouble?" Walter's frequent clashes with the Osages were well-known here in the Cherokee settlement. He had been called upon by the fort commander more than once to defend his actions.

"No. He is there on business. The government will put a new Choctaw agency at Fort Smith. Walter hopes to sell supplies to the Choctaws moving to Miller County."

"Bah," now Jesse sounded skeptical. "Choctaws not come out here. Washington men say they can go and or they can stay in Mississippi. They build big fine houses in Mississippi. They have buried their ancestors there. They will not come to Arkansas."

Edmund remembered his conversation with McKee Folsom at the Fort Smith meeting. His former classmate had concurred with Jesse's assessment. As long as the move to

Arkansas was voluntary, there would likely be few Choctaws willing to do so.

"The Creeks, they come," Jesse went on. "Colonel Brearley is going to Little Rock to meet their scouts."

Edmund had no doubt that Jesse knew what he was talking about. The man was not much older than Edmund, but he had traveled widely in the region and was conversant in a dozen Indian languages. He kept abreast of news that spread faster than wildfire among the various tribes.

"You know them Creeks?" Jesse asked. "From Georgia?"

"I know a few," Edmund responded. "I took the ferry at Indian Springs sometimes. Many Creek families lived in that area."

"Yes, that be right," Thomas added. "The McIntosh people, they come."

Edmund digested this news thoughtfully. If the Creeks in Georgia were being forced out west, the Cherokees would likely also feel the same pressure. He was glad he had made the move with Walter and Bettie seven years earlier. Even though Arkansas politicians weren't very happy that the government was sending Indians to their territory, still it was better here than the outright hostility and harassment Indians continually faced in the southeastern states.

He knew that most members of the Indian nations in the south were determined not to be forced from their homelands. But Edmund had witnessed the relentless pressure placed upon the Osages to vacate land promised to the Cherokees. If enough pressure was applied, would any of the Indians be able to stay in their homes? Was there a place far enough from the states that Indians would be allowed to be free and live according to their ancestral traditions?

"So can we have credit," Thomas asked drolly, interrupting the store clerk's thoughts. "We pay you in gold when we get back."

It was a joke and all three men knew it. The Webbers never extended credit.

"You can pay in gold," Edmund agreed with a grin. "But I'll take it right now."

The Chisholm brothers paid with a few gold coins and also traded two enormous buffalo hides they had taken in the hunt. Edmund threw a length of oilcloth into the trade to wrap the supplies and walked out with them where they loaded the items onto their horses.

"Will you stay out west?" he asked them as he shook hands with both men.

"Maybe so," Thomas said with a shrug.

"Maybe so we'll go to Texas," Jesse laughed. "Like other bad men."

Edmund joined the laughter. Though the Mexican province was filling up with American settlers, it was also an attractive hideout for fugitives from the law. He had seen a Wanted poster nailed to a tree when he had gone to Fort Smith. Scrawled across the sketch of the wanted man were the letters "G.T.T." He had asked Rev. Washburn what the letters meant.

"They stand for 'Gone to Texas,'" the minister explained. "Fugitives can hide there from the law since Texas is a part of Mexico, not the United States."

"Maybe we'll all go to Texas," Edmund added. "Some Cherokees have already settled there."

"Maybe so," Jesse nodded. Then the two brothers mounted their horses and turned their heads to follow the trail along the bayou.

Edmund watched them until they were out of sight. He still wished he could go with them. Maybe that would satisfy the restlessness and longing he felt in his heart.

CHAPTER NINE

Cornwall
August, 1826

Cornelia tried to hold her tears in check as her mother drew her close for a final embrace. Her parents had driven her to the stage stop to join the Kingsbury family and now it was time to board. Her trunk had been securely fastened on the roof of the coach and she held her traveling valise tightly, praying she hadn't forgotten to pack some essential item.

For this leg of her journey she had chosen to wear a brick-colored traveling suit that complimented her auburn hair and hazel eyes. Hopefully it would disguise the clay-red dust that would likely settle everywhere and on everyone inside the stage.

She had never traveled such a long way from home before. A mixture of fear and excitement caused her heart to pound and she wondered if her parents could feel it when they hugged her goodbye.

"Our prayers go with you, dear," her father was saying. "We are very proud of you."

"Thank you, Father."

"Write whenever you can," Julia added while still holding onto her daughter's arm. "I want to know you are safe."

"I'll be safe," Corrie tried to reassure her. "Cousin Cyrus has made this journey often. He says with the new steamboats, it won't take much more than a month to reach Chattanooga. Then it's just a day to New Echota."

The driver completed an inspection walk around the coach. He stopped by Corrie who was the only passenger who had not boarded.

"May I help you aboard, miss," he asked in a not-so-subtle hint that he had a scheduled to keep.

"Oh, of course." Corrie squeezed her mother's hand one last time, then allowed the driver to help her negotiate the rather high step into the stagecoach. She took a seat next to John Kingsbury, the four-year-old and his seven-year-old brother Cyrus, Jr., called Russ.

Electra sat next to Russ and Rev. Kingsbury was next to her on the opposite end of the stiff leather seat. Across from them sat two men who looked like traveling salesmen and an elderly woman with her son who said they were returning home to New York.

Corrie had barely settled the skirt of her suit into place when the driver hefted himself up top, released the brake and snapped his whip in the air over the horses. The animals leaned into the traces and the coach was set in motion with a jerk.

Corrie was glad she had a seat by the window. She waved goodbye to her parents and watched them seem to grow smaller as the coach pulled away from town. In no time, the stage was rocking in rhythm to the horses' easy trot and they entered the sunny countryside. She was sure the coach would soon grow quite warm and was glad she had packed a fan in her valise.

The dainty piece of luggage also held a few books she planned to read to the boys on the journey. It would take four days to reach Pittsburgh where they would board the steamboat that would travel the Ohio and Tennessee Rivers to reach Ross's Landing near Chattanooga.

As she had expected, John and Russ quickly grew tired of being confined to the coach and it took her and Electra a great deal of enterprise and imagination to keep them entertained. As was typical of most men, Cousin Cyrus left the care of his sons to the women, intervening only when the boys became particularly rowdy. Most of the time, he engaged the other passengers in conversation.

As they crossed Pennsylvania, they had opportunity to meet a wide variety of fellow travelers, each with interesting stories to tell of their reasons for taking the stage. But all seemed interested in these missionaries on a journey that would take them to Georgia and Mississippi to work among the Indians.

"Aren't you afraid?" one woman asked Corrie after introductions had been made on the coach leaving Scranton. "I mean, they can be so unpredictable, so, so . . . uncivilized." It was apparent that the woman was searching for words that would not seem unkind, yet they struck Corrie as quite ignorant.

"I suppose," she said, feeling her face flush with irritation, "if you consider predicting a lunar eclipse or having your final essay read by the President, or paying the most charming compliments or creating an entire dictionary in your native tongue unpredictable and uncivilized."

A look of shock and then of doubt crossed the woman's face. 'I doubt that any Indian has done any such thing," she sputtered.

"I have met each of the young men who did exactly that," Corrie countered. "And furthermore . . ."

She was interrupted by Rev. Kingsbury. "It has been my experience," he said quietly, but firmly, "that any individual remains ignorant or uncivilized only if denied the opportunity to learn. The schools we are building among America's native people are making a tremendous difference in their lives."

The woman opened her mouth as if to argue with the minister, but apparently could think of nothing to provide counter evidence. She closed her mouth and suddenly seemed to take a great interest in the scenery outside.

Corrie looked down to the fan she held in her lap lest a flame of triumph be seen in her eyes by any of the other passengers. She silently gave thanks that Cyrus had intervened to keep her from saying something she would have regretted. Something about having fallen in love with such a young man. No one needed to know about that.

Later in the evening as she and the Kingsburys ate supper in the dining room of the inn in Williamsport, Corrie apologized for her outburst earlier that day.

"I shouldn't have spoken in anger," she said contritely, "but I find such attitudes so wrong and . . . so unchristian."

"It was a perfectly natural response," Electra said, patting Corrie's hand in sympathetic agreement. "You, better than most people, know what education can accomplish for those who have been given the opportunity to learn."

Cyrus gave his wife a look Corrie had seen him give his sons several times over the past two days. "Nevertheless, dear," he said, "a soft answer is better than giving in to anger. You will find yourself facing criticism for choosing to work among the Indians, Corrie. You must learn how to deal with it in a way that reflects your Christian values."

Now Electra looked contrite. "You're right, of course, dear. I'm still learning that myself, Corrie. Don't feel badly."

"You will find that in time you can sit at the dinner table with someone you completely disagree with and still maintain a civil tone. Heaven knows I have had to," Cyrus said ruefully.

Both women smiled, remembering the meal with the mission board at the Tuttle home.

But Electra's voice took on a saucy tone, "Oh, goodness, Corrie, I do hope he isn't talking about us!"

Corrie joined in the laughter around the table, but tucked that bit of advice away for the future. Somehow she knew her future would always involve work among the Indians she had come to know and respect and . . . love.

The port of Pittsburgh was bustling when they arrived two mornings later. The hack they had hired deposited them and their luggage near the berth of the steamboat *Velocipede*. The Kingsburys and Corrie made their way up the gangplank to board the boat with the enormous paddlewheel at its stern.

"These boats are always trying to break their own speed record," Cyrus commented as they took some time to walk around the upper deck. "But river levels are low this time of year, so the captain will have to be cautious as well."

Though the missionary's family had traveled this way before, it was a first for Corrie and she was excited to finally start the river portion of her journey. They would dock at several port communities along the Ohio before entering the Tennessee River at Pekin in Kentucky. From there the river meandered through the hills of western Tennessee and northern Alabama before reaching Chattanooga.

Like many other passengers Electra and Corrie spent much time during the warm days aboard the *Velocipede* seated on deck chairs near the stern. The churning paddle created a slight breeze and dispersed a fine mist of water over the deck. It helped to keep the passengers who gathered there cooler than they would have been in their small cabins below deck.

John and Russ had quickly made friends with a couple of other boys also traveling with their families downriver. They spent their days exploring the big boat though Electra insisted they report their whereabouts to one or the other of their parents on a regular basis.

Cyrus sometimes sat with the two ladies, but just as often he would find another passenger to visit with among those who occupied chairs on deck. Corrie admired his ability to engage anyone in conversation, always finding something he could talk to them about.

As they began their second week of the river journey, Corrie sat with Electra working on a needlework sampler. Nearby, Cyrus conversed with an older woman dressed in black, presumably a widow. She saw him draw out his small, worn Bible and thumb through it until he found a passage to read to the grieving woman.

"Your husband has a gift for finding people with a need, doesn't he?" Corrie noted to Electra.

"Yes," her cousin agreed, "but he would say it doesn't require any special gift. Every one of us has some need, some question or struggle. He's developed the art of being a good listener. I suppose that is his gift."

"Not everyone can do that," Corrie noted. "I can see he has a passion for it."

"His passion is working among the Indians," Electra added. "It has been for nearly ten years. But he feels a certain urgency now more than ever."

"Why?"

"If you followed the last Presidential election, you saw no doubt that every politician is promising a solution to the 'Indian problem.' What they mean, of course, is that they want the Indians to go away – either by complete assimilation into American culture or by removal west or sadly by complete annihilation. Cyrus is working as hard as he can to help the southeastern Indians navigate this dangerous time, giving them the tools of education and the hope of Christianity."

"He doesn't believe they have long to find their own solution, does he?"

"No, pressure is mounting on them, more with every election. Unfortunately even the Indians aren't in agreement about how they can survive this. You must have noticed that among the students at the mission school."

"Yes," Corrie agreed, thinking about the sometimes vigorous debates held around the dining table at her parents' home. She kept her needle busy, steadily pulling the thread through the canvas while her mind returned to the three young Cherokees who were frequent guests in the Tuttle home.

"I remember the friendly arguments John, Edmund and Elias would have," she said. "John favored assimilation, believing education and Christianity would give the Cherokees respect and provide them with legal recourse to protect themselves. Edmund thought this required too much compromise and the loss of their identity, their culture and traditions, so he favored moving west. Elias was more pragmatic. He thought the Cherokees should avail themselves of every opportunity to be educated and well-informed so they can retain their sovereignty wherever they might live."

"And how was their debate resolved?"

"It never was," Corrie smiled ruefully. "I think each man walks his own path, each one hoping he will reach the right destination."

"It is the same among the Creeks, the Choctaws and Chickasaws and the Seminoles. They don't agree among themselves and it creates distrust and division. If they are not careful, the politicians will exploit that division and they will lose through diplomacy what they fought so hard for in battle."

"So Cyrus fights for the missions and defends them to all the naysayers."

"Like a bulldog," his wife smiled.

The following day the *Velocipede* reached Pekin. Here the boat would dock and any passengers continuing on the Tennessee River would transfer to another steamboat aptly named the *Tennessee*.

Cyrus told Corrie that the little river port had once been a Chickasaw trading post. It was little more than that now, but its advantageous location at the Ohio-Tennessee river juncture would ensure its growth.

While luggage and trade goods were transferred between the boats, the Kingsbury party disembarked, bought some crackers and cheese at the trading post and sat under a tree on the riverbank to eat their dinner. They were pondering getting a nap when the steam whistle of the *Tennessee* announced to passengers that it was time to board.

Within an hour, the boat had pulled away from the dock and its big paddle churned the water of the smaller river. In another two weeks they would arrive at Chattanooga and Corrie's new life would begin.

"I think we'll end our discussion here," Rev. Washburn told the Bible study class as he glanced toward the Seth Thomas clock on a table at the side of the chapel. "We'll continue in this chapter next week."

After the closing prayer, the class dispersed. Attendance by the older students was required for this Wednesday afternoon class, but a few of the church members who lived close by also came.

Edmund helped the minister collect the Bibles that the class used and stored them in the pulpit at the front of the room. The students hurried to the dining hall to join the younger children in some afternoon treat that Miss Thrall would have prepared for them. Edmund thought he would join them as well.

As he and Washburn stepped out of the chapel, they were met by James Orr.

"We have visitors," the farmer told the two men. "Colonel Brearley has brought a delegation of Creeks. They are headed to Fort Gibson but have asked if they might spend the night here."

"We would be glad to host them," Washburn stated. "Are they in the dining hall?"

"They are just going in. I gave them a tour of the mission while waiting for your class to conclude." Dwight Mission was a large compound, with a number of log and frame buildings, including two water mills – one for grinding corn and one for sawing lumber.

"Thank you, James." Washburn turned to Edmund. "Do you speak any Creek, Webber?"

"I know a few *Muskoke* words," he said.

"I wonder if they have an interpreter with them?"

"If they are the McIntosh group, most will probably speak English," Edmund explained. "They have Scottish ancestry, like me."

"Do you know them?"

"I have met Chillicoth McIntosh at Indian Springs," the Cherokee explained. "He goes by Chilly. He is probably one of the delegates. Elias wrote to me about his father being killed for signing the removal treaty. He and his sister have been living near New Echota since then. Her husband was also killed."

They reached the dining hall and stepped inside to find five Creek delegates dressed in their traditional colorful clothing, adorned with beads and ribbons, with feathers stuck in their turbans.

Colonel David Brearley, a retired veteran of the most recent war with England, stood with the men while they waited for Miss Thrall and some of the other women to bring refreshments from the kitchen.

Brearley operated a trading post near Dardanelle and had served as the U.S. agent to the Cherokees for the past few years. He had just recently been assigned the task of assisting the McIntosh Creeks, as they were being called, in their move west.

When Washburn and Webber entered the room, Brearley turned from the man he had been talking with.

"Rev. Washburn," he said, extending his hand. "Thank you for your hospitality. We've had a long ride from Lewisburg today."

"We are pleased to have you and are eager to meet those who will be our new neighbors." Washburn shook hands all around with the five Creek leaders while Brearley gave their names.

As Edmund had expected one of the men was Chilly McIntosh. After shaking hands with Washburn, the young man turned to Edmund. "You look familiar to me," he said.

"Edmund Webber," the Cherokee introduced himself. "I met you once at the Indian Springs ferry."

"You live here?"

"Yes, I came out seven years ago with my brother and his family."

"Is this is a good land?" Chilly asked. At his words the other men turned to hear a fellow Indian's view of Arkansas Territory.

"I think it is," Edmund said. "Good bottom land for crops. Plenty of rivers. I know that is important to your people."

"We have always lived along the rivers and creeks; even our ancient ones built their mounds there." This information came from the man introduced as Roley McIntosh. Edmund knew him to be Chilly's uncle.

At this time, Abigail Washburn and Cynthia Thrall stepped into the dining room from the kitchen, each carrying a tray of food and serving dishes. They were followed by Sophronia Hitchcock and Minerva Orr, also bringing in food to serve their guests. The kitchen sat just behind the dining room, connected by a covered dog trot.

Washburn invited their visitors to be seated and then the women served biscuits and cheese with plenty of hot, black coffee. The children had already eaten and had been dismissed for a time of play before supper.

"You've had a long journey," Jacob Hitchcock noted after their guests had been given time to eat the light meal.

"We travel by boat from Coweta," the man named Benjamin Perryman said. "But the river too dry at Little Rock."

"The Arkansas is too shallow right now for the steamboats," Brearley explained. "So we borrowed horses and have followed the military road from there. We hope to reach Fort Smith in a couple of days and then Fort Gibson after that."

"Pardon me for saying so," James Orr said, "But I thought the area around Fort Gibson was bought for the Cherokees."

"The western boundary of Lovely's Purchase is the Verdigris River which flows into the Arkansas right there at Three Forks where Fort Gibson is located. So the Creeks will be looking over the land west of there between the Verdigris and the Arkansas."

"I have hunted there," Edmund volunteered. "It is prairie except along the rivers where there is plenty of timber, mostly oaks, walnut and hickory. Lots of pecan trees too."

"Do the Osages still hunt there?" Perryman asked.

"Yes," Edmund admitted. "We always keep a careful eye out for Osages or Wichitas."

The delegates exchanged concerned looks and spoke to each other in their language.

Brearley spoke when it grew quiet again. "I have assured these men that it is the intent of Colonel Arbuckle at Fort

Gibson to protect the Creeks from the Plains tribes. I plan to locate an agency for the Creeks at Three Forks. I've already discussed purchasing a building from the fur trader, Colonel Chouteau.

"If you choose to settle along the Arkansas and Verdigris, you will be quite close to the fort. The Osages themselves found refuge there this summer following a Pawnee uprising."

"Promises of protection have not been honored in Georgia," Perryman stated with bitterness in his voice. "General Jackson calls us his good friends because we fought with him against the Red Sticks. But he says he can't protect us in Georgia; we must move west to be safe. How can we know if we will be safe out here?"

"Colonel Arbuckle is not General Jackson," Brearley stated firmly. "He has no ambition to be President."

Some of the men smiled at the agent's blunt assessment of current political realities. In truth, Arbuckle had fought against the Red Sticks himself during the most recent war. Jackson had parlayed his victories at Horseshoe Bend and New Orleans into political capital. Arbuckle simply served wherever the military sent him and now found himself in the middle of an area Jackson was determined to turn into an Indian territory.

CHAPTER TEN

Chattanooga, Tennessee
September, 1826

Corrie was saying goodbye once again, this time to the Kingsburys who were preparing to leave Chattanooga for Mississippi. They had spent a week with the Worcesters at the Cherokee mission but were now anxious to get back to their own work among the Choctaws. Corrie would wait at Brainerd for Elias and Harriet to come for her and move her to New Echota.

For some reason this goodbye seemed almost harder than when she had left Connecticut. Back then she could only imagine what life would be like in an area still considered the frontier. Now she'd seen it and she realized it was going to take some adjusting to dusty towns with no sidewalks and few stores and scattered farms consisting of log cabins and primitive amenities.

Corrie had accompanied the Worcesters to Ross's Landing to see the Kingsburys again board the *Tennessee* bound for Alabama. Then they would follow the Natchez Trace to Mayhew Mission.

"I'm going to miss you two," Corrie told John and Russ who stiffened and acted embarrassed when she tried to hug them. Electra was not so reluctant to receive her hug. The two women had become good friends on the journey and it was hard for them to part.

"How do you do it, Electra?" Corrie whispered as the two women embraced.

"Look past the differences," she advised, fully understanding what Corrie was asking. "Look for those things we all share in common – love of family, times of fellowship, good food."

The two laughed and Corrie felt some of her fears melt away. "I'm going to miss you."

"You're going to be just fine."

Cousin Cyrus stepped closer to also offer advice to the young woman. "You are far better prepared for mission work than most, Cornelia. You have had the good fortune to get to know some of the very people you'll be working with. You've already come to love them and that's all it takes to find a home on a mission field."

Corrie felt her face flush at the minister's words. What did he know of her love of Cherokees – a certain Cherokee? Had her mother said something to them? But she could read nothing in the face of Cyrus or Electra that said they knew the secret she still held. The secret she could not seem to let go.

Corrie stood with Samuel and Ann and watched the family board the steamboat. The boys didn't hesitate to rush to the place at the rail where passengers would wave to folks who had come to see them off. It was awhile before the boat was released from its moorings and the whistle announced that the gangplank was to be raised.

A few minutes later, the chug of the engine sent a shudder through the boat and the paddle slowly turned. Corrie and her hosts waved until the boat was well out into the main channel and pushing its way south.

"Shall we take some refreshments before we drive back to Brainerd?" Samuel proposed to Ann and Corrie. "The tavern serves tea and scones."

"That would be lovely, dear," Ann agreed. She was a petite woman with blonde hair and gray eyes. Though nothing had been said, Corrie could tell that Ann was in the family way and Samuel was being quite solicitous of his young wife.

They enjoyed their tea while Ann shared some of her experiences at the Cherokee mission. "We've only been here a year now, but we've come to love it. And wait until you see the woods in autumn. I didn't think anything could be as lovely as New England, but it's really quite beautiful here."

Corrie had already admired the mountains rising up in the distance in folds of blue. "I'll look forward to that."

"Come up and see us when the leaves start to turn," Samuel suggested. "You and the Boudinots. We'll drive over to Lookout Mountain and take a picnic."

Ann gave her husband a bemused look. "I will be otherwise occupied about the time the leaves are turning," she smiled.

Corrie saw Samuel's face flush crimson. "Of course, my dear," he said. "I'm sorry I forgot."

"You can still come up," Ann turned to Corrie. "We'll have a new baby that we'll want to show off in early November."

"I'll look forward to that as well," Corrie grinned.

Two days later, Harriet and Elias arrived at Brainerd. They spent a day visiting with the Worcesters, the two men full of plans for the printing press that had finally arrived.

"My dream is to start a newspaper," Elias revealed as they stood with their wives and Corrie around the large black machine set in a little storage building that had been cleared to create the printing office.

"That will take money," Samuel stated.

"I think I can persuade the National Council to provide some funds," Elias countered. "The rest I can raise. I've received invitations to speak from some churches up north. Not everyone in New England hates me." His smile was rueful.

"We'll print some samples for you to take with you," Worcester offered. "Give them an idea of what we can do. I'm working on a way to print both in Cherokee and English on the same sheet."

"He's done nothing but tinker with that type since it arrived." Ann shook her head in mock annoyance, but Corrie could tell that she was proud of her husband.

Harriet had been quiet since they had arrived causing Corrie concern. Later that evening, before they retired for bed she questioned her friend. Harriet confided, "Elias and I will welcome our own little one next year. I'm just feeling a bit poorly right now. Nothing to be alarmed about."

"I'm happy for you, Harriet," Corrie said, trying hard not to feel just a wee bit jealous. "But you shouldn't have made the trip from New Echota if you weren't feeling well."

"It comes and goes," Harriet smiled. "Otherwise I'm fine. And you know it wouldn't have been proper for you to travel alone with my husband. We can't be causing a scandal." She giggled at her words. Corrie laughed too, happy that her friend had put that pain behind her.

The next day, Corrie and the Boudinots started their journey back to New Echota as dawn crept over the mountains. They reached Chattanooga and decided to rest a bit at the waterfront tavern because Harriet was feeling nauseous.

They were sipping coffee while Harriet nibbled on crackers when the door of the dining room opened and the tall man Corrie had met in Cornwall stepped inside. He removed his hat and looked around the room for a table. His eyes lighted with surprise when he saw Corrie.

He crossed the room to stand at her elbow. "Miss Tuttle," he said with a bow. "What a delightful surprise to see you here. You are certainly a long way from Connecticut."

"Yes, Mr. . . ." Corrie could not recall his name.

"It's Ackley, Oliver Ackley."

"Mr. Ackley. These are my friends Harriet and Elias Boudinot."

Corrie thought she saw a slight narrowing of those green eyes as Ackley acknowledged the introduction. "My pleasure," he said, but the words were clipped and his voice lacked any warmth.

The young man turned his eyes from his cool appraisal of Elias to look at Corrie. "How long will you be visiting Georgia?" he asked.

"I've come to stay," Corrie replied. "At least for a time. I have taken a position at the Mission School at New Echota."

"A mission." Again Ackley's words were cold, but he quickly hid the disdain from his face. "They are fortunate to have you, I'm sure."

"Thank you." Corrie wondered if she should continue to engage the man in conversation. He seemed to have no intention of moving on to another table, but she felt quite hesitant to ask him to have a seat at theirs.

"I didn't realize you were from Chattanooga, Mr. Ackley."

"I'm not," he replied quickly. "My father's farm is west of here. There isn't any land to be had in Chattanooga for anyone but the Ross family, it would seem."

He turned back to Elias, with a challenge in his demeanor. "Daniel Ross is building quite the empire, isn't he? With his sons Lewis in Tennessee, John in Georgia and Andrew in Alabama, he controls thousands of acres of prime farmland, but has not a single acre available for sale."

Elias frowned at the man's words. "We hold our land in common," he explained. "Our law doesn't allow a Cherokee to sell land to anyone who isn't a citizen of our nation."

"Your nation?" Oliver repeated with incredulity. "These are the United States, twenty-four sovereign states. You are here with our permission."

Elias threw his napkin on the table and looked as if he would stand. "You are here with *our* permission," he countered with steel in his voice.

Corrie felt a tremor of shock run through her. She had never see Elias so angry, not even in the midst of all the ugliness in Cornwall. He was normally affable and good-natured, but he now looked as if he might challenge Mr. Ackley to step outside.

Corrie looked at Harriet and saw the same shock on her face. Her friend also looked rather green as if she were about to lose the crackers she had been steadily eating in an effort to settle her stomach.

The young woman laid her hand on her husband's arm. "Elias, I don't feel well. I need some fresh air."

Immediately concern for Harriet replaced the look of anger on the Cherokee's face. He stood, reached into his pocket and flipped a coin to the table. Then he helped his wife to stand also. "Please excuse us," he said quietly.

Corrie stood also to leave, but Ackley moved away from Harriet's chair thus blocking her from following the couple.

With a genuine look of remorse on his face, he said to Elias, "I'm so sorry. I did not mean to offend."

"Nor did I," Elias said. Then he and Harriet walked to the door.

Oliver turned to face Corrie. "I apologize to you as well. I had some bad news this morning and I'm afraid I let it get the best of me. Please forgive me. I hope you will not hold it against me."

"I accept your apology, Mr. Ackley. But I must be going."

"Let me walk you to the door, Miss Tuttle. It's the least I can do."

"Alright," she said with a nod of her head. She took up her reticule and Mr. Ackley laid a light hand on her elbow. The room was filled mostly with men, so Corrie was grateful to have an escort.

At the door, Ackley paused. "I travel through New Echota occasionally on my way to Savannah," he said. "My father's factor has an office there. Might I call on you at the mission?"

Corrie was surprised at his request. She had been aware of the man's interest even in Cornwall, but had not thought their circumstances would ever allow for a social call. She was torn about what answer she should give.

He was certainly a handsome man and seemed to have money, education and good manners. He was not as tall as Edmund or nearly as charming, but he was attentive. Yet she hardly knew him and he also seemed to bear some animosity toward Cherokees. All these thoughts flitted through her mind while he waited with an expectant look on his face.

"I suppose," she finally said, "if you are ever in New Echota. Do you know where the mission is?"

"I'm sure I can easily find it. New Echota is a very small place."

"Well, perhaps we'll see each other again."

"I will see to it." Ackley gave a bow and then held the door open for Corrie to pass through.

"Good day," she said.

"Good day, Miss Tuttle."

She hurried to the carriage where its team of horses was tied to a hitching post. Elias and Harriet stood by the seat of the vehicle. She was taking a sip of water from the tin canteen the cook had filled for them at Brainerd. The young woman then dabbed at her mouth with a dampened handkerchief.

"Harriet has fed the bushes," Elias said when Corrie reached them. His voice was gently teasing and any sense of anger from his encounter with Mr. Ackley seemed to have dissipated.

"Hmmh," Harriet tried to sound annoyed.

"Are you feeling better?" Corrie inquired.

"Yes, much better. Let's get on our way. We have a long drive."

Elias helped Harriet and then Corrie into the carriage, then crossed behind it to untie the horses before pulling himself up into the seat. He turned the horses toward the road that headed south. Corrie glanced back at the tavern with its six over six windows and thought she saw Mr. Ackley standing at one of them, watching. Perhaps such interest should have felt flattering, but for some reason it made Corrie feel on guard. Telling herself she was being silly, she turned and settled back in the carriage seat and the three friends were soon engaged in conversation.

Oliver turned away from the window once the Boudinot carriage was out of sight. He had spotted a friend when he entered the dining room and now made his way to that table.

"Well, Ackley what brings you to Chattanooga?" his former school chum asked as Oliver took a chair.

"I brought another offer to Daniel Ross for that acreage along the south ridge," Oliver explained while nodding to the serving girl who brought out a cup and a pot of coffee. "But it's not for sale."

"When are you going to give up on that? Ross isn't going to sell, none of those Cherokees are. It's their law."

"Everyone has their price, Richards, you know that."

"Perhaps. But paying with your life is a mighty high price just to strike a deal. Their law says a Cherokee selling land to a non-Cherokee is committing treason."

"A barbaric law," Ackley groused as he took a sip of the hot drink. "One of the many reasons the Cherokees need to move west."

"You'll be waiting a long time for that," Richards drawled.

"Just until Jackson is elected."

"You really think he can accomplish that?"

"He said he would in his last campaign."

"Politicians say a lot of things when they're on the stump." Richards shook his head. "He'll have to convince Congress."

"Maybe not," Ackley countered. "The states are the true authority in government. If they have Jackson's support, they can do what Georgia has already done to the Creeks – strike a deal, get a treaty written to their advantage and send them west."

Richards didn't seem convinced. "I still wouldn't make any plans for the south ridge if I were you. The Cherokees are getting educated . . . real fast. They won't be easily pushed out of their homelands."

"Perhaps they can be persuaded," Ackley said thoughtfully. He glanced back at the window that looked out toward the mountains. "Maybe they would listen to a trusted friend."

"You have a 'trusted friend' hiding in your pocket?"

"Perhaps," Ackley smiled and then dug into the plate of flapjacks the girl had placed before him. "Perhaps I will very soon."

The air felt crisp on a morning in early fall as Edmund swung his ax to split another length of kindling. He hadn't been able to work at this task for the past week because of the heavy rains that had inundated the area. The ground was soggy and the wood wet, but he would stack it into a lean-to by his cabin to let it dry out.

He'd been outside since dawn, using his horse to drag a fallen tree from the woods nearby then saw it into lengths to fit the fireplace in his small cabin. Edmund had built just a one-room home with a covered porch. It sat at the edge of a stretch of timber that ran up into the hills. He was in sight of Walter's much larger home with its many outbuildings, but far enough away that he did not feel he was a part of the plantation.

Beyond Walter's finely furnished double cabin lay the rich river bottom land just harvested of its cotton. He couldn't see the river, but he knew it was running high with a strong current. The bayou was also full, as well as the several creeks in the area that fed into it.

His work and the welcome sunshine were making him warm, so he paused to remove the chambray trade shirt he wore. He settled back into the rhythm of heaving the ax and hearing the satisfying thunk of it when it struck the wood.

He tossed the split kindling to one side and reached for another length of wood when he saw Harry running along the footpath that connected his cabin to the rest of the Webber land. If there was an errand to be run to Mr. Edmund, Harry was always quick to volunteer. He had come to expect a penny as compensation for his effort.

"Mr. Edmund," Harry was already calling even before skidding to a stop by the tree stump where the Cherokee worked.

"What is it, Harry?"

"Miz Webber says you need to come," Harry gulped, "to the store."

"What's wrong?" Edmund could sense the urgency in the lad's effort.

"The bayou's comin' out of its banks," the boy explained. "It'll reach the store 'fore too long. Mr. Webber wants to move the stuff to higher ground."

Before Harry could finish, Edmund had pulled his shirt back on and set his ax on the porch. "Wait here, Harry, while I get my horse. Then we'll ride down."

Harry nodded his compliance and hopped up to take a seat on the porch floor with his feet hanging off. Edmund strode to his barn and quickly put a halter on his horse. He threw a blanket over the paint's back, but didn't bother with a saddle.

He mounted in one fluid motion then trotted the horse to the porch. "Come on, Harry," he said while leaning far over toward the boy. "Take my hand."

Harry grasped Edmund's hand with both of his and was easily pulled up to sit astride in front the interpreter. Then Edmund clicked the horse into a trot and followed the path down to the military road that wound along the river bank. They soon turned onto the trail that would take them to the Webber trading post.

When they arrived they found that Walter had brought his two large wagons from home and had backed them to the two doors of the mercantile. His hostler and blacksmith, a burly Negro named Malachi along with the man's two sons were loading merchandise into the wagons as quickly as they could. Edmund lowered Harry to the ground then dismounted himself and tied his horse to the hitching rail at the front of the store.

Walter nodded to his brother as he came out of the store with an armload of mink pelts. These were some of the most valuable items in stock and the Scotch-Cherokee trader would not want them to be ruined by a muddy flood. Edmund hurried inside and looked around trying to determine what else was of greatest value to be saved.

He grabbed a Spanish saddle, intricately carved and inlaid with silver. Quickly he added it to the growing pile of stock in the wagons. What they could not fit in the wagons they lifted to higher shelves or into the rafters of the building.

Walter hastily stuffed papers from the back desk into a carpetbag, then looking around, he seemed satisfied that they had done the best they could to save as much merchandise as possible.

All the men exited the building. Walter went to a lean-to at the back and hauled out bags of dried corn. With the other men, he piled them around the two doors of the store. These might not stop all the water, but perhaps they would slow it down. They might also keep out the snakes that would surely accompany the flood.

Edmund glanced again at the bayou. The waters had risen so much it was impossible to tell where its normal banks were located. Already the stream had covered the footpath in front of the store. Edmund helped Harry climb into the back of one of the wagons then went to remount his horse. The animal was skittish as it eyed the rising water.

Walter climbed onto the seat of one wagon and told Jerome, Malachi's younger son, to drive the other wagon. Before they could set the horses in motion, they heard a call. It sounded like a girl. The men turned to see who was approaching the store from the north.

Lucinda Ballard, on horseback, came around the corner of the building. "We need help," the seventeen year old said in Cherokee. "Our horses are trapped."

"Where?" Edmund asked.

"On the rise behind the house," the young woman explained. "They're completely surrounded by water."

Edmund looked at Water. His brother said, "Take Malachi and Peter. We'll take the stock home, then come join you."

Edmund nodded then slid from his horse and tossed the reins to Malachi. "May I ride with you?" he asked Lucinda. At her assent, he nudged her horse to the hitching rail. Using it as a step, he climbed onto the roan and settled behind the girl. Edmund had to admire her pluck. She had ridden without saddle or bridle with her fingers tightly twined into the horse's mane.

With Malachi and Peter on Edmund's horse, they splashed through the water following the trail as best they could toward the Ballard farm. Rabbit Ballard raised horses and had built a reputation for having some of the best stock in Arkansas. Edmund had acquired his own paint from among Ballard's stock.

Edmund was uncomfortably aware of his nearness to Lucinda and wondered if he should have found another horse to carry him to the Ballard farm. But there had been little time and Lucinda seemed unaffected by their shared ride. Her focus was on getting home as quickly as the rising waters allowed.

The trail branched away from the bayou and they left the water for a time. They reached Chief Jolly's peach orchard and quickly rode through it, bending low to avoid the branches. Here Jolly's son Price had a cabin with his young family. As they passed it, they saw Price's younger sister on the porch. "Price has gone to help," Colista said.

"*Wado*," Lucinda called her thanks. The two young women were good friends.

Continuing on they reached the Ballard farm which sat between Spadra Creek and the Illinois Bayou. It was in a pleasant valley with rich pastureland, but subject to flooding. Edmund saw Mrs. Ballard hastily working to clear items out of their cabin which was already surrounded by a few inches of water and would soon be inundated.

Lucinda pressed the mustang on past her home unconcerned that her long skirt was being splashed by the muddy water. The girl had a great love of the horses her father raised and was anxious to reach the hillock where about a dozen of their stock stood above the water, but were completely surrounded. The animals were frightened and bunched together under a giant cottonwood.

When they reached her father, she brought the horse to a halt. Edmund dismounted quickly and helped Lucinda down. Malachi and Peter were not far behind and also quickly jumped from Edmund's horse.

Having visited the farm to purchase his horse, Edmund knew there was a wash that ran between the cabin and the hill where the horses had sought refuge. Normally the small ravine held little water, but today it provided an outlet for Spadra Creek to overflow toward the bayou. No doubt they would have to wade fairly deep water to get to the horses then coax the frightened animals through the water back to safety.

Rabbit Ballard and Price Jolly stood ankle deep in water, considering how best to get the horses off the hill.

Edmund looked to Malachi who worked with horses every day. "What should we do, Malachi?"

"We needs to get hackamores on all of them."

Rabbit nodded. "Have rope." He pointed to a coil of rope on the ground nearby, outside of the mud.

The men walked to the coil and Ballard took out a knife and cut it into lengths to snub around the nose of each horse. The men took two coils each.

"There are eleven," Rabbit said. "I will get three, you must get two each."

The men nodded while they knotted their ropes.

"I can get one, father," Lucinda said.

"No, daughter," Ballard shook his head. "They are afraid and will be hard to manage."

"I can get Kalanee," she returned. "He trusts me."

The raven-black horse was a favorite of the young woman. She rode him often and the pony followed her around like a pet.

Her father studied the horses which were becoming even more agitated.

"You must turn back if the water is too deep."

"I will," Lucinda agreed.

Still reluctant, Ballard gave his daughter one of the rope hackamores. Then with a nod to the men, he led the way into the muddy water. The others followed in single file, with Lucinda just behind her father. All were wearing moccasins and the soft soles allowed them to feel the ground that they could not see.

Edmund kept a watchful eye on Lucinda as the water rose to their waists when they reached the wash. He also scanned the water's surface looking for the v-trail of water moccasins – the poisonous snake common along the waterways. Clearly Peter was keeping an eye out too for he pointed toward one off to their left. The rescuers moved right to avoid the cottonmouth.

The water became shallower as they climbed the rise and Ballard spoke softly to his horses to try to calm them. His words seemed to have no effect at first. The horses continued to paw at the ground and snort in agitation. They were bunched so tightly together they seemed like one frightened animal.

Lucinda stepped out from behind her father and called to her pony.

Hey, Kalanee, my pretty boy."

The small black horse lifted his head, his ears flicking back and forth at the familiar voice. He looked over the back of another horse and nickered softly.

All the men spread out and carefully approached the horses in a semi-circle. Lucinda kept talking softly to the stallion and it finally managed to press through the crush of the other horses and walked tentatively toward the young woman.

The stallion's actions seemed to pull the attention of the other horses away from the rising water. They eyed the pair with curiosity. Ballard was able to slip his rope onto the closest horse. The mustang shied and swung its rump around, but Ballard held onto its head, speaking softly to it. He pinched the horse's nostrils to firm his control over it. Soon the animal calmed and stood still.

The other men followed suit, working to get the makeshift hackamores on the horses. When all had been secured, Ballard again led the way, coaxing the two horses he held into the water.

Edmund found himself fighting to control one mare who seemed especially frightened of the water. She nearly pulled him off his feet at one point as she refused to set foot into the rising flow and tried to jerk her head away.

"Nanyi," Lucinda scolded the mare. "Behave."

The mare dropped her head as if embarrassed and gave Edmund no more trouble. The group slowly led the horses back across the expanse of water. Walter and Jerome arrived on horseback and left their mounts to wade into the wash and assist in pulling the still skittish animals to safety.

The effort of pulling the horses against the heavy current left them all winded. They stood for a while, stroking the horses and talking softly to calm them and to catch their breath. Ballard walked among them, running a practiced hand over his stock to see if any horse was injured. None seemed too worse for the frightening effort though the mare named Nanyi had a cut on one foreleg.

"I thank you," the stockman said. "If you please, we will lead them to the north corral. It sits high and rarely floods."

Again they all followed Ballard with the horses they had secured. Within fifteen minutes they reached the high corral and led the horses inside the split rail fence.

"Good stock," Malachi observed as they stood for a moment watching the horses gathered around a stack of hay.

"I buy from an Osage named Bird," Ballard explained.

Walter harrumphed his contempt for the Osages but Ballard ignored him.

Edmund looked down at his wet and muddy clothes. Everything was likely ruined. The horses were covered in mud as well and would require a hard brushing once it dried. He made a mental note to come back tomorrow to help with the task.

After a few moments the group returned to where they had left their own mounts. They found Mrs. Ballard with the four younger children waiting in their loaded wagon.

"Do you have a place to stay?" Price Jolly asked.

"My sister lives up in the hills. We will spend the night there. The water should be down by tomorrow."

Then Rabbit shook hands all around again thanking the men for their help. He and Lucinda walked to the wagon and the others went to their horses. Lucinda looked back toward Edmund and raised a hand, mouthing her thanks. "*Wado*."

He nodded and watched as she climbed into the wagon. Her dress was soggy and even the ends of her long black hair showed traces of mud. But her blue eyes held admiration as she smiled his way. It made him smile too.

CHAPTER ELEVEN

Running Waters, Georgia
November, 1826

Elias turned his carriage onto the long tree-lined drive that led to the home of John and Sarah Ridge. Ahead Corrie could see the white colonial-style home through the row of trees. Its windows glowed from candlelight that sparkled behind the lace curtains. She felt as nervous coming to this supper as she had for her first fall dance back in Cornwall.

The invitation to the Ridges' dinner party had arrived by messenger last week at the New Echota mission where Corrie had been settling into her new job. It had come as a pleasant surprise to the young housemother. She had hoped to see her old friends from school soon and was curious to visit the home Sarah had written about. She sent a reply back by the same courier accepting the invitation.

Now as the carriage approached the house, Corrie smoothed the light blue taffeta fabric of her skirt, hoping she was dressed appropriately. Harriet had assured her that she looked lovely when she and Elias had called for Corrie for the drive to Running Waters.

While they enjoyed the warm fall day, Elias explained that the dinner party would likely be attended by many members of the National Council, which served as the government of the Cherokees. Elias no longer taught school at the Moravian mission. He had been hired as clerk for the National Council and oversaw many of the day-to-day operations of the Cherokee government.

The Boudinot carriage reached the house and the horses pulled it around the circular drive to stop at the front door. Before Elias could alight from the vehicle, a young Negro man, about fifteen or sixteen, hurried to hold the reins while Elias helped Corrie and Harriet alight. They walked toward the door while the young man jumped into the carriage and directed the horses toward a side yard where other vehicles had been parked.

The sight of the slave had immediately assailed Corrie's conscience. In her excitement to see Sarah and John, she had forgotten that they kept slaves. Now she felt a twinge of regret for accepting the invitation without thought. She had promised herself when she took a job in the South that she would do nothing that would appear to condone or accommodate the practice of slavery.

Yet here she was, being greeted at the door by another servant who offered to take their wraps. Corrie felt trapped and wondered how she would make it through supper. She could hardly refuse to join the party now so she surrendered her ivory shawl and smiled her thanks at the older Negro man with graying hair. She remembered Cousin Cyrus's advice about sitting at a meal with someone you disagreed with and promised herself that she would keep her remarks pleasant and soft.

The threesome entered the foyer where a sweeping staircase led to the second floor. Through double doors, Corrie could see Sarah, her blonde hair shining in the candlelight. She turned from talking to an older Cherokee man and caught sight of Corrie and the Boudinots. She quickly excused herself and came to greet them at the doorway.

"Corrie, it is so wonderful to see you," she said, pulling her friend into an embrace.

"Yes, it is, Sarah," Corrie replied, trying to match Sarah's enthusiasm. "Thank you so much for the invitation."

"Well, I knew you had to be included when Harriet told me you had arrived. It's like old times, isn't it? All that's missing is Edmund."

"Yes," Corrie said tightly. Could this evening get any more awkward?

"Come, all of you," Sarah went on, not noticing Corrie's strained reply. "Let's make sure Corrie meets everyone. Some of our guests have children who attend the school at New Echota, so you might have met them already."

In accordance with proper etiquette, Sarah led Corrie and the Boudinots to the oldest and most important couple in the room to start her introductions.

"This is Chief Pathkiller and his wife Peggy," she said to Corrie. Then turning to the couple who were dressed traditionally, she spoke Cherokee to explain who Corrie was.

When she heard Sarah finally say her name, Corrie spoke. "It's a privilege to meet you."

She didn't know if she should offer her hand or curtsy. What was the proper protocol for meeting an Indian chief? Why hadn't she asked Harriet on the way here?

Elias translated Corrie's greeting and then the couples' response. "Pathkiller counts it a pleasure to meet you as well. Peggy hopes you are well settled at the mission."

"Yes, I am. Thank you."

After Elias had translated, Sarah said something more in Cherokee, then slipped her arm through Corrie's and led her to another couple standing nearby. She whispered close to Corrie's ear. "You're doing fine. They are the only ones who speak no English."

Corrie released the breath she had been holding in a sigh of relief. After that Corrie was greeted warmly by John before being introduced to his father Major Ridge and his mother Suzie. Then she met Elizur and Esther Butler, who worked at a nearby mission, James and Mary Starr, whose farm was near the Waties' and Charles and Nancy Hicks, the second chief and his wife. By this time the names were beginning to run together and Corrie was sure she would not remember who were the Vanns, the Rosses and the Foremans.

The man named Crawling Snake, she would probably never forget. She prayed that the start his name gave her had not been noticeable.

Sarah did her best to make Corrie feel comfortable, but since much of the conversation around her was being spoken in Cherokee, the housemother felt rather out of place. She knew a few words in the native language, thanks to Edmund, but not enough for conversation. Corrie stayed close to Harriet while Elias made the rounds shaking hands with the men in the group.

After about twenty minutes, Sarah nodded to John who raised his voice to get their crowd's attention. "I believe supper is ready to be served. Please join Sarah and me in the dining room."

The guests strolled across a hall to the large room where two long tables dressed in fine linens, china and silver candlesticks waited. A fire crackled in a large rock fireplace at one end of the room. Except for making sure Pathkiller and his wife were seated next to John at the head of the first table, Sarah indicated the guests could be seated where they chose. Elias pulled out chairs for both Harriet and Corrie then took his seat next to his wife.

"Well, what do you think?" Harriet asked her friend quietly.

"Wouldn't the good people of Cornwall be shocked at how far 'beneath herself' Sarah has wed?" Corrie replied looking around the well-appointed room. Though not as fine as the Huddleston home, it was far and away more richly furnished than most of the houses in her hometown. Mrs. Huddleston would have frowned at Sarah's casual way of entertaining, but she would not be able to fault her decorating style.

John called for quiet by tapping a knife against his water goblet. "We will ask Dr. Butler to offer thanks for our meal."

All bowed their heads while the missionary doctor stood and said a brief prayer. Then Sarah nodded to the three house slaves who stood at the sideboard in gray uniforms. Quickly they set baskets of hot rolls on the tables and served the traditional Cherokee soup *kanuche.* This was followed by quail with a cornbread dressing and roasted potatoes.

Quiet conversation flowed gently around the room. The food was delicious, but Corrie found it hard to eat. She felt guilty about enjoying a meal prepared and served by slaves. It went against her sense of right and wrong. She resolved to keep her opinions to herself, get through this evening, and find an excuse not to return to Running Waters.

"Chief Pathkiller truly was pleased to meet you, Corrie." Elias interrupted her thoughts. "He is very traditional in his thinking on most subjects, but he does value education and those who are bringing it to our nation."

"How long has he been chief?" Corrie asked.

"Oh, my," Elias thought for a moment. "As long as I can remember. He is quite venerated among our people."

"He fought in the Revolutionary War," Harriet added.

"He's a hero then."

"Well," with a twinkle in his eye, Elias explained, "he actually fought for the British."

Corrie knew she had a surprised look on her face. She didn't know what to say.

Harriet smiled. "I was surprised too. Elias loves telling about Pathkiller and Dragging Canoe leading Cherokee warriors to battle at Chickamauga."

"We love good stories like that," Elias defended himself as the dessert plates were set out. "Pathkiller is one of only a handful of the old warriors left." He sounded almost wistful.

It's true," Harriet said. "The Cherokees are wonderful storytellers. You'll probably hear many of the stories from your students. Just remember that the Cherokees don't mind telling tall tales."

"I guess every culture has them," Corrie said as she took a bite of the honey cake. "Like the headless horseman and Rip Van Winkle."

"Exactly," Elias agreed.

The meal was winding down and the servants removed the dishes from the table. John stood, thus announcing an end to the supper. "If you gentlemen will join me in the library, we'll leave the parlor to the ladies."

Everyone rose then and went to the separate rooms. The men would talk politics while they smoked and the women would enjoy coffee while they talked about the men. Many Cherokees were temperance people and alcohol was not served at Running Waters.

Corrie sat quietly with the other women, trying to follow the conversation. Sarah did her best to translate both Cherokee and English for those who might need assistance in understanding. Corrie admired Sarah's poise, her brilliance, mother would say. The Ridges had successfully melded their two cultures in a lovely home. It was sad that slavery existed in both cultures.

Sarah was explaining that the chicory she was serving had been grown at Running Waters. Corrie didn't care for the bitter taste so only took a few sips to be polite. She was developing a headache and hoped that Elias would decide soon that they needed to start back to New Echota.

At one point the ladies heard raised voices coming from the library. The men apparently were arguing about something. Mrs. Ross made a comment in Cherokee and the other women broke into laughter. Sarah covered her mouth to hide her own smile and chose not to offer an English translation. Corrie supposed she would never know what had been said and thought it was just as well.

She glanced through the lace curtains and saw movement outside on the circular drive. John had called for the carriages to be brought forward and the men were strolling out of the library to collect their coats, retrieve their wives and take their leave of the beautiful home.

Elias came for Harriet, carrying her wrap as well as Corrie's shawl. They paused at the front door to extend their thanks and goodbyes to the Ridges.

Sarah again hugged Corrie. "Thank you for coming," she said and Corrie could tell that her presence had been deeply appreciated by her school chum. "If Harriet doesn't mind, maybe we three can meet at her house some time. I hardly had a chance to really visit with you."

"I would like that," Corrie agreed. She sensed that Sarah understood her discomfort at Running Waters.

"I'll pick a date and let you know," Harriet enthused.

"Then I hope we'll see each other again soon, before Harriet's confinement," Sarah said. Then the three stepped onto the front porch and waited for their carriage to be brought forward. Elias helped the ladies up and they were soon traveling back down the long drive. A nearly full moon gave silver light to the cool evening air.

They rode in silence for a while, but Harriet soon asked, "What were you men arguing about? We could hear you from the parlor."

"The same thing we always argue about," Elias sighed. "James Starr said we should never have allowed the federal road to be built through our nation. He said we ought to look into more settlement out west. That, of course, angered John and his father . . . Ross as well. To even suggest such a thing is the same as treason to them."

"Mrs. Starr said their farm is near the road. The traffic on it has doubled over what it was last year. Folks using the federal road don't seem to respect that they are in a sovereign nation," Harriet told him.

"It's a double edged sword. A good road allows us to move our product to market and bring goods in that we need. But I understand Starr's concern. It brings a lot of people into the nation, all seeing our land and wanting it for themselves."

Corrie had listened to the exchange quietly, not familiar enough with the political issues to have yet formed an opinion.

"Do you think it's treason to move west?" she finally asked.

"No," Harriet replied quickly. "At least I don't. Edmund isn't wrong to be out in Arkansas or Bettie either. Don't you think, Elias? "

"I can see both sides of this issue," Elias said, in his customary tactful manner. "I don't fault anyone for trying to provide a good life for themselves and their children. Bettie's happy out west. Her children are in school at Dwight Mission.

My greatest concern is that we are in danger of becoming two nations instead of one. The distance makes us strangers."

Yes, Corrie thought. *Distance certainly does that.*

A few days later, Corrie sat on a little stool at the work table in the mission kitchen peeling apples. In the two months that she had worked here, she had overcome her homesickness but she still felt a sense of loneliness. Thankfully there was always plenty of work to keep her busy and keep her mind off her home so far away. Besides serving as housemother, she assisted with other chores including kitchen and laundry duties.

She now lived in a two story cottage that housed the few students who boarded at the school. Upstairs a Cherokee-Creek widow named Jane Hawkins resided with her young son. Three other boys were boarded there. Downstairs Corrie was in charge of six girls aged seven to thirteen. She found the girls to be sweet but rather shy and since their English was limited and her Cherokee even more limited, they depended upon Jane sometimes to help with communication.

Corrie found Jane also to be very quiet, but she could not blame the young woman. Hers was a tragic story. Her father William McIntosh and her husband Sam Hawkins had been both killed for signing the Indian Springs Treaty. In a single day, her world had been plunged into a dark sadness.

Because her mother had been Cherokee, Jane had left the Creek Nation to reside at New Echota. She would stay until her uncle and brother returned from Arkansas Territory. Then she planned to travel west with other members of the McIntosh clan and start a new life for herself and her young son Pinkney.

Corrie glanced across the work table where Jane sat also working on the apples. Mrs. Hannah Sanders, wife of the mission's director, felt it was cool enough now to undertake making apple butter. Stirring the cooking apples over a fire was an hours-long affair and not something she wanted to attempt while the weather had remained warm.

It had been unseasonably warm and very rainy through the fall months. Everyone had welcomed the cold snap that had finally frosted the trees with color. Now they worked to preserve several bushels of apples that had been donated to the mission by the plantation owner John Ross.

Jars of canned apples lined the shelves in the root cellar. Other apples had been sliced and were drying by the fireplace. Today, they would use the big cauldron set over a fire outside to make the apple butter. The workers would take turns stirring the apple and spice mixture to keep it from burning.

The women couldn't resist snitching a slice of apple now and then while they worked. They would laugh when someone caught them enjoying a bite of the tangy fruit.

"Good apples," Delight Sergeant said sheepishly when Jane pointed at her with a smile. Delight was a Cherokee woman a little older than Corrie who worked as a kitchen helper at the mission.

"It was good of Mr. Ross to give them to us," Mrs. Sanders agreed.

Corrie had learned that the Ross family was a large one among the Cherokees and apparently was wealthy as well. Mr. Ross's plantation sat across the river from John and Sarah's home. She had met Ross and his wife Quatie at the dinner at Running Waters. Like John Ridge, Mr. Ross was a member of the National Council. Corrie sensed there was a bit of rivalry between the two men.

Having filled a large bowl with chopped apples, Corrie carried it out to the yard beside the kitchen to add to the cauldron. Lem Starr, an older man who was simple of mind, was adding more wood to the fire. A gentle and always smiling soul, Lem did odd jobs at the school in exchange for a home-cooked meal.

Corrie smiled at the man and was rewarded with a dazzling grin that split his face. Back home, someone like Lem would likely have been institutionalized. But the Cherokees had no such institutions. It was the responsibility of the community to care for those in need.

His neighbors had built him a little cabin near the Council House and made sure it was always stocked with firewood and food. But Lem didn't have to eat at home. He would be welcomed at any table in the community. Corrie knew Harriet and Elias had fed him more than once.

She carefully added the apples from her bowl to the big pot as Delight came to take up the long paddle used to stir the mixture. Corrie noted the time on the little watch she kept pinned to the bib of her apron. She would come and take her turn at the paddle in a half hour, but right now she was hoping there might be some coffee still warming in the pot set among the fireplace coals.

Corrie was walking back toward the kitchen when she caught sight of Elias striding quickly up the trail from town. The young woman paused at the kitchen door and waited on Elias.

"Hello, Corrie," he greeted her while nodding to Lem and Delight.

"Elias, how are you? And how's Harriet?"

"We are both well, though Harriet is complaining of swollen ankles."

Corrie smiled. "Well, she will soon be past that," she commiserated. "A baby will make it all worth it."

"Yes," Elias agreed. "And speaking of that, we received a letter from the Worcesters. Ann gave birth to a girl. They named her Ann Eliza."

"Oh, that's a pretty name. And they are well?"

"Yes, despite the sickness that has been a problem this fall."

Corrie waved a hand toward the kitchen. "Would you like some coffee?"

"I cannot stay long. I am on my way to Brainerd." He patted the satchel he carried. "I just came to ask you to join Harriet and me for supper this Saturday. Can Mrs. Hawkins watch the children?"

"I believe she would," Corrie confirmed. "I look forward to a visit. But what takes you to Brainerd?"

"I have been visiting with Dr. Butler. There has been so much sickness; he thinks it is from the floodwaters. Something called cholera. He wanted help in getting information to people about boiling their water for drinking and cooking. So I am going to have Samuel print some broadsheets for me. We can distribute them among the people."

"Dr. Butler was by here to advise us to do that," Corrie confirmed. "It is good that you can print something to get the word out."

"Yes, though the Cherokee grapevine spreads news quickly, they need the information to understand why this precaution is necessary."

"Will you stop by your house before you head to Brainerd?"

"I am on my way there now."

"Then tell Harriet I will see her on Saturday."

Elias nodded. "Until then," he said. Then he continued his quick pace along the trail toward his home.

Corrie glanced again at her watch. She would have time for a quick cup before relieving Delight. It was cool enough that she wouldn't mind standing at the fire, enjoying the fragrance of the spicy apples.

After the mixture had cooked down, the women ladled the thick, grainy apple butter into crocks while it was still bubbling hot. Once the crocks had cooled slightly, they would apply wax and add the lids. The wax, softened by the warm containers, would provide a tight seal and they would enjoy the apple butter on their biscuits and flapjacks for months to come.

Later that day after school had been dismissed, Corrie sat with Macie Cornstalk at a spinning wheel in the parlor of the cottage. The girls were learning to spin and weave and since Corrie had learned these skills from her mother, she was happy to help the girls practice. Two other girls were carding cotton, using paddles with teeth to pull the fiber into workable strands.

"That's good, Macie," she encouraged the girl at the spinning wheel. "Pull the thread strong and steady." Macie nodded, her brow knit in concentration. It took some practice to learn just the right tautness to use for a smooth thread.

Corrie heard a knock at the front door but since Jane went to answer it, she paid it little mind. She was concentrating almost as hard as Macie was.

"Miss Cornelia," the other housemother interrupted her focused thoughts. "You have a gentleman caller."

Corrie looked up in surprise. "Is it Mr. Boudinot?"

"No. I do not know him." Jane held out a printed calling card. Corrie took it and read the name. Oliver Ackley. She didn't recognize it at first, but she glanced toward the door and saw the tall man with the striking green eyes and then remembered him.

She felt a mixture of emotions. Part of her was flattered that he seemed to feel such an interest in her. Part of her wished he didn't feel such an interest in her. She could not say that she felt the same way.

But she could not rudely let him wait at the door. Her mother would be appalled if she did. So she stood and thanked Jane then crossed the parlor, aware of the curious interest from the girls and the other housemother.

"Mr. Ackley," Corrie greeted him. "What a surprise."

"Here as promised," Oliver gave a slight bow. He looked beyond Corrie to the parlor to see four sets of eyes watching him. "Could we, perhaps, go for a walk?"

Corrie felt a hesitancy that she couldn't explain to herself. Mr. Ackley seemed a perfect gentleman so why should she be reluctant to stroll around the mission grounds with him?

"Perhaps a short one," she finally agreed. "I'll need to get the girls to supper in about a half hour."

"That will be perfect," he said while Corrie reached for her wool shawl hanging on a stand by the door. "I must be in Savannah so I cannot stay long."

Corrie turned to Jane. "I won't be gone long." Then she stepped out the door and pulled it closed and the two strolled along the path that ran among the mission buildings.

"You are traveling through on business?" Corrie began the conversation as she had been taught in etiquette class.

"Yes," Oliver replied as he placed a hand on her elbow. "I will meet with our factor tomorrow about our cotton and tobacco crop. I have a few other appointments in Savannah as well."

"You grow cotton and tobacco on your father's . . . farm?"

Corrie knew that both these crops were labor intensive and often involved slave labor. She wondered if this was the case on the Ackley farm, but she couldn't ask a question that was tantamount to inquiring about someone's financial position.

"We have about one hundred acres in each," Oliver replied, but offered no more information.

"Are you traveling by stage?"

"Yes. It's not the most comfortable means of travel, but this is a short trip so I didn't want to bother with a carriage."

"Oh." Corrie was running out of questions to ask.

"Will you . . ."

"How do you . . ."

Both spoke at once and then stopped in the awkwardness of not knowing one another well enough for flowing conversation.

"You first," Oliver offered.

"I was just going to ask if you planned to overnight at the inn in New Echota."

"No, never there," Oliver responded, his tone flat and somewhat condescending. "I plan to stay in the capital, Milledgeville."

The New Echota tavern and inn which sat by the livery on the federal road was owned by the Vann family. Corrie had never visited it, but it seemed clean and pleasant enough from what she had been able to observe. Mr. Ackley obviously thought it beneath him.

Silence lingered for several more steps. They had reached the trees at the edge of the property and turned back toward the cottage.

"How do you like living in Georgia?" the gentleman asked. "I hope you have found the South to be agreeable to you."

"Oh, yes. The people here have been very welcoming. I enjoy my work with the students."

"You don't find you miss more civilized environs? There is little opportunity for culture or entertainment here among the Cherokees. It's rather a hardscrabble life isn't it." Oliver waved a hand toward the modest buildings that made up the mission.

"I didn't come for culture and entertainment," Corrie replied evenly, trying to keep annoyance out of her voice. "But I haven't found either of those things lacking here." She almost launched into a description of the dinner party at Running Waters, but thought better of it.

Oliver looked unconvinced and seemed about to say something more himself, but also appeared to check his words.

"Still, a woman of your refinement surely misses the nicer things found in New England," he said. "Life among the Cherokees must seem primitive compared to your life there. I wish I could offer you something more than just a pleasant fall walk, but I'm afraid even Milledgeville or Athens would seem provincial by New England standards."

"Well, as I said, Mr. Ackley, I didn't come to be entertained. I find my work is rewarding and my friendships enjoyable."

"Yes," he seemed to frown. "You are friends with the Boudinots."

"And I've made new friendships here," Corrie added, thinking of Jane and Delight and the sweet students she cared for.

They had returned to the cottage and halted at the front door. "As I said, I can't offer much as entertainment, but I wonder if I might take you for a carriage ride the next time I visit. I could bring my sister as a chaperone if you would feel more comfortable with that."

Corrie thought this was a very considerate gesture, one some suitors might not offer. It softened her thinking about the man.

"Perhaps," she finally said. "If there isn't a problem with getting time away from the school."

"Even missionaries need time off, don't they?" Oliver smiled.

"Yes, I suppose," Corrie said demurely.

"I will write you with a formal invitation then," he offered. "Address it to Miss Cornelia Tuttle?"

"Yes." Corrie wondered how he had learned her given name since she didn't recall ever sharing it with him. She supposed he had asked in town when getting directions to the school. New Echota was small enough that everyone knew the school staff. Many of them attended the church service held at the mission each Sunday.

"Until we should meet again," Oliver said, doffing his bowler hat. "I hope you have a pleasant evening." He opened the cottage door for her but did not step inside.

"Thank you. And to you as well."

Corrie watched him return up the path while she stood in the door. His step seemed jaunty and he appeared pleased. She had begun this encounter not liking the man, but now she couldn't think of the reason why.

Oliver returned to the livery in New Echota just a few minutes before the stage was set to pull out bound for Milledgeville and then Savannah. He never liked traveling through the Cherokee and Creek lands, always leery of trouble from the Indians who lived along the federal road. He sensed their resentment of outsiders traveling through even though several of them operated ferries, taverns and trading posts along the route and made good money from those travelers.

Ackley resented the prosperity of these enterprising businessmen. It was much easier to press for their removal if the Indians were viewed as poor, uneducated pagans who threatened the security of the good people of Georgia and Tennessee. Schools, churches, and thriving businesses all belied this view and they needed to be stopped. What a shame that the pretty Miss Tuttle was a part of the problem. Hopefully he could use her friendship with Cherokees like Ridge and Boudinot to further his cause for Indian removal.

It seemed a stroke of good fortune, the following evening to find himself dining with the governor of Georgia. His father's factor, Shelby Townes, invited Oliver to join the dinner party at his home.

After supper the men gathered in Townes' study, a spacious room lined with walnut panels and filled with overstuffed leather chairs. Townes' houseman poured each of the men a drink and passed around cigars that the factor boasted had come from the islands. Soon the air was filled with a blue haze while the men let the alcohol relax their minds and their tongues.

Having completed his duties, the slave slipped out of the room to take a seat in the hall outside the door to be at Townes' call. For the men in the room, he had become invisible.

A portly man named Richardson turned to Oliver after a few minutes of quiet indulgence in the niceties of liquor and tobacco. "So you are from Tennessee," he drawled, looking the young man up and down. "Friends of General Jackson, I suppose."

"My father is friends with him. They served in the militia together," Oliver provided. "I have had the privilege of dining in his home."

Some of the men seemed impressed. "Will he run again in '28?" another asked. "We need a Southerner back in office."

"I believe that is his plan."

"Good," Governor Troup stated. "Jackson understands what we face down here. He sees the need clearly for moving the Indians west."

"To be fair President Adams did manage to get a treaty with the Creeks," said a fellow factor named Calvert. "Shouldn't they be moving out of Georgia soon?"

"Not soon enough," someone murmured into his glass. A few of the men chuckled.

"It wasn't Adams," Troup countered. "It was the Indian Commissioner who negotiated that treaty. Rich isn't it? Adams doesn't even know enough but to appoint a man as Indian commissioner who hates the Indians."

A guffaw spread across the room. Oliver had met Commissioner Montgomery in Washington City and knew the governor's assessment was true. The man had no love of Indians.

"We still need Jackson as President," Troup continued. "I have not been able to get the Cherokees to even agree to a meeting. Jackson has fought alongside the Cherokees; he knows them and I think he'll be able to persuade them of the wisdom for moving west."

"The problem with the Cherokees is that they view themselves as a sovereign nation," Oliver interjected. "They feel no need to deal with the states. They will only negotiate with the federals."

"How do they even know what the word sovereign means?" Townes asked snidely. More chuckles followed his question.

Oliver knew it wasn't the Cherokees who were ignorant but rather Townes himself. But he kept that thought silent.

Some of the men were pouring themselves a second drink. Oliver would have liked one, but decided against it. He wanted his wits about him until he had made his point.

"The states are sovereign as well," he stated quietly but emphatically. "We don't kowtow to the federal government. We have the right to govern ourselves as we see fit."

"So what do you propose we do?" Troup asked, turning to give his full attention to the young Tennessean.

"Suspend the sovereignty of these Indian tribes. Require them to follow state laws. It will be such a noxious idea that they will want to move west. They have no desire to be law abiding citizens."

This brought several of the men forward in their seats.

"We couldn't do that."

"Who would stop us?"

"Certainly not Adams. Cursed Yankee doesn't know up from down." Knee-slapping laughter erupted now.

Oliver watched the men through the smoke haze. Enough liquor had been consumed now that everything would be laughable from this point forward. But he saw the speculative look on the governor's face and he knew he had made his point. He tossed back the final dregs of his glass and went to help himself to another generous pour.

CHAPTER TWELVE

Webber Plantation, Arkansas Territory
November, 1826

Edmund sat on an overturned nail keg on his porch in front of a makeshift table of planks resting on two more kegs. He worked with a small awl and mallet to punch holes into a piece of deer hide. He was fashioning a new pair of moccasins for himself. Using thin strips of the same hide he would sew together the upper and lower portion of his new shoes.

He had spent several days sewing beads onto the tongue of the moccasins, something Bettie teased him about. She said he needed a wife to do such fine needlework for him. Edmund had simply shrugged, not wanting to discuss the matter.

He wished he had finished the shoes earlier, but had put it off for a time, content to wear an old pair that was comfortable but growing too thin for winter. All morning he had heard the sound of gunfire coming from the woods that ran behind his cabin up toward the Ozark foothills. Several men from the community were quail hunting today, flushing out the coveys that found cover among the thick trees.

As he pulled the leather thread through the holes he had created, he thought he might have time to join the hunters. Walter's man Jerome had told him the coveys were especially thick this year. The birds needed to be thinned to keep the flock healthy.

After the hunt the community would gather at Bettie's house to help clean the birds and roast some of them for a feast this evening. The rest would be hung in smokehouses around the community beside the hams and sides of bacon harvested earlier this fall. The Jollys had killed two enormous razorbacks and shared the meat from the feral hogs with their neighbors.

Edmund pulled the second shoe onto his foot and tested the fit. The moccasins were tight, but he knew the leather would stretch with time. He went inside, took down his musket then grabbed his powder horn and a small leather bag filled with nuts and dried fruit – a gift from Bettie. She seemed to fear that he would starve if she didn't keep him supplied with food.

He paused at his barn to find a large cotton sack that had held oats. Then he set out at a lope toward the woods, running as silently as the deer that sometimes crossed the field behind his cabin. Edmund spent the afternoon enjoying the hunt and the redolent smell of the forest. He never caught up with the other men who had worked their way down toward the river. So he bagged the birds he had killed and returned home to clean up before going down to Bettie's.

He was pulling on a clean shirt when he glimpsed out the window to see Harry running up the path to his cabin. He smiled at the boy who never walked when he could just as easily run. Edmund owed Harry a penny for the day of the flood so he fished around a catch-all tin on the hearth until he found two coins. He met Harry at his front door.

"Mr. Edmund," Harry began, breathless as usual. "Miz Webber says to come. The party's 'bout to start."

"I was just on my way down there," he said, pulling the door closed. He reached for the bag of quails he had set on the porch.

"You got a passel, didn't ya?" Harry observed, his eyes big.

"Yes, the Lord has blessed us with plenty."

"They's a whole wagon load at the big house."

Harry hopped off the porch and pattered alongside Edmund as he walked. "Where are your moccasins, Harry?" the interpreter asked.

"Don't wear 'em lessen it's cold," Harry shrugged. "That way they won't wear out and Mattie can wear 'em after me."

"I see. That is very thoughtful of you, Harry." Edmund suspected the truth was that Harry simply preferred the freedom of bare feet. He had felt that way when he was Harry's age.

"I owe you some money, I believe." Edmund reached into his pocket and displayed the two pennies.

Eyes big again, the boy reached for them. "Thank you, Mr. Edmund!"

"Do not spend that all on candy."

"Why not?"

"If you save one of them, you can collect some more pennies to go with it and then buy something better than candy."

Harry scrunched his face in thought. "Like a whistle?"

"Yes," Edmund smiled. "Like a whistle or maybe something even better someday."

Harry dropped the pennies into his own pocket. "That is a very good idea," he said as if he had just come to understand the concept of saving.

As they reached the yard of the Webber home, Harry dashed off to join other children playing near the firepit being prepared for the quail roast. Edmund added his birds to the pile that filled the Ballard wagon. Men and women both were cleaning the birds, saving the feathers to stuff pillows and mattresses. The downy feathers would dry through the winter and then fill new bedding come spring.

"Oh, this one's pretty," Colista Jolly said, holding up a feather with beautiful colors and markings. "I'm saving this one for my dance shawl."

The best feathers would be used to adorn dance regalia, jewelry and clothing. The men especially liked to tuck bright feathers into their turbans.

Once the first birds were cleaned, they were placed on spits to roast over the firepit. Some of the younger folks were assigned the task of turning the spits often to ensure even cooking. Soon the aroma from the fire blended with the smell of corn cakes being fried in bacon fat in Bettie's kitchen.

By the time the sun had set most of the quail had been cleaned, washed and salted. The harvest was divided among the various families according to their need, wrapped in long cotton tow sacks and set aside to be taken home after the meal. Now it was time to eat.

The women set large pots of hominy and beans, pans of corn cakes and the quail on makeshift tables set up in the yard. They dished up the food and served the men, then the children, then themselves.

Edmund dried his hands after washing up at the horse trough. He was planning to help himself to the tantalizing food, when Lucinda Ballard approached him carrying a plate piled high.

"For you," she said, holding it out to him.

"*Wado*, Lucinda." He took the plate and walked with her back toward the circle of blankets around the fire. "Have you eaten?"

"I will get my plate now. Will you save me a seat?"

"Yes."

He found a spot next to Bettie who scooted over to allow plenty of room for Lucinda as well, a sly smile on her face. "She likes you," the woman whispered.

"Do not start, Bettie." Edmund shook his head. All the women in the community seemed to have matchmaking plans for the handsome young man, but he was in no hurry to marry.

"I just say that it is good for you to have friends here since all your school friends are in New Echota."

"Not all of them," Edmund said, looking down at his plate, his voice low.

"Yes," Bettie returned. "Even your Cornelia. She is in New Echota too."

"What?" the young man looked at his sister-in-law, surprise on his face.

"Did not my brother write to you? Cornelia is working at the mission school at New Echota. I got a letter from Harriet yesterday."

"I have not heard from Elias in a while." Edmund felt stunned. Cornelia was living in Cherokee Nation? Was this true?

Before he could question Bettie further, Lucinda returned and sat down beside him cross-legged on a grey and white trade blanket like the ones Walter always kept in stock at the store. She wore a dress of different shades of blue calico that made her eyes seem to sparkle in the firelight.

For a time, conversation was limited while everyone ate. But soon plates emptied and some went back for seconds while others got a drink of water from the gourd dipper tied to a bucket at the well. Some of the men pulled out pipes and the air was quickly filled with the sweet smell of tobacco.

Bettie and Lucinda visited back and forth both trying to draw Edmund into their conversation.

"Are your horses good after the flood?" Bettie asked.

"Yes, most are."

"Did Nanyi's leg heal?" This was Edmund's question. After Edmund had helped Walter clean and re-stock the store following the flood, he had visited the Ballards to help clean their horses.

"My father has kept her leg bandaged to be safe. She will drop a mule soon."

"I did not know he bred mules."

"He sells them to a freighter from Batesville. He says the Spanish mustang give the mules stamina for hauling freight across the prairie to Santa Fe."

"It is your job to ride the horses for exercise, isn't it?" Bettie said in a question that Edmund could tell was leading somewhere.

"Yes," Lucinda confirmed.

"You should go riding with her, Edmund." Bettie's face was the picture of innocence, but Edmund knew she was scheming.

"I always ride on Sundays, after church." Lucinda looked hopeful. Edmund felt trapped.

"I could ride with you then," he offered, "unless Rev. Washburn needs me to help with something at the church."

"I would like that," Lucinda smiled.

Edmund sighed and threw a look at his sister-in-law. She ignored him.

Lucinda rose to take their plates to the kitchen where Etta and Jennie were washing dishes in a big tub normally reserved for laundry. The families who had gathered for the communal hunt were packing up their wagons to return to their homes.

The young woman in blue met Edmund as he helped Bettie fold blankets. "I have to go," she said. "I will see you on Sunday, Edmund."

"Yes," Edmund smiled. "See you Sunday."

He watched her walk toward the Ballard wagon, her dark hair swinging down her back. When she was out of hearing he turned to ask Bettie more about what Harriet had written concerning Cornelia. But his sister-in-law had moved to the fire and was talking now with Walter. He didn't want to question her in front of Walter, so he stacked the blankets on the porch of their cabin, picked up his sack of plucked birds and took the path back to his own home.

He was curious about Corrie's move to New Echota. Why had she made such a choice? Had something happened in Cornwall? But no matter how much he pondered it as he walked through the quiet darkness, he could find no answers, no reason to think that anything had changed between them. Whether in Cornwall or New Echota, she was still hundreds of miles away and she still wasn't Cherokee.

The path between the Boudinot farm and New Echota was muddy and Cornelia kept an eye on the hem of her skirt so it didn't drag through a puddle. Elias was walking her back to the mission after she had dined with the Boudinots on a rather cold December day.

"You have been quiet all morning, Elias," Corrie observed when the mission buildings came in sight. "Is something wrong? Harriet seems fine."

"She is fine, but I have asked her to stay at home," Elias replied. "Dr. Butler says the influenza is spreading."

"First cholera, now influenza," Corrie shook her head. "Several students have missed classes because of it."

"I am afraid Chief Pathkiller has it as well."

"It must be hard for him . . . at his age. Is his wife Peggy well?"

"So far she is. But you are right; it is hard for Pathkiller. He has taken to his bed. We are all concerned for him."

"I'm sorry. I know you admire him very much."

"He is one of the last old warriors," Elias agreed. "Very traditional, very resistant to change. But I respect him for that. He has fought for our people in many battles; he has earned the right to his opinion."

Corrie hesitated before asking her next question. "If he passes, what will happen? Does Mr. Hicks become chief?"

"Yes, Charles Hicks is second chief. He has been managing the government on behalf of Pathkiller for some time now anyway. I am meeting Hicks at the Council House and then we will visit Pathkiller this afternoon. We have some important matters to discuss with him."

"Is something wrong?"

"We have received a letter from the Governor of Georgia. He says we should follow the Creeks and give up our lands within Georgia. If not, he claims he has the authority to suspend our sovereignty and take our land."

"But he can't do that, can he?"

"Not according to the treaties we have signed. But I don't think treaties matter to Governor Troup."

Corrie could tell that Elias was very troubled. "I'm sorry the Cherokees are facing this," she said. "I am praying for you."

"Thank you," Elias said as they reached the door of the student cottage. "That is the best thing that any of us can do. I will see you in church tomorrow."

"Goodbye, Elias."

Corrie waited at the door as Elias turned to go. She watched him walk to the mission corral where he had left his horse, his head bowed as if he were in prayer or perhaps deep in thought.

Elias reached the Council House and found Mr. Hicks waiting inside, reading a book. Hicks had an extensive library and Elias rarely saw him without a book in his hands. Together they mounted their horses for the ride to the venerated old chief's cabin which was nestled at the base of a hill surrounded by the woods where Pathkiller had long hunted and fished.

They found Peggy in the yard, drawing water and Elias quickly dismounted to help her carry the heavy bucket into the house. It was a thatch-roofed log cabin with a dirt floor and a stone fireplace in the center. The crackling fire was the only light in the room. Elias set the water bucket on a table with two cane-bottomed chairs beside it.

"Is he awake now?" Hicks asked in a low voice. He had secured both horses and followed Peggy inside.

"He sleeps much," Peggy answered. "But he will be happy to see you." She crossed over to the low bed where the old man slept. He thinning grey hair formed two long braids and he was propped up on several pillows. His breathing seemed labored and Elias felt his stomach clutch at how frail the chief looked.

"Wake, Pathkiller," his wife said as she nudged his shoulder gently. "You have visitors."

The man's eyes opened slowly and he turned his head to see who was calling at his house. Seeing the two men, he nodded and gestured for them to come to his bed.

Peggy began to drag the chairs over, but Elias took them from her and set them near the chief. Peggy went back to making soup, but kept a watchful eye on her husband.

"You come with frowns upon your face," the chief said in a wheezing voice. "Are you afraid I am going to die?"

"We are concerned about you," Charles confirmed.

"Everyone dies. I do not fear."

"Death does not have to be feared," Elias said and Charles nodded. Both men had chosen the Christian faith, finding hope in it at a time in their nation when hope was threatened. "God, our Great Spirit, has promised us eternal life with him."

Pathkiller nodded slowly, almost imperceptibly. "You speak of the white man's religion."

"No," Charles gently contradicted. "Truth does not belong to any one people. It belongs to everyone, no matter the color of their skin."

Pathkiller's gaze met the eyes of Charles and then Elias. "I have heard the story from the preacher men. A Son who loved us enough to die for us. It is true?"

"Yes," Elias confirmed while Charles nodded. "I believe it is true." He lightly touched the gnarled fingers of the old man.

Pathkiller was quiet for a long moment but finally nodded again. "Then I will believe too. Then I will go to the Great Spirit when I die."

"Yes." Elias couldn't say anything more for a moment as tears filled his eyes. It was hard to see one of his heroes now resigned to death, but there was joy too in knowing his soul would be at peace.

A quiet, reverence seemed to settle upon the room. Even Peggy stopped chopping carrots and stood quietly. No one spoke for several minutes and Pathkiller closed his eyes. Elias was afraid he had passed from this life at that moment, but after a time his eyes opened again.

"Something more troubles you," he whispered.

"We have a letter from the Georgia governor," Charles explained. "We need to form a response."

But Pathkiller shook his head. "Do not tell me of it," he requested. "Let me die while our nation is still strong and proud and free. I do not want to hear what he says. I cannot fight anymore."

The two visitors exchanged a look. "We will take care of it," Charles assured him. "Sleep in peace."

Pathkiller nodded then closed his eyes once more. The men were about to rise to leave when Pathkiller spoke again. "You must start your newspaper," he said, looking directly at Elias, his eyes clearer than they had been. "You must tell the truth."

Elias nodded, unable to speak for a moment. "I will," he finally said.

"I sleep now." Pathkiller's eyes closed again and he folded his deeply veined hands across his frail frame.

The men quietly returned their chairs to the table and Elias took one of Peggy's hands. "I will ask my mother to come to you tomorrow," he told her.

Peggy nodded. "*Wado*."

"Can we do anything for you?" Hicks asked. "Do you need firewood?"

"Yes. The ax is on the back porch."

They exited the little cabin and went around back, then took turns chopping a log that someone had dragged to the yard. Elias carried several armloads into the house and stacked the kindling by the fireplace. Then they bid Peggy goodbye and solemnly rode back to New Echota.

"You finally have his blessing to begin your newspaper," Hicks commented quietly as they approached the Council House. "I think God softened his heart today."

"He couldn't have given me a greater benediction," Elias agreed. "I am honored to have his trust. I will dedicate the first edition to Pathkiller."

"I will bring the matter to the National Council," Hicks offered. "I think they will fund it, at least in part. There is money in the education fund and a newspaper is certainly a means of educating our people about the threats we face. We must stand together as one."

Elias nodded his thanks. As the men prepared to part ways, Hicks gripped the younger man's shoulder to offer comfort and encouragement. "We will fight in our own way," he said. "Use your pen as a sword."

"I will do my best," Elias promised.

“See you at church,” Hicks said and the two men parted ways to return to their homes. Elias set out briskly in the waning daylight, feeling both humbled and excited at the prospect of starting a newspaper. As far as he knew, this paper would be the first printed by a native nation. As soon as he reached his house he would send a letter to Worcester asking him to bring his printing press to New Echota. They had a battle to wage.

CHAPTER THIRTEEN

New Echota, Georgia
December, 1826

Cornelia checked her appearance in the small mirror above the bureau in her room. The invitation to a carriage ride had arrived three days earlier from Oliver Ackley. As promised he was bringing his sister and they would call upon Corrie at the mission in the afternoon.

She had chosen to wear her brick red traveling suit and had spent the morning ironing it while the girls were in class. Now she didn't want to get it wrinkled so rather than sit and take up her embroidery work as Jane was doing, she walked between her room and the front door.

Jane watched her nervous pacing with sympathetic amusement. "You have never had a gentleman caller before?" the Creek woman asked.

"No. I mean, yes I have, but not really," Corrie knew she was making no sense but she didn't want to explain that her only other suitor had been Edmund and he had never really called on her. They sat together at church and attended a school play or church picnic together, but it was always in their group of six.

She smiled remembering the time they had all gone to the brook to ice skate after it had frozen solid. The Cherokee boys were terrible at ice skating and the girls had teased them unmercifully.

The other housemother saw the smile and heard the sigh that followed it. She was about to comment when they heard the clop of horses' hooves and knew a carriage approached the cottage. Corrie was reaching for her coat when Jane stopped her. "You sit," she said. "I will answer the door. You do not want to appear too eager."

"Yes, *Etsi*," Corrie said and the women exchanged a smile.

Corrie took her seat and was demurely pulling her needle through the canvas when Oliver's knock sounded at the door.

Jane opened it to admit Mr. Ackley and a pretty girl about age fourteen who he introduced as his sister Dolly. Corrie rose to greet them and offered them a seat in the little parlor. Oliver glanced at Jane and declined saying they should take advantage of the fine afternoon weather.

He helped Corrie don her coat and the three of them stepped outside to the waiting carriage. It was a fine black phaeton with a matching set of black Tennessee Walker horses. Oliver helped Dolly into the vehicle, then gave Corrie his hand to help her as well. It seemed to her that his hand lingered in hers just a moment longer than necessary while she settled onto the leather seat. Then he walked around and climbed inside so that Dolly sat between them.

Mr. Ackley turned the horses and directed them to the trail that would take them to New Echota and the federal road. He kept the horses to a slow walk so the women weren't jostled too much on the unpaved trail.

"I hope the day isn't too cold for you, Miss Tuttle," Oliver said solicitously. "If you'd like it, I have a lap robe under the seat."

"No, I'm fine," Corrie replied. It hardly seemed cold to her but Dolly Ackley was dressed as if the weather were quite cold. She held a fur muff and her deep green coat and hat were also trimmed in fur.

"I hope it doesn't snow," the girl said. "That will just ruin my plans at Aunt Ophelia's."

"I'm driving Dolly to our Aunt's home in Athens," Oliver explained. "She'll spend some time there while on break from school."

"Oh, where do you attend school?" Corrie asked.

"I'm a freshman at the Staunton Female Institute in Virginia," Dolly replied. "That's where my mother attended as well. She's from Virginia and insisted that I complete my education there."

"Do you enjoy school?"

"Most usually," Dolly sighed, "but we have a very strict housemother. She never lets the boys who call go beyond the visitors' parlor and they can never stay after sundown."

"I'm sure she wants you to focus on your studies," Corrie smiled.

"But the whole point of going away to school is to make a proper match," Dolly explained as if Corrie should know such things. "Mother says there are hardly any appropriate young men around Lynchburg. We are simply surrounded by Cherokees."

Oliver gave a little cough as Dolly finished her sentence, but he did not succeed in keeping Corrie from understanding the sentiment Dolly expressed. She had certainly witnessed such attitudes in her own hometown, so she wasn't shocked that this young girl held them as well.

"I thought we might drive toward Lookout Mountain," Oliver interjected. "Have you had a chance to visit that area?"

"No, but several friends have suggested I need to," Corrie replied. "I hear it's quite lovely."

"It's not at its best in winter, of course, but the vistas are more open without leaves on the trees. I know of a pretty waterfall."

"Oh, yes, the falls are lovely," Dolly confirmed. "But we'll have to bring you back in spring when the dogwoods are in bloom."

"Yes, we must," Oliver agreed. "If that would be agreeable with you, Miss Tuttle?" He looked around his sister to gauge her reaction.

"It sounds . . . lovely," Corrie said.

They continued their ride, heading north on the road toward Chattanooga. Dolly chattered on about classes and boys while sparing Corrie and her suitor from awkward conversation. The girl was the perfect chaperone, lively and fun and seeming to genuinely enjoy this outing.

Corrie imagined that the pretty blonde with the same green eyes as her brother had many suitors calling on her. She would make a wonderful hostess for some genteel home in the future.

They reached the spot where a brook – Dolly called it a creek – tumbled over fallen boulders. Oliver halted the carriage and helped the women alight then they strolled for a time along the bank with leaves crunching beneath their feet. Corrie was delighted with the scene and thanked Oliver for bringing her to view it.

"It's a nice spot for a picnic," Oliver stated, "but I didn't plan one for today. I thought the ground would be too damp and cold."

"Oh, it would be," Dolly agreed. She gave a shiver and stuffed her hands further into the fur muff. "But it will be perfect this spring."

Corrie smiled at what this Southern girl thought was cold. She had been surprised at how warm it was so close to Christmas. At home, they would have pulled out the sleds and ice skates by now following many inches of snow. She wondered if she would ever see snow while in Georgia.

Since Dolly seemed cold, Oliver walked the women back to the carriage, helped them aboard and then handed the small quilt to Dolly to spread over her lap. Then he turned the carriage back toward New Echota.

They were all three quiet for a while on the journey back to Corrie's home. Finally Oliver cleared his throat and spoke in a casual tone. "Have you ever visited Arkansas Territory, Miss Tuttle?"

His question startled Corrie. How did he know about Edmund? She glanced at him out of the corner of her eye, but saw nothing on his face to explain his question. He was looking at the road, steering the horses around its gentle curves.

"No," Corrie said, finding her voice. "Why do you ask?"

"I know there are missions among the Cherokees in Arkansas," he explained, now looking at her. "I didn't know what your work experience might include."

"Oh," Corrie said, feeling a rush of relief. It had been a completely innocent inquiry. "No, this is my first mission work at New Echota."

"Parts of Arkansas are very similar to our mountains here," he went on. "But they are wholly unspoiled, awash with game, and the prairie beyond has huge herds of buffalo, deer, elk. I understand that the Cherokees who have moved there are prosperous and happy. It surprises me that more Cherokees haven't followed their leaders west where they could find peace and an idyllic life."

Corrie doubted that an idyllic life truly existed anywhere. But she knew that Edmund had thought the mountains where he lived were beautiful and he was happy with his decision to move there.

"But this is the Cherokee's ancestral homeland," she said. "I can understand why it would be hard for them to leave."

"No harder than for them to stay," Oliver returned and Corrie thought she heard an edge to his voice. "Game is becoming scarce back here. Their way of life is threatened. And they hardly use the land the government has given them."

Dolly added, "They have millions of acres of land not in production. Father says it's a travesty."

Corrie wondered if the girl really understood what a travesty was or if she simply repeated what her father had apparently impressed upon both his children.

"They have the right to do whatever they choose with their land," she said, feeling defensive. She could imagine the reaction of Elias or John to these words.

"Certainly," Oliver said, his conciliatory smile not quite reaching his eyes. "But they could have twice as much land out west. President Jefferson purchased the Louisiana Territory for the Indians. It's a beautiful land."

"Have you been there?"

"No," he admitted. "But a friend of my father's has lived there for a time while serving as agent to the western

Cherokees. He and my father fought together at New Orleans."

"Colonel Brearley, you mean?" Dolly asked.

"Yes. Colonel Brearley visited us earlier this year while traveling to Georgia. He's now helping the Creeks prepare to move west. He sees it as a positive development for them and hopes the government will create a special territory just for Indians where they can't be harmed by unscrupulous white men."

Corrie considered his words for a moment. They echoed a sentiment she had heard expressed by Rev. Sanders at the mission. Too often men of ill repute brought whiskey and gambling into the Indian settlements all with the intent of cheating them.

The minister's protests to the government agents seemed to fall on deaf ears. That was one reason he and other missionaries strongly urged the Cherokees to pass temperance laws. At least they could try to control the sale and consumption of alcohol by their own people.

"I suppose it would be good to be able to keep out those who would try to corrupt the morals of Indian youths," she said.

"Exactly." Oliver seemed to pounce on her words. "A move west would protect their children. It would give them opportunity and peace and a better life."

He reached into the inside breast pocket of his coat and pulled out a small pamphlet. "You should read this treatise. It was written by a missionary named Isaac McCoy. He agrees with Brearley about moving the Indians west. He makes some very good points." He held out the paper to Corrie.

She took it and glanced through it briefly, catching a heading titled Aboriginia Territory. She tried to return it to Oliver, but he waved a hand. "Keep it," he said. "I have another one."

She tucked the paper into her own pocket, wondering about this missionary's premise. Would it be better for all the Indians to move to their own territory? She couldn't imagine Elias or the Ridges agreeing to that.

They continued the drive back to the mission, talking about Dolly's plans for her week's visit with her aunt. The rest of the Ackley family would join Dolly there at Christmas.

Talk of Christmas made Cornelia homesick again. This would be the first time she had ever celebrated the holy day without her family. Her small salary from the mission society didn't afford her the opportunity to travel and it would have required too much time even if she had the money.

She would spend the morning helping the children with their Christmas program at the mission, then spend the afternoon with Harriet and Elias. They had invited Jane and Pink to join them as well, for all the boarding students were home for the Christmas break so the cottage would be empty.

They arrived at the mission and Oliver pulled his carriage to the door of Corrie's home. He helped her out and Dolly insisted on walking Corrie to her door as well. She gave the housemother a hug as she bade her goodbye.

"Oh, I'm so happy to have met you," she said and her broad smile proved her sincerity. "I hope we become good friends."

Corrie returned the smile. "I hope so too," she agreed and she meant her words as well. Dolly was a charming young lady and she had thoroughly enjoyed the outing with her and her thoughtful brother.

He took Corrie's hand and bent over it as if he were going to kiss it. But he stopped short of doing so and Corrie felt a little disappointed. His dark eyes held hers for a moment. "I hope you have a happy Christmas, Miss Tuttle."

"Yes," Dolly concurred.

"Thank you. The same to you both as well."

"May we count on you for another outing?" Oliver asked. "Perhaps when the weather is a little warmer."

"I would like that," Corrie smiled while Dolly clapped her gloved hands.

"I'll be home again at Easter," Dolly confirmed and it seemed as if the date for a picnic was thus set.

Oliver bowed again and then led his sister back to their vehicle. Corrie watched from the door as he turned the horses and set off. Dolly turned to look back and wave and Corrie returned the gesture. She was chuckling at the girl's enthusiasm as she stepped inside the house.

Oliver skillfully directed his horses back to the main road and the siblings settled back for the long ride on to Athens.

"Did I do all right, Olly?" the girl asked after a time.

"Yes, little sister," Ackley smiled, seeming quite pleased. "You did just fine."

Three days later, a package for Corrie arrived among the mail Lem had picked up for the mission at the New Echota Trading Post. Corrie opened it to find a slim leather-bound volume of sonnets. Inside the book was tucked a crisp white handkerchief trimmed with hand-crocheted lace.

A note from Mr. Ackley wished her a happy Christmas from him and from Dolly. He also asked for permission to correspond with her and gave her his address in Tennessee where she could reply.

Corrie found his attentions flattering. She hadn't expected to be courted while she worked at a mission in the Cherokee Nation. After all the same reasons for ending her relationship with Edmund would exist for any other Cherokee man and she had little expected to meet anyone else here at the heart of their nation. She might have left Cornwall, but her parents would still face censure and scorn if their daughter behaved in a "scandalous" manner.

Mr. Ackley presented some interesting possibilities. She told herself to be careful, however. Mr. Ackley might own slaves and she could not do as Sarah had done and overlook that. But it didn't hurt to dream a little and she found her thoughts during the Christmas break going often to the man with the striking green eyes.

On a cold January morning, Edmund stepped out onto his porch just as a rim of pink dawn lined the eastern horizon. He wore a heavy deer-hide coat and had taken the time to wrap a turban on his head. He usually preferred an English hat, but the day promised to remain cold and the wool turban would be warm.

Edmund planned to get to the store early to help Walter sort and price a bundle of buffalo hides his brother had brought back from the trading community of Three Forks near Fort Gibson. Normally Walter bought or traded for the hides with the Chickasaws, but he had run out of the large wooly robes early this winter and knew he could get more at the Three Forks trading posts. Walter would have to overlook the fact that they likely had been traded by the Osages, his sworn enemies. Ever since a cousin of theirs had been killed in a clash with Osages six years ago, Walter had wanted nothing to do with the Osages except to exact revenge.

Edmund sighed as he thought about his brother's hardened attitude. He had long suspected that Walter resisted Christianity because his brother understood such attitudes would run contrary to the teaching and example of Christ. He was not willing to let go of his grudge just yet. Edmund prayed he would soon. Bettie was growing as a Christian and he knew Walter had noticed the change in his wife.

Edmund had made coffee and now his hands wrapped the tin mug while his breath visibly mingled with the coffee's steam. He watched the light spread across the landscape revealing a heavy frost that almost looked like snow. In the distance he heard again what had drawn him outside.

The lone howl of a wolf sounded in the woods. It was the mating season for wolves and the lonesome cry of a young male made the hair stand on the back of his neck. It was a haunting sound, beautiful but also a little frightening. Edmund almost held his breath to see if the wolf would get a reply.

The young Cherokee stood for a long moment, hearing nothing but the creaking of tree limbs in the cold air. Then even more distant, he heard another wolf's call, the response of a female. The male wolf sent up an excited yip that ended in a long, drawn out howl. Edmund caught a glimpse of the beast running among the trees. He smiled.

The cold had quickly cooled his coffee so with another glance toward the sun just peeking over the hills, he returned inside to cook some ham and potatoes for breakfast. While he worked, his mind turned back to the wolf and he wondered if the male belonged to the pack he had seen earlier in the week. After spotting the eight powerful animals chasing a deer, he had changed his route to stop by the Ballard farm and warn them to keep their horses close to home. Of course, Mrs. Ballard had invited him to stay for supper.

The following day, Edmund was returning from Dwight Mission and had been skirting the woods, keeping an eye out for the small herd of elk he had seen that morning. Coming out into a clearing he halted, noting quickly the direction of the wind. A wolf pack had a large bull elk caught in its circle. Thankfully Edmund was upwind from the wolves or they might have turned their attention to him.

He crouched and watched as the circle of wolves tightened around the old elk. At first the animal had rushed around the clearing looking for an escape, but as the wolves moved in, the old man of the herd dropped his head, seeming resigned to his fate.

When the wolves began to growl and bare their teeth, Edmund rose and skirted around the edge of the clearing to continue home. He understood the need for this kill for both the pack and the herd but he didn't want to watch. The wolves would take what they needed and leave the rest to smaller scavengers and a necessary balance would be maintained in nature.

Now Edmund dished up his breakfast and sat at the small table he had drawn close to the fireplace. He bowed his head to give thanks and then ate quickly, still remembering the snarls of the wolf pack and the bowed head of the old warrior of the woods.

A gust of wind sent curling fingers of cold past the shutters on his window and he felt a shiver run down his back. *Just the cold*, he told himself, trying to shake off the image of the old bull elk. *It's just the cold.*

CHAPTER FOURTEEN

New Echota Mission
January, 1827

Corrie reached for a fresh iron sitting on the grate in the fireplace. She and Delight had worked all morning doing laundry in the little outbuilding behind the mission's kitchen. Lem kept them supplied with firewood and had helped them string rope inside the building to hang the clothes of the boarding students. A cold mist had hung in the air all morning making it impossible to dry the clothes and bed linens outdoors.

The housemother had lost count of the number of calico dresses she had ironed, but was finally working on the last one. The girls' garments were called tear dresses because the calico was torn in long strips to form the tiers of the skirts. Always bright and colorful, the dresses usually were trimmed in matching ribbons and sometimes had yokes with beads. The beautiful handwork on the dresses made them a challenge to iron, however, and Corrie breathed a relieved sigh when she pulled the last one from the laundry basket.

She heard Jane coming down the stairs. The other housemother had been putting clean sheets on the boys' beds.

"Something is wrong," she said as she reached the bottom step.

Corrie looked up from her work. "What?"

"The children are leaving school. It is not time."

Glancing at the mantle clock, Corrie could see that Jane was right. For classes to be dismissed this early, something must be wrong.

They both walked to the front door and opened it to look out. Miss Ermina Nash, the girls' teacher, was walking three of the girls to the cottage. The students were huddled together under her big umbrella and Corrie could tell they were upset.

She reached for them to pull them inside. "Come in, girls. Take off your coats and warm up by the fire."

"I'll bring the other three along," Miss Nash said then turned to hurry back to her classroom. In the meantime, Jane's boys were dashing across the mission yard to reach the cottage. Jane hustled them inside and took them upstairs to assist with changing into dry clothes.

When Ermina Nash returned with the other three boarders, Corrie insisted she come inside as well. The two women stood near the door and Jane joined them.

"What has happened, Miss Nash?"

"We just received word from Mr. Hicks," the teacher said in a hushed voice. "Chief Pathkiller has died."

"Oh, no," Corrie and Jane both gasped. It should not have come as a shock for everyone knew he had been ill. But it seemed as if a great tragedy had struck the nation. No wonder the students were upset.

"Mr. Hicks will be chief now," Ermina said. "He has called for a fortnight of mourning so Rev. Sanders decided to dismiss classes for that time. The parents of your boarders will probably come to get them in the next day or so."

"This is a great loss," Corrie murmured, thinking of how revered the old chief had been. "Will there be a funeral?"

"I haven't heard." Ermina pressed her lips into a thin line. "Who knows if there will be a funeral or some pagan ritual. Most of his clan are not Christians."

"But Rev. Sanders baptized Pathkiller," Corrie reminded her. "Surely Peggy will want a Christian burial."

"Well, it all remains to be seen. I suppose we will hear something by the end of the day." The teacher glanced toward the girls huddled together near the fireplace. Some were crying and they all looked frightened. "I can't believe they are taking on so."

"Pathkiller was the father of the nation," Jane said softly.

"Hmmh," Miss Nash replied. "I still don't like them missing two weeks of school. I'll be hard pressed to have them ready for final exams as it is with all the sickness we've had this year."

Corrie had always found Miss Nash to be a rather prickly sort of woman. She was not unkind to her students, but she was a strict, no-nonsense teacher who liked things done a certain way.

"I appreciate you walking the girls over, Miss Nash," Corrie said. She was anxious to see the teacher on her way so she could try to provide some comfort to her young charges.

"I'll be in my classroom should you need me. I'm going to write out some reading assignments for my students. Perhaps they can continue to study even during this break."

"That sounds good, Miss Nash." Corrie handed her the black umbrella she had stood by the door. Ermina took it and stepped outside into the persistent drizzle then carefully picked her way around the puddles back to the school building.

Corrie closed the door and crossed the parlor to the fireplace, reaching out to hug her girls one by one. Jane went upstairs to also offer what comfort she might to the boys.

"I am so sorry, girls," Corrie said as she sat with them on the floor by the hearth. "I know you are very sad. It is hard to say goodbye to someone we love."

"What will happen to us? Now that Pathkiller walks no more among us?" Macie asked as she swiped away more tears from her cheeks. As the oldest of the girls, she seemed to understand that Pathkiller's death had national significance.

"Mr. Hicks will be chief now," Corrie explained. "He will take care of you, just as Pathkiller did."

"What does die mean?" Sehoya Woodall lisped around a missing front tooth. At only seven, she didn't seem to understand exactly what was making everyone sad.

Corrie sent up a prayer for guidance in what to say. She placed a hand over her heart. "Can you feel your heartbeat, girls?"

They all copied the housemother and nodded in response.

"When someone dies, it is like they fall asleep. But their heart stops beating and they don't wake up again here on earth."

"On Turtle Island?"

"Yes," Corrie smiled at the beautiful imagery of earth. "But if that person knows Jesus, then they will wake up in heaven to begin a new life there with him."

"Did Chief Pathkiller know Jesus?"

"I believe he was trying to know Jesus," Corrie answered. "Remember Rev. Sanders telling us in church how the chief asked for baptism?"

Solemn nods came from the girls.

"So now he lives in the Happy Lands?" Macie asked.

"Yes, I believe he does, Macie. In a place where no one is sick or sad and no one ever has to be lonely or afraid."

"Then I'm glad," Sookey Martin said and the other girls nodded again.

Corrie was relieved to see the tears had dried. "Your parents will come for you so you can stay with them for two weeks. Why don't we pack what you want to take with you."

Smiles greeted her now. Few children were sad about a break from school. They all stood and went to the long bedroom they shared and began to plan for their time at home.

They received word that evening that a funeral would be held at Pathkiller's home the following day and he would be buried near his cabin. Then a memorial powwow would be held at New Echota in a week, giving Cherokees from across the nation time to come.

As expected, all the boarders were picked up by their parents and taken home to mourn together the loss of one of the last full-blood chief of the Cherokees. Most of the men who now held leadership positions were of mixed racial heritage. It was an end of era for the Cherokees and was felt deeply by all who understood its significance.

Jane had received a letter from her stepmother at Indian Springs telling her that her brother and uncle had returned from their exploratory trip to Arkansas. She planned to use the time off to visit them at Indian Springs. Enough time had passed since the signing of the removal treaty that the hard feelings against the McIntoshes had subsided. She felt safe to venture back into the Creek lands.

Because they would not be attending the funeral, Corrie and Jane decided to walk in to New Echota together with three-year-old Pinkney running ahead or lagging behind the whole way. Jane bought stage tickets for herself and Pink at the livery and then they walked to the trading post to do some shopping.

As they strolled through town, they noticed clusters of people gathered at the tavern, the livery, the blacksmith shop. All were talking in hushed tones, many wearing black arm bands on their coats. The sense of sadness lay like a mantle over the community. The women spoke little while in town and neither found much of interest at the store. Jane bought a penny peppermint for her son and some beads for the moccasins she was working on.

As they walked back to the mission Corrie asked, "When will you travel west, Jane?"

"It will most likely be late summer," the young mother said while keeping an eye on her son. "We will wait until after the crops are in and the river levels rise. It will take that long to pack and dispose of our livestock and other items we can't carry with us."

"I will be sorry to see you go. I have enjoyed our friendship."

"I have as well," Jane smiled, but there was sadness in her eyes. "Thank you for accepting me."

Corrie shook her head. "Thank you for accepting me."

They walked a little further and Jane said, "You should come with us, Miss Cornelia. We will need schools for our children in our new homeland."

"I'm not a teacher," Corrie said, feeling her heart speed up at the thought of going to Arkansas.

"It is a big land, I think. We will need someone like you to care for our children as they learn. Someone who does not judge children by the color of their skin."

Corrie was surprised that she felt torn about Jane's invitation. She had friends here in New Echota and work that she enjoyed. Besides that, going to Arkansas would stir up old feelings that she had tried to put away.

Corrie went to spend the day with Harriet while Elias attended the powwow for Chief Pathkiller. Knowing the dancing and eulogies would last well into the evening, the women sat down to supper without Elias. Harriet was dishing up some warm bread pudding to follow their potato soup when her husband burst through the door of the house.

"Elias!" Harriet exclaimed, her spoon halted in mid air. "What is wrong?"

Clearly the young man was upset as he made his way to sit at the dining table. "Nancy Hicks sent word to the powwow," he said, seeming almost dazed. "Charles is ill . . . deathly ill. I went to Creek Path Mission to ask Dr. Butler to attend him. I fear the worst."

"Oh, no," Harriet said while reaching to grasp her husband's hand. "I'm so sorry, Elias."

"What will we do without him?" Elias raked his fingers through his hair. "Our nation will be in peril."

Corrie could hear an almost desperate fear in his voice and there were tears in his eyes. She knew from her visits with Harriet, that Elias was very close to Mr. Hicks. While he had admired Chief Pathkiller, Elias looked upon Charles as a mentor and friend. They had shared a deep Christian faith and a desire to lead the Cherokee nation to that faith.

Charles had an almost evangelistic fervor after his conversion at the Moravian mission. When he was baptized he chose a new name for himself . . . Renatus, the Latin for "born again." He wanted even his name to bear witness of his faith.

"We will pray for him, Elias. His faith is strong." Harriet assured her husband. Corrie nodded in agreement.

"I know, but several have died from the influenza," Elias said. "I just have this awful feeling." He shook his head as if to remove the dark doubts from his mind.

Corrie rose and poured a cup of coffee for Elias, setting it on the table in front of him. He smiled his thanks, but the worry did not leave his eyes.

"We cannot lose him, not now," he said after a sip of the hot liquid. "Georgia officials are circling like vultures as it is. I saw one at the powwow, taking notes. If Charles dies they will use his death as a reason to attack our sovereignty. They will say we have no one to negotiate with the federal government, no on to lead us or speak for us."

"But that is hardly true," Harriet protested. "You have the National Council and many fine, well-educated leaders."

"It won't matter. If we don't have a chief, they'll have their excuse to overrun us."

"Who becomes chief if Mr. Hicks dies?" Corrie asked.

"That's just it. It's not clear who will be chief. We have no succession law. We've never even voted for a chief before. Pathkiller assumed the role because he was a revered warrior and a descendant of other chiefs. Charles was selected as second chief ten years ago."

Corrie was beginning to understand her friend's concern. The lack of written laws would be another issue Georgia politicians could use against the Cherokees.

"Most of the National Council is at the powwow, aren't they?" Harriet asked.

"Yes, I think so."

"Then you need to be there too. They will want to stay close to New Echota so a decision can be made if . . . if Mr. Hicks does pass away."

Elias nodded slowly. "They may meet through the night. Will you be alright if I am gone?"

"Of course. Corrie can stay, can't you?"

"Yes," Corrie agreed quickly. "School is still out. I can stay with Harriet for the next few days."

Elias turned the cup in its saucer, pondering what to do. "If you're sure you'll be alright."

"I will be," Harriet said firmly, stroking her abdomen where their child grew. "You are clerk of the Council. You need to be there. And if the meeting runs through tomorrow, Corrie and your mother and I can put together a meal for you all. Just send word."

Elias looked relieved and grateful. "Thank you, my dear. I don't know what I would do without you." He swallowed the last of his coffee and stood. Harriet walked with him to the door.

"Pray for us as well as Mr. Hicks," he said, looking over her shoulder to include Corrie in his request. "This is a critical time in our nation."

Then he stepped outside into the darkness and sprinted down the trail to New Echota.

CHAPTER FIFTEEN

New Echota
Winter 1827

Two days later Charles Hicks also died. Though the Cherokee-Dutch leader had not been as revered as Pathkiller, his loss was felt just as keenly. After a mourning period for the chief, the National Council held an emergency session, debating how to keep their government operating until an election could be held for a new executive. They appointed William Hicks, the younger brother to Charles, to serve as an interim chief.

"We must get our laws in writing," John Ridge stated to a group of men gathered at the entrance to the Council House after the emergency session had closed.

"Agreed," John Ross said and the other men nodded. "Not just a succession plan either. We need a full constitution that guards our sovereignty."

"I propose calling for a constitutional convention to meet one month from today," Major Ridge added. "We are perfectly capable now of joining the world's nations as a democracy."

"Then we will return in a month," Elias concluded. "There is little time to spare. That letter of 'sympathy' from Governor Troup might as well have been another threat against us."

Standing a little apart from the group was Samuel Worcester. He and his family had moved into a building at the mission just the week before. He had brought the printing press and was ready and willing to begin work for the Cherokees to commit their government documents to print.

Samuel stepped back out of the way as William Hicks approached the cluster of leaders.

"Men," he said as he shook hands all around. "You do me a great honor to serve as your chief."

"Thank you for your willingness to serve," Major Ridge said. "We have just decided to call for a constitutional convention. If you will send runners . . . ."

"Wait," Elias interrupted. "Worcester can print something by the end of today. The runners can carry it but we can also send it by post." He threw a look to his friend who nodded.

"You can print in Cherokee?" Hicks asked Worcester

"Yes, in Cherokee and English."

"Good. Elias, you and young Ridge write something up. I will sign it."

"We will work on it this afternoon," John agreed.

Those members of the Council not from New Echota made their way to their horses and vehicles to return home.

Elias, John and Samuel began the walk to the Boudinot farm. Corrie was still staying with Harriet and Sarah Ridge and Ann Worcester were also visiting at the Boudinot home. The women would no doubt have a meal prepared and would be anxious to hear the outcome of the Council meeting.

As they traversed the trail, the men were quiet, each one appearing deep in thought. There was much to be done and little time to complete it. Having the printing press at the Cherokee capital would greatly aid the task before them.

"What an amazing godsend your printing press is," Elias spoke his thoughts out loud.

"God's timing is perfect, my friend," Samuel agreed.

"We can discuss the newspaper this afternoon, as well," John added. "At this critical moment in our history, we must keep our people informed."

"You can also inform others who are sympathetic to your cause," the missionary said. "I know it can seem as if you stand alone with enemies all around you, but there are many people who want justice for you. They need to hear from you. I think you'll have readers from around the world."

They reached the Boudinot home and were greeted by the smell of the roasted turkey Harriet and Corrie were taking from the big oven set over the fireplace coals. Sarah was setting the table where every available chair had been placed while Ann fed little Ann Eliza in the parlor.

Harriet and Sarah went to greet their husbands and Samuel took a seat on the parlor's sofa to speak to Ann. Corrie was left standing alone in the kitchen cutting the cornbread into squares and pretending not to care that she had no one to greet. The only thing that kept her from feeling sorry for herself was another letter from Mr. Ackley tucked away in her pocket. Mrs. Sanders had asked Lem Starr to bring it to Corrie from the mission.

Shortly everyone came to the dining table after the sleeping baby was secured in a basket on the sofa. Elias held out a chair for Corrie to be seated. "Thank you for being here for Harriet," he said quietly. Corrie smiled to acknowledge his comment.

After Samuel offered grace, the conversation flowed as the food was shared around the kitchen table. The men reported on the selection of William Hicks for interim chief and the decision to call a constitutional convention.

"We'll be able to print our own documents," Elias declared as the meal drew to a close after a dried peach pie had been devoured. "And eventually start our newspaper."

"You need to give this newspaper a name," Sarah said as the women began to clear the table. Harriet was about to carry a pot of water from the fireplace, but Elias stood and took it from her and poured its contents into a large dishpan. Then he crossed to a desk in the parlor and pulled out sheets of paper, a pen and inkwell and returned to the table.

"What shall we call it?" he posed the question, looking around at everyone in the crowded room.

"Cherokee News," John proposed with a twinkle in his eye.

"How original," Sarah countered drolly from where she stood behind her husband, wiping a plate dry.

"I knew she would say that," John laughed.

"Cherokee Messenger?" Ann suggested, turning slightly from the dishpan, her hands soapy.

Sarah considered it. "That's better, but still not quite right. This newspaper should reflect where we are in our history."

"You mean 'not dead,'?" Now it was John's turn to speak with an ironic tone. "That is what Governor Troup has declared."

"Exactly," Samuel mused. "The Cherokee Nation is not dead. You have been dealt a terrible blow with the deaths of two great men, but you have not been defeated. You will rise from these trying circumstances."

"Like the phoenix of mythology," Elias added thoughtfully. "It rises from its own ashes to soar again."

"The Cherokee Phoenix," John and Sarah said together.

"It definitely sends a message," Worcester nodded.

"A bird that is born again," Elias said. "Charles would have liked that."

He looked down at the paper in front of him then dipped the iron-tipped pen into the ink. In bold letters, he wrote across the top. *Cherokee Phoenix*.

For the next half hour, ideas were tossed around fast and furiously like a good game of stickball. What articles should be included in the first issue and who would write them was discussed with growing excitement. Sarah offered to write news of the missions, even stating she would write under John's byline.

"You don't have to do that," John told his wife. "We Cherokees have no problem listening to a woman's voice."

"But if this newspaper will be sent to supporting churches in New England . . ." Sarah let her words trail off. Everyone in this room knew about attitudes back home. People there were easily scandalized and the fledgling *Phoenix* could ill afford to offend individuals who might offer financial support.

Ann Eliza began to fuss so Corrie volunteered to see to her since Ann was still up to her elbows in dish water. She changed the baby's diaper then brought her to stand in the kitchen door.

Corrie had said little during the planning of the newspaper, having little experience with such matters. She nuzzled the little girl's nearly bald head. Samuel called the few wisps of white-blonde hair on his daughter "peach fuzz." Corrie had yet to eat a fresh peach, and so wondered what the fuzzy fruit was like when just picked.

"The newspaper aside," Elias said, "we need to get the call for a constitutional convention printed. We will have time to pursue the newspaper after we have our government set in order." It was understood that Elias would be editor of this newspaper.

"I spoke with Slithering Snake before we left the Council House today. He is in full support and as speaker of the Council he should call it into special session."

Sarah laid a hand on her husband's shoulder. "John, why do you insist on calling him that? It's sounds so . . . ominous."

"It is the literal translation of his name into English," John reminded her. Clearly they had had this discussion before.

"But Crawling Snake sounds less threatening."

"Snakes don't crawl. They slither."

Corrie tried to hide a smile and a shudder and couldn't stop herself from glancing around. Just hearing the words slithering snake made her want to make sure one wasn't anywhere near her.

"I'm afraid I agree with Sarah," Ann said, finally drying her hands after giving the last dish to Harriet. "If someone besides Cherokees is going to be reading this newspaper or other documents, you don't want to use ominous sounding translations."

"But just calling him Snake is inaccurate," John groused. "The literal meaning is a snake that is moving."

"What about Moving Snake?" Samuel proposed looking at Ann to gauge her reaction.

"That's better, I think," his wife agreed.

"Still . . ." Sarah seemed to like her translation best.

"Going Snake?" Elias asked, looking around. "What do you think, Harriet? Corrie?"

Harriet simply shrugged and tried to hide a tired yawn behind her dishtowel. She looked to Corrie to answer.

"I think Going Snake seems less threatening," her friend said carefully. "It sounds like the snake is moving away from you instead of coming toward you."

O "Then it's Going Snake," Elias said firmly. He had just made his first editorial decision. The task of printing in two languages would likely prove to be the greatest challenge he would ever face. Getting this newspaper to press would also prove to be a long process, but he couldn't wait to get started.

Edmund offered the final prayer at the Dwight Mission church one Sunday in late February. The service today was well attended because the weather had warmed and the trails were relatively dry. Every seat in the little chapel was taken and some of the men stood at the back wall. If the church and school continued to grow, the missionaries would soon have to build a larger structure.

Washburn reminded the congregants that the Women's Temperance Society would meet on the following Tuesday afternoon. Abigail Washburn led this group and Edmund knew from Bettie that the women in the Illinois Bayou community enjoyed their meetings each month. Though the production and introduction of alcohol was forbidden by law in the Cherokee Nation, whiskey stills were common back in the hollers and the women had pledged themselves to keeping it away from their families.

Edmund did not act as interpreter for the women's meeting because Persis Lovely filled that role. The older woman, widow of Major William Lovely, had long lived among the Cherokees and spoke their language quite well. It was easy to forget that Mrs. Lovely was not Cherokee herself.

She was such a respected fixture in the community that many of the Cherokees called her *Etsi*, their mother.

Her husband had been appointed agent to the Cherokees in 1813 when the first Cherokee migration west began. The Lovelys had settled on the east bank of the bayou and had established a good farm there with a plum orchard said to be one of the best in Arkansas Territory.

As folks mingled and visited at the conclusion of the service, Mrs. Lovely approached Rev. Washburn and Edmund who greeted folks just outside the door. She spoke in English to the minister and though she had long lived in the South, Edmund recognized that she still retained her Boston accent.

"Good sermon, Rev. Washburn," she said when the minister shook her hand.

"Thank you, Mrs. Lovely. I'm glad to see you could be here today. You didn't have trouble fording the bayou did you?"

"No. Jeb drove me," she replied with a wave toward the Negro man who waited by her wagon. Edmund didn't know if Jeb was a slave or a freeman. He had worked at the Lovely farm for as long as anyone could remember.

"But I have a problem," Persis went on, "and I could use some assistance."

"What is it, *Etsi*?" Edmund asked concerned by the distressed look on the woman's face.

"An extremely large and violent razorback has taken a liking to my plum orchard," she explained. "It could kill my trees with its digging. Night before last it mauled my dog so badly I had to shoot the poor thing to end its suffering. It has made Jeb and me both rather afraid to walk the property and if something isn't done, we won't be able to get the potatoes planted in time."

"I could get a few men to come and take care of it," Edmund offered.

"Would you? I would be so grateful. Neither Jeb nor I are good enough with a gun to go after it ourselves. And the animal is just too dangerous to not get a good clean shot on the first try. I don't see well enough and Jeb has a slight tremor from that bad accident he had a few years ago. So we really do need some help."

"I am sure some of us can come to your farm tomorrow or Tuesday at the latest."

"Well, try to make it tomorrow. I have the Temperance meeting on Tuesday, you know."

"Yes, ma'am," Edmund agreed. "We will be there tomorrow."

Edmund mentioned Mrs. Lovely's request over dinner at Walter and Bettie's home following church. Walter quickly agreed to go with his brother to take the wild boar.

"Can I go too?" Walt Jr. asked.

"Me too?" Charles added, not to be outdone by his brother.

"You have school tomorrow," Bettie responded before Walter could.

"We could miss a day of school," Walt mumbled around a spoonful of hominy. He was not particularly interested in book learning. He preferred the lessons of the woods. But a stern look from his father kept him from saying more.

"Come down early," Walter instructed Edmund. "We will take Bettie to the store, then go to Lovely's farm."

"I will be here at sunrise," Edmund agreed, sending a sympathetic look to the boys who ate the rest of their meal in silence.

All the Webbers traveled by wagon to the trading post early the next day. The boys would walk to school from there and Bettie would open the store for trade while the men were away. Walter pulled the wagon behind the building and helped his wife down then lifted the boys out of the wagon bed.

Edmund unhitched the team and saddled them while Walter checked the store. Then the brothers rode the horses up the bayou trail to the ford. Splashing through the cold water was not easy. The horses did not seem to relish the effort and had to be spurred a few times to enter the fast flowing stream.

Once on the other side, they headed southeast to the valley where Mrs. Lovely lived in a small cabin. Persis came out onto the porch to greet them when they rode into her yard.

"I thank you for your help," she said in Cherokee. Walter would not have conversed with her otherwise. "Can I get you some coffee?"

"Maybe afterwards," Edmund said as both men dismounted.

"Jeb saw the boar up near the spring this morning," the woman went on, waving a hand toward the north. "There is a hickory grove up there. It likes the mast."

Water nodded as he unsheathed his musket from its scabbard behind his saddle. Edmund checked his powder horn a second time and then the men walked across the unplowed fields toward the spring that fed into the bayou.

The morning was chilly and a low fog clung to the hills. The farm was in a pretty location and Edmund could understand why Mrs. Lovely had stayed here even after her husband's death. She had no children except for the many Cherokees who considered her a second mother. She had cared for a little Osage girl for a time but the child had died and was buried beside Major Lovely under a massive oak near the house.

They passed the little burial ground as they crunched through fallen leaves and dried grasses. It surprised Edmund when his brother paused a few seconds to look at the carefully tended graves.

They continued on in silence for a while, their eyes scanning the ground for signs of the razorback. Edmund could tell that Walter had something on his mind. He was a man of few words, however, so Edmund did not expect his brother to share his thoughts.

Shortly they spotted the hog's footprints under another oak. They crouched down to examine them. From their depth it was easy to tell the animal was a large one.

The brothers preceded carefully, their eyes scanning the woods that lined the creek up ahead. They didn't want to happen upon the tusked animal unexpectedly. They crossed the still unplowed potato field watching their footing carefully on the uneven ground, their guns at the ready but pointed down.

Walter's voice was low when he spoke and it almost startled Edmund.

"Have you ever had to forgive someone?" he asked.

Surprised, Edmund didn't answer for a moment. What had brought such a question from his brother? Walter was a product of both his Scottish and Cherokee ancestry where clan loyalty and revenge were more often the rule than forgiveness. To forgive was seen as weakness by men like Walter.

"Yes," Edmund answered, "I have." His thoughts turned to several instances when he had made that difficult choice. He thought of Corrie who had never answered his last letter. Though he knew it was partly his fault, it still had hurt and for a while he had found it a struggle to forgive what had seemed like an insult.

"It is hard for me," Walter said. "The wolves war inside me. Someone told me that it takes more strength . . . more courage to forgive than it does to fight."

"This is true," Edmund agreed. The two had stopped walking but neither looked at the other. They kept their eyes on the woods. "Who told you this?" As far as he knew his brother had never once attended a church service where he might have heard the message of forgiveness.

"Wah-She-Hah," Walter said.

Edmund knew this name. In English it meant Star That Travels. It was the name of an Osage warrior who also served as an interpreter at a mission – Union Mission on the Neosho River.

"I spoke to him at Fort Gibson last moon," Walter explained. "He will not fight me though I have bid him to do so for the sake of his friend who was killed. I do not know what to do with a man who will not fight me."

"He has chosen to forgive?"

"Yes. That is what he says."

Edmund knew from this that Wah-She-Hah must be a Christian. The Osages followed the law of vengeance as faithfully as the Cherokees or Scots.

"He has chosen the upward path . . . the more difficult path."

"I do not know how to do this," Walter said.

"I do not believe anyone can without the help of God," Edmund offered.

Walter just shook his head and began to walk again. Edmund thought to pursue the matter but decided to let it go for now. He would pray for his brother instead.

They reached the tree line and slowed their steps, their moccasins making little noise in the damp woods. Up ahead they finally caught a glimpse of the large boar. It was rooting around the base of a hickory tree, nose to the ground. Like bears, the wild hog would eat anything and was a danger to other animals and humans.

The men stopped and crouched by another tree. Walter pulled some tufts of grass and tossed them into the air to judge the wind. Unfortunately to stay upwind of the animal would mean staying behind it with no clear shot of its head.

"I'll circle around," Walter whispered pointing in the direction he would take.

Edmund nodded then stood to check his loaded musket and take aim should the animal turn in his direction. He waited for his brother to come around behind the boar his gun also at the ready.

Once in place on the other side of it, Walter deliberately stepped on a stick to create noise hoping to draw the animal's attention and cause it to raise its head. But the hog was intent on its foraging and continued to feed on the dry hickory nuts.

Both men held their stance, patiently waiting for the best shot. Finally the large animal paused when the movement of a squirrel caught its eye. Raising its head, the hog turned toward Edmund and the young Cherokee took the shot. But the hog had moved too fast and the musket ball hit it in the fat of its shoulder, only wounding it. Walter had no clear shot at all.

With a squeal the animal charged and Edmund had no choice but to move quickly out of its way. The wounded animal was not nearly as fast as it normally would have been and Edmund could outrun it which he was determined to do. He needed to get well out in front of it so he would have time to reload.

As he crossed the potato field he saw Mrs. Lovely out in her yard, hanging her wash on the line. He feared that if the boar caught sight of the woman it would turn toward her.

"*Etsi*, get inside!" he called to the older woman. She looked over the clothesline and quickly realized what was happening. "Jeb, get the cow back into the barn," she called, then she hurried up the porch steps and into the cabin.

Edmund raced to the porch thinking to take his stand there where he could catch his breath and load the musket for a second shot. He had just leapt onto the floor of the porch when Mrs. Lovely stepped out, holding her own musket loaded and ready to fire. She thrust it toward him and took his gun. Then she hurried to load it, tamping down the powder like a skilled hunter and adding a new mini ball.

Edmund fired the woman's gun at the charging beast and this time made the kill shot. At almost the same time, Walter fired from where he had followed the animal. With another squeal and shudder the animal went down.

Persis handed Edmund his now loaded gun. He took it, admiration in his grin. "You are fast, *Etsi*!"

Persis shrugged but her smile said she was pleased at his compliment. "You don't live out here as long as I have without learning a few things."

The two men approached the animal cautiously, knowing not to assume that it was no longer a threat. Walter nudged it carefully with his foot and was satisfied that the boar was dead.

"Do you want the meat?" he asked Mrs. Lovely.

"I can always make room in my smokehouse," she nodded. "But Jeb can take care of it. Come inside for some coffee and my gingerbread."

Edmund was happy to comply. The men leaned their rifles against the wall of the house and stepped inside to its comfortable warmth. She motioned them to seats around the table in the single room and pulled a pot of coffee forward to the hot spot of her pot-bellied stove. Then she removed plates from a cupboard and placed generous squares of the still warm gingerbread she must have baked this morning.

She set the cake before each man then poured three cups of coffee and joined them at the table.

"You did not get a clean first shot, did you?"

"Sorry, *Etsi*. I did not."

"Well, you outran the ornery critter," she smiled with a look of her own admiration. "That is what I knew I could not do. I thank you again for coming out to help me."

"We are happy to do so," Walter said.

Edmund looked at his brother, surprised for the second time today. Walter usually did not care to converse with a white person, always pretending not to understand English. But Mrs. Lovely knew him well enough to keep her comments in Cherokee and Walter seemed willing to overlook the fact that she was not a tribal member.

"I had another visitor just last week," Persis said, as she sipped from her cup. "Colonel John Nicks. You know him?"

"I have met him at Fort Gibson," Walter said. "He is sutler for the fort."

"Yes, and he is a territorial legislator. He tells me that he is going to introduce a bill in the next session to create a county out here and it will include the Cherokee land. He is going to call it Lovely County in honor of my husband."

"I have heard this," Walter said. "They hope to make Arkansas a state and need counties to show they have adequate government. We may have to get a new treaty to protect our land . . . the land your husband purchased for us from the Osages."

"Those politicians think they can appease me by honoring my William. But you know I had to fight them to keep my land after the last treaty was signed even though you included my name in it. They wanted to force me to move because I am not Cherokee."

"It was not our doing, *Etsi*," Edmund said.

"We do not want to force you off your land," Walter added. "The treaty said anyone not a citizen of our nation would have to leave. But we consider you one of us."

"I do not blame you," Persis said as she stared into her cup. "But I am getting too old to fight this same fight. I do not want to leave my land. I hope the next treaty gives some consideration to a tired old woman who just wants to die here and be buried beside her husband."

"We will remember you, *Etsi*," Edmund stated firmly and his brother nodded.

The men had finished their refreshments and rose to take their leave of the feisty widow. She walked with them to the porch and thanked them again for their help.

"Have a safe journey," she told them as they took up their guns and mounted their horses tied to the porch rail. The brothers headed back toward the bayou, both quiet again with their thoughts.

Finally Edmund questioned his brother. "You think of Mrs. Lovely as one of us?"

"Yes. She knows us, our language, our traditions. She does not try to change us or make us white."

"But she is white. Can a white woman truly have a place in our nation?"

Walter turned to his younger brother and looked at him so closely that Edmund was forced to look away. He spoke quietly, "Yes, some white women can."

Edmund said nothing but after a few moments stole a glance at his usually stern-faced brother. Something was changing in Walter and he wasn't sure exactly what it was or why it was. Perhaps the prayers he and Bettie were praying for a softened heart had found a clear shot.

CHAPTER SIXTEEN

New Echota
Spring 1827

"Thank you for a lovely day," Corrie said as Oliver helped her from his carriage. They had returned to the mission after spending much of the day on their spring picnic. The trees were quite beautiful putting on their new green leaves. The small, white-blooming dogwoods scattered among them had looked like lacy parasols.

Oliver and Dolly had brought a basket of food prepared by their aunt's cook and they had spread out a blanket beside the brook to enjoy the meal. The weather had been pleasant, requiring only a light shawl and Corrie had enjoyed the outing tremendously. After so much sadness at the mission over the past few months, the excursion had been a welcome one.

Dolly did not walk with Oliver as he escorted Corrie to her door, but waited in the carriage.

"I enjoyed our outing very much, Miss Tuttle," Oliver said. "Thank you for agreeing to it."

"It was my pleasure," Corrie smiled. They paused when they arrived at the door, and Corrie wondered what Mr. Ackley thought of her humble home. She had gathered from his letters that the Ackleys were a family of some means.

His father had been wounded in the last war and still carried a mini ball in his leg, making it difficult for him to walk. This was the reason Oliver was the one to travel so often on behalf of the family business. His letters had been postmarked from places such as Nashville, Savannah and New York.

He had another sister who was married and lived in Nashville and a brother who had died, but he didn't explain how or why. He had expressed his sympathies for the Cherokees who had 'lost their leaders,' as he put it as if Pathkiller and Charles Hicks were the only leaders they had. He seemed to feel this was one more reason why they should consider moving west.

Mr. Ackley always seemed solicitous toward the Cherokees, but Corrie could sense that he didn't really feel comfortable around them. Neither did Dolly. They never lingered long at the cottage and always refused her invitation to stay for a cup of tea.

"I wonder if we might plan another outing," Oliver was saying. "Perhaps to Athens? My aunt tells me there is to be a spring choral concert at the college next month. We could drive down on a Saturday and attend the concert that evening. Then you could stay with Aunt Ophelia and we could attend church Sunday morning. I could drive you back on Monday."

Corrie was pleased with how completely proper and thoughtful Mr. Ackley could be. She was sure Jane would be amenable to watching all the boarders while Corrie went to Athens. Jane was planning another trip to Indian Springs in a few weeks to help her stepmother begin to pack up the plantation so Corrie could repay her kindness then.

"That sounds wonderful, Mr. Ackley. I would enjoy that."

"Very good," he smiled. "I will write you all the details in a few days. I look forward to it."

"As do I."

He opened the door for her, doffed his hat, then waited for her to enter the cottage. From the door she watched him as he returned to the carriage and waved again to Dolly when they pulled away.

She knew she was smiling broadly when she turned to face Jane who had come downstairs to greet her.

"He makes you smile," Jane stated in a matter-of-fact tone, but she was not smiling.

"Yes, he does," Corrie admitted.

"He does not like Indians."

Corrie's smile disappeared. "I don't think it's dislike, exactly," she said, vaguely aware that she was making excuses for him. "He actually seems very concerned about what you face. He just isn't comfortable around Indians. I don't suppose he has had much opportunity to get to know them . . . you. I hope he has not offended you. If I thought he had . . ."

Jane shrugged. "It does not matter." She seemed resigned to being the target of men's distrust and anger. Sadly she had experienced it in many ways.

"Yes, it does matter," Corrie said firmly. "I will speak to Mr. Ackley about it."

"Sometimes we women simply have to accept the way our men are."

Corrie shook her head. "No, I don't accept that," she said.

Jane smiled sadly. "You will learn, Miss Cornelia."

Corrie opened her mouth to argue, but Jane had turned away to take a seat by the fireplace. She took up her needle and continued to sew beads on a new pair of shoes for Pink.

The housemother hung her bonnet and shawl by the door then closed it slowly looking out on the pretty spring day. Jane's words bothered her because they expressed the concern that she had felt but had not honestly identified. She didn't want to believe that Oliver was as ill disposed toward Indians as that awful editor Isaiah Bunce.

She walked to her room to change into a work day dress, recalling Oliver's reluctance to come into the cottage. He was such a well-mannered man, even courtly in some ways. Perhaps he simply felt it would be inappropriate for him to linger in her home, especially since her parents were not here.

As she worked to fasten the buttons up the back of her cotton gown, she felt convinced that this must be the reason for Oliver's behavior. She would give him the benefit of the doubt because she didn't want to believe the worst of him. She was growing quite fond of him.

A few days later, Samuel Worcester came to the cottage after school. Jane opened the door at his knock and invited him inside. He stepped in as Corrie came into the parlor.

"Elias sent a note by Lem," he said after greetings were exchanged. "Harriet has had a baby girl and is now receiving visitors. Ann is anxious to go and we wanted to see if you would like to accompany us, Miss Tuttle. You, as well, Mrs. Hawkins."

"You go, Miss Cornelia," Jane said. "I will watch the children."

"We could ask Miss Nash to stay with them," Corrie suggested. The Boudinots had invited Jane to dinner during the school breaks and she knew Harriet would welcome a visit from her today.

"I will go another day," Jane said. "Please take my happy wishes to them."

"Well, if you're sure," Corrie smiled. "I'm just as anxious as Ann to see that new baby."

By horse and wagon, it took only about a quarter hour to reach the Boudinot farm. Corrie held Ann Eliza during the journey, marveling at how much the girl had grown.

They found Harriet and her newborn in the parlor after Susanna Watie welcomed them at the door. The Worcesters and Corrie oohed and cooed over Harriet's daughter who had a thatch of dark hair. Harriet had named the baby Eleanor after her mother.

"Did Dr. Butler attend you for the birth?" Ann asked while she held Eleanor, sitting beside Harriet on the settee.

"No, Elias's mother was here," Harriet explained. "She has been a godsend, staying with me for the past several weeks while Elias has been at the convention."

"How is the work going?" Samuel asked. "I haven't been able to keep up with it as well as I would like. Rev. Sanders has me teaching two classes of upper mathematics to some of the boys."

"Slowly," Harriet replied, hardly looking at Worcester. She seemed to have eyes only for her daughter. "Some days he comes home pleased and some days he's frustrated.

"I can imagine," Ann interjected. "It cannot be easy to form a new government."

"They are using the U.S. constitution as a guide, but there are still so many unique issues and long-held traditions among the Cherokees that must be taken into account. And you know one of their most prized traditions is speechmaking. Every single member of the council gets up to speak on every single article. It's taking far longer than Elias anticipated."

"But such vigorous debate ensures that every voice is heard," Samuel said. "It will give strength to the final document."

"That is everyone's hope," Harriet said. "I just hope this little one isn't half grown before Elias gets to spend time with her." She reached over to stroke the baby's cheek causing the girl to open her bright black eyes.

"He will not let that happen," Corrie smiled. She could just imagine Elias's pride in his daughter.

Susanna had prepared supper for them and came to the parlor then to let them know the meal was ready. The baby girls slept in a large basket Susanna had made while the adults ate and continued to discuss the constitution.

"Stand tells me the Ridges are firm in saying no more sale of Cherokee land," Susanna told them. "I am not sure my older son agrees."

"Surely he doesn't want to see your nation diminished," Samuel responded.

"He wants to keep options open," the Cherokee woman said. "Who knows what we will face in the future."

"I suppose that might be wise," Ann said.

"Still . . ." her husband mused, "solidarity will be important if the Cherokees are to resist the effort to force them west. Politicians like General Jackson will try to find any wedge they can use."

"Hopefully the laws they make now will serve us well into our future," Susanna added and all nodded their agreement.

The convention was recessed for spring planting but the work continued through April and into May. Corrie was busy helping her girls with their preparation for final exams and assisting with work in the big kitchen garden.

After supper one evening she was lighting the lamps in the cottage and happened to look out a window to see that a light was coming from the print shop where Samuel worked when he wasn't teaching. She wondered why he was working late and then noticed Elias and John approaching the shop from the New Echota trail.

Corrie hadn't seen either of the men in a few weeks so she told Jane she was going to walk over to the shop for a moment. Jane looked up from helping one of the students with spelling words and nodded.

Corrie strolled the path through the mission grounds, enjoying the soft breeze and the gentle light of dusk. She reached the print office just before John and Elias did and the three friends greeted one another.

"Are you here on official business?" she asked.

"Yes," Elias smiled while holding up a thick sheaf of papers. "The Council voted approval of the final draft of our constitution today. We have a new democratic government."

"That's wonderful."

"It is wonderful," Samuel echoed Corrie's sentiments as he stepped out of the shop to greet the delegates. "Are you two satisfied with the final results?"

Both men shrugged. "There were compromises required," John stated. "I suppose there always is. The important thing is that we now have an interim government in place. We will hold elections next year."

"Will Mr. Hicks continue as chief?"

"Yes, with Going Snake as second chief. John Ross will be president of the National Committee and my father will be speaker of the National Council."

"Like the Senate and the House of Representatives?" Corrie clarified.

"Yes and we have set up a court system. John Martin will be chief judge and will be able to appoint a marshal to oversee law enforcement. What we have to do now," Elias turned to his missionary friend, "is get this document into print."

"Let's get started then," Samuel smiled and waved the men into his office.

Corrie bid the men good evening and walked back to the cottage, thinking that she would share this good news with Oliver when they went to Athens on Saturday. He seemed so concerned about their tenuous position here in the east, she was sure he would be happy to learn of this development.

"Surely you jest!" Oliver exclaimed when Corrie mentioned the completed constitution on the drive to Athens. She saw a look that seemed like anger cross his face, but he quickly looked away so she could not be sure. His reaction surprised her.

"No," she said somewhat timidly. "They now have a government with three branches just like our federal government. They will be printing the constitution as soon as they can get the type set for it."

"Unbelievable," the gentleman said with a tight jaw. He shook his head as if to try to clear out an unwelcome thought.

"It should help them retain their homeland, don't you think?" Corrie asked, aware of a new undercurrent between them. Up until this moment, they had been enjoying the drive on a fine spring day. Now their pleasant conversation seemed to have made an abrupt change and she wasn't sure why.

"Yes, of course, it will," Oliver agreed. His hands tightened on the horses' reins and his eyes looked straight ahead.

Corrie remained quiet and her suitor made no attempt at conversation either. The silence stretched on for an uncomfortable amount of time and the only sounds were those of nature, the clop of the horses' hooves, the call of birds, a gentle breeze stirring the leaves. Everything outside the carriage seemed peaceful and serene, but not so inside the vehicle.

Finally she could stand the silence no longer. Taught to keep a conversation going, Corrie cast about her mind for another topic to discuss.

"Tell me about your aunt," she said. "She is so kind to offer me accommodations."

Oliver blew out a deep breath and seemed to bring his thoughts around. "Aunt Ophelia is my mother's older sister. Her husband teaches at the college and they have a home on campus. They raised several children – all grown now – so they have plenty of room. We'll be able to walk to the lecture hall where the concert will be held."

"Oh, that should be pleasant."

"Yes, it should." Finally Oliver turned to look at her and offered Corrie a smile. Whatever had distracted him seemed to be gone now. For the next several miles, they continued to talk about his aunt and cousins and the College of Georgia located in Athens.

Oliver stopped at a couple of roadside taverns along the drive for a needed break, but did not offer to purchase refreshments at the Cherokee-owned businesses. He had packed a picnic for their noon meal and stopped once at a clear, fast-running stream to refill a canteen with water.

It was late afternoon when they arrived in Athens and halted at a red brick, federal-style home at the edge of the campus.

Oliver looped the reins through the metal ring of a hitching post out front then helped Corrie step down from the carriage. She was tired and glad for the journey to end.

Oliver walked with Corrie up the brick sidewalk to the door. He rapped the knocker and within moments the door was opened by a Negro woman in a maid's uniform. Corrie felt her heart sink. Once again she had failed to consider that she might be waited on by slaves. She was starting to wish she had not agreed to this outing, but her heart had wanted it so much.

"Good afternoon, Mr. Oliver," the woman greeted him and opened the door wider to allow them to step into an entry hall. To the right a staircase curved up to the second floor.

"Good afternoon, Jessie," Oliver returned the greeting. "This is Miss Tuttle, my aunt's houseguest."

Jessie nodded and smiled. "Welcome, Miss Tuttle. Mrs. Buchanan has been expecting you."

As if summoned, Oliver's aunt entered from a room at the end of the hall.

"Oh, Oliver, you're here," she said with a decidedly Southern drawl. "I hope your journey was tolerable."

"Yes, Aunt Ophelia. It was pleasant enough and certainly made more so by the company of Miss Tuttle."

"So you are the Miss Tuttle I've been hearing about," the older woman said taking Corrie's hand into her own two. She was a petite woman with dark hair, graying at the temples. She wore a stylish dress in the color of irises.

"It's a pleasure to meet you, Mrs. Buchanan," Corrie said. "Thank you so much for allowing me to stay in your home."

"The pleasure is mine, dear," she said. "But don't let me keep you standing here in the doorway. You must be tired. Jessie will show you to the room we have ready for you. We'll let you freshen up then come downstairs to the parlor here." She indicated the room to the left that Corrie could see was decorated in shades of green and cream.

"If you'll follow me, Miss," Jessie said in a pleasant tone. She led the way up the stairs. Corrie heard Oliver give instructions to someone about getting their bags from the carriage and seeing to the horses.

"Where is Uncle Thad?" he asked.

"He's keeping late office hours," Ophelia explained. "It's finals week and the time students come begging for leniency."

The two of them laughed and then their voices faded as they entered the parlor.

Jessie led Corrie to a lovely bedroom at the back of the house with a bank of windows that overlooked a rose garden. The maid showed her the accommodations, including a pitcher of water and basin with a towel and soap sitting near, and a large wardrobe for her clothes.

Shortly a man came to the door carrying Corrie's traveling valise. He set the bag on a chair by the door.

"Thank you, Joseph," Jessie said. Then she turned to Corrie. "Would you like me to unpack for you?"

"No," Corrie said. "Thank you, that's kind of you, but I can manage."

Jessie looked at her more closely. "You're not from Georgia, are you, Miss?"

"No, I'm from Connecticut."

"What brings you down our way?"

"I work at a mission at New Echota."

"You're a missionary? Is that in the Creek lands or the Cherokee?"

"Cherokee."

Jessie shook her head. "You're brave."

"I hardly think so. I have found nothing to be afraid of."

"People's scared of Indians around here," Jessie said. "Guess they just don't know nothing different."

"But I have many friends among the Cherokees," Corrie assured her.

Jessie seemed skeptical but said nothing more about Indians. "Well you let me know if you need anything, Miss Tuttle. There is a bell pull by the door. Just ring for me and I'll be right up."

"Thank you, Miss . . .?" Corrie felt she shouldn't call the woman by her first name.

"It's Mrs. Russell," Jessie supplied. "But you can call me Jessie. Everyone does."

"Thank you, Jessie."

The maid nodded and then slipped out the door, closing it quietly behind her. Corrie sank onto the big featherbed wishing she could stretch out on it and rest a bit. But she feared she might fall asleep and keep her hostess waiting downstairs. So she removed her hat, then unpacked her valise, hanging her gowns in the wardrobe. She crossed to the washstand and poured out a little water to wash her hands, face and neck with the delicately scented soap.

After she dried her hands with the soft towel, she checked her appearance in the wardrobe mirror, repinning a few errant curls. Satisfied that her traveling suit wasn't terribly wrinkled, she made her way back downstairs.

In the parlor, Corrie visited with Oliver and Ophelia for a time before Mr. Buchanan arrived. Then they went to the dining room for a light supper that Jessie served from a large walnut sideboard. After the meal everyone went to change for the concert. Corrie wore her blue taffeta gown, the only dressy item she had brought from home.

The Buchanans walked with Oliver and Corrie across the campus to the lecture hall. The concert was quite good with several choral groups from the school performing as part of their final exercises. During intermission they enjoyed teacakes with coffee, tea or wine.

Walking home in the waning daylight, Corrie had to work to hide a few yawns. The day had begun very early for her and even earlier for Oliver. For that reason Ophelia suggested they all retire for the night as soon as they arrived back at the Buchanan home.

"Come to breakfast at your leisure, Miss Tuttle," she said after walking with the young woman upstairs. Oliver and Thaddeus Buchanan remained downstairs, for cigars Corrie supposed. "We always serve ourselves before church. I give Jessie the morning off so she can go to church as well."

"Oh, alright," Corrie said, thinking that was very kind of the woman. She found Ophelia to be pleasant and interesting. This introduction to Oliver's family made her appreciate him even more.

Corrie stepped into her room to find that Jessie had left an oil lamp burning with a low flame. She crossed the room and turned up the light, then changed into her nightdress and brushed out her hair.

After she settled into the comfortable bed, she felt the need to pray for guidance. She knew that she could easily come to care for Oliver Ackley, but also knew it might not be wise. Her heart was torn. And as she drifted off to sleep the smiling face of Edmund Webber came almost forcefully to her mind. Then her heart was torn even more.

The next day, they again walked across campus to the chapel for the morning worship service. Afterwards they enjoyed a late dinner then Ophelia invited Corrie to take a stroll through her garden out back. She was quite proud of her roses and wanted the young woman to enjoy their fragrant blooms.

Mr. Buchanan and Oliver went into town on some business and were gone for a good part of the afternoon so the women took tea with biscuits and slices of fruit and cheese in the parlor in place of supper. After clearing away their dishes, Jessie returned to light the lamps for the ladies.

The maid paused at the parlor door and spoke to Mrs. Buchanan. "I have set the sourdough to rise, ma'am, for cinnamon bread in the morning. Since we'll have breakfast early with Mr. Oliver and Miss Tuttle I wonder if I could go on home now?"

"Have you left something out for the men to eat in case they didn't eat in town?"

"Yes, ma'am. There's a platter of sliced beef and cheese with bread on a shelf in the cold cellar. Mr. Buchanan knows where I always leave him something."

"Very good, Jessie. Have a good evening then."

"Thank you, ma'am. I'll be here early in the morning."

Corrie knew her face registered surprise at this exchange. "Jessie doesn't live here?" she asked after the housekeeper had departed.

"No, she has a house full of children," Ophelia explained. "Her oldest girl watches them while Jessie works."

"Then she isn't . . ."

"A slave?" the older woman finished Corrie's query when she hesitated. "No. Mr. Buchanan and I are opposed to slavery."

"I didn't know any Southerners . . ."

Ophelia nodded in understanding as Corrie floundered for words. "Yes, I suppose you Yankees have been told every

Southerner owns slaves and treats them badly. But it isn't true. In fact, most Southerners don't own slaves either because they can't afford to or because they believe the practice is wrong. My husband and I are in the latter category."

For some reason Corrie felt tears spring to her eyes. "I'm so glad to know that, Mrs. Buchanan."

Ophelia smiled and reached over her chair arm to pat Corrie's hand. "Why don't you call me Aunt Ophelia," she said with a twinkle in her eyes. "We're kindred spirits, aren't we? And perhaps we'll be family someday."

Corrie felt her cheeks warm at the suggestion that she might marry Oliver. She wasn't yet sure that she wanted this, but learning that Oliver's aunt and uncle didn't support slavery gave her hope. Perhaps his parents felt the same way.

She had never had the courage to ask about it and Oliver had never given her even a hint of his position on the issue. He seemed far more focused on the Cherokees for some reason.

The household rose early the next day and enjoyed a light breakfast of Jessie's wonderful cinnamon bread with sausages and coffee.

The hostler Joseph brought Oliver's carriage around and loaded their bags and a picnic basket Jessie had filled with plenty of food. The Buchanans walked with the young couple to the vehicle and Ophelia extended an invitation for another visit soon.

"Thank you so much for your hospitality," Corrie replied, but did not feel free to agree to return again. Oliver didn't indicate if he had plans for another visit with Corrie. It left her feeling uncertain. He had remained courteous this weekend, but had seemed distant.

But as they took the road back to New Echota, their conversation was amenable and their stop for a picnic in a glade where rhododendrons bloomed was enjoyable. When Oliver walked Corrie to her door several hours later, she was tired but happy.

"Dolly will be home for the summer soon," Oliver said after he opened the door and set her valise inside. "Shall we plan another outing?"

"Yes, I'd like that."

"I'll write you the details then." He gave a little bow and then turned to walk back to his carriage. Corrie stepped into the cottage only then realizing she hadn't invited him inside and she had never once brought up his seeming reluctance to socialize with Indians.

She sighed. There were so many things to consider in her relationship with Oliver. His attentions were courtly, but never suggested anything more than a casual interest. Men were so confusing some times.

CHAPTER SEVENTEEN

Illinois Bayou
June 1827

Edmund put away the ledger book at the trading post and rubbed his tired eyes. The crowded back area of the store which passed for an office was dimly lit with only one small window. He had been recording transactions in the ledger for most of the day and was glad to be done with it now.

Most of Walter's customers bartered for the goods from his store so there were few cash transactions to record. Usually his customers brought in pelts and hides taken in the hunt, but Walter had begun to accept a pledge of corn from the upcoming harvest or for livestock.

The government was making contracts with most every trader and large tract farmer in western Arkansas to have the promised provisions for the Creeks who were moving out here. Colonel Brearley had purchased one of the Chouteau trading posts at Three Forks and was enlarging it to serve as the Creek Agency where he would dispense the food staples, farm implements, blankets and other provisions promised to the Creeks in the Georgia removal treaty.

Walter wanted to be able to provide some of the corn, beef and pork the government had pledged to these tribal members for the first year in their new homes. So he was now accepting bushels of corn or a litter of pigs in exchange for goods in his store. In another couple of weeks, the corn harvest would begin and Walter wanted an accounting of whom he would need to collect corn from.

Edmund had worked to complete the bookkeeping before he left today. The Neosho District Missions Conference would begin on Sunday and Dwight was hosting the event this year. Rev. Washburn had asked him to be available for the preaching services that would be held during the conference.

The students at Dwight had hand written posters inviting the community to attend. These were placed in all the trading houses in the area, at the dock and even tacked to trees at crossroad corners. They planned to preach the opening and closing days at Dwight with additional services offered in the Mulberry and Piney communities further to the west.

Washburn was hoping that offering a meal between the morning and afternoon services would entice some of the farm families to come for at least one day of the conference. The ministers from Harmony, Neosho, Hopefield and Union Missions, as well as Dwight, would all take turns giving sermons at the two-week event and Edmund would act as interpreter.

As he prepared to leave for the day, Edmund paused at the front of the store where Walter was dickering with Rattling Gourd over some beaver pelts. When the two men had shaken hands on the transaction, Rattling Gourd left with a bolt of muslin, an iron skillet and several candles.

Walter jotted down the items traded on the back of a used envelope. His bookkeeping method was casual at best and was one reason why Edmund had worked all day to sort and enter everything into the big green ledger.

"Remember I will be working at Dwight the next two weeks," Edmund told his brother.

Walter nodded. "I will be here to watch the store."

"I think Bettie would like to attend one of the services, but I am not sure I will be able to drive her. Perhaps you could bring her before you open the store?"

Walter simply grunted and Edmund could not tell if this was assent. But it wasn't an outright refusal so he would hope. If Walter brought her, it would be his first visit to the mission.

"Do not forget, Bettie wants you to come to supper tonight," Walter now reminded him. "She has also invited the Ballard family."

Edmund ignored the knowing look on his brother's face. "Of course, she did," he sighed. "Tell her I will be there."

Walter chuckled and Edmund took that moment to leave. He did not want to get into a discussion about how he needed to settle down and get married. Lucinda Ballard was pretty and he enjoyed her company. Her interest in him was flattering, but he did not feel the same interest. She just wasn't . . . . He just wasn't ready.

The young man took some time currying his horse after he rode home. The paint had a tangle of cockleburs in his tail and had been twitchy the whole day. Afterwards Edmund brushed his clothes and black felt hat, applying a little tallow to the bright cardinal feather he stuck in the band.

He couldn't say why he wanted to look his best. Maybe he liked the admiring look in Lucinda's eyes or maybe he just wanted Bettie to think he was trying to move on from another pretty girl.

Edmund walked down to the big double log cabin anticipating what Bettie and Etta would have cooked for supper. He waved to Harry who was stacking firewood by the kitchen wall after his older brother split the kindling. He saw that the Ballards' wagon was already pulled into the yard.

He stepped into the house and was greeted by the fragrance of food already being placed on the dining table. He saw Mrs. Ballard and Lucinda helping Bettie and Etta set out plates of elk steaks, bowls of hominy, beans and collard greens and baskets of corn muffins. Lucinda smiled at him and he returned the smile while hanging his hat on a peg by the door.

He approached the table just as Walter and Rabbit Ballard stepped into the room from the back porch. It was then that Edmund saw a young man, tall and gangly, standing by the door. He looked familiar but Edmund could not recall ever hearing his name. Perhaps he had seen him at one of the recent stomp dances.

Bettie invited everyone to take a seat and to his surprise the young visitor quickly pulled out Lucinda's chair and then sat down beside her before Edmund could. Bettie asked Edmund to pray over the food, something that Walter tolerated when they had guests.

Then as the food was being passed around, Lucinda introduced the young man. "This is Roddy Hildebrand, from over Piney way."

Piney was a three-day ride from the Illinois Bayou. Edmund wondered what had brought the young man here. He knew the Hildebrands, a Cherokee-Dutch family, operated a mill over on the Baron Fork Creek. Had he come to call on Lucinda? And why did that make Edmund want to smack him in the face?

He saw Bettie give him a look of reproach as if to say he had waited too long. He huffed out a frustrated breath and thought he heard his brother chuckle again. The rest of the meal was miserable.

Edmund excused himself shortly after supper concluded. He told Bettie he had promised to be at Dwight early the next day to help build a brush arbor for the conference. With guests coming from the other missions, the chapel would not hold everyone expected to attend the preaching services.

He stomped back to his cabin, chiding himself for being upset. What right did he have to expect Lucinda to wait on him? She had every reason to accept another man's courtship. They had never had anything but a casual friendship. But Bettie's reproach was correct – he had dithered too long and now he was once again alone.

Edmund arrived early at Dwight and had time to sit down to Miss Thrall's breakfast of ham, biscuits and eggs before joining Jacob Hitchcock and James Orr at the clearing chosen for the brush arbor. By the time they had raised the corner poles, Edmund had worked up a sweat in the June warmth and had prayed through his anger. He recognized that his pride had been hurt but he wasn't really angry at Lucinda. He was really angry at himself.

The men covered the roof of the arbor with a bramble of vines and small brush taken from the nearby woods. Long, split pine logs would provide seating and if there was a need for it, others could sit on blankets around the open-air arbor and still hear the singing and preaching.

Edmund was washing up for the noon meal when two wagons pulled into the mission compound. The visiting ministers had arrived, traveling together from Union Mission north of Fort Gibson on the Texas Road. Harmony Mission was located in Missouri and had been started at the same time as Dwight and Union. The farm missions, Hopefield and Neosho, were located in between Harmony and Union, both along the Neosho River.

Their visitors stiffly climbed down from the wagons and were greeted by Cephas and Abigail Washburn. They had camped at a point along the military road out of Fort Smith and had been traveling since before dawn.

The staff at Dwight all came to welcome their visitors while handshakes and introductions were made all around.

"Your timing in impeccable Rev. Vaille," Abigail noted. "We were just about to sit down to dinner. But I'm sure you'll want to freshen up first. Mr. Orr will show you to your quarters. The boys' dormitory will be where you'll be staying."

"Thank you, Mrs. Washburn."

Nathaniel Dodge and his wife Barbara were attending from Harmony but Benton Pixley, the director of the Neosho Mission, came without his family. From Hopefield were Will Requa and Rev. William Montgomery. Also visiting from Union were Dr. Marcus Palmer and his wife as well as the boys' teacher Abraham Redfield.

Over dinner they discussed plans for the conference. Primarily the event was a chance for the mission leaders to take a much needed break from the never-ending work at their respective stations. It was a time to plan joint preaching tours, discuss issues with the tribes they served and share encouragement and prayer. The annual event was one of the highlights on the missionaries' calendar.

They lingered over servings of huckleberry cobbler and coffee, enjoying the camaraderie of like-minded individuals.

"I am fighting envy, Washburn," Benton Pixley said at one point with just a little bitterness in his tone. "You have a wonderful operation here. I don't even have a church or school at Neosho."

"We are blessed," Washburn acknowledged. "The Cherokees have had two hundred more years of interaction with Americans than the Osages so they are comfortable with us and our institutions. And we are greatly aided by having the Cherokee language in writing."

"I have been three years trying to learn Osage and I am just now getting an understanding of their phonetics. Requa is the best among us at speaking the language."

Will Requa acknowledged the compliment with a nod and by raising his coffee cup. "Montgomery and I are working on a children's primer. Getting it printed will be our next challenge."

"My prayers are with you," Pixley said. "Seems like the Board's budget gets tighter every year and we get no help from the Osage agent."

Rev. Montgomery agreed. "We have seen the major only once in the past year. He lives in St. Louis and does little to actually serve the Osages. I'm afraid Hamtramck may succeed in getting the farm missions closed."

"All the Osage missions are in flux," Rev. Vaille noted. "Their treaty from 1825 requires them to move out of Lovely's Purchase and Missouri. Colonel Arbuckle hasn't pressured the Osages to move yet, but with the Creeks soon to arrive, that may change. Then we will have to decide whether we move with the Osages or stay and try to work with the Creeks."

"I can't see Harmony Mission lasting much longer," Nathaniel Dodge noted. "Pawhuska and Walking Rain, the chiefs near us, have both moved their villages to the Neosho. The remainder of the Osages in Missouri will soon follow. Then we will definitely have to move."

"Do you know if the Creeks are amenable to missionaries and the work of the church?" It was Abraham Redfield, a teacher and lay preacher who posed the question to Edmund.

"My friend Elias writes to me that there is a strong Baptist work among the Creeks in Alabama, but not so much among those in Georgia."

"Since the McIntosh group will be coming from Georgia, perhaps we can get a work started among them," Dr. Palmer said. "We already preach at Fort Gibson every other week; maybe we could add a service at the Creek Agency."

"You'll be heading up a second Cherokee mission soon, Palmer. So, it will fall to you, Abraham, if we are to start working with the Creeks," said the Union director.

"I will be happy to give it a try," Redfield said.

"I can assist him," Rev. Montgomery volunteered, "at Creek Agency and at the fort."

"How proficient are the Creeks in understanding English?" the doctor asked. "The delegation that visited last year spoke the language, but are they the exception?"

Every eye turned to Edmund as the only person in the room who had much knowledge of the Creeks.

"Most of the Lower Creeks have intermarried with the Scottish. So there is a basic understanding of English among them. It is less so among the Upper Creeks in Alabama who are mostly full blood."

"Let's plan on trying to meet with Roley McIntosh after the Creeks arrive," Vaille proposed. "We could do a preaching tour next summer, if they are interested."

"Sounds good," Redfield said and the other ministers nodded. From here the discussion turned to plans for Sunday's services. Monday would be a day of travel to the Mulberry community to set up for preaching on Tuesday.

"I'm looking forward to visiting Mulberry," Dr. Palmer said, casting a look at his wife Clarissa who sat at an adjacent table with her fellow teachers Eliza Weeks and Minerva Orr who taught the girls at Dwight. The Palmers planned to be established at the Mulberry mission by the end of the year.

The remainder of the afternoon was spent in rest, most of the traveling missionaries taking the opportunity to nap. After supper they gathered in the chapel to practice singing hymns. Elias had sent copies of three songs translated into Cherokee. Edmund and Abigail Washburn had worked to learn them so they could lead the congregation. The Dwight staff, who had all learned Cherokee, lifted their voices in the hymns set to the familiar old tunes.

"That is beautiful," Barbara Dodge said when the voices faded.

"You should hear our congregation sing," Abigail replied. "We have some wonderful voices and the Cherokees love to sing."

The singing continued through a few more hymns then Washburn gave a brief devotional and called for a time of prayer for the upcoming services. Afterwards everyone parted for the night. Edmund stayed at the mission, spreading out a pallet in the dining hall.

The next morning after breakfast, Edmund was helping Mr. Orr carry the pulpit from the chapel to the brush arbor. He saw Walter's wagon approaching the mission, but as it got closer realized that it was Jerome driving the vehicle, not his brother. Walter must have given permission for some of the slaves to attend the special meeting for the bed of the wagon was full.

When Bettie approached him, he smiled and asked, "Walter would not come?"

"He said he might for the last service."

Edmund nodded. "We will keep praying, Bettie."

The service was well attended by others who lived in the area. The Dwight Mission church was growing and all the missionaries were pleased that at least one of their stations was having success.

The remainder of the conference was spent in holding services at Mulberry, Piney and Philips Landing, across the river from Fort Smith. Edmund traveled with the ministers who spoke at two services in each community. Though these gatherings were not as well attended as those at Dwight, still there seemed to be an interest in matters of faith.

Near the Mulberry stomp grounds Edmund walked with Dr. Palmer and Jacob Hitchcock, looking over the site for the new mission. Hitchcock and a couple of their Cherokee friends had come over last fall to cut some of the tall pine trees that grew in abundance in the area. These had now cured and were ready for constructing a school and home for the Palmers.

The doctor seemed pleased with the location. "Sure is different from our prairie home at Union," he said as his eyes roamed over the mountains that rose to the north. "With this pine forest it seems more like New England."

"Mrs. Lovely calls those the Boston Mountains," Edmund told him. "She says they remind her of home."

"My wife will like it here. She sometimes misses Connecticut."

"I know how she feels," Edmund said almost under his breath. Then he quickly turned and walked away.

At the New Echota council ground, Corrie sat on a quilt with Jane, Ann and Harriet with their babies watching a game of stickball. Elias and Samuel were gathered with a cluster of men under the nearby sycamore trees, discussing hunting and politics and the likely outcome of the upcoming election for Tennessee governor. Sam Houston was running and he was known to be a friend to the Cherokees so most in the group were hopeful to see him in the governor's house.

It was the time of the Green Corn Festival and the hot summer day had been spent among friends, enjoying the games and good food. Ann was feeding her eight-month-old girl small bites of fresh peaches. Ann Eliza would almost shudder at the tartness of the fruit, but she eagerly opened her mouth for more. The women laughed at her sweet, funny face.

Corrie was enjoying the peaches as well. They were "bend over" peaches Elias had said – so juicy that they all had to bend over to take a bite to keep the juice from running down their chins and arms.

"These are so good," Corrie said after finishing her second peach and wiping her hands with a cotton napkin. "I know now why there are so many orchards around here."

"We plan to take cuttings with us when we move west," Jane said, smiling at Corrie's appreciation of this southern fruit. "Hopefully Arkansas Territory will be a place where the peaches can grow."

"When will you be leaving, Jane?" Harriet asked.

"In just over a month. Next week I will go down to Indian Springs to get my household goods packed. It will be a big work. I have put it off as long as I can."

"I can help you, if you need me," Corrie volunteered. "School won't start until September so I'll be free."

"That is kind of you. *Mvto* . . . thank you."

"We would help too, Jane, if we didn't have babies and husbands to look after," Ann assured her.

"I know," Jane said. "I understand."

"I know how hard it is to leave home," Harriet said then looking at Ann and Corrie, she added, "we all do, in fact. But none of us had to pack up an entire household and move to a virtually unknown area. I know this must be hard for you."

"In many ways it is. My husband and my parents are buried here and it is unlikely I will ever be able to return to visit their graves." Jane's eyes held a sad and far-away look. "But in other ways it will be a relief to go. There are people camping out on our land, just waiting for us to leave so they can claim it."

"Can they do that?" Ann asked in disbelief.

"Chilly and Uncle Roley have sent letters of complaint to the Indian Commissioner. But it does no good."

The women all shook their heads at the injustice.

"Elias's sister Bettie has written to me about Arkansas Territory," Harriet said. "She had to move everything just as you are, but she seems happy there now. I hope you will be too."

The others nodded in agreement, but Corrie had to look away for a moment. Harriet's mention of a letter reminded her that it had been weeks since she had received one from

Oliver. She was surprised at how much she cared and how frightened it made her feel. She worried that when his aunt and uncle had learned that she worked as a servant they had convinced him the she was an unsuitable companion.

Earlier this morning, Harriet had sensed Corrie's mood and had coaxed the matter from her. Though she was sympathetic, she had not seemed particularly sorry to learn that Oliver had not written. She didn't seem to think he was suitable for her.

"Perhaps it just wasn't meant to be, Corrie," she had whispered as they walked along behind the Worcesters to the council grounds. "Perhaps there is someone else who you are supposed to be with."

Corrie understood what Harriet wasn't saying out loud. Her friend had never given up hope that she and Edmund would marry. But Corrie had put that hope behind her long ago. She wouldn't dwell on it now. It seemed she must also put the hope of Oliver behind her as well, and she couldn't shake this new sadness.

The men joined them and Elias immediately reached down and took a peach from the basket at Harriet's feet. He bent over to take a big bite of the fuzzy fruit. After enjoying the tart sweetness for a moment, he said, "Guess what Worcester brought with him today?"

"What?" Harriet asked.

"Show her, Samuel."

The missionary printer reached into his back pocket and pulled out a folded sheet of paper. He handed it to Harriet with a satisfied smile.

Harriet took it and read the first few sentences printed in English. "Is this the constitution?"

Samuel nodded proudly.

"We finally finished the translation," Elias said.

"There are a few typographical errors we need to correct," the missionary printer said. "But it should be ready to print by next week."

"That is marvelous," Harriet smiled in congratulations. "You two have worked long hours on this."

"Yes, we have put off the newspaper and the hymnal and other projects to get the translation completed. But it is done at last and we can now distribute it throughout the nation in both languages. I plan to send it to some of the major newspapers as well." Elias sat down by his wife and took the paper she held to look it over once again.

"He's as proud of this as he is of Eleanor," Harriet laughed.

"Not true," Elias countered and now bent over to kiss the dark hair of his sleeping daughter.

"You're getting her all sticky!" Harriet protested playfully.

"No, I am not," Elias said leaning close to his wife to nuzzle her cheek.

"Stop it!" Harriet playfully pushed him away. "I don't want your peach juice all in my hair." She tossed her napkin at him and he wiped his hands and face to the laughter of the others in the group. Even Jane seemed to enjoy the banter between the couple.

After a few moments, Samuel asked, "Will you send a copy to Chief Jolly?"

"I am not sure," Elias said thoughtfully. "I do not want him to think we are trying to suggest how he should govern the western Cherokees. I may send it to Edmund and let him show it to Jolly."

"Yes, send it to Edmund," Harriet agreed, giving Corrie a look. "I'm sure he'll be interested in what's going on back here in New Echota."

Corrie simply looked away.

CHAPTER EIGHTEEN

Nashville, Tennessee
July, 1827

Oliver walked into the dockside tavern in Nashville with his sister Daphne and her husband Jason Edwards. He had just arrived on the steamboat *Red River* after a months-long trip to New York to meet with several textile mills to discuss the cotton crop that would be harvested soon. It was the type of work that should have been handled by their factor, but his father didn't trust the man to be aggressive enough so had sent Oliver instead.

The threesome took seats at one of the tables and ordered tea and the daily special of catfish and black-eyed peas with rice. Daphne caught Oliver up on all the happenings in Nashville since he had had last visited.

"You need to read the Nashville paper as soon as possible, Oliver," Jason said. "It reports that the Cherokees have written a constitution and formed a real government with a court system and bicameral legislature."

Oliver sighed. "I had heard that from Miss Tuttle, but had hoped she misunderstood. So it is true?"

"Yes, it's true," Jason confirmed.

"Are you still seeing that young woman in Georgia?" Daphne asked.

"I'm not sure it's worth the effort anymore," Oliver replied. "I'm beginning to feel she will not be as helpful to our cause as I had hoped."

"Is it a chore to court her?" Jason asked after the serving girl had set their plates in front of them. It was a moment or two before Oliver replied while they ate the flaky fried catfish.

"She's a pretty young woman," he said, "and intelligent enough for conversation. But she is a servant after all. Can you imagine mother's reaction to her? That's why I took her to Aunt Ophelia's. She thought Miss Tuttle was wonderful."

"Aunt Ophelia looks at the world through rosy glasses," Daphne said dryly. "She thinks everyone is wonderful."

"Still, I don't think you should give up on trying to convince this woman of the expediency of a Cherokee removal, if she has the ear of Cherokee leaders as you say," his brother-in-law argued. "Heaven knows we're getting nowhere with our politicians. Neither Crockett nor Houston has done anything on this issue in Congress."

"Careful, Jason," his wife warned with lowered voice. "Sam Houston is sitting at one of the back tables right now."

Jason glanced over his shoulder. "Let him hear me," he said, but he lowered his voice as well. "Let everyone hear. We don't need Houston as our governor."

Oliver said nothing for a while as they finished the meal but he kept sending angry glances toward the table where Congressman Houston sat with another man.

"Do you know who that is with Houston?"

Jason looked again. "That's Colonel John Allen; one of the richest men in Tennessee. You know he's backing Houston in the governor's race. His plantation on the Cumberland isn't anywhere near Cherokee lands so he has nothing to lose or gain by their removal."

"Why is he backing Houston?"

"Political power," Jason chuckled without mirth. "Allen craves a place in the governor's circle. He'll even throw in his daughter to get it."

"What do you mean?" Daphne asked. "You're not talking about marriage to Eliza Allen are you? She's barely sixteen; she's Dolly's age. Houston must be twice as old as her."

"That's the rumor along lawyer's row. Of course the arrangement is contingent upon Houston getting elected and Eliza turning eighteen. So a long engagement will fill the society columns and give all the matrons of Nashville something to titter about."

Poor girl," Daphne tsked. "She'll have no say in the matter."

"So Houston gets a wife and money for his campaign?"

"Yes, and he needs both," Jason nodded. "He doesn't come from an aristocratic family and has no wealth. He's more comfortable with the Cherokees than with Nashville society. He has his friendship with General Jackson and his military reputation, but that's all."

"It has been enough for him so far."

"And with Colonel Allen's money, he'll probably have the title of governor soon."

"All the more reason for you to remain friends with that girl in Georgia," Daphne said. "Our dear brother may have served with Sam Houston, but I don't think we can count on him to see our side of this issue or to do anything to remove the Cherokees."

"Maybe it will be Houston who'll remove," Oliver mused. "I hear that his Cherokee 'father' lives in Arkansas. Maybe we should encourage Houston to go live with him."

"And how do you propose to do that? He can't govern Tennessee from there and I don't see him giving up the governor's office if he gets it."

"There are always ways to get someone out of office," Oliver smiled over his teacup.

"Such as?"

"Scandal, Jason. Nothing beats a good scandal."

Jane stood at the door of the cottage at the New Echota Mission watching the road from town. Her brother Chilly was coming by wagon to take her and Pinkney to the McIntosh plantation. Corrie would join them, as well. There was not much coming off the garden right now so Corrie wasn't needed for the task of canning vegetables. Mrs. Sanders had agreed to let Corrie travel with the other housemother to help with the packing.

Soon the rattle of the wagon could be heard coming around the bend and the two women went to collect their things for the trip. Corrie had packed just a few necessities since they expected the work would take only a couple of days. Cook had prepared a big basket of food for them to take as well.

Pink, now four years old, raced down the stairs and out the door to wave to his uncle who brought the wagon around to the front of the cottage.

"Can I ride up with Uncle Chilly?" Pink asked his mother who had followed him out the door.

"Yes, you may. But first help Miss Cornelia with the food basket, please."

Pink took the basket from Corrie and hefted it into the wagon bed. It was almost too heavy for him to manage.

Chilly stepped down from the wagon seat and Jane introduced him to Corrie. He nodded to her but said nothing in way of a greeting. Then he opened up the wagon bed, lifted down a little wooden stool and helped Jane and Corrie climb into the wagon. They settled on an old quilt spread out over the rough wooden bed.

Pink scrambled over the front wheel and took his seat as his uncle returned to release the brake and start the two horses that pulled the wagon. The women quickly found that the best place to sit was directly behind the driver where the dust didn't swirl as badly. Corrie pulled out her fan and tugged her bonnet brim forward to cover her face better. The drive would be a hot one, but would not take as long as the drive to Athens.

Taking a different route than Oliver had, they quickly left the Cherokee Nation and moved into the Creek lands. Jane pointed out the homes of friends as they neared the McIntosh plantation. It was clear that these homes were being packed up for the journey west. Belongings were crated and piled into wagons. The corn harvest was complete and the removal would begin soon.

All along the route they witnessed the encroachment upon Creek lands by Georgia citizens. Some were living in tents; others had already occupied homes that had been cleaned out. Technically the land still belonged to the Creek Nation, but eager homesteaders cared nothing for technicalities. Many of these squatters stared angrily at the wagon as if Chilly and Jane were the intruders instead of them.

"Did your father own slaves, Jane?" Corrie asked as they turned off the main road to follow a long trail through cotton fields now lying fallow.

"Yes, several dozen. They are Uncle Roley's now."

Corrie grimaced, but said nothing.

"I know you don't approve, Miss Cornelia," Jane said. "But it is an old practice. We Creeks adopt our slaves in a sense. They become a part of us."

"And they will travel west with you?"

"Yes, they will go west."

Within a few minutes Chilly directed the horses to pull in front of a two-story frame house. It was not nearly as fancy as the Ridge home, but was larger than most of the small log or frame dwellings they had passed. A wide verandah stretched across the front of the plantation home.

There was evidence of the fire that had been set to the home two years earlier to drive William McIntosh out before he had been shot. Some windows were boarded on the first floor and the verandah posts were slightly charred.

They went inside to find the household in a state of controlled chaos. Stacks of books, clothing, linens, dishes, cookware and other household items waited to be packed into crates and barrels filled with straw.

An older woman was directing two Negroes as they all worked to fold muslin sheets as tightly as possible. They were all speaking *Muskoke* and Corrie felt quite out of place.

Jane steered her friend over to this woman who seemed to be in charge of the packing.

"Miss Cornelia, this is my Aunt Muskogee; she is Roley's wife." Then to Muskogee she said, "Miss Tuttle and I work together at the Cherokee mission in New Echota."

"Hello, Miss Tuttle," Muskogee greeted her in English and to Jane she added, "We have not touched your things, Jane. We did not know what you would want to take."

"Mostly just necessities," Jane replied. "Corrie and I will get started." She looked around for Pink who was playing with a number of older children, half siblings to Jane, Corrie supposed, or perhaps cousins.

"Pink, you stay here and obey Aunt Muskogee," she said, catching hold of his hand so she could get his attention. "Do you understand?"

"Yes, *Etsi*," Pink replied.

"You turn him into a Cherokee?" Muskogee asked with a raised eyebrow.

"That is what he hears at school," Jane explained. "He speaks *Muskoke*, Cherokee and English, sometimes all in the same sentence."

With a further admonishment to behave, Jane let him return to his play. She directed Corrie to follow her through the kitchen and out the back door. Here they found other slaves sorting through mounds of corn ears. Some were to be taken to the mill to be ground and sacked to take west; some of it would be sold to help finance the journey. The government was supposed to pay the Creeks for their land and improvements, but so far no money had arrived. The McIntoshes would finance this first migration west out of their own funds.

"My home is out back here," Jane explained as the two woman walked toward a smaller cottage sitting on a rise and overlooking the Chattahoochee River. Jane's people almost always located their homes near a stream of water which is why the English settlers had given them the name Creeks.

As they reached the entrance, Corrie caught sight of movement near the river. It looked like a group of squatters had a camp there. It made her think of vultures, circling a dying lamb.

Inside the home they found most of the furnishings covered with cloths. It was clear that someone had cared for the cottage while Jane was away. There was no dust or cobwebs, but the house had a musty closed-in smell.

Jane paused for a moment and Corrie could tell that she was battling her emotions. She had lived here with her husband and baby until that fateful day when her father and husband had been killed.

All over again, Corrie felt admiration for this young woman. She could have become bitter from these awful circumstances, but she bore the sorrow with grace and dignity.

She remembered Jane's comment about having to live with their husbands' decisions. She wondered if the men who made treaties and brokered land deals considered the upheaval their decisions would create for their families. She felt a flash of anger at the situation Jane now found herself in. She would say goodbye to this home and to all that was familiar and dear to her.

Corrie stood quietly looking out the front window toward the river to give Jane time to collect herself. She was aware when her friend pulled a handkerchief from her apron pocket and wiped her face.

"I am alright now, Miss Cornelia," she said in a husky voice. "We should get started."

Corrie turned and crossed the room to slip an arm around Jane's shoulders. "Tell me what to do. Where do you want me to begin?"

Jane led the way to the kitchen, a lean-to at the back of the house. The two women began sorting through cookware with Jane deciding what she would take with her and what she would have Chilly try to sell. She chose to keep only a few items, the bare necessities. While they worked her brother arrived with two slaves bringing crates and setting them in the parlor.

Jane thanked them, then went to a bedroom and brought a quilt to line the first crate. They filled it with the pots and kettles, utensils and serving ware. Then they moved to a hutch in the dining room where Jane had kept her china.

"What a pretty pattern, Jane," Corrie said as she pulled the pieces out to set on the table.

"Sam gave me the set as a wedding gift," Jane said softly. "He ordered it from England." Her words faltered and she sat down suddenly in one of the dining chairs. Swamped with emotion again she laid her head on the table and gave in to the tears.

Corrie felt her own tears coursing down her cheeks in empathy. She laid a hand on Jane's shoulder and silently prayed for the young woman while her sorrow found release. But Jane soon raised her head and mopped her face once again.

"I am sorry," she said.

"Don't be. It's perfectly understandable."

"But we have no time for tears." Jane looked over the spread of china on the table. "I did not plan to take this with me," she said with a wave of her hand. "But I cannot leave it."

Corrie had found plenty of cotton and linen napkins and tablecloths in the drawers of the hutch. "We can wrap each piece," she said. "Do you have another quilt?"

"Yes, in the bedroom."

Corrie went for it and filled another crate. Then they carefully wrapped only a few pieces of the china set. "I will not need all of it," she said. "Pink and I may live with Chilly when we are first arrived."

All afternoon they filled the crates with clothing, bed linens and a few precious knick knacks from the mantle and bedside tables. A couple of Pink's toys were squeezed into the space.

At suppertime Muskogee came to the door and invited the two friends to eat at the big house. Afterwards they rested in bentwood chairs on the verandah while a little breeze helped cool the evening air. Corrie sat quietly while most of the conversation was conducted in *Muskoke*.

"Will you be finished in the morning?" Jane's aunt asked in English. Corrie appreciated that the older woman thoughtfully included her in the question.

"Yes, we just need to add straw to the crates and then the men can close them up," Jane responded.

"Will you take any furniture?"

"Only the rocker. Sam gave me that when Pink was born."

Muskogee nodded. "Roley tells me he knows of a trader in Milledgeville who will take all the furniture. He hopes he will give him a fair price, but who knows."

Jane sighed, "I am sure it will not be what it cost us."

"No, nothing will cover what this will cost us."

They retired for the night shortly afterwards, Corrie and Jane sharing a room with her half sister Rebecca. The next day they finished the packing after breakfast and were soon on their way back to New Echota.

They stopped for the noon meal at the McIntosh tavern at Indian Springs. It was evident that the staff there was also packing for the journey. They ate a meal of beans and cornbread with mustard greens. Pink grew restless and roamed the dining room, charming other patrons with his smile and accepting bites of cobbler from a woman at the other end of the large room. Being located at the ferry crossing, the tavern still saw a steady business of travelers on the federal road.

"Chilly and I both worked here when we were younger," Jane told Corrie. Her brother, a man of few words, had finished his dinner quickly and gone out to see to their horses.

"Did you wait tables?"

"Yes," Jane smiled with a nostalgic look on her face. "I taught Hawk everything he knows." She looked up at the Creek man who was replenishing their coffee.

"Good *mihia*," he said, "good teacher."

"Are you going west, Hawk?"

"Yes, I am getting packed. I will help Chilly load the wagons soon."

The man he spoke of stepped inside then and nodded to Jane.

"We should go," she said. "Come, Pink."

The little boy ran to his mother and took her hand. Soon they were on their way again. Instead of riding on the wagon seat with his uncle, Pink chose to sit in Jane's lap. He seemed to sense her sorrow and fell asleep to the rocking of the wagon.

As they passed through the Cherokee capital, Chilly turned to look at his sister. "Do you want me to burn it?" he asked.

"Burn what?"

"Your cottage. Our stepmother wants the big house burned so the squatters can't have it."

Jane was quiet for a long time. "You decide," she said at last. "But do not tell me if you do."

Her brother nodded and they spent the last mile of the journey in silence.

CHAPTER NINETEEN

New Echota Mission
August, 1827

When Corrie stepped into the cottage she saw a stack of mail waiting on the little table by the door. Mrs. Sanders must have brought it for the two women while they were away. Glancing through the stack of letters and packages, she was pleased to see that several were addressed to her. Corrie's birthday was just a few days away and no doubt most of the missives contained birthday wishes.

She handed two envelopes to Jane and then took the rest of the mail to her room to open after she had unpacked from the trip. The larger package contained a new dress from her parents and Corrie was pleased with the soft green batiste fabric.

A smaller package contained a set of combs from Sarah Ridge with a short letter that wished her well and also announced the birth of her baby, a little boy they named John Rollin. A note from Harriet extended an invitation to dinner for the following day and another long letter from cousin Electra told about the Kingsburys and their life at the Choctaw mission in Mississippi.

Lastly was a letter from Oliver. She recognized his bold handwriting and felt her heart trip at the sight. She had almost given up on hearing from him again.

He apologized for the long delay in writing her, explaining that his father had sent him to New York on business. He proposed another picnic before Dolly returned to school in Virginia. They would both call upon her the following week. Corrie glanced at her new dress and knew exactly what she would wear.

On the day of the picnic, Corrie took extra care in arranging her hair, wanting to look her best. She let Jane get the door when the knock came and was seated with her embroidery when Oliver stepped just inside. Jane excused herself and went upstairs. Corrie offered Oliver a seat but he said Dolly was waiting and they should be on their way before it grew too hot.

Oliver chose a different location for this picnic, but one still on Cherokee land. As Oliver brought the horses to a halt, Corrie wondered how this man from Tennessee seemed to be so familiar with the Cherokee woodlands.

This spot stood in the shade of a rock wall where a little stream of water trickled downward into a natural basin. The water was cold in spite of the August sunshine and so clear they could see the pebbles that settled at the bottom of the pool.

"Doesn't that look like gold?" Dolly asked as the two women washed their hands while Oliver spread out a quilt for them to sit on.

Corrie looked down at the little flecks of rock that did seem to glisten in the light that filtered through the trees.

"Yes, I suppose it does," she said. "It's probably what they call 'fools' gold.'"

Dolly seemed disappointed. "Wouldn't it be fun if it was gold?" she grinned.

"Yes," Corrie laughed. "Then we would be rich. I've never had that experience before. Although I suppose this would really be Cherokee gold."

Dolly's smiled faded at her words. "Is it terrible to be poor?" she asked, seeming sincere and not snide.

"It's not terrible to have little money," Corrie assured her. "Especially when you are rich with faith, family and friends and a purpose in life."

"Still," Dolly said thoughtfully, "it would be better to have all those things and money. Aren't we young ladies supposed to find a husband with that one important attribute?"

"I suppose that is the goal for some young ladies," Corrie said. "But not everyone can have that. We must learn to be grateful for whatever God gives us in life."

"You wouldn't turn down a marriage proposal from someone who had money though, would you?"

Before she could stop herself Corrie glanced at Dolly's brother, looking handsome and gentlemanly carrying the picnic basket from the carriage. "No, I wouldn't," she said and felt a flush heat her cheeks. Then she hastily added, "Not simply because he had money."

Dolly slipped her arm through Corrie's and pulled her to the picnic spread. They enjoyed cold chicken salad with deviled eggs and peach fried pies. Corrie had to appreciate Oliver's effort to make their outing enjoyable. He had ordered the meal be packed for them from a tavern along the route and clearly had at some time scouted out this pretty setting for the picnic.

The meal was spent in quiet conversation but Oliver never once hinted at the topic of marriage. He seemed more interested in hearing about the Cherokees, asking who among them might be interested in going west.

When the meal was completed, Corrie and Dolly packed up the metalware dishes while Oliver went to fill their canteen with water. He seemed to linger for a time at the basin so Corrie folded the quilt and then the two women walked to the carriage to stow the items under the seat.

Dolly leaned close to Corrie as they stood there and said in a low voice, "I don't care what Mother and Daphne say. I think you're a completely appropriate match for my brother. He needs to forget all this Cherokee worry or find someone else to convince them to move."

Her words puzzled the young housemother. "What do you mean, Dolly?"

The girl glanced back and saw Oliver approaching them. "Nothing," she said. "Forget I said anything."

"Are you ready, ladies?" her brother asked.

"Yes," Dolly said hastily. "But we simply must stop at that tavern on the way. I need to use the little house at the end of the lane."

Oliver laughed as he helped the women into the carriage. "Yes, little sister," he said.

During the ride back to the mission, Corrie's mind worried over Dolly's comment. Obviously there was a family objection toward her, a simple mission worker with no dowry. But what had the girl meant about the Cherokees? She didn't understand and didn't know how to ask.

The Mulberry Mission site was silent as several men rode their horses into the little clearing. Mr. Hitchcock had told Edmund that the heat and a terrible outbreak of the summer fever had delayed construction. The double log cabin being built for the Palmers was halfway completed but nothing had been done on any other buildings. It would be impossible to begin school this fall. Washburn had sent word to Union Mission explaining the delay.

The men with Edmund were acting as delegates to a council that would be held at the home of Chief Blackcoat in the Piney community. His brother Walter, Chief Jolly with his son Price, Sequoyah and Spring Frog, Rabbit Ballard and Thomas Chisholm made up the group traveling west. Chisholm had just returned from his trip to the mountains with his brother.

These men would be joined at Piney by John Rogers who was a business partner with Colonel Nicks, having a mercantile near Fort Gibson. Rogers was married to Chief Jolly's sister. Also attending would be Rogers' son-in-law, John Flowers who acted as the attorney for the western Cherokees.

Edmund carried the copy of the constitution Elias had sent to him. He had shown it to Chief Jolly and shared the news of the deaths of Pathkiller and Charles Hicks. Jolly called this meeting to discuss the need for a clear plan of succession for chiefs of the western band.

The council met in the open air in the shade of tall trees near the Baron Fork Creek. After a day of speeches and discussion, the men chose to depart from the tradition of having hereditary chiefs and hold elections in the fall. They agreed to have three chiefs knowing that epidemics and natural disasters could affect them just as it had their eastern brothers. The interim chiefs chosen at the council were Jolly, Blackcoat and Walter Webber.

"Colonel Nicks is making plans for Lovely County," Rogers told the group. "He wants to start a town where he'll build a post office and county courthouse."

"Where will this town be?" Blackcoat asked.

"Somewhere on the military road between Fort Gibson and Fort Smith. Close to the river. He expects steamboats will soon reach Gibson, if they can get past the falls on the Arkansas. He will call the town Nicksville."

"Of course he will," Walter said with irony in his voice. The other men smiled.

From his coat pocket Mr. Flowers took out a letter and told the men the Indian Commissioner had requested that the western Cherokees send representatives to Washington for a new treaty negotiation.

"Why do they want a new treaty?" Spring Frog asked.

"To take more of our land," Blackcoat responded in a graveled voice.

"The politicians in Little Rock want us to move further west. New settlers come to the territory and they want our land," Jolly said. "But we will hold Lovely's Purchase with a tight fist. The Osages are leaving it and we must claim it quickly or the President will move some other people onto it."

"I think the governor hopes to move us even further west. He doesn't want to lose any more territory to Indians." Walter offered this opinion.

"I believe the governor is willing to sacrifice the part of Lovely's Purchase that is west of Fort Smith," Flowers countered. "But Nicks and other legislators don't want to. That is why they have created this county – to provide it with government so that more settlers will come."

"So who of us will go to Washington to protect our claim?" asked Edmund.

Chief Jolly looked around the group and pointed to the men he would assign the task. "Blackcoat. Walter Webber. Sequoyah. Be ready to leave at the Persimmon Moon. Mr. Flowers, will you accompany them as well?"

The attorney nodded. "I think you need to consider moving more of your people into this area," he advised. "Or at least mark the corners of land you claim."

"We will make Piney our capital then."

"What are we to do if the government men want to take our land east of Fort Smith?" Walter asked.

"If they insist on this, then you must insist on being given all the rest of Lovely's Purchase," Jolly stated.

"We need more hunting land too," said Spring Frog.

"We will ask for a hunting outlet to the west where we can chase the buffalo on the prairie," Sequoyah added.

The men nodded and soon the council ended with the pipe being passed around their circle.

It was a week before school was set to start and everyone at the New Echota Mission was preparing for the return of the students. Corrie and Jane, with Delight's help, had thoroughly scrubbed the boarding house after spending a week stuffing new feathers into mattresses and pillows. Delight would replace Jane as housemother after she departed in a few days.

Corrie hummed softly while she spread freshly laundered sheets on the girls' beds. Jane was working upstairs and Delight had gone to help in the kitchen so the house was quiet. The silence gave her too much time to think. She had worried over Dolly's obvious slip of the tongue at the picnic, but could not reach a conclusion about what her words meant. Was Oliver courting her in the hope that he could use her influence on Cherokees? That seemed ridiculous. She hardly had any influence and certainly couldn't and wouldn't try to persuade her friends to give up their homeland.

At times, Corrie considered writing to Oliver demanding that he tell her where their relationship stood. At other times, she wanted to never hear from him again. She had cried quietly in her room each evening for the past week. Nothing made any sense to her right now. She was beginning to wonder if she should leave New Echota.

"Miss Cornelia," Jane's voice interrupted her tortured thoughts.

Corrie looked up at the worried tone of her friend. "What is it, Jane?"

"Pinkney has a fever," the mother explained. "It seems very high to me. He does not want to get out of bed and you know that is not like him."

Corrie knew that was certainly true. Normally Pink was a perpetual motion machine, on the move from morning to nightfall.

"What can I do to help?" she asked.

"Could you get Mrs. Sanders to come check on him?"

The mission director's wife had some medical experience and usually handled any sickness or injuries among the staff and students.

"Yes, I'll get her right away."

Corrie left the cottage and Jane returned to her room upstairs. The little boy laid still, his dark hair matted with sweat. She again touched his forehead and his eyes opened. They were glazed with the fever and seemed bothered by the light. His mother crossed the room to the washstand and dampened a cloth then returned to his bed and gently sponged his face.

Shortly Mrs. Sanders bustled into the room a little breathless from climbing the stairs. Jane moved out of the way so the older woman could examine the little boy. Corrie stood in the door to offer any assistance that might be needed.

"Light a candle so I can see his throat," the nurse instructed.

Jane hurried to comply and held the light close so the woman could peer into his mouth.

"Not swollen," Mrs. Sanders said quietly. Then she felt behind his ears and along his neck. Satisfied with that, she lifted the boy's night shirt to examine his stomach. A red rash spread across his abdomen.

Jane gasped and covered her mouth.

"Is it . . . ?"

"I'm afraid it may be measles," the director's wife stated as she lowered the nightshirt then felt Pink's forehead. "Might he have been exposed to them when you went home?"

"No one there had them," Jane replied.

"Perhaps at the tavern where we stopped for dinner," Corrie suggested. "Pink visited with all the other guests."

Jane sat down on the bed quickly as if her knees had given out. "I should have kept him at our table," she said. "That woman gave him some of her cobbler and wiped his mouth with her napkin. Could he have gotten them that way?"

"Possibly," Mrs. Sanders answered. "I'm no expert on such matters, but I think that might have been enough to expose him."

"Oh, this is awful," Jane moaned.

"Now don't blame yourself," the nurse said. "We'll get Pinkney through this. But you'll want to keep him isolated and yourself too."

She turned to look at Corrie. "Have you had close contact with him since his fever developed?"

"No, Delight and I have been so busy with cleaning neither of us have held him or fed him."

"Then we'll hope no one here but Jane has been exposed." She turned to the worried mother. "Watch yourself for any symptoms and wash your hands thoroughly after caring for Pink."

"Should we move out of the boarding house? The students will arrive soon."

"No, I don't want to move him. The Worcesters have built a nice big house. I will ask if the boarders can stay with them until Pink is well. Delight can help Ann."

"I can help Ann too," Corrie stated. "Or stay and help Jane."

"Why don't you help Jane, dear," Mrs. Sanders decided. "You can fetch their meals so Jane doesn't have to get out."

Corrie nodded and Jane sent her a look of gratitude. Mrs. Sanders left, saying she would ask Cook to prepare some hot broth for Pink.

"Can I do anything for you, Jane?"

The mother shook her head, worry clouding her eyes. "Chilly will be here any day and he will be angry. I do not know if we should try to travel now, but we cannot ask everyone else to wait on us."

"You don't think they could wait a couple of weeks?"

"It is important to travel at this time of year because of the water levels on the rivers."

"Of course, I forgot," Corrie could understand why Jane was so upset. "But you said there would be two groups traveling west. Can you go with the second group?"

"Yes, I suppose," Jane sighed. "Do you think the mission will let me stay?"

"There is plenty of work to go around. To be honest I don't think Delight was looking forward to being a housemother. She would rather help Cook with the baking and such."

Jane nodded then looked down at her sleeping son. "Chilly may insist that we go anyway. I cannot know what he will decide."

"Surely he won't wish to expose others to the measles."

"I cannot say what Chilly will want."

It was two days later when Jane's brother arrived at the mission. He had left the wagon train on its way to Alabama where they would be joined by a few other Creeks from that section of Creek Nation to go west. They were to board a steamboat on the Tennessee River.

Corrie greeted Chilly at the door and explained briefly that Pink was sick. She could not read any reaction on the man's face. He didn't seem like an unkind man, but he did seem stoic and stern.

Jane heard their voices and came downstairs.

Chilly spoke to her in *Muskoke*. "You are not ready to go?"

"We are packed," Jane said. "But I do not think we should leave now. Pinkney is very sick."

"How sick?"

"Come see for yourself." Jane waved for him to follow her upstairs. Together they stood at the foot of the boy's bed. Chilly questioned him and Pink responded in a frail voice. He was clearly quite ill and miserable from the itching rash. The chamomile mixture Mrs. Sanders had sent over offered only slight relief.

Chilly looked hard at the boy then turned to his sister. "You do not wish to go now?"

"The decision is yours, brother. You are his uncle."

In Creek culture the maternal uncle of a child, especially a boy, had more say in the upbringing of that child than anyone.

"This disease can spread to others?"

"Yes, Mrs. Sanders says it can."

Chilly nodded and looked unhappy at this news. "You will stay for now," he said. "I will come back for you. But it may be many moons before you will see me again."

"I know. I am sorry."

Chilly turned to go back downstairs where Corrie waited on the settee by the fireplace. Jane trailed behind him and they stood in the door of the house for a time, talking in low serious tones. Then her brother walked to his wagon. Jane stood at the door, watching him drive away, tears streaming down her face.

CHAPTER TWENTY

New Echota Mission
Fall, 1827

"Come along, girls," Corrie told her young students as they walked to the kitchen. "Don't dawdle. Cook is waiting for us."

"What is dawdle, Miss Tuttle?" Sookey Martin asked.

"It means to walk slowly," their housemother explained. "Which is what you girls are doing."

"Like Pink?"

"Pink is slow because he tires easily. He's still recovering from the measles," Corrie reminded them. "But you don't have that excuse. Don't you want to learn how to bake bread? You'll get to eat what you make."

"That is what we fear," Macie said, her face dead-pan serious.

Corrie laughed. Macie had already perfected the ability to tell a joke with a deceptively straight face.

"Oh, it won't be that bad," Corrie said, unable to master the same expression.

"Can we have peach jam with our bread?" Sookey now wanted to know.

"I think Cook will let you enjoy some. If you listen carefully to her instructions. Right, girls?"

The five students nodded and picked up their pace on their walk to the kitchen.

Corrie planned to use the time while the girls were practicing their baking to pen a letter bound for home. She had confided some of her worries about Mr. Ackley to her mother and Julia Tuttle had asked for more details.

Corrie hardly knew what to tell her. She had been so charmed by the man with his chivalrous manners and dark green eyes. Her interest in him had been more than a passing fancy. She had truly hoped something serious would develop between them. But she had grown to doubt that Mr. Ackley had ever felt anything but a passing fancy toward her.

As she stepped out of the kitchen, she almost ran into Lem Starr who was stacking firewood by the door.

"Hello, Mr. Starr," she greeted him knowing she would get a smile from Lem. He seemed perpetually happy and lacked any artifice.

"*Siyo*, Miss T." Lem had never been able to pronounce Cornelia's name, either first or last and so she had told him to call her Miss T. With his Cherokee accent it sounded like Miss D.

"How are you on this fine fall day?"

"Me good," he replied. "I got me a big buck hunting last week. Tom going to dress it out for me. Good eating." He rubbed his stomach and grinned even bigger.

"That will be nice," Corrie smiled. "You like venison?"

"Venison good," the older man nodded. "Hunting good too. Plenty big bucks in the woods."

Corrie knew many men in the community had been hunting over the past few weeks and comments after church told her that the venison harvest would be abundant this year. She couldn't claim to enjoy the gamey meat as well as her friends, but she was glad that there would be plenty of meat to fill the smokehouses found on every farm.

"Did Tom take you hunting?" Tom was Lem's young cousin, the son of James Starr who was a member of the National Council.

"No, I go alone. I know the game trails myself."

"I'm sure you do. You know your way through all the woods around here, don't you?"

"Yes." The man had finished piling the kindling in a neat stack and now fumbled into his coat pockets.

"I found something," he explained as he took out a small rough rock about the size of a pea and held it out on his palm for Corrie to see.

She lifted the rock and found it surprisingly heavy. Facets of the stone seemed to glisten in the autumn sun. "That's a pretty rock," she said, handing it back to him.

"You can have it," Lem offered with a shy smile. "I know there is some more like it."

"Why, how sweet of you," Corrie said. "*Wado*. Thank you!"

She was about to slip the gift into a pocket when a familiar voice behind her gave her a start. She turned to see Oliver standing a few feet away. Beyond him at the corral fence, his smart black carriage and two horses waited. Corrie had been so absorbed in her conversation with Lem that she had failed to notice Mr. Ackley's arrival. He had not sent a note to tell her he planned to visit.

"Rocks for gifts," Oliver stated flatly, clearly indicating what he thought of such a thing.

"A thoughtful gift," Corrie replied holding it up briefly to admire before dropping it into her apron pocket. She didn't see the look of surprise that now filled Oliver's eyes. He quickly masked it with a smile.

"I realize you didn't expect a call from me today," he said. "But I was in the area and wondered if we might enjoy a walk on this lovely day."

Corrie turned to speak to Lem but the older man was already shuffling away from her, shaking his head as if dismissing something unpleasant. Both Corrie and Oliver watched him for a moment. Oliver had a speculative look on his face, and his green eyes were narrowed. But he quickly smiled when Corrie turned back toward him.

"I suppose a walk would be nice," she said.

Oliver offered his arm and Corrie slipped her hand through it. She noticed the young man made no effort to draw her close to him in the way that Edmund . . . in the way that some young suitors might have. She sighed and they began their stroll, side by side but seeming miles apart.

As they approached the print shop at the west end of the mission compound, Corrie saw Elias step out the door and into their path. The couple stopped and waited for Elias to reach them, then Corrie made introductions. She wondered if Elias would remember the encounter with Oliver in Chattanooga. Remembering that Oliver had always refused her invitations to visit Elias and Harriet became one more reason to doubt this man.

Clearly both men remembered the earlier exchange between them. They eyed each other like two fighters in a boxing ring.

"This is the Mr. Ackley you have been seeing for the last year?" Elias asked Corrie.

"Yes." Corrie felt defensive and didn't know why. She could spend time with whomever she chose. "I told you and Harriet about Mr. Ackley."

"You failed to say we had met before." Elias's words seemed cold but his gaze was directed toward Oliver and not Corrie. He seemed to be sizing up the impeccably dressed man. "May I ask you, sir, what your intentions are toward Miss Tuttle?"

The question surprised Corrie but after the initial shock, she actually felt relief. It was a question she had longed to ask but had feared looking like a coquette trying to secure a proposal.

"I don't believe that is any of your business," Oliver replied, his tone as cool as Boudinot's had been.

"Miss Tuttle is a friend of mine and she is a like a sister to my wife. I only ask out of concern." Here Elias sent an apologetic look to Corrie. "I do not want to see her ill used."

Oliver seemed to bristle at the suggestion that he was using Corrie and his jaw hardened. To admit that he was in fact using her to influence this very individual was something he would never do. But he was not going to be backed into declaring a commitment to a more personal relationship.

"I met Miss Tuttle in Cornwall. When I learned she was working here I hoped to offer her friendship knowing she was a long way from home and living in less than desirable circumstances. I thought a diversion now and then would be welcomed. I meant no harm and have never behaved in an ungentlemanly fashion. Have I?" He turned to Corrie for agreement.

"You have always been a gentleman," Corrie murmured. In her head she added *and nothing more.*

It was a moment of revelation for her. Oliver had no intentions of being anything other than a friend offering diversions for her "undesirable circumstances." And she, Cornelia Elizabeth Tuttle, had been a fool! She was so angry at that moment she could have chewed lead and spit bullets. But she didn't know who she was most angry with – Elias, Oliver or herself.

Elias saw the flash of anger in her eyes. "Would you like me to walk you to your door, Corrie?" he asked quietly.

"I can see Miss Tuttle home," Oliver stated coldly.

"I'm fine, Elias," Corrie said. She didn't want him to see her home and see just how upset she was. "I think I would like to return home now, Oliver."

"Of course."

The two adversaries exchanged a last malevolent look then Oliver hurried to catch up to Corrie who was already walking purposefully toward the cottage.

"I'm sorry if I upset you," Oliver hastened to say when he reached her.

Corrie was about to relent in her anger and accept his apology. Oliver always seemed so sincere when he expressed regret. But he wasn't finished speaking.

"I think your 'friend' presumes a great deal in thinking he needs to question me. That is the trouble with these Cherokees. They always presume upon the good graces of the citizens of Georgia and Tennessee."

"Your good graces?" Corrie stopped and turned to look at the man. She could feel her face growing warm in anger again.

"We have been infinitely patient with these people. We are growing tired of seeing the economy of our noble southern states held hostage to their waste of our land." Oliver seemed to be warming to his argument as well.

"It is their land!"

"Yet they do next to nothing with it," Oliver countered. "Oh, a few mixed bloods have attempted some sort of enterprise, but most are content with a cabin and a corn patch."

"The Cherokees and Creeks live according to their ancient traditions. That is their right."

"Their right? They hold millions of acres of land and it has no economic value whatsoever. Abundant timber could be harvested and milled. Rich river bottom land could produce cotton and tobacco. It would double the southern economy."

"It would give *you* more land," Corrie said, suddenly seeing what Oliver's intent had been all along.

"It would give the South more land." Oliver seemed determined to justify his actions. "Don't you see? We don't merely want it; we need it if we are to retain an equal economic footing with the northern states."

"So this is about slavery?"

"It isn't about slavery; it's about survival. Soon enough people here will grow tired of watching the land wasted; they will demand that the Indians give it to those of us who will turn it to good economic use. If the Cherokees leave now they will get a good price for their land, but if they wait . . ." His words seemed to hold a threat.

"And you want me to try to convince them of this?"

"You would be doing them a great service."

"I don't think so, Mr. Ackley. It isn't my place to tell them what to do, even if I agreed with you."

"But they . . ."

Corrie held up her hand for silence. "I don't think you need to call on me again. Goodbye, Mr. Ackley."

She turned onto the path that led to the cottage door, angry with Oliver and herself. Mostly she was angry that hot tears now filled her eyes and threatened to spill down her cheeks. She would not let him see her cry.

Corrie hurried inside and practically ran to her little bedroom; her only sanctuary is this crowded busy place. At that moment she wished she had never come to New Echota Mission.

Oliver stared at the closed door for a few moments, his anger visible on his face. Then another thought seemed to enter his mind and he turned quickly to retrace his steps to his carriage.

Starting the horses with a snap of his whip, he steered them toward the road to town. It was the road that Lem Starr had taken in his slow, awkward gait. Ackley caught up with the man before he entered the little village of New Echota.

"Would you like a ride?" he called while he slowed his horses to keep pace with the simple man.

Lem stopped to look up and Oliver halted the carriage. The older man looked frightened; he clearly didn't care for strangers having been treated poorly by some in the past.

"No," he said, shaking his head. "I walk just fine."

"I can take you anywhere you want to go."

"You take me to Tom's?"

"Yes," Oliver said, having no idea how far this Tom's place might be. "Get in."

Still Lem hesitated so Oliver set the brake and stepped down then took Lem's arm none too gently and pushed the old fellow onto the leather seat. He hurried around to enter the carriage himself and set the horses in motion.

"Where does Tom live?"

Lem pointed forward, "Down this road."

Oliver visibly controlled his temper. This day had not gone at all well, but perhaps this old man could turn things for the better.

"I saw you gave Miss Tuttle a gift," he said, keeping his voice quiet. "That was nice of you."

"You mean Miss T?"

"Yes, Miss T. Where did you find that rock? It was very pretty and I would like to give my sister a stone like that."

"I found it."

"*Where* did you find it?"

"In the woods." Lem gestured to the northeast toward the mountains. Oliver sighed. The man could probably never find his way back to that location.

"Were there any more pretty rocks there?"

"Yes. Some."

"Could you show me where they are?"

Lem shook his head firmly. "No."

Oliver barely suppressed a growl. "Could you *tell* me where they are?"

"I was tracking a deer . . . big buck . . . ten points. Tom is going to give me them antlers."

"Yes, yes, yes. Where was the deer?"

Lem screwed up his face as if trying to recall. Oliver waited nearly holding his breath.

"Holly Creek."

"Holly Creek," Oliver repeated. "I think I know where that is. You're sure that was where you saw the pretty rocks?"

"Maybe so."

Oliver grimaced, but kept his temper. He didn't need to alienate the man or call attention to the fact that he was giving a Cherokee a ride in his carriage.

"How much further to Tom's house?"

"Down the road."

They continued east through town while Oliver tried to get the man to give him more specific clues as to the whereabouts of his find. But Lem could be no more specific than the fact that it was along a game trail. After what seemed like a very long time, he pointed to a log cabin.

"That is Tom's house."

Oliver immediately pulled the horses to a stop. "Let's keep the pretty rocks a secret, shall we?" he proposed to the man as he carefully climbed down.

"A secret?"

"Yes, you like secrets, don't you?"

"No." More emphatic shaking of his head.

"Oh, forget it then." Oliver could not suppress his growl this time.

"I can do that," Lem grinned. "Tom says I am good at forgetting."

"Good. Then let's forget that you and I ever spoke."

"Alright."

Lem grinned again then shuffled toward the cabin and Oliver wasted no time turning the carriage around and heading back toward the federal road that would take him to Chattanooga and then home. He eased back on the seat and gave the horses their head, his eyes roaming over the mountains that rose to the east.

"Gold," he mused aloud causing the horses to prick up their ears. "And more than just a few flakes. They've been mining gold for a couple of years in North Carolina. Why shouldn't there be more in Georgia and Tennessee – most of it in Cherokee lands."

He threw a backward glance toward New Echota and tightened his grip on the reins. "Just one more reason for them to move, Miss Tuttle. With or without a word from you."

"Well, what do you think?" Elias asked the group of friends who had gathered at one of the tables in the dining hall at the mission. They had just completed a Christmas meal together following a special service at the chapel.

Ann Worcester held up one of the pages of newsprint that Elias had spread on the table after Delight and Corrie had cleared away the dishes. Delight had stayed in the kitchen to help Cook clean up but had insisted that Corrie return to visit with her friends.

"It looks wonderful to me," Ann said of this rough edition of the *Cherokee Phoenix*. "What are you dissatisfied with?" She turned to her husband with a quirk of her eyebrow.

"It's very difficult to get the column lengths correct," Samuel replied. "Translations of an article from Cherokee into English or English into Cherokee doesn't take the same amount of space. We have struggled with it for quite some time."

"This isn't a problem if we are printing in only one language at a time," Elias explained. "But to print both in a single publication is proving to be a challenge."

"I think people will understand that challenge," Harriet offered. "Don't you, Corrie?" She seemed to be trying to draw her quiet friend into the conversation. Corrie had barely spoken two words during the entire meal.

"Yes, I'm sure they will," Corrie said with little interest or emotion.

The young woman saw the look of concern that passed between Harriet and Jane, but she couldn't muster up any enthusiasm. She had been in a depressed mood since she had sent Mr. Ackley packing and no amount of cajoling from her friends had lifted her spirits.

Secretly she was considering returning home at the end of the school year. She loved the students she cared for, but overall her time at the mission seemed a failure. She felt like she was a failure and now wondered what she had been thinking to come here.

Jane was peering over Ann's shoulder to get a view of the newspaper. "What have you written about?" she asked Elias. The Creek woman was fortunate that her father had provided her with a good education. She could read English and had learned to read Cherokee while working at the mission.

"Front page is about the Tennessee governor's election," he said. "Sam Houston will replace William Carroll when he is inaugurated next month. There is also a report on the first session of our legislature."

"This is so exciting," Ann said. She well knew how long Elias and Samuel had worked on developing the template for their newspaper. "When will a first edition come out?"

"Should be within a month or so," Worcester answered. "We're getting very close."

"We'll have to hold some type of celebration when it's printed," Harriet said. "And you must send it to Chief Jolly and Edmund. This will be another way to keep everyone connected."

"We owe a debt to Sequoyah for giving us our own written language," Elias agreed. "Without it the distance might have separated us completely."

"Speaking of that," Harriet interrupted. "Have you heard from your family, Jane? Have they arrived in Arkansas yet?"

"I received a letter from my aunt Muskogee. She posted it at Memphis," Jane answered. "She says there are nearly 800 of them making the journey. They are traveling on a steamboat pulling two keelboats behind it loaded with their baggage. It makes the journey very slow. She says there has been much sickness and everyone is tired but glad that they are halfway there."

"I can't imagine 800 people being crammed into one boat," Ann said. "How difficult it must be. And sickness would certainly spread easily in such crowded conditions."

"That is what I fear and Muskogee does as well."

"Were they joined by others in Alabama?" Samuel asked. "I hear some of the Baptist missionaries working there have decided to also move west and are urging their congregations to go as well."

"Yes, Muskogee says they visited with the leaders in Alabama and they told their people if they wanted to go, they would part in peace. In fact, Uncle Roley smoked the pipe with Yahola while they were at Wewoka."

"So they left on good terms?" Elias asked.

"I believe so." Jane said no more and Corrie could understand why. It must have taken a determined effort for her uncle to smoke the peace pipe with the men who had condemned his brother – Jane's father – to death. Not to mention that he and Chilly and Jane's husband had also been found guilty of treason and sentenced to die.

"John has dealt with Yahola and Big Warrior. He says they came to regret their hasty actions. It created a lot of fear and animosity not only among their own people, but among outsiders as well."

Everyone at the table was quiet after Elias spoke. Those regrets came too late for Jane and her family.

"Do you know when your brother expects to return for you?" Ann asked after a moment.

"It will likely be next fall before he can get back. He will want to get his family settled, some type of housing built and the first crops planted."

"That is life on the frontier," Samuel mused. "Be assured, Jane, that we are all praying for your family. And praying that you will be able to join them soon."

"*Mvto*. I thank you."

The conversation then turned to other things including plans for the return of the students after the Christmas break. Corrie heard little of it as she stared out the dining room window. She just couldn't bring herself to care about anything. She hated feeling sorry for herself. She had only to look at Jane to know that her circumstances could be much worse. But it didn't help. She felt so weary of life that she couldn't even cry anymore.

Harriet had tried to console her when she had confided to her friend about ending her relationship with Oliver, but it helped very little. Corrie knew that Harriet hadn't been truly sorry that she would no longer be seeing the man from Tennessee.

She tried to smile when the group stood to pull on their winter wraps and gather up children to return to their homes. She saw the worry in Harriet's eyes and whispered, "I'm alright," when her friend hugged her.

"Are you?"

"Yes. I will be. Don't worry about me."

"But I do worry, Corrie. I want you to be happy and I know you're not."

"You can't fix this, Harriet. Nothing but time will."

"Will you come to supper on Friday? Before classes start again."

"Yes. I'll be there."

"We'll come and get you. It's too cool for you to walk."

"I'll be ready."

"Then I'll see you on Friday."

Her friend reached down and picked up Eleanor and the little girl with dark hair and eyes threw a kiss to "Aunt Corrie." This was the only thing to bring a genuine smile to the housemother's face.

The Boudinots parted from the Worcesters at the hitching post by the chapel. Elias helped Harriet into their buggy then lifted Eleanor to sit on her mother's lap. As they drove home, Harriet said with resolve, "We have to help Corrie."

"Why?" Elias asked. "Is something wrong?"

"Are you blind?"

"No." Elias said and looked surprised when Harriet huffed. "What?"

"She's miserable," Harriet explained while rolling her eyes. "She broke up with that Oliver Ackley and now she's simply miserable."

"Good riddance to him, I say."

"I feel the same way, but don't you dare say that to Corrie."

"Why is she miserable? She should be glad to be rid of him. It was clear to me that he hates Indians and I only met him twice."

"Love isn't logical, Elias."

"She didn't love him, did she?"

"I don't know. I don't think she really did. But I think she hoped for love. And I want that for her. We have to get her and Edmund back together."

"Uh, that's going to be a little difficult," Elias stated emphatically. "He's a thousand miles away."

"But it's not impossible," Harriet countered, looking thoughtful. "I'm going to write to Bettie and tell her what's going on here. I think she'll know what to do."

"Well, leave me out of it," Elias said. "You women take care of it. I just want to be able to print a newspaper in two languages."

CHAPTER TWENTY-ONE

Allenton Manor, Tennessee
January, 1828

Oliver followed Daphne and Jason up the wide sweeping staircase in the Allen plantation home east of Nashville. A narrower but no less opulent set of stairs then continued to the third floor ballroom. Here two massive crystal chandeliers sparkled with candlelight and illuminated the couples who gathered beneath them in the first social event of the year.

This was the first of three inaugural balls being offered for Sam Houston, Tennessee's new governor. The Ackleys had been invited by the John Allen family due to their military connection to both Houston and his mentor General Jackson. Most of Nashville's elite were present as well as all the area planters.

On Oliver's arm, Dolly fairly quivered with excitement. Now seventeen, her parents had deemed her old enough to attend the event. Daphne had several potential young suitors in mind for her sister. She also planned to introduce Oliver to a few eligible ladies.

As they entered the ballroom, Daphne leaned close to Oliver and nodded toward a dark-haired beauty across the room. "See, there is Millicent Longstreet. She'd be perfect for you, Oliver. Her father owns nearly every acre south of Murfreesboro. Now that you're free of that servant girl in Georgia, you need to consider your options."

"I hardly have time to court anyone, Daphne," Oliver countered. "Father keeps me on the road half the year looking out for his interests."

"Well, his interests need to include finding you a suitable wife."

Dolly stuck out her bottom lip in a pretty pout. "I think Miss Tuttle was perfectly suitable," she interjected. "She was very sweet."

Daphne gave her sister a patronizing smile. "I'm sure she was, dear. Now come with me. I want you to meet someone." She guided the girl toward a group near the windows while giving Oliver another nod toward Millicent.

Oliver seemed in no hurry to do his sister's bidding. His eyes were on another young woman in the center of the room. "I see John Allen," he said to Jason. "Is that his family with him?"

"Yes, his wife is one of the Lynches and that's Eliza, the sacrificial lamb."

Oliver smiled at Jason's sardonic tone.

"She's pretty."

"Don't get interested in Eliza, Oliver. She's off limits and everyone here knows it even if a formal engagement hasn't been announced yet."

"I understand. But where is the man of the hour? I don't see Houston."

Jason looked around. "He's at the back," he said with a nod toward the other end of the room. Oliver caught a glimpse of the new governor and the shock of white hair that identified his friend Andrew Jackson. Also in their group were other Tennessee politicians and men of means.

"Come, I'll introduce you to some of my colleagues." Jason led Oliver toward the refreshment table where a group of men stood. Jason practiced law in Nashville, an occupation Houston had engaged in before entering politics.

Oliver stood at the fringe of the group listening to them talk shop, but offering few comments himself. He was out of sorts and had been since Miss Tuttle had so handily dismissed him. Two excursions to the Smokies trying to locate a game trail on Holly Creek had so far yielded nothing except a couple of close encounters with Cherokee hunters wielding muskets.

Out of the corner of his eye, the young man kept watch on Eliza Allen. He could recall having met her a few years ago when she still wore her skirts short and her hair long. Now she looked the part of a future governor's wife in an off-the-shoulder gown and piles of curls atop her head. She clearly was trying to look older than her seventeen years. Oliver wanted a chance to speak to her.

He saw the opportunity after the center of the floor had been cleared for dancing and a small chamber ensemble began to play. Eliza stood to the side of the room visiting with Miss Longstreet so Oliver wove his way around the edge of the dance floor toward the two young women.

He knew Daphne was pleased to see him approaching Millicent, but she was probably shocked when Oliver led Eliza out onto the dance floor. The young woman had received few invitations to dance this evening as if most of the men in the room had received the message that she was off limits. If the governor had been paying any attention at all to her, Oliver might have refrained as well. But Houston had his back to the dance floor and seemed engaged in a rigorous debate with his fellow politicians.

"I don't know if you remember me, Miss Allen," Oliver began as they moved onto the parquet floor. "I'm Oliver Ackley; we met a few years ago."

"I think I recall. You're Daphne Edwards' brother, aren't you?"

"Yes, that's right."

They chatted for a while about the weather and the excellent music provided by the chamber group while they kept the three-quarter time of a waltz.

"I hope I'm not speaking out of turn," Oliver finally said, "but I understand that congratulations are in order for you. Or should I say for our esteemed governor? He's the lucky one."

A pretty blush pinked Eliza's cheeks. "Thank you," she murmured not seeming particularly thrilled at the reason for his congratulations.

"I must say I think you are very brave."

"Brave? Why?" Eliza looked puzzled.

Oliver lowered his voice as if sharing a confidence. "I know it is the desire of most women to have children. To give that up must take a great deal of grace and courage."

"What do you mean?"

"You know my brother served with Houston at Horseshoe Bend. Surely you know the governor was badly injured there?"

"Yes, I had heard that."

"His injury left him incapable of . . ." Oliver let his voice trail off as understanding caused Eliza's cheeks to flame bright red. Oliver said no more. He really had no idea if his implication was true though that was the crude rumor he had heard at a public house in Lynchburg.

The young woman now blinked back tears as the dance came to an end. Oliver walked her back to the edge of the floor.

"Please forgive me for speaking out of turn," he said, sincerity in his voice, but not in his eyes. "It was not my place and completely inappropriate. I hope I haven't upset you."

"No," Eliza said with a false smile. "Your concern is unwarranted."

"I'm glad to hear that." Oliver gave a bow and then walked away to find Millicent Longstreet. As he danced with this young woman he saw Eliza hastily leave the room and a satisfied smile crossed his face. This was turning out to be a very good evening indeed. A whisper was better than a shout when planting seeds of doubt.

"I doubt that Walter will be home before summer," Edmund said in response to Old Blair's question about his brother's visit to Washington. "These negotiations always seem to drag on for months – many moons."

"Hope he not give away the store," the older man cackled around missing front teeth.

"So do I," Edmund laughed with him. "That would put me out of a job."

"You have good work to do at mission," Old Blair said. "I see new mission is 'bout finished."

"I need to ride over to Mulberry and see how Mr. Hitchcock is coming. You are right; I think the school is about complete."

"When new preacher come?"

"The Palmers won't come until school ends at Union Mission. Three moons from now."

Old Blair nodded as he pulled his coat fashioned from a trade blanket closer around his thin shoulders. The two men were sitting in rockers by the stove at the trading post, passing the time since no customers had come in all afternoon. "Weather sure be cold now."

"Yes," the young clerk agreed. "The snow has not had a chance to melt."

"Jesse Chisholm been to Pine Bluff. Says the Creeks are there. Three boats full of them and their stuff."

"I saw that in the *Gazette,*" Edmund confirmed. "They should arrive at Three Forks in another few weeks. Might stop here for a time."

"Cold time to travel. Many sick, he says."

"There has been a lot of sickness along the river. I hope the snow melts and raises the river levels so the steamboat can get over the falls."

So far, no paddle wheeler had ever made it past the falls on the Arkansas just above its juncture with the Illinois River. If the steamer carrying the Creeks couldn't make it over the tumbling water, the emigrants would probably have to walk the last forty miles to their new lands. Mules would be hired to pull the keelboats over the riffles and on upstream to the trade community where the Creek Agency was located.

Their conversation soon melted into a comfortable silence and after a few more moments Old Blair was asleep. His head dropped forward and his turban slipped askew over one eye. Edmund smiled at the elder's gentle snores then rose quietly to stand at the front counter and resume reading the *Arkansas Gazette*. He hoped there might be some news of their delegates in Washington City and a hint of how the negotiations were going.

Walter had attended treaty negotiations before but this was his first time to travel to the capital as an elected chief. He warned Edmund and Bettie before he boarded a steamboat that he and the other delegates would likely be gone for the better part of a year. According to Walter, the government negotiators always insisted that the Cherokees get to Washington as soon as possible, but then took their time in meeting with them after they arrived.

"They think if they make us wait, we will grow impatient and agree to everything they demand from us. They think we need to get back home to take care of our farms. They do not know that we Cherokees look out for one another and no one's farm is neglected. No one can wait more patiently than an Indian. We do not get in a hurry."

Edmund knew the truth of Walter's words. Most Indians had no use for clocks or calendars. Keeping to an hourly schedule had been one of the hardest adjustments for him while attending school in Cornwall.

He had just finished the newspaper and was pouring himself a cup of coffee at the stove when Bettie and Patsy Blair stepped into the store.

"Here he is," the elder's daughter-in-law said when she saw him asleep in the rocker. "I spend half my time looking for him."

"You should start here first," Edmund teased.

"I should," the woman said. "But you would be surprised at how many rocking chairs this old man is comfortable in around here."

"No, I wouldn't," Edmund laughed and the women joined him.

Patsy gently shook the man awake and helped him rise. "Supper is ready, Father. Time to go."

Bettie held the door open for them and watched as they took the trail north to their home. The Blairs were keeping an eye on Sequoyah's farm while he was in Washington. She pulled the door tightly closed against the winter chill.

"Did you bring mail from Dwight?" she asked.

Edmund nodded toward the back office. "It is on the desk."

Bettie walked to the back of the store. "Light a lantern," she called. "It is getting dark."

He lit a slim piece of kindling at the stove and touched it to the wicks of the candles in two lanterns. Bettie returned with a letter from Georgia and settled in one of the rockers to read it by the lamplight. Edmund stood at the counter with his coffee and watched the lengthening shadows through the six-paned window.

As his sister-in-law perused the letter, Edmund noticed that she kept glancing up at him. It made him curious about its contents. Finally she folded the pages and returned them to their envelope.

She sat quietly for a moment just looking at him and it made him feel self-conscious.

"Anything wrong?" he finally asked.

"Harriet sends her regards."

"That is nice. She is well? And Elias and Eleanor?"

"They are well. But Harriet is worried about her friend Cornelia."

"Cornelia?"

"Yes, you remember her?"

"Of course. I remember Cornelia." Edmund kept his eyes on the window. "Why is Harriet worried about her?"

"She has been hurt."

Edmund nearly choked on a sip of coffee. "Hurt? How?"

"By some white man."

"You mean physically hurt?" He set down his cup and looked ready to charge out the door.

"No," Bettie shook her head and patted her chest. "She has been heart hurt."

Varying emotions played across the young man's face as he stared at Bettie. He tried to look indifferent but didn't succeed. "What happened?"

"They were courting, Harriet says. Long time. But Corrie told him to go. Now she is sad."

"So she ended it?"

"Yes."

"Then why is she sad?"

Bettie gave him a look that told him she thought he was being a stupid man. "She has lost hope. You know what that is like."

Edmund turned to look out the window again. The only sound for a long moment was the crackle of the fire in the stove.

"You should write to her."

"Me?" Edmund sounded incredulous. "Why?"

"She needs a friend."

"She does not want to hear from me. She would not write back."

Bettie shrugged. "The letter would not be for you; it would be for her."

"So I am supposed to write to her knowing she will probably not respond?"

"Yes."

Edmund shook his head and took another sip of coffee, not looking at his sister-in-law. It was a crazy idea. He would not do it.

"Send it to the New Echota Mission," Bettie said, ignoring his unspoken refusal. Then she rose and walked to the back office leaving him to argue with himself until time to close the store.

Corrie set plates filled with crumbled cornbread covered with sausage gravy in front of Sookey and Sehoya then went to the dining room sideboard to pour cups of milk for the other boarders. The group of students was seated near the fireplace for the February morning was cold.

She was dishing up a plate for herself when the door opened and the Worcesters entered the hall followed by Elias and Harriet. She was surprised to see Harriet. Elias sometimes ate breakfast at the mission if he got an early start at the print office, but Harriet and Eleanor normally were at home on the farm. She wondered what the occasion was that had brought them here for breakfast. Then she noticed the stacks of newsprint in the two men's hands.

"Hear ye! Hear ye!" Samuel called out as he held up a newspaper for everyone to see. Corrie read the large banner heading: *Cherokee Phoenix*.

"First edition?" Rev. Sanders asked. "You finally have it printed."

"Finally," Elias said. "Volume one is dedicated to Pathkiller and Charles Hicks."

The staff applauded, sharing the two men's excitement. Then they gathered around the printer and editor to get copies of the *Phoenix*. Harriet and Ann dished up plates of the bread and gravy for themselves and their husbands then found seats at the long tables and began to feed their little girls.

Corrie brought her copy of the newspaper and joined her friends. "You must be very pleased."

"Yes," Ann agreed. "Now we might see our husbands once in a while."

The housemother looked over the newspaper. She had been at New Echota long enough to be able to read and speak Cherokee. She saw Elias listed as editor and a byline for John Ridge. A message from Chief Hicks was also on the front page.

"Will it be a weekly paper?" she asked as the men joined them at the table.

"A monthly at first," Elias answered. "Then in time we hope it will become a bi-weekly. We have to cover a large area with readers in three or four states."

"At the very least," Samuel added.

"John and Sarah have invited us all to Running Waters for a celebration. It will be this coming Saturday," Harriet told her friend. "You're invited too, Corrie."

Corrie shook her head. "I don't think I will be able to make it."

She could tell that Harriet wanted to urge her to come, but decided against it with a sigh.

"Perhaps we can have dinner for everyone at our house soon," she offered instead.

"I don't know if I can get away from the mission," Corrie responded but when she saw concern in everyone's eyes, she added, "but I'll see."

She rose then to help the girls wipe their hands and faces and then put on their coats for the walk to their classroom. Miss Nash frowned on tardiness so she didn't want them lingering too long over breakfast.

As they prepared to exit the dining room, Corrie took up her own coat and hurriedly pulled it on so she could walk with them to class. She needed some fresh air even if it was frosty cold. She took the long way getting back to the dining room, hoping to avoid more well-meaning efforts by her friends to help her "get over it."

When she returned, she found most everyone had left the dining hall. She discovered a stack of mail addressed to her sitting on top of the newspaper she had been reading. Mail was often distributed during mealtime but she wouldn't take time to read it now. She slipped the envelopes into one pocket of her coat and folded the *Phoenix* so that it would fit in another pocket. Then she went to help clean up the breakfast dishes in the kitchen.

After helping chop vegetables for soup, Corrie donned her coat again and walked with Jane back to the cottage. She went to her bedroom and pulled her reading material from her pockets and placed it all on her bedside table. Then she fixed herself a cup of tea and pulled her long braid down from its knot, thinking she might take a little nap after reading her mail.

She was still feeling a little frustrated with Harriet, her sister-friend who seemed determined to help her move on from her disappointment with Oliver. *I know she means well*, she thought as she fingered through the letters in her lap.

Corrie wanted to move on, she really did. She was tired of feeling tired. She didn't want to wallow in self pity, didn't want pity from others, didn't want . . . .

Her fingers stilled when she reached the last envelope even as her heart pounded in her chest. This envelope, addressed to Miss Cornelia Tuttle, was written in a hand she still recognized after three years. She stared at it for the longest moment, following the florid, looping letters of her name.

"Edmund," she whispered. Her fingers were shaking so badly she could barely pull up the wax that held the flap in place.

Why had he written? She quickly reached into the plain brown envelope to pull out a single sheet of paper. She was about to unfold it when a thought entered her mind. Had Harriet put him up to this? Had she written to him to tell of her failed romance? How humiliating. Was this to be one more expression of pity and concern?

She frowned at the thought, not sure now if she wanted to read this missive. She held it unfolded for another long moment as if gathering courage to face what it held. Finally she opened it and read the salutation: My dearest Corrie.

It was the way he had begun every one of his letters to her. All of them were still tucked away in the bottom of her trunk and tied into a bundle with the ribbon from the bouquet she had caught at Sarah's wedding.

Edmund had grinned at her blush when she caught it and whispered to her that her new name would be Girl who Fights for Flowers. She had hit him with that bouquet and acted miffed, but she had kept the ribbon. She had forgotten all about that . . . until now.

Corrie took a deep breath and began to read. The letter was a casual telling of news from his home. He had built a cabin in a clearing below a hill that overlooked the river. Dwight Mission was doing well, so well in fact that they were beginning a new mission in the Mulberry community. He thought they might have to build a larger school at Dwight but they were waiting to learn the outcome of a new treaty his brother was working on in Washington City. He had heard that the Creeks had arrived at Pine Bluff and were expected to reach the bayou before long.

The letter was friendly, but rather impersonal. No mention of her recent embarrassment; no expressions of sympathy or concern. For that she was grateful.

She reached the end of the letter and saw a black splotch as if the pen had lingered over the paper long enough for a drop of ink to fall between the closing words "Your" and "devoted friend."

Friend. Is that all she was to every man she had ever cared for? The word hurt. She was about to wad the paper and toss it into a corner when she caught sight of a post script.

"Please write back."

Those three words were like a knife to her heart and in that moment she understood something she had never fully realized. She had hurt Edmund, hurt him deeply. It must have taken a great deal of forgiveness for him to write this letter and risk being hurt again.

She didn't know what she would write, but she decided then and there that as soon as her heart stopped pounding and her hands stopped shaking, she would write him back.

CHAPTER TWENTY-TWO

Illinois Bayou
February, 1828

Edmund heard the whistle of a steamboat as he was moving a stack of buffalo hides closer to the front of the store. He paused in his work, annoyed with himself that the sound created a spark of hope in his brain. It was only two weeks since he had written to Cornelia. She would barely have had time to receive it and certainly there was not time for a letter to have come from her. So he told himself to ignore the whistle and keep working.

Shortly Price Jolly entered the store with his cousin Tsiana. A recent widow, the attractive young woman was back at Dardanelle following a period of mourning at her parents' home near Fort Gibson. Her late husband, David Gentry, had owned a large plantation east of Mrs. Lovely's place and Edmund knew Price and his father had been helping Tsiana manage it until she could sell it to another Cherokee family.

"Do you keep the riverboat schedules here, Edmund?" Price asked as they approached the trade counter.

"Yes," Edmund pointed to handbills hanging on the wall by the window. Most of the steamboat captains left their schedules at all the business houses along the rivers. Though weather conditions and river levels impacted travel, most of the riverboats that plied the Arkansas tried to maintain a regular schedule.

Price and Tsiana turned to look over the advertisements.

"The *Neosho* should be here on Wednesday," the young man said, pointing to one of the bills. "We can try to get you on that." His cousin nodded.

Turning back to Edmund, Price explained their question. "Tsiana is returning to her parents' home. We thought she could board the *Facility* when it arrived today, but it is overloaded. The Creeks are traveling west."

"I had heard they were in Arkansas."

"Their captain does not travel on the Sabbath, does he?"

"No, I do not think he does. So they will be at the Dardanelle landing through Monday."

"I have never seen a boat that full," Price went on to say. "The women and children were on the steamboat and the men were on two keelboats pulled behind it."

"We will be neighbors with the Creeks once again," Edmund noted. "Especially if we secure all of Lovely's Purchase at the treaty negotiations."

"Have you heard how the negotiations are going?"

"Walter is not one to write much. I have not heard anything. Has your father?"

"Just a letter from Sequoyah saying they had arrived safely. He has been invited to dinner with every politician in town, including the President."

"I suppose they admire his work – to invent a written language is significant."

"Yes. My father hopes Sequoyah's presence will help us in the negotiations. That is why he sent him."

While they had been speaking, Edmund noticed a group of Creeks walking the trail from the river landing. Their clothing, though similar to that worn by the Cherokees, made them easily identified. Soon several men and a few women entered the store. Price and Tsiana thanked Edmund for his help then exited to give more room in the crowded trading post.

The young clerk greeted the visitors and spent the next hour assisting them with small purchases. He recognized Chilly McIntosh from his visit last year. Before the Creeks left, Edmund invited them to Dwight Mission for church services the following day. He gave directions to the site and assured them they would be welcome to attend.

"*Mvto*," one man who had introduced himself as Hawk Childers replied. "We are all very weary of travel. A visit to church will be good."

Chilly gave the same kind of disparaging grunt that Walter usually gave when invited to church. "Better to hunt," the man said.

Hawk simply shrugged his shoulders. "Some of us will be there tomorrow." Then he filed out with the rest of his people.

True to his word, Hawk arrived at Dwight the next morning with a few other Creeks. Following the worship service he introduced another young man named John Davis. John was from Alabama, he explained, after shaking hands with the interpreter. Edmund thought he looked as if he had some African heritage. A new convert to Christianity, he had listened closely during Rev. Washburn's sermon.

"Are there churches where we go?" the young Creek asked in English.

"I know services are held at Fort Gibson," Edmund replied. "But the only real church is at Union Mission. It is north of the fort on the Texas Road."

"I would like to help begin a church among us," John explained. "I had hoped to learn more of the Bible at school, but my family needs me to help get us settled here."

"You should visit with Rev. Vaille at Union," Edmund suggested. "I believe they would help you with schooling. There might be work there as well."

John nodded thoughtfully. "*Mvto*. I will visit Union as soon as I can. I want to do what you do – share the teaching with my people. There are not many believers yet among us, but we want to worship in our new land."

"I am sure the missionaries at Union will help you in any way they can. They are eager to see a work among your people."

The Creeks declined an invitation to stay for dinner following the church service and took the trail back to where the *Facility* sat docked at the landing. Edmund watched them as they walked south toward the river. They seemed tired and cautious. What uncertainly must fill their hearts as tomorrow they would begin the last leg of their journey to a new home.

With a good snowmelt that week, the *Facility*'s captain was able to press his boat through the rough water at the falls. The sound of the boat's whistle when it arrived at Three Forks brought everyone outside to witness the historic event. The first steamboat had made it past the Arkansas falls.

Colonel David Brearley heard the whistle and stepped out of the log building where the Creek Agency would operate. He joined some of the fur traders in walking down to the river bank to catch a glimpse of the *Facility* as it left the Arkansas River and eased into the channel of the Verdigris River.

The Creeks had chosen land lying between these two rivers. It was rich bottomland thick with hardwood trees and choked with river cane. Now these travel-weary individuals lined the rails of the boats eager to catch a glimpse of the land the McIntoshes had chosen for them.

When the *Facility* was finally tied to the rock ledge that served as a landing, planks were lowered from the first keelboat. Roley and Chilly exited the boat and Colonel Brearley approached them to shake hands with these two leaders.

"I was expecting you much sooner," he said.

"The boats are heavy and our way was slow," Chilly explained. "Some are sick and we are all weary."

"I'm sure you are. Come with me to the Agency and we'll discuss housing for your people. I will send someone to Fort Gibson to alert Colonel Arbuckle of your arrival."

The McIntoshes walked with their agent to the log structure. Here Brearley explained that he had secured tents to be put up south of his building in a jut of land called French Point that sat between the Verdigris and Neosho Rivers. On the east bank of the Neosho sat Fort Gibson and the garrison was prepared to provide protection for the new emigrants.

While the men talked, a soldier from Gibson arrived. Lieutenant James Dawson stepped inside and was introduced to the two Creeks. "I will be your liaison with the fort," Dawson said as he shook their hands. "I have already ordered a detail of soldiers to start erecting tents for you. I know you'll want to de-board as soon as you can."

"Yes," Roley agreed.

"If you'll come with me, I'll show you where you will stay for the time being. As soon as you're ready, I can take you and your heads of households to choose individual home sites. We'll assist with harvesting logs and clearing land for crops."

Dawson continued to talk as the men walked south along the Texas Road to the point where it veered east to a ferry landing on the Neosho. The Point had once been the site of an Osage village but it was vacant now and the soldiers were quickly setting up the temporary housing of canvas tents.

Satisfied with these accommodations, the McIntoshes returned to the boats and assisted the Creeks with coming ashore. Some of them were in tears as they stepped onto the riverbank. They had brought the coals of their ancient council fires and here they soon would ignite them again.

"Here," John Flowers said, as he pointed to a map rolled out on a conference table at the War Department's offices. The hand-drawn chart clearly marked the juncture of the Three Forks. "The treaty our nation and your nation signed with the Osages gives us the land as far west as the Verdigris. You must honor this treaty. We want all of Lovely's Purchase."

"You are only a few thousand people," Indian Commissioner Montgomery argued emphatically. "We will only agree to everything west of Fort Smith."

Flowers turned to the three Cherokee delegates and they conferred, speaking in their native tongue. Sequoyah reminded him, "We must have hunting lands. This section of

Lovely's Purchase is wooded and hilly and few buffalo come here. We must have prairie."

Flowers nodded and turned back to the commissioner. "We will agree to this portion of Lovely County," he said, "if you will add a hunting outlet to the west."

"The Creeks will be settled west of the Verdigris."

"Then give us what is north and west of the Arkansas. Here," he pointed again to the map, encircling a long strip of land that ran all the way to Mexican territory.

"That land has barely been explored or mapped," Montgomery argued. "We would have to survey it."

Walter spoke in Cherokee, "No surveys."

"The Cherokees do not allow surveys," Flower stated.

"Then we have nothing to discuss," Montgomery said, visibly annoyed. "I think we need to conclude our meeting for today. I will take your request to the Secretary."

The Cherokees' attorney frowned, but finally nodded. "When will we meet again?"

"I will send word to you about our next meeting date." With that the commissioner turned on his heel and walked out of the room, leaving a clerk to gather the maps and his notes and follow in the man's trail. The delegates watched them go then took their own leave of the office building on Pennsylvania Avenue.

"Montgomery will make us wait a few weeks," Flowers predicted as they approached the small hotel where they were staying. The long drawn-out negotiations were frustrating but the delegates held to their resolve to get the land they were requesting.

"It is only his own time that he wastes," Walter said as they climbed the steps to the room they shared. "Arkansas does not want the outlet land. Secretary Barbour will agree to our demand. We will wait as long as he takes. Who are we dining with tonight, Sequoyah?"

A few weeks later Edmund joined students and staff in the dining room at Dwight following the Wednesday Bible class. Miss Thrall, the plump and pleasant cook, always had biscuits or cookies for everyone.

Jacob Hitchcock was there, having returned from the river landing where the *Neosho* was docked. He carried the mail pack and Edmund eyed it with curiosity.

"You'll never guess what arrived in the mail, Edmund," Hitchcock said as he set the heavy canvas bag on one of the tables and reached in to take out the mail.

"What?" Edmund asked, despising the fact that he sounded too eager.

"This!" Hitchcock stated, unfurling a newspaper to reveal its front page. "The *Cherokee Phoenix*!"

Rev. Washburn joined Edmund to look over Hitchcock's shoulder at the newspaper he spread on the table. "This is the paper you told me about, Edmund?"

"Yes. Bettie's brother is the editor."

"It's in two languages," Hitchcock marveled and his words brought other staff to look over the edition. Then he folded it and handed the paper to the interpreter. "It is addressed to you, young man. You get to read it first, but I expect we'll all want to look it over when you're done."

"Certainly," Edmund agreed. He took the paper, squelching a feeling of disappointment. Why did he set himself up for this? He knew he should never have written to Corrie.

"Oh, that's not all for the Webbers," Hitchcock added, while thumbing through the canvas bag. "Here's the rest of your mail."

"Thank you," Edmund glanced at the handful of letters and was surprised that the top one was in Walter's hand, addressed to Bettie. He would need to get it to her right away. She was beginning to worry about her husband's long absence.

"I must get over to the store," he said. He snatched a molasses cookie from the tray on the next table and then pulled on his coat for the walk down the bayou trail. He was almost to the trading post when he thought to look through the other letters. Elias had written both to him and to Bettie.

There was also a letter to her from her mother Susanna. And lastly he found an envelope addressed to him in a dainty hand. He almost dropped it in his surprise. She wrote him back!

CHAPTER TWENTY-THREE

New Echota Mission
Spring, 1828

It was a glorious spring day, the kind to make one forget the three days of thunderstorms that had preceded it. Corrie sat in a bent willow chair on the little front porch of the cottage enjoying the sunshine. Tomorrow would be the final exercises for school then her boarders would return home for the summer.

Harriet and Elias were going to travel to Cornwall to take Eleanor to meet her grandparents. They had invited Corrie to go with them and she had saved enough money that she could afford the trip. She was looking forward to seeing her parents and was starting to feel homesick again for her childhood home.

Gone was her desire to quit her job at the mission, however, and return to Cornwall to stay. Over the past months she and Edmund had exchanged three letters and while she felt cautious about their resumed relationship, she also felt happy and hopeful.

They had kept their correspondence casual – just two old school friends catching up on their lives. Neither had revealed any secrets of the heart. Edmund's letters were always entertaining and often made her laugh out loud when she read them. He had always been the wit among their group with his dry sense of humor and willingness to tease. Corrie found herself often remembering school days when the six friends had spent most of their free hours in each other's company.

She was chuckling when Jane stepped out of the house to join her on the porch. "You are smiling," she said as she took the other seat.

"It's a pretty day," Corrie said as a way to explain her bright demeanor.

"Yes," Jane agreed with a smile of her own that told Corrie her friend knew it wasn't merely sunshine that made her happy. Corrie felt almost as close to Jane as she did to Harriet and she had never tried to hide the fact that she was receiving letters from a gentleman. Beyond that she had said little about Edmund. There was really not much to tell, except that they were old friends.

"Have you seen Pink?"

"He's playing with Ann Eliza by the print shop," Corrie pointed to the two youngsters across the yard. "Ann came to have dinner with Samuel, I think.

Jane glanced at the sun, her clock. "I should get my son washed up for dinner. Cook and Delight will be setting it out soon."

"Yes, I'll go over and give them a hand. See you there."

Jane had to call Pink three times before he reluctantly came to the cottage. He endured the scrubbing his mother gave his hands and face to wash away the mud he had collected from the puddles in the path between the mission buildings.

The dining room was crowded. With final exams taking place this week, the teachers had urged parents to be sure their children were in class. Most of the crops were planted by now so attendance was up.

Lem Starr was also there having brought the cook a mess of fish he had caught this morning. The man might have little book knowledge but he knew every good fishing hole in the Cherokee hills. He took a seat at the table where Corrie sat with Jane and the Worcesters.

"I hear we'll be having fish for supper thanks to you, Lem," Samuel smiled.

Lem rubbed his stomach. "Cook fixes fish good."

Everyone smiled their agreement and after grace was offered, enjoyed the ham and beans she had prepared. Conversation flowed around the room in a mild roar. The children were excited that school was almost finished for the year.

"The Black Horse Man gave me a ride again," Lem said to Corrie.

"The black horse man?" she asked, puzzled at his description

"The Tennessee man," Lem explained. "Him comed to see you sometimes. But not for a long time."

"You mean Mr. Ackley?"

He nodded. "Black Horse Man."

"Why did he give you a ride?" That Oliver would offer Lem a ride seemed completely out of character for the man.

"Him looking for pretty rocks like I gave you."

Corrie pondered Lem's words for a moment, suspicious of Oliver's motives. She had never shown anyone else the rock Lem had given her, assuming it was a bit of fool's gold. Why would Oliver have an interest in finding more? Had Lem stumbled upon an actual piece of gold?

"Did he find any pretty rocks?"

"Yes. Him did. Him happy. So him give me a ride after I showed him."

Concern filled her mind. Lem was too simple a soul to realize that his knowledge of a source of gold might create problems for him. It might create problems for all of the Cherokees who owned the land that Lem roamed so freely.

"Don't tell anyone about the pretty rocks, Lem," she advised. "Except for your family. Tell Tom. Will you do that?"

Lem nodded, then shook his head. "Black Horse Man said not to tell anyone. Will he be mad because I told you?"

"No," Corrie said though in truth she thought Oliver probably would be angry. "But don't accept any rides from Mr. Ackley again."

Lem nodded. "Not ever again."

Oliver impatiently tapped the counter of the assayer's office in Athens. The man had taken the tiny pebble Oliver had presented him and was now examining it in a back room. It was taking far longer than he would have liked and he kept glancing out to the street hoping no one else would enter the small office.

The assayer finally returned to the front. "Well, it's gold alright," he said.

Oliver held out his hand for the rock. It might be small, but this man had confirmed that it was valuable and he wanted it back.

The assayer placed the rock on Oliver's palm.

"Where'd you find it?" Curiosity was written on the man's face.

Oliver hesitated. "I have a friend who has done some prospecting in North Carolina," he lied smoothly. "He gave me that. I thought he was just playing a joke on me. I expected you to say it was fool's gold."

"No, your friend has found the real thing," the assayer confirmed. "I hear a lot of folks are heading into the mountains over there, expecting to get rich. Most of them are going to be disappointed though."

"Why do you say that?"

"Most folks think they're just going to pick up chunks of gold lying around on the ground. They don't realize mining gold is hard work. Most will give up as soon as it proves too hard for them."

"Yes, I suppose you're right," Oliver agreed. "Well, I thank you for your time."

"Sure." The man pushed up his wire-rimmed spectacles and looked closely at Oliver. "Let me know if you want to sell that," he said. "I'll give you a good price."

Oliver carefully slipped the rock into his pocket. "I will," he said. "But I'm thinking I'll just keep it as a souvenir."

The assayer shrugged. "Suit yourself."

Oliver thanked him, put his hat back on and stepped out onto the brick street. A dozen possibilities lay before him with this discovery and he needed to give some thought in how to proceed.

He hoped his lie would keep the assayer from guessing that he had found his tiny chunk of gold in Georgia. There might come a time when Oliver would be glad for the word to get out about it, but he wanted it kept secret for now.

He hoped that afflicted old Cherokee could be trusted to stay silent, but Oliver doubted that he would. His thoughts turned to Cornelia. Lem had given her a piece of gold. Oliver didn't think the woman realized what she had, but he couldn't be sure. Whatever course of action he took, he would not let an old Cherokee or an uppity female get in his way.

Edmund stood at the rail of the *Neosho* watching in fascination as the gulls that followed the boat swooped up and down above the churning wake of the paddle wheel. It was his first time to travel by riverboat since he had returned from school four years ago.

He was traveling to Union Mission for the annual missions conference. It would be his first time to visit this outpost in the Osage lands. Rev. Washburn had asked him and Jacob Hitchcock their buildings manager to attend because rumors were circulating that the Cherokees were going to have to move into this area of Lovely's Purchase. If this was to be the case, then Dwight Mission and the new Mulberry Mission would have to move as well. They would look over the area while conducting their preaching circuit this summer to get an idea for new locations.

Bettie's letter from her husband had stated that the treaty negotiations were complete and the delegates would be traveling home as soon as it was approved in the Senate. In his usual taciturn manner, Walter had given few details of the treaty's contents. But there was a buzz of speculation in the *Arkansas Gazette* about it and the consensus seemed to be that the Cherokees were once again being forced to move further west.

Edmund turned his attention to the brown waters of the Arkansas River. The troops at Fort Gibson did their best to keep the river clear of dead trees and other debris that would hinder the riverboats. But there was little they could to do clear the multitude of sandbars or ensure a heavy enough flow of water at the falls to allow passage over them. Boat captains never knew if they would make it all the way to Three Forks or would be halted at the falls where a ferry and livery now operated at a spot called Illinois Station.

The boat paused at the Sallisaw Creek landing. The town of Nicksville lay just north of here. Occasionally Edmund would catch a glimpse through the trees of travelers on the military road that closely followed the river.

The *Neosho* reached the falls in late afternoon and with just enough water in the channel, the pilot jammed the boat through the rapids. The boat then dropped anchor for the night and they reached Three Forks the following morning.

Edmund, Hitchcock, the Washburns, and the Palmers secured a mule-drawn wagon to carry them up the Texas Road to Union. Dr. Palmer drove, knowing the route blindfolded he said, after eight years of working at Union before his transfer to Mulberry. They reached the mission in time for the evening meal.

Edmund was pleasantly surprised to find the young Creek John Davis working as a farm assistant at the mission. John accompanied the preachers for their speaking engagements at Creek Agency, Fort Gibson and Nicksville.

While the conference was being held at Union, the sawmill there was running almost non-stop. The Creeks were building cabins with pine logs harvested in the nearby hills, but they wanted plank floors and window frames sawn from the walnut and oak trees growing in abundance on their land.

It was on their journey back to the bayou that Edmund made mental notes of such natural assets in the region. He had hunted here numerous times, but had never considered living here before. He wondered if Walter would be home when he got back. If so the brothers might return sometime soon to select a new location for their homes.

Rev. Washburn joined him on deck, taking one of the low chairs beside him.

"I'm glad we haven't built the new wing on the school. It would have been a real waste of the board's money if we have to move," the minister noted. "But we will be bursting at the seams when school begins this fall."

"I think a move is likely," Edmund sighed.

Washburn waved a hand toward the riverbank. "It's less than a hundred miles away from Dwight, but it seems primitive out here, doesn't it? Except for Three Forks, the fort and Nicksville, we've hardly seen a single structure and nothing in the way of a true settlement."

"We will have to start over if we come here. Just as the Creeks have." Edmund couldn't keep a little bitterness out of his voice.

"I know. It isn't fair."

"Some Cherokees are going to Texas. They think Mexico will treat them fairly. But I have my doubts. I am not sure there is a fair place on Turtle Island."

"Not one occupied by humans," Washburn agreed wryly.

Edmund laughed, his dark mood lifted. "That sounds like something I would say."

The minister chuckled too. "You're rubbing off on me, Edmund. And that's a good thing. I have to admire your steady faith in the midst of such trying circumstances."

"At least we have the Lord on our side."

"Yes. He has a way of bringing things around for our good."

The interpreter smiled and nodded with a thoughtful expression on his face. "Yes, I believe he does."

"Gone?" Oliver narrowed his eyes as he stood face to face with the Indian woman. "What do you mean she's gone?"

Jane held the door of the cottage half closed. "Miss Cornelia has gone to her home in Connecticut. She is not here."

Oliver looked as if he did not believe her. He tried to look around her into the parlor of the boarding house. Jane thrust the door open further and waved a hand. "Would you like to come inside?" she challenged him.

His eyes darted around the front room as if seeking corroboration of the woman's words. "No," he said at last. He turned on his heel and hurried back to his black carriage. Quickly he turned the horses and started out of the compound. But almost as suddenly he pulled back on the reins to slow his horses to a walk.

Jane watched him go. There was no regret on her face for leading Mr. Ackley to believe that Corrie was gone permanently. She had never liked this man who so obviously did not like her. She stepped out on the porch to continue watching him. The man was peering into windows and around every corner of the buildings as he passed them. Was he looking for Miss Cornelia? Or someone else?

CHAPTER TWENTY-FOUR

Cornwall, Connecticut
July, 1828

Corrie dabbed at the corners of her mouth with a napkin after she finished a piece of cranberry pie. "Oh, Mrs. Carroll, that was wonderful," she said to the housekeeper who was clearing away a few of the dinner dishes. "You and mother have spoiled me this month fixing all my favorite dishes."

"Thank you, Cornelia." Mrs. Carroll's eyes twinkled as she spoke. "It was my pleasure."

"We wanted you to enjoy your visit, dear," Julia smiled. "I hope you have."

"I have, Mother," Corrie grinned. "Or should I say *Etsi*?"

Jonathan Tuttle leaned back in his dining chair. "I feel as if we have all those Cherokee students back again," he smiled. "You have become quite proficient in their language."

"It was a necessity," Corrie shrugged. "All my girls were willing little teachers."

"You care for them, don't you?" Julia asked.

"Yes, they were all very sweet. Rarely gave me any problems. Jane, on the other hand, sometimes had her hands full with the boys."

"I don't know how many people asked me if you weren't afraid to be living among Indians. Please tell me you never were."

"No, I was always treated respectfully. Some of the more traditional members could look rather fierce at times. Especially when they were playing stickball." Corrie shook her head. "That game can be brutal – they consider it training for battle, I think."

Pastor Tuttle chuckled. "I have seen the lads at Westminster play lacrosse with the same fervor. They all seem to have something to prove."

He glanced at the Seth Thomas on the mantle. "I need to get back to my study, ladies, to finish my sermon for tomorrow." He dug through the mail that had sat on the table through dinner. "You might want to read the mission newsletter, Corrie." He handed the publication to her.

"I should help with the dishes first."

"Nonsense, dear. You take that and relax in the parlor. Mrs. Carroll and I will see to the dishes." Julia shooed her daughter into the other room.

Smiling, Corrie sat on the little sofa and opened the monthly report from the missions board. She was feeling sleepy after the wonderful meal and found it hard to concentrate. But her heart sped up when she saw an article about Dwight Mission. Just that name made her think of Edmund.

According to the article the Arkansas Territory mission would have to change locations because of a new treaty just signed by the western Cherokees. Despite this, however, Dwight was growing and funds being raised to expand the school. Two new teachers were needed as well as support staff such as housemothers and custodians. The article ended by urging readers to prayerfully consider accepting a call to mission work out west. Corrie got the impression that the board was finding it difficult to fill these new positions.

She set the paper down thoughtfully. She couldn't go to west could she? Would Edmund think that terribly forward of her? As if she were chasing after him? Would he even want her there?

She shook her head to clear the whirl of thoughts, hopes, doubts. She couldn't go. She had a commitment to New Echota Mission. But the idea was stuck in her mind. She would have to pray about it; not make a rash decision on a whim.

She put the mission publication down and picked up the New Haven newspaper. The Tuttle household still did not subscribe to Mr. Bunce's paper. He was joining in the chorus of supporters of Andrew Jackson's campaign promise to move all the Indians west if he was elected President.

Corrie saw that the front page was filled with news of the campaigns of President Adams and General Jackson. It was considered in bad taste for the two candidates to actually campaign for themselves so much of the work was done by proxies.

A supporter of Adams had written a lurid piece accusing Mrs. Jackson of bigamy and her husband of knowingly engaging in the scandalous relationship. This was old news, but its salacious nature no doubt sold extra copies of the paper.

The tone set by the New England writer was quite different from the newspapers in the South that for the most part printed only glowing reports about the famous Indian-fighting general. Except for the *Cherokee Phoenix*, of course.

Corrie shook her head in disgust at the sordid nature of politics. She was about to read more when her father opened the door to his office so she hastily set the newspaper back on the table by the sofa. It was considered unseemly for women to read such "tripe," as her father called it.

She rose and followed him into the kitchen where he poured himself a cup of coffee.

"If you don't need me, Mother, I think I'll go upstairs and take a little nap."

"That's fine, dear. Don't forget that the Golds and the Boudinots will be here for supper."

"I'll come down in a bit and help with the preparations."

"Thank you, Corrie, but you sleep as long as you need. I want your last two days here to be restful. You'll start a tiring journey back to New Echota on Monday."

Walter and Edmund dismounted their horses to wait their turn to board the ferry on the river above Fort Smith. The garrison was empty of soldiers now with most of the Seventh

Infantry transferred either to Fort Gibson or Fort Towson down on the Red River. The Webbers, along with Price Jolly and Rabbit Ballard were scouting locations for their move west.

Edmund lifted his hat while they waited, to allow a bit of breeze to cool his sweat-soaked hair. The day was warm and would only grow warmer as they traveled, following the military road along the river toward Fort Gibson.

When the hand-hauled ferry bumped the shoreline, the Cherokee men led their horses onto the flat, wooden boat. They each stood close to their mounts to keep the animals calm for the trip that took several minutes. At this time of year the Arkansas River was not very deep, but it was wide and it took some time to get across.

They walked their horses up the dirt ramp on the opposite bank and then mounted them and resumed their ride on the hard packed road built and maintained by the Gibson troops. The trail crossed several creeks, most of them nearly dry in the rainless heat.

The men reached Illinois Station and found the place busy. Freighters used the road for hauling goods to Mexican locations such as San Antonio and Santa Fe. The owner of the way station kept mules that river captains would hire to get keelboats over the falls and on to Three Forks.

Pausing here to eat some of the provisions their women had packed, they discussed how best to use the land.

"The old ones will settle in the hills around Piney," Ballard predicted. "They don't require much land. I need flatter land and more acreage for my horses. I want to be close to the way station."

Walter nodded. "I want the river bottom land near here. Your father will as well," he said to Price.

The younger Jolly agreed. "If you want the Arkansas land, we will take the Illinois River land. I think Spring Frog plans to locate along the Canadian."

The Illinois and Canadian Rivers clearly had been named by early French traders who had operated in the area years ago. These smaller rivers emptied into the Arkansas within a few miles of one another.

"Sequoyah wants a salt spring," Edmund said as he bit into a plum from Mrs. Lovely's orchard. "There's one on Skin Bayou, he says."

"My father wishes to give the Salt Branch of the Illinois to John Flowers as payment for his services in Washington City."

"There are some white men mining that salt, aren't there?"

"Yes, the Bean brothers. But they will have to move. Anyone who isn't Cherokee will be ordered out by the government."

"What about Mrs. Lovely?" Edmund asked, concerned about the widow.

"She will wing the first government man who dares to try to move her," Walter chuckled.

The other men laughed. Mrs. Lovely's skill with a musket was well known and well respected.

"My father will do everything he can to protect her property," Jolly assured them.

A boat's whistle sounded just then and the men rose from where they sat beneath a giant sycamore tree and walked down to the river bank. Soon the *Facility* came into view. They watched as the boat's crew tied up at the way station's landing. The steamboat would not be able to traverse the falls today. The rocks that created the tumbling water were quite visible in the parched river.

A few passengers de-boarded and made their way to the livery. Two were in military uniform and two more in civilian clothes but they were clearly traveling together. They exited the stable shortly, mounted on horses the liveryman rented. They headed north toward Fort Gibson.

The rivermen unloaded freight from the steamboat and piled it around the way station. It was likely bound for Mexico and a freighter would soon pick it up to continue its journey westward.

Edmund watched his brother watch this activity with a shrewd look in his eyes.

"A store would do well here," he observed. Then he turned to Edmund. "You build near here and you can watch the store for me." It didn't sound like a request, but rather an order.

Edmund felt a rod of resistance straighten his spine. "I will wait to see where Dwight locates," he countered. "I will try to build close enough to your store and the mission that I can continue to work for both."

Walter's eyes narrowed. Edmund rarely stood up to his older brother, but this time he did not intend to be pushed into a decision that would only benefit Walter. He knew Dwight Mission was seeking more staff. He knew they would need housemothers at their new location. He knew of a certain housemother he hoped might come to work there. He wanted his home close by. Whether he would find the courage to actually ask Corrie to come west remained to be seen. He still wasn't sure about that.

Corrie's legs felt wobbly as she stepped off the gangplank of the *Red River* steamboat at Ross's Landing in Chattanooga. A month of nearly constant motion on the rivers made dry land seem unstable somehow. As Elias saw to their luggage, she and Harriet found a place to sit in the shade of a counting house.

"Oh, good, there's Samuel," Harriet said after a while. She pointed to the road that led to the wharf where Worcester brought the mission's carriage to a halt. "Eleanor, come here," she called to her daughter who was picking up rocks nearby.

"I'll get Eleanor," Corrie volunteered. "You find Elias."

She carried the little girl to the two-seater vehicle and greeted the missionary. Samuel assisted her into the back seat, then went to help Elias carry their luggage and place it in the boot of the vehicle. Soon they were on their way south, the women riding in back and the men up front.

"Ann packed food for you," Samuel announced after he had guided the horses through the waterfront traffic. He reached under the front seat to pull out a basket. Elias handed it back to the ladies and Harriet distributed cucumber sandwiches made with sourdough bread and squares of gingerbread.

After they had enjoyed the light meal, Eleanor climbed into her mother's lap and was soon asleep.

"Did the *Phoenix* get out alright?" Elias asked.

"Only a day or two late," Samuel grinned ruefully. "But both issues were mailed on time. John did a fine job as editor in your absence."

"Good," Elias said. "Any news I should know about."

"Not news exactly," Samuel frowned, "but something of concern."

The man's worried tone caused Harriet and Cornelia to lean forward to hear what he had to say.

"What?"

"A rumor has started around that gold has been discovered in the Smokies in Georgia – on Cherokee land."

"Gold," Harriet said. "You mean the metal?"

"Yes, dear," Elias teased. "Not some of your cousins."

Harriet stuck out her tongue at her husband and they all laughed.

Samuel quickly sobered though and added, "A number of Cherokees have reported seeing strangers roaming the woods around their homesteads. It has everyone a bit on edge."

Corrie thought of Lem and instantly felt concern for her friend. "How did the rumor get started?"

"No one knows for sure. I certainly haven't seen any gold."

"I doubt that it is true," Elias stated. "I have hunted all over those mountains and have never seen anything."

"I have," Corrie said quietly. Everyone looked at her in surprise. "At least I think I have."

"What do you mean, Corrie?"

"Lem gave me a little rock a few months back."

"Lem Starr?" Samuel asked.

"Yes. He just thought it was a pretty rock and so did I at first. But he later told me that Oliver Ackley asked him to show him where he found it. And I guess he did."

"Ackley," Elias muttered to himself. "I knew that man was trouble."

"Do you think Mr. Ackley told someone else? Is that how the rumor started?" Harriet asked.

"It could be." Corrie looked worried. "Or Lem might have said something. I told him not to, except for his family. But you know he wouldn't understand why it should be kept quiet."

Elias still looked doubtful. "One or two nuggets hardly make a gold strike." He looked back at Corrie and saw her worried expression. "I will talk to Lem," he told her, "and have him show me what he showed Ackley. This is probably much ado about nothing."

"Thank you, Elias," Corrie said. "I hate to think my association with Oliver might cause problems for you."

"You are not to blame for anything that man does," Harriet protested.

"Still," Corrie sighed, "Sometimes I wonder if I should have come here. If I should be here."

"God orders our steps, Corrie," Worcester said quietly. "Trust his guidance. I don't think your work here has been a mistake. Those little girls you have cared for have seen the Lord in you and felt his love through you. That is never wrong."

"No it isn't," her best friend agreed.

They fell into silence then in the drowsy heat of afternoon. But Samuel seemed to be worrying over something. Corrie could tell just from watching his silhouette that he was chewing his lip as if pondering a matter, or praying about it perhaps.

"You know, Corrie," he said slowly, "I received a letter from Cephas Washburn at Dwight Mission. They are desperate for more workers out there and he invited me to come."

"You are not thinking about going out there, are you?" Elias asked in surprise.

"No, I wrote him back and told him I feel my work is here," Samuel assured the editor. "I recommended Emmanuel Newton who just left Harmony Mission in Missouri. And I told Jane about it. She might find work there when she moves. If you're feeling uncertain about being at New Echota, Corrie, perhaps the Lord might be leading you to Dwight."

Corrie sucked in a breath in surprise of her own. "I don't know . . ." she said looking over at Harriet.

Her friend actually had a hopeful expression on her face.

"I have a commitment at New Echota; school is about to start."

"Rev. Sanders already knows Jane is going to be leaving at winter break," Elias said. "Miss Sergeant will take over for her."

Samuel added, "And they have hired a new woman. A Miss Stetson, Ellen, I think. She's from Virginia."

Corrie got the impression that the three friends in this carriage were helping her pack her bags for Dwight. Why? Why was everything and everyone pointing her toward Dwight? Was this from God? Or was it simply her own heart being pulled like a compass to her true north?

It was several weeks before Elias caught up on his work at the print office so he could take Lem hunting. James Starr and his wife Mary had been keeping the old man close to their home during this time. Rumors continued to circulate about gold in the Cherokee mountains, but Elias had yet to hear of any concrete evidence. So far, most of the tales were being told among the Cherokees, but word would soon spread further.

If there were riches in the mountains, it might be a great boon to the Cherokees. But the newspaper editor knew that the lure of such riches would bring hundreds or likely thousands of intruders into their land. He couldn't see how the Cherokees could successfully keep people out of the rugged, timbered and largely unfenced terrain.

If gold truly had been discovered, the pressure on the Cherokees to give up those ancestral mountains would intensify. He had little hope that Georgia authorities would make any effort to police the area and if individual Cherokees tried to protect themselves from trespassers, the law would not come down on their side.

These thoughts weighed heavily on him as he rode into the yard at the James Starr homestead. As he dismounted, Starr came out to meet him. Elias had sent word about his purpose and he could tell the older man wanted to speak to him about it.

"Tom is helping Lem get a horse saddled," James said.

"You do not mind me taking him out to the mountains, do you?"

"No. Lem has wanted to go hunting for weeks but we have not let him. He is very smiling today that you are taking him."

"What do you think of his story? Do you think there is any gold out there?"

Starr shrugged. "I went with him up there after he told Tom about it and about Black Horse Man. I did not see anything to make me think there is gold."

"Miss Tuttle at the mission showed me the nugget Lem gave her. It looks real to me, but we have not had it assayed."

"Is that the Miss T. he talks about?"

"Yes. She is kind to him and he is sweet on her, I think."

The men smiled and then watched as Lem led a horse from the barn.

"Do you think he just cannot remember where he found the rock he gave Miss Tuttle?" Elias asked.

"Lem is not good at talking," Starr replied. "But he does not get lost in the woods. He may not be able to tell someone where he found it, but he is able to go right to the spot. He is one with the land."

Elias nodded and then turned to greet the old man who walked with an odd gait as if one leg were slightly shorter than the other. Tom helped him mount his horse, then handed him a bow and quiver of arrows. Lem hunted the old way.

The two men took a trail going east that steadily climbed into the hills starting to show their fall colors. They let the horses take their time in picking their way around boulders and through ravines until reaching a fast flowing stream.

Here they dismounted and led their horses along Holly Creek, watching for animal tracks or scat. Elias came to quickly understand what he had often been told about Lem. The man might be slow of wit and speech, but he easily identified animal tracks that were so faint Elias would have missed them.

"Bear," Lem said pointing to scat. "Two cubs."

"Is that fresh?" Elias asked, looking around the area. He did not want to accidentally happen upon a protective mother bear.

"Old," Lem shook his head. "She gone."

They continued following the stream, at one point pausing when they heard the distant scream of a panther. Though the sleek black cats were fewer in number now, a few still roamed the remote, heavily timbered area. The horses nickered nervously.

"Long way," Lem said. "Over on Cohutta mountain."

Elias smiled in admiration. Lem's ears and eyes worked perfectly. Soon Holly Creek turned southward and spilled over fallen rocks that had slid down the mountains sometime in the distant past. Lem led his horse to a quiet pool and let the animal drink. Elias did the same.

Pointing to the creek, Lem said, "That is the shiny rock place."

Immediately Elias crouched beside the stream and studied the clear water, his eyes searching the rocks that formed the streambed. Like James Starr, he did not see anything that might be gold.

He stood. "I do not see any shiny rocks."

"Have to cross," Lem stated. "I hold your horse."

It was clear that Lem had no intention of crossing the creek. Perhaps in his mind, that area represented unwanted attention and trouble. Elias sighed and stepped into the frigid water. Careful not to slip in the flowing stream, he reached the other side and stepped out around a large boulder.

Studying the ground, he still did not see anything resembling the nugget Corrie had shown him. He looked up the hill that rose above the creek, feeling a mixture of relief and frustration. Something caught his eye. He stepped up on the boulder and then around it to another one. Behind the roots of a scarlet-leafed dogwood he saw a thin ribbon of rock in the hillside. He unsheathed his knife and scraped off a few flakes into his palm. He held his hand out to catch the light. The flakes glistened. He dropped them carefully into the knife's pouch.

Then his looked straight down behind the boulder he stood on. In the dim light he could barely make out the rain-washed grit resting on the ground at the base of the hill. Most of it was fine as sand, but a few pebbles and rocks were mixed in. Shiny rocks – dozens, hundreds of them. His heart began to pound. This find would mean either a boon or doom for the Cherokees. In his heart he knew it would be the latter.

Elias reached down and collected a few of the larger pebbles and added them to his knife pouch. Then he crossed back to Lem.

"Is this where you brought Black Horse Man?"

Lem nodded. "Him not cross the creek. Not want to wet his boots. Him find little rock there." The older man pointed to the quiet pool then held up his thumb and finger to show the size of the pebble Ackley had found.

"But he did not see what is over there?"

"No. Not James either."

Elias nodded in understanding. Maybe, just maybe, they could protect that hidden vein of gold.

The two men continued on, following the creek and speaking little. Lem took a buck, a fat, four-pointer. Elias took a shot at another but missed.

Lem grinned at him. "Shiny rocks make your hands shake," he joked.

"That is the truth," Elias agreed.

They paused at the sun's zenith to eat some jerky then retraced their steps along the creek with Lem's buck tied to the back of his horse. They reached the Starr farm near sundown.

James came out and gave Elias a questioning look.

"We found it," was all Elias would say. "I will bring it to the National Council."

James nodded solemnly. Monetary riches weren't important to a traditionalist like Starr. But he could understand the ramifications of finding gold on Cherokee land.

"Stay for supper?" he asked while his son Tom helped Lem take his horse back to the barn.

"I think I will get on home," Elias said. "Thank you anyway."

Starr nodded again. Neither man seemed to want to say anything more.

When their new government met at the Council House in New Echota a few weeks later, they authorized the formation of the Cherokee Mining Company and passed a law restricting access to the mountains by intruders. Elias printed the text of the law in the *Phoenix* but buried the English version on page three at Samuel's suggestion.

Chief Hicks traveled to the Georgia capital to meet with Governor Troup to request his help in restricting access to the Cherokee land. Troup had seemed intrigued with the information but showed no interest in aiding the Cherokees.

It was three weeks later when the Council received word from the statehouse in Milledgeville. The Georgia legislature had passed a law making it illegal for Cherokees to mine the gold. If conflicts arose between the Cherokees and gold prospectors, the governor warned, the Cherokees would not be allowed to press charges or testify against such intruders. They had been, in effect, told to stay off their own land.

CHAPTER TWENTY-FIVE

Illinois Station, the Indian territory
October, 1828

Edmund and Jerome both grunted with the exertion of lifting the big pot-bellied stove up the stairs into the new trading post. Ever the businessman, Walter had decided to build his store first before completing his new home near the Forks of the Illinois River. The Webber family would live in a back storeroom until their house was finished.

With the stove set in place, Jerome went back out to bring in the sections of the vent pipe. He handed the parts to the younger Webber then went out again to help with unloading the wagons filled with trade goods.

Bettie brought in an armful of fabric bolts, set them on a shelf and then watched Edmund attach the pipe to the stove and then climb a ladder to push the other end out the vent hole cut in the side wall.

"Does it seem right?" he asked, looking down from his perch.

"Yes, but we won't know for sure until we light a fire."

"Do you want me to start one?"

"No, it is too warm today. Walter can light one tonight if we need it." Though mid October, the daytime temperatures were still comfortable.

Edmund quirked an eyebrow in an unspoken question. His brother was not adverse to work; he could outwork anyone if there was a need to do so. But he also wasn't opposed to getting someone else to do the work for him.

Edmund could imagine that it would be Jerome or Peter who would haul the wood and start the fire this evening. Edmund would be on his way to Nicksville before then.

"Walt Jr. is glad his father chose to live here," Bettie said as her two boys carried armloads of canned goods to a back shelf.

"Why?" Edmund ask as he descended the ladder and again checked the vent pipe's connection to the stove.

"Because he will not have to learn how to spell a new name for where he lives. Illinois Bayou . . . Illinois Station."

"Little study required," Edmund smiled. His nephew was not one who wanted to spend much time with books or school.

"He was disappointed to learn that he will still have to attend school."

"Will you send them to Dwight when it is moved or to the other mission near Piney? They are going to name it Fairfield, Rev. Washburn says, instead of New Mulberry."

"The boys will continue at Dwight, since you will be working there."

"Even though Walter gave money to the Fairfield Mission?"

"Were you surprised by that?" Bettie asked. "I know I was when he told me."

The leaders of the missions in the region – Dwight, Mulberry, Union and Hopefield – had met with Colonel Nicks and Chief Jolly at Nicksville to discuss moving Dwight and Mulberry out of Arkansas. Since Lovely County would cease to exist, it no longer needed a county seat. Colonel Nicks offered to sell the courthouse and post office to Dwight for a fair price. While the men were estimating the costs to move and rebuild the Mulberry school, it had been a shock to everyone when Walter had offered a generous donation to the mission.

"I have to admit, I was surprised," Edmund replied. "He said it was for you, that you had asked him or at least he implied that."

"I never asked him; I just told him I would try to help both missions any way I could."

Edmund nodded, looking thoughtful. "He is changing, is he not?"

"More than you know." Bettie looked around to make sure her husband was not within hearing. "He has visited the Fairfield place several times. He says he goes to make sure his money is being spent right. But he stays and talks with Dr. Palmer."

Edmund could barely keep his mouth from popping open. "Dr. Palmer does not speak much Cherokee. Does Walter talk with him in English?"

Bettie shrugged to say she wasn't sure. "Maybe so. He tells me some of what they talk about. Dr. Palmer answers his questions about God."

It might seem like a small thing to someone who did not know his brother, but Edmund knew this was a major change in Walter Webber. And if he had changed in this matter, perhaps he had, or would, change in other ways as well.

Edmund stayed until after supper then rode the fifteen miles to Nicksville. He was bunking in the old courthouse along with Mr. Hitchcock and James Orr. They were working to get the cavernous brick structure ready for the new school semester next year. They would have space for twice as many students as the school on the bayou. Two teachers – Emmanuel and Mary Newton – would transfer from Harmony Mission for the next semester. Edmund knew they still needed housemothers though.

The men took a break from construction work the following week to attend the Pumpkin Moon Rendezvous held each fall at Three Forks. There was much talk at this gathering of Indians and traders about the Indian policy being pushed by the government.

Just last month Creek, Choctaw and Chickasaw leaders from Alabama and Mississippi had toured the area looking over land the government was offering them south of the Arkansas River. Jackson's campaign pledge to move the

Indians was popular so President Adams was pushing for the same thing, hoping for votes, no doubt.

"Seems like the voting back east is going to have a lot to do with us out west," Jacob Hitchcock observed in Cherokee as the group from Illinois Station rode south following the Rendezvous.

"The eastern Cherokees soon will vote for a chief, too," Edmund added. "Either John Ross or John Ridge seems to be the most likely choice according to the *Phoenix*."

"Ross will win," Walter said. "The full-bloods will favor him over Ridge."

"Why do you think that?"

"Ridge has a white wife."

The coldness of his brother's statement washed over Edmund like a winter rain. "And you think that disqualifies John Ridge?" he asked after a moment, his voice harder than he meant it to be.

"I did not say that." Walter looked at his younger brother. "Our skin is but a shell that holds our spirit," he explained. "That is our true self and by it we should judge and be judged."

Edmund was surprised by his brother's words and shared a look with the mission superintendent who was smiling.

"Those are wise words, Mr. Webber," Hitchcock noted.

"*Wado,*" Walter said, smiling too.

Edmund was certain that he was witnessing something of a miracle.

Corrie sat with a group of friends after supper at the Boudinot farm. The atmosphere seemed somber despite the laughter of the children playing in the parlor. This was a farewell meal for Jane and Pinkney who would leave New Echota after Christmas. Her brother Chilly had returned for them from the Indian territory.

Beside this, the news that General Jackson had won the popular vote in the Presidential election was disturbing to the Cherokees and the other tribes in the southeastern states.

What Adams had started in regard to the Indian removals, Jackson was sure to accelerate.

"Maybe we should all be going west," Sarah Ridge said glumly. She had taken her husband's loss of the election for chief personally. She had heard the comments and knew she had been a detriment to his campaign. It gave her great sympathy for Rachel Jackson, the much vilified wife of the new President.

"We cannot be forced off our land," John countered as everyone knew he would. But it seemed to Corrie that his words held less vehemence than they might have before the election. The circumstances surrounding them continued to worsen.

"I know," Sarah said. "But sometimes it just seems futile to fight."

"Chilly says the land is good out west," Jane offered quietly. "I dread the long journey, but I think I will be glad when we arrive."

"But we are going to miss you," Ann replied. The others nodded, especially Corrie who had come to think of Jane almost as a sister.

Quiet reigned around the table for just a moment then Harriet stood to gather the dishes. Corrie and Jane were quick to help them, insisting that Ann and Sarah see to their little ones. The Worcesters had added a second daughter to their family recently. The men retired to the parlor to try to talk over the chatter of Pink and Ann Eliza.

The three friends made quick work cleaning the dishes, not saying much as they worked. As the last dish was dried, Corrie felt her heart pounding. If she was going to speak up, she needed to do so now. She pulled a letter from her pocket.

"I received a letter . . ." she began and Harriet almost squealed in response.

"From Edmund?" her friend asked with excitement in her eyes.

"No." Corrie could feel her cheeks grow warm. "It's from Rev. Washburn at Dwight Mission. I had sent an inquiry about a position there."

"Oh," Harriet seemed terribly let down. "What did he say?"

"He says they have a great need for workers there and if I am interested he would welcome me to work as a housemother at their new location."

"What are you going to do?" Harriet asked, as she took the letter Corrie held out to her.

"I'm torn," Corrie confessed. "I'm not sure what I should do and would like your advice."

Harriet smiled as she quickly perused the mission letter. "You know that I have always thought God brought you and Edmund together just as he did Elias and me. Going west would be an opportunity for you to see if there is a future for you two together." She handed the letter from Washburn back to her friend. "You and Edmund have been corresponding haven't you?"

"Yes," Corrie said. "And I keep hoping that he'll invite me again to come out there. But so far he hasn't. And I'm hesitant to go unless he does. Besides that I don't think I have enough funds for the journey. I spent my savings going back to visit my parents this summer."

Harriet sighed. "I would loan you the funds, but Elias and I spent our savings as well going to Cornwall."

"I have the money," Jane surprised Corrie by saying. "The government has finally paid our family for my father's property. Chilly is bringing my share when he comes to get us. He thought I might want to purchase something for the trip since I sent most of my things with him last year. I would be happy to pay for your steamboat ticket."

"I couldn't let you do that, Jane."

"I would like to have you travel with me, Miss Cornelia," the young widow confessed. "Most of my family went west last year. Those who will be traveling on this trip are from southern Georgia or Alabama. I know only a few of them. It would be so good to have a friend going with me."

"But would there be room for me?" Corrie worried. "I wouldn't want to add to crowded conditions."

"There are far fewer of us going this time. A good number of our people have chosen to stay and purchase land here or move to Alabama and live among the Creeks there. But it will be a slow journey hauling all the household goods behind the steamboat."

"God seems to be providing a way, Corrie," Harriet gently nudged her.

Corrie drew in a deep breath and let it out in a sigh. "I just wish I knew how Edmund felt. I have this fear of arriving at Dwight Mission and seeing shock or disapproval on his face. I cannot presume that he would welcome me. And how awkward would it be for him to have me there? I know I hurt him in the past and I certainly don't want to do that again."

"You could write to him and just honestly ask him how he would feel about you taking a position at Dwight," Harriet suggested.

"But my letter couldn't get there and his response back before Jane has to leave."

Harriet and Jane exchanged concerned looks, but neither could offer a solution to their friend's dilemma.

Edmund heard the steamboat whistle and he quickened his pace. He carried a letter in his hand but in some ways he felt like he carried his heart inside it. He hurried to reach the steamboat landing at Sallisaw Creek directly south of Dwight Mission. For some reason he felt an urgency to make sure this letter was sent on its way aboard the *Neosho* heading down the Arkansas River toward the Mississippi. It needed to reach Georgia as quickly as possible.

The day before, he had interpreted at a brush arbor service at Walter and Bettie's new home at Illinois Station. Dr. Palmer had preached a sermon for the upcoming Christmas season and at the end had called for penitents to come forward for salvation. Walter led the way and nearly forty others among their neighbors followed the chief's steps.

It had been a most remarkable day. At the meal that followed the arbor service, Walter gave his brother a forearm to forearm handshake in the closest thing to a show of affection he had ever given. Then the brothers sat together and talked while enjoying the roasted quail and turkey shared at the communal dinner.

"Bettie tells me you have a woman in Georgia," Walter said at one point in the conversation. Edmund felt uncomfortable at the personal nature of the remark and almost denied it. But he stopped himself.

"Yes," he said quietly so others at the table wouldn't overhear. "I do."

"So why is she there while you are here?"

"I did not think you would want her here."

"Maybe so I would not have . . . yesterday."

"But today?"

"Today is a new day. I am a new man. And Georgia is too far away to have a woman."

So now Edmund ran, fearful that the *Neosho* would pull away from the dock before he could reach it. His lungs burned as he sucked in the cold air. He reached the landing as the rivermen were pulling in the ropes that secured the boat to its mooring. He dashed down the long wooden wharf toward the steward who was about to raise the gangplank.

"I have a letter . . ." he huffed, too winded to say more.

"Well you made it just in time," the boatman grinned. He held out his hand and Edmund placed the precious missive into it. The steward glanced at the address. "New Echota," he read. "You are in luck. We're carrying a government packet from Colonel Arbuckle for the new chief back there. I'll put yours with it and it will arrive in just a few days."

"Thank you," Edmund said, amazed at the timing. It wasn't luck, he knew. Something . . . someone . . . was at work in the heavens.

Chilly McIntosh sat in the dining hall at New Echota Mission warming up with a cup of coffee while waiting for his sister to say her goodbyes among the mission staff. At the cottage Jane embraced Corrie and the two young women clung to each other for a moment. When they parted Jane asked, "Are you sure you will not come with us?"

Corrie sadly shook her head. "I don't think I can right now. Perhaps I will go west in the future. I hope you understand."

Jane nodded, appearing equally sad. "We have to follow our men, do we not? Even if that means waiting for them to catch up to us."

Corrie couldn't help but laugh at Jane's words. How true they seemed to be for her. She had actually packed her trunk, believing, hoping that by some miracle she would get a letter from Edmund. But none had arrived.

"I'm going to miss you, Jane. Please write to let me know when you arrive safely."

"I will. It likely will be spring before we are there."

The two women left the cottage and walked together to the dining hall where Pink waited with his uncle. Then Chilly helped Jane and her son into his wagon where their luggage was already loaded. Corrie stood with Hannah Sanders and waved as the wagon pulled out of the mission yard.

"I thought for sure you would be going with Jane," the motherly woman said to Corrie. She had explained her situation to the mission directors without much detail about Edmund. They simply knew she was praying about going west and searching for God's will.

"I thought I would go too," Corrie said. "But it was not to be right now. Perhaps it never will."

Hannah nodded but said nothing more. Corrie knew the older woman was aware of her correspondence with the interpreter for Dwight Mission but she had never pried into her personal affairs.

Corrie walked back to the cottage. It was empty now because all the boarders were at home for Christmas break. The house seemed cold and as Corrie walked to her room she was swamped with a feeling of loneliness that she had never felt before. Was she being stupid . . . stubborn? She couldn't help but feel that she had made a terrible mistake.

She threw herself across her bed and might have given into tears but a knock sounded at the door. Corrie almost chose to ignore it, but everyone at the mission knew she was here in the cottage. It would be rude to pretend otherwise. With a sigh, she rose and went to answer the door.

Mrs. Sanders waited outside.

"I'm so sorry, dear," she said as she held out two pieces of mail. "I should have given you this earlier. I don't know where my mind was."

"That's alright, Mrs. Sanders," Corrie replied as she took the letters. She could see one was from Electra Kingsbury. "Thank you."

"Certainly." The woman turned away before Corrie could invite her inside. So the housemother closed the door and crossed the parlor to sit by the fireplace. She was about to open Electra's letter when she glanced at the other piece.

Edmund's hurried handwriting nearly leaped off the page at her. Forgetting Electra's letter, Corrie hurriedly pried up the wax seal and pulled out the page. Scanning it quickly, she saw that Edmund's brother Walter had come to faith in the Lord. He was almost finished building his new house. He told her that Dwight Mission needed housemothers, a fact that she was already aware of.

She flipped the page over and there were the words she had longed for. "Please pray about coming west," he wrote. "I want you here with me."

She stood quickly, a sense of panic running through her. Jane was already gone. She hurried to the door to scan the road but Chilly's wagon was not in sight. What should she do?

She prayed even as she rushed to the table where the children did their school work. She found a sheet of paper and then located a pen and inkwell. Her fingers were trembling as she opened the bottle of ink, dipped in the pen's nib and hurriedly wrote.

"I will come west. Traveling with the McIntosh group. Should arrive in the spring."

Without thinking she started to write "Love," but stopped herself after she had formed the "o." Should she use this word that was in her heart? Would this still be presuming too much, reading too much into Edmund's letter? Thinking desperately, she finally wrote, "Looking forward to seeing you soon." Then she signed her name and blew on the ink to dry it while she searched for an envelope and her sealing wax.

When the envelope was addressed and the ink dry, Corrie grabbed her coat and was pulling it on as she nearly ran to the mission kitchen. Finding Mrs. Sanders working with Cook and Delight she asked the women, "Is Lem here? I need someone to post a letter for me."

"I haven't seen Lem in weeks, dear," Hannah responded as she wiped flour-dusted fingers on her apron. "I'll have my husband post it. He's going to New Echota this afternoon."

"Thank you," Corrie said. "I am going to try to catch Jane and Chilly. I have decided to go west after all. I hope this is not an inconvenience, Mrs. Sanders."

The missionary smiled a knowing smile. "Go, my child. I hope you find happiness."

Tears sprang into Corrie's eyes at the woman's kindness. "Thank you," she whispered and then turned to run to the print shop. Elias would be working there today; she could see his carriage parked outside the door.

Bursting into the office, Corrie was greeted by a surprised look on the editor's face.

"Corrie, what is it?" he asked, his concern clear.

"I have decided to take the position at Dwight Mission, Elias. I heard from Edmund just today. But Chilly and Jane have already gone. Can you take me to catch up with them?"

Elias set down his pen and quickly closed his own bottle of ink. Then wiping his fingers, he stood and reached for his overcoat.

"Let me hitch up the horse," he said. "Are you packed?"

"Yes, my trunk is ready. You'll just have to load it."

"Then let us get started," he grinned. "Harriet would never forgive me if I delayed even one second."

Corrie returned his smile, knowing Elias was exactly correct. Wouldn't her friend be thrilled when Elias told her? "Thank you, Elias. I will meet you at the cottage."

Within fifteen minutes they were on the road to Bridgeport, Alabama where the McIntosh party would meet the steamboat on the Tennessee River. It was only after they had driven for awhile that Corrie remembered Harriet's comment once about her riding alone with Elias. Would tongues wag if someone should see them? Oh, she just didn't care! Let her cause a scandal!

"Can we catch them, do you think?" the housemother asked at one point. "I hate to take you away for long."

"My carriage is much lighter than McIntosh's wagon," Elias assured her. "We will be upon them before long. They will not be in a hurry."

True to his prediction, they soon crested a hill and saw Chilly's wagon in the distance. Elias kept his horse at a steady trot and they slowly gained on the heavier vehicle. Corrie felt herself willing the distance to close between them. She could see that Pink was sitting between the adults and Jane had her arm around the boy's shoulders to keep him warm.

"Jane," she called when she thought they were close enough that she might be heard. But her voice did not carry over the sound of the horses.

Soon, however, Chilly became aware that another vehicle was approaching from behind and he directed his horses closer to the right side of the dirt trail. He glanced back and must have recognized Corrie for he said something to his sister.

Jane looked back and surprise registered on her face. Chilly whoa'd his team. Elias pulled alongside the wagon and halted his horse as well. The two men nodded to one another.

"Is your offer still good, Jane? Can I go with you?" Corrie asked eagerly.

"Of course," her friend replied. "But what changed your mind?"

"I received a letter." Corrie held it up, knowing her friend would need no other explanation.

Jane smiled just as everyone else had when learning that Edmund had finally asked Corrie to join him out west. She spoke to Chilly in *Muskoke* and he set the brake and then climbed down from the wagon bench. Jane also scrambled down over the large wheel.

The two men transferred Corrie's trunk to the wagon.

Corrie turned to Elias and took both of his hands. "Thank you so much, Elias. You are a true friend. Tell Harriet I am sorry that there wasn't time to see her and say goodbye."

"I will tell her. She will understand. You must tell Edmund that I said it was about time."

Corrie laughed. "I will." Then Elias helped her into the back of the wagon and Jane and Pink joined her there, huddling together under a big blanket behind the wagon seat. Elias turned his carriage and set off at a slower pace back to the mission. Chilly started his team again.

They camped by the side of the road that evening and arrived at Bridgeport the following day. Jane's uncle Roley had secured berths for the women and children on the *Tennessee*. Behind the steamboat were two keelboats where the men would ride with their baggage.

It took two days for the baggage to be loaded. While the Creeks camped at the waterfront a local congregation opened its doors and fed the emigrants. It was a pleasant surprise, given how Indians were often received, and all of their party were grateful for this kind gesture.

When it came time to board the big steamer, Corrie expected to feel some moment of doubt or regret. She was not usually given to such impetuous actions. But even as she and Jane and Pink found places to sleep in the dormitory style second deck, she felt only a certainty that this was right.

CHAPTER TWENTY-SIX

Nashville
March, 1829

Oliver and his brother-in-law Jason Edwards stepped out of the public house where they had met and shared a drink. They were on their way to supper at the home of Nashville's district attorney given in honor of Andrew Jackson. The supper was to be a send-off for the President-elect who would begin his journey the next day to Washington City for his inauguration.

A quiet meal had been arranged in place of a ball out of respect for the grief of the general. His beloved Rachel had died suddenly at the Hermitage and the sadness still lingered in the Tennessee capital. Oliver and Jason wore black armbands over their suit coats and the women would all wear black gloves in a show of mourning.

Jason sent a Negro porter to bring his carriage around front. They were attending alone because Daphne was with child and Dolly was away at school. Oliver had chosen not to ask the winsome Miss Longstreet to accompany him, given the somber nature of the affair.

While they waited for the carriage, Oliver stepped over into the shadows of the shrubbery to have a quick smoke of a hand-rolled cigar. He had just gotten a good draw on it when a low voice nearby startled him.

"Glad to catch up with you, Mr. Ackley." The voice was raspy and had a thick backwoods drawl.

Oliver turned to see the man who emerged from the shadows. A gristly beard covered his lower face and a hat was pulled low over his eyes.

"I told you not to try to meet with me in public."

"No one will see us here," the man countered. "You ain't easy to catch up to." He looked around just to assure Ackley that they were alone. "Me and Pete did the deed. Now we want our money."

"You found the creek . . . and the gold?"

"We found it. Like you said, that old man led us to it . . . after we persuaded him a bit. Some Cherokees were working the vein in the hill, but we ran them off."

"I didn't want anyone hurt."

"Don't worry about it. We secured the site. Pete's watching it. Ain't nobody but you gonna work that mine."

"What about the old man?" Oliver asked, drawing nervously on his cigar and watching Jason out the corner of his eye.

"He won't be leading anyone else to that gold," the man snickered.

"I said I didn't want anyone hurt. I don't want that on my hands."

"We didn't hurt him. Just took him further back into the mountains. Took his horse and left him there."

"Where? Where did you leave him?"

The man screwed up his face as if trying to recall the route he and Pete had taken. "Up near Wilson's Bend," he finally said. "Left him down in a ravine."

Oliver threw down his cigar and ground it under his heel in a gesture of frustration. "That's in Tennessee, you fool. You should have left him in Georgia. The authorities there wouldn't care what you did to an Indian. You wouldn't even be prosecuted. But Tennessee has a governor who is sympathetic to the Cherokees. This better not come back on me."

"He ain't gonna find his way out. And he don't know about you. He thinks some black horse man did it. The man is teched in the head."

Oliver saw that Jason's carriage was pulling up to the front walk of the tavern. Hastily he pulled out his wallet and counted out the promised money while the henchman watched eagerly.

"Go back and help Pete keep the area safe. I'll be out there myself as soon as I can get away."

The man nodded and gave a mock salute. "Pleasure doing business with you." Then he slid back into the shadows.

Oliver met Jason at the carriage. It was pulled by two of the sleek black Tennessee Walkers the Ackley farm was famous for. The men embarked and Jason steered the horses onto the street and through traffic toward the Belmont.

Oliver drummed his fingers nervously on his knees, his agitation over the recent encounter barely hidden. He stared at the backs of the horses and suddenly his eyes widened. "Black Horse Man," he muttered.

"What?" Jason asked.

"Nothing," Oliver replied but he cursed under his breath.

By the time they reached the home of their host, Oliver had composed his features. The two men left their vehicle with a slave then climbed the stairs of the massive white-columned porch. Stepping inside and into a large parlor Oliver's eyes were immediately drawn to the guest of honor who towered above most of the men there. Governor Houston stood near Jackson making Oliver's eyes narrow. More than ever, the governor seemed to be an enemy – a personal enemy whose political power was greater than ever now that his mentor was to be President

Oliver quickly scanned the crowded room searching for the governor's young wife. She stood at the opposite end of the parlor near the fireplace surrounded by other women hoping to secure her attention.

These matrons of Nashville society would never have orbited around poor Rachel Jackson as they did Eliza Houston. Rachel had been tainted with scandal. If the Houstons were to find themselves in such a position, they would no doubt feel the same cold shoulder. It would certainly reduce Houston's power.

Surrounded as she was, Oliver knew he couldn't speak to her so he followed Jason and joined his colleagues queued near the well-appointed bar where a smartly-dressed houseman poured drinks.

"Houston's probably begging Jackson to take him to Washington," one lawyer wagged.

"Why do you say that?" Oliver asked as he accepted the brandy snifter offered him.

"There's trouble in the governor's house," another man responded, his voice low. "I hear that Mrs. Houston is not happy."

"If she complains to daddy, Houston's in trouble for sure. He's announced he's going to run for a second term. But he won't win without Colonel Allen's money." The men were enjoying the joke at the governor's expense.

"Perhaps he'll go to Texas instead," a third man quipped.

"Perhaps he should," a plantation owner replied. "We need Texas. The government is giving everything north of the Red River to the Indians."

The jesting continued but Oliver stopped listening. Given his earlier conversation with Eliza he doubted she would want to have another one with him. But perhaps he could speak with her mother. Mrs. Allen stood just a few feet away. Mothers wanted their daughters to be happy, didn't they? He casually made his way toward the colonel's wife.

By the end of the evening Oliver had whispered a few suggestions here and there that Eliza's only hope for happiness was to leave the governor.

"But that would be scandalous," an elderly woman had gasped, waving her fan vigorously. "It could ruin him."

"Yes, sadly so," Oliver said, looking truly sorry. "Sadly so."

Three weeks later the Nashville newspaper blared the headline: "Governor Houston Resigns!" The details surrounding his abrupt departure from office were scarce but that didn't keep speculation from running rampant. No one in Nashville was shocked that Eliza had left the governor's mansion and returned to her parents' home. Rumors of marital discord had circulated since the couple had returned from their wedding trip.

But no one had foreseen that the humiliation of his wife's departure would actually force Houston's resignation. And no one seemed to know where the former governor was now that he had left the statehouse grounds. This marital scandal had driven the man to seek refuge in the home of his friends from childhood.

The steward of the *Red River* steamboat looked up from the manifest he held in his hands while checking in passengers boarding the luxury vessel docked on the Cumberland River at Nashville. Surprise registered on his face when he saw the man who matched the name on the passenger list. Governor Sam Houston with his signature cane in hand climbed the gangplank. His flat brimmed hat was pulled low and his head was down but that didn't keep the steward and some of the other passengers from recognizing the shamed man.

Houston paused to speak to the steward. "I want my privacy," he said. "Do you understand?"

"Yes, sir. Meals in your room then?"

"Yes. This boat goes to Illinois Station doesn't it?"

"No, sir, I'm sorry. We don't go up the Arkansas River. We go up the Red River. You'll have to change boats at Paducah."

"What boats will be available there?"

"The *Facility* goes to Creek Agency and the *Neosho* goes to Fort Gibson. Either will take you to Illinois Station."

"Very well. Can you see to securing my ticket at Paducah? I don't care which boat it is – as long as it goes to Illinois Station."

"I'll see to it, sir."

The steward then gave his passenger directions to his private stateroom. When the governor had moved away, the man pulled his handkerchief from a pocket and mopped the sweat from his brow. The captain would never allow any of his employees to gossip about their passengers, but no doubt word would soon spread along the river that Houston was heading west.

Corrie and Jane took another turn around the deck of the *Tennessee*, enjoying the early spring sunshine. They stayed on deck whenever possible because their quarters below were stuffy and the air stale. Three months of travel and they were two thirds of the way through the journey.

When their boat had spent two days docked at Decatur, Corrie had used the time to post a letter to her parents explaining her decision. She had also written a more complete letter to Edmund. She still could not give him an exact date of her arrival at Dwight Mission. Because the *Tennessee* only traversed the river for which it was named, the McIntosh group would have to change boats in Paducah.

Roley McIntosh had already made arrangements with Captain Pennywit for them to travel aboard the *Facility*. This steamboat was larger than the *Tennessee* so the women were looking forward to having more room in steerage. The first class staterooms would be off limits to them, however.

The Tennessee River for the most part flowed through a sparsely settled area of the state and towns were few and far between once they left Alabama. So it was a surprise when they landed at Paducah to read a newspaper announcing the resignation of Tennessee's governor. It was an even greater surprise when word spread through the passengers on the *Facility* that Governor Houston had come aboard.

Corrie had only seen a sketch of the famous politician once in the Savannah newspaper. She couldn't help but scan the clusters of other passengers also on deck this April afternoon looking for Houston.

"Is that him?" she quietly asked Jane when she spotted the man with a cane.

"I think so," Jane replied in an equally quiet voice. She understood the gossip spoken in *Muskoke* that made its way around the boat and passed it along to her friend. "They say he drinks a bit."

In truth Houston was never drunk, but also never completely sober. He carried a slim silver flask in his pocket and sipped from it occasionally where he sat brooding in a deck chair near the paddlewheel.

"Does anyone know why he resigned?"

"His wife left him, I hear. He could not face the scandal."

Corrie felt empathy for the man. She knew all about facing scandal. She supposed it was bearable if a couple could face it together as her friends had done. But to face it abandoned and alone – that must be very hard indeed.

"He is going to his Cherokee father, they say."

"Who is his Cherokee father? Was he adopted?"

"He grew up among the eastern Cherokees on Hiwasee River. But I do not know who his father is."

Corrie tried not to be obvious as she studied the man. How interesting that they both were traveling west to live among the Cherokees. She hoped for Houston's sake, as well as her own, that they both could find happiness at the western edge of the frontier.

As they traveled down the Mississippi toward Memphis, it seemed to Corrie that the crowds of people at each port of call were larger than usual. She supposed everyone was hoping for a glimpse of the governor. But he made a point of staying below deck while the boat was docked.

At Little Rock the landing was especially crowded and Corrie saw a newspaper reporter with pad and pencil in hand. He would be disappointed if he expected an opportunity to speak to the celebrated vagabond.

Corrie, Jane and Pink went ashore to be off the boat for a while. Everywhere they went they heard the whispers of gossip. When they passed a laundry that also offered baths, they took advantage of the opportunity to feel clean again.

The river level was high on the Arkansas from the spring rains and this slowed the boat even more as it pushed through the fast running current. It was an overcast day in early May when they reached a small dock called Sallisaw Creek. From Mr. Whitson, the steward, Corrie had learned that this was the closest landing to Dwight Mission, but that many of the Cherokees had settled close to Illinois Station.

After the boat was tied to the wharf, Corrie found the solicitous man. "Could you check to see if there is anyone from Dwight Mission here?"

"Certainly, Miss. I think I see Mr. Hitchcock. He always brings the mail."

"Oh, good," Corrie said, trying to hide her disappointment that it wasn't Edmund waiting to meet her. "I will probably be getting off here then."

"Yes. Let me see to the mail and then I'll have your trunk brought up."

"Thank you."

Corrie hurried below deck to get her shawl and travel valise. Jane took her hand and walked with her up the stairs. Corrie could feel her heart pounding. She was really finally here. She kept drawing in deep breaths to try to steady her nerves.

When the steward approached them, Jane slipped her arm around Corrie's shoulders sensing her friend's need for support at this critical moment in her life.

"I spoke with Hitchcock, Miss Tuttle," Whitson said. "He tells me that their interpreter, a man named Webber, is working at the store at Illinois Station. He's expecting to meet you there. Do you want to get off here or go on?"

"How far to Illinois Station?" Jane asked. Corrie couldn't seem to speak.

"We'll be there within the hour."

"She'll go on to Illinois Station."

Corrie nodded.

"Very well. I'll see to your trunk."

After the riverman had walked away, Corrie turned to her friend. "I didn't think I would be this nervous. It's been four years since I've seen him. Will we even recognize each other?"

"You stand out among us, Corrie," Jane smiled. "I think he will know you."

Except for Corrie and Sam Houston the only passengers remaining on the *Facility* were Creeks. The governor was now standing at the rail having learned from the steward how close he was to his destination.

Jane stood with Corrie at the rail not far from Houston. Several of the Creek passengers were also on deck looking over the land so close to where they had come to live. Behind them on the keelboat, most of the men were also on deck. The question for them was whether the *Facility* could get over the falls. If not they would walk the rest of the way to Creek Agency.

Corrie watched the shoreline where the trees were dressed in their pretty spring green. They quickly moved out of the gently rolling hills and the land became flat. She could see cotton growing in the fields.

There was a crowd at the Illinois Station dock. Corrie tried to focus on every face but did not see Edmund.

Mr. Whitson walked up behind them. "I see the chief," he said, pointing to a Cherokee wearing a turban and having mutton chop sideburns.

Across the way, Houston raised a hand to greet someone on shore. It was the chief who returned the gesture.

Corrie tried to remember who was chief of the western Cherokees. It seemed like Walter Webber was.

"Is that Walter Webber?" she asked with a sharp intake of air.

"No, that is Chief Jolly. He is Mr. Houston's adopted father."

"Oh," Corrie felt a great sense of relief. She didn't want to get tangled up in Houston's scandal. She had had enough of that already.

Still she did not see anyone who even looked like Edmund. Finally she raised her eyes from the dock up to the bank of the river. A large mercantile stood like a sentinel above the falls and across the front of it a sign read, "Webber's" written in both Cherokee and English. Someone stepped out the door of the trading post. When he turned from pulling the door closed, Corrie saw the handsome face she had been searching for.

Edmund hurried along the trail from the store as it wended down to the wooden dock. He stepped up next to the chief and the two men spoke briefly.

The gangplank was being lowered and Houston made his way toward it. Corrie realized that Edmund was not aware that she was aboard the *Facility*. She wanted to call his name but her throat seemed frozen.

Finally as Houston walked by her, Edmund caught sight of Corrie. His face split into the widest smile she had ever seen on him. He worked his way through the bystanders toward the point where the gangplank would rest. He planted his feet at the end of it and waited, his eyes never leaving Corrie's face.

Jane squeezed the young woman's shoulders. "Go, Miss Corrie."

"Oh, Jane," Corrie said turning to face her friend. "How can I ever thank you?"

"You can thank me later. I will write to you at Dwight Mission and we will arrange to meet. But now you must go. He is waiting for you."

After a quick hug, Corrie gripped her valise and then followed the governor down the gangplank. When she reached Edmund he took her hand to help her step onto the dock, but he did not let it go. With his other hand, he reached for her bag and she released it to him.

For a moment it seemed as if neither knew what to say. He led her along the dock, weaving between the throng of bystanders some of whom had gathered around the chief and his returning son.

When they were away from the crowd, Edmund said, "Your journey was a long one."

Corrie ducked her head. "Far longer than it should have been." There was regret in her voice.

He understood her meaning.

"What matters is that you are here now. I think the timing was for a divine reason."

"Do you?"

"Yes. There is a season for everything." They walked toward Webber's trading post.

Corrie looked around at the place she hoped to share with Edmund. "Then I think this season is going to be beautiful."

Edmund gave her a teasing smile and nodded in agreement. "Welcome home, my pretty girl. Welcome home."

BOOKS BY JONITA MULLINS

The Neosho District
The Marital Scandal

The Missions of Indian Territory
Journey to an Untamed Land
Look Unto the Fields
Come to Lovely County

Glimpses of Our Past
A Look Back at Three Forks History
Life Along the Rivers

Adventures of American Kids
Making a Point

Haskell: A Centennial Celebration

A Kitchen on the Frontier

The Jefferson Highway in Oklahoma

The Whatsoever Things

Jonita Mullins is a popular speaker on topics of history and inspiration. She also offers history tours in and around her home community of Muskogee, Oklahoma. More information is available on her books, gifts, tours and preservation projects at her website: okieheritage.com